The typewriter sat in front of me as I struggled to try to provide a proper ending to my latest story. It was an adaptation of the events at the blasted heath outside of Arkham, Massachusetts. I'd struggled to put to words the wild story told to me by a sickly strange looking man named Ammi. A tale of flora and fauna corrupted by an unknown substance from space. It was not that the local legend wasn't a good subject for weird fiction, it was that I was afraid I would be beaten to my adaptation of it.

There was also the fact that events were possibly a little too close to home if I were to try to sell it to local publishers. Arkham's appetite for the macabre was greater than any market outside one of America's largest cities but the issue of groundwater contamination following the building of the local reservoir had been a gradually growing concern for the past decade. There were some who believed unknown metals or chemicals were slowly driving the citizens to madness or an early grave.

Was it exploitative to write a tale where the origins of this ever-increasing rise in infirmity or death was the cause of an alien life form carried to our world from distant galaxies? Perhaps, but it would also sell a lot of magazines.

Or so I hoped.

THE BOOK OF HASTUR

FEATURING STORIES BY

C. T. PHIPPS ~ TIM MENDEES ~ DAVID HAMBLING
MATTHEW DAVENPORT ~ ANDREA PEARSON
ERIC MALIKYTE ~ DAVID NIALL WILSON

MACABRE
Ink

Contents

Foreword

"It is kind of thee, O Hastur," so he prayed, *"to give me mountains so near to my dwelling and my fold that I and my sheep can escape the angry torrents; but the rest of the world thou must thyself deliver in some way that I know not of, or I will no longer worship thee."*

— Ambrose Bierce, "Haita the Shepherd"

"For I knew that the King in Yellow had opened his tattered mantle and there was only God to cry to now."

— Robert W. Chambers, *The King in Yellow*

"I found myself faced by names and terms that I had heard elsewhere in the most hideous of connections — Yuggoth, Great Cthulhu, Tsathoggua, Yog-Sothoth, R'lyeh, Nyarlathotep, Azathoth, Hastur, Yian, Leng, the Lake of Hali, Bethmoora, the Yellow Sign, L'mur-Kathulos, Bran, and the Magnum Innominandum — and was drawn back through nameless aeons and inconceivable dimensions to worlds of elder, outer entity at which the crazed author of the Necronomicon had only guessed in the vaguest way."

— H. P. Lovecraft, "The Whisperer in Darkness"

"There is a whole secret cult of evil men (a man of your mystical erudition will understand me when I link them with Hastur and the Yellow Sign) devoted to the purpose of tracking them down and injuring them on behalf of monstrous powers from other dimensions."

— H. P. Lovecraft, "The Whisperer in Darkness"

Hastur is not only one of the most famous of the evil eldritch entities that imperil humanity in the Cthulhu Mythos, but also one of the most nebulous. That is because he is almost solely a product of other authors taking his name and description before expanding upon it in unique as well as terrifying ways.

In a very real way, this is because Hastur is not a creation of H.P. Lovecraft himself but a borrowed concept that was, itself, a borrowed concept. Ambrose Bierce made him the god of some poor pagan shepherd in the middle of the wilderness before the name was adopted by Robert Chambers for his sanity-twisting horror novel about a weird play somehow linked to it. Chambers also mentioned Carcossa, Hali, the Hyades, and the Yellow Sign.

H.P. Lovecraft picked up his football and threw Hastur in among his Great Old Ones. But there's no story about Hastur. No, *The Dunwich Horror*, *The Call of Cthulhu*, or even *The Dream Quest of Unknown Kadath* do not elaborate on the character like Yog-Sothoth, Cthulhu, or Nyarlathotep. In terms of Lovecraftian "canon", we know Hastur exists and is probably a baddie due to the names he's accompanied by as well as the fact he has a cult devoted to doing harm to the Mi-Go. Hastur isn't even an enemy of humanity, he's got problems with a bunch of fungi from Yuggoth.

It is the much-misunderstood August Derleth, original HPL superfan, that created much of what would later be embraced as fact about Hastur in the *Call of Cthulhu* tabletop game among other sources. Ridiculed ideas like Hastur is Cthulhu's brother and an air elemental. Hastur would also become like Beetlejuice or Bloody Mary in that he was equated with the "Unspeakable One" so that if you said his name three times, he would possess you.

Hastur!

Hastur!

Hastur!

Huh, I guess he's busy. However, the terrifying nature of Hastur has endured and many artists have taken the bare bones nature of the Great Old One to make their own dark interpretations. I have no evidence to support this but am inclined to think the Crimson King of Stephen King's Dark Tower series (especially since Nyarlathotep is linked to Randall Flagg) is one. The first season of *True Detective* has the

King in Yellow linked to the series of rapes and murders performed by a twisted cult in Louisiana. He has even tangled with the Doctor of Doctor Who fame in the Virgin New Adventures line.

My first exposure to Hastur was the "Old Man Henderson" gaming story where a deranged Scottish American Arkhamite obsessed with lawn gnomes ended up permanently killing the Great Old One in what is almost certainly apocryphal but hilarious nevertheless. A friend of mine had him as his favorite Great Old One simply because of a piece of fan art that stuck in his brain of a tattered yellow robed wizard with no face.

So what does that mean for our stories in this book series? The Books of Cthulhu series are a collection of pulpier more action-orientated tales than your typical Lovecraftian fare. Hastur, however, defies description and our stories will go in interesting directions because of that. He is a god of madness, art, shepherds, death, decay, and many other subjects as his worshipers attribute to him — or perhaps he is a place — or perhaps he is an idea. Either way, he is the last Great Old One to remain truly mysterious and thus undefeatable.

So ask yourself: have you seen the Yellow Sign?

And if you have, run.

Weird Tales with Randolph Carter

By C. T. Phipps

The typewriter sat in front of me as I struggled to try to provide a proper ending to my latest story. It was an adaptation of the events at the blasted heath outside of Arkham, Massachusetts. I'd struggled to put to words the wild story told to me by a sickly strange looking man named Ammi. A tale of flora and fauna corrupted by an unknown substance from space. It was not that the local legend wasn't a good subject for weird fiction, it was that I was afraid I would be beaten to my adaptation of it.

There was also the fact that events were possibly a little too close to home if I were to try to sell it to local publishers. Arkham's appetite for the macabre was greater than any market outside one of America's largest cities but the issue of groundwater contamination following the building of the local reservoir had been a gradually growing concern for the past decade. There were some who believed unknown metals or chemicals were slowly driving the citizens to madness or an early grave.

Was it exploitative to write a tale where the origins of this ever-increasing rise in infirmity or death was the cause of an alien life form carried to our world from distant galaxies? Perhaps, but it would also sell a lot of magazines.

Or so I hoped.

"Randolph!" A voice spoke from the hallway outside my study. It shook me out of my reverie and brought me to the present. I was inside my study with a noisy thunderstorm outside and the hearth in the chamber burning brightly. There was no bust of Pallas with a raven on the top to complete the horror writing mood, but I was otherwise close to the perfect circumstances for the creation of chilling tales.

"It is polite to knock before entering, Harley," I replied, not getting up from my seat at the desk.

I'd inherited the property from my late father, and it was far more than a professional writer could afford on the meager payments to his mad imaginings, but it was still large enough to surprise me with the kind of visitors that sometimes showed up.

"Would you have heard me, old friend?" Harley Warren inquired, entering. "I know the kind of place your mind goes when writing."

Harley Warren was thin, clean shaven, and starting to go bald. He dressed well though his suits were years out of fashion and patched due to his complete lack of desire to keep with the times. He was quite wet, and I could tell he'd arrived without an umbrella. There was also a brown paper wrapped bundle under his right arm.

"No," I replied. "Unlike you, I cannot afford servants."

"I'd buy you one, but you can't own people anymore," Harley said, making a less than pleasant joke.

Harley came from money in the way that fish came from water. His ancestors dated back to the time of the Puritans and had made fortunes equal to the Washingtons as well as the Jeffersons. Sadly, with the same means. Supposedly, Harley's ancestor Hobert Warren had believed Ben Franklin to be a mystical rival of legendary warlock Joseph Curwen.

Unfortunately, Harley had no interest in business and neither had his immediate ancestors, becoming instead embroiled in the secret societies that feuded constantly among New England's upper crust. Masons, fraternities, and mystical groups with delusions of spiritual power. The last three generations of Warrens had been part of them all.

Harley was the last of his line and was very likely to spend the rest of his family's money chasing phantasms that, however entertaining I found them, would leave him as bankrupt as a writer for *Weird Tales* or its local equivalent, *Outlandish Stories*. That would be, however, at least a decade or two of frivolous spending chasing ghosts.

"Is there any reason you're darkening my door this stormy night?" I lit myself a pipe and began smoking, taking in a deep whiff of tobacco. My mother had encouraged me in the habit to calm my nerves.

"I cannot show up for no reason other than your charming company?" Harley asked.

I narrowed my eyes. "Not normally no. I remind you that you left last year to scour the globe for secrets of the unknown."

Harley took a seat in my grandfather's leather-bound chair across from me. "A worthy use of my time if there ever was one. What I have to show you tonight is enough to change both our lives forever."

Harley was a man prone to such bold proclamations and I frequently found myself disappointed by the results.

Harley unfolded the brown paper wrapping around his package and revealed its contents. It was a yellow leather volume with crinkly paper that had a golden clasp around it. A strange squiggly trio of lines was on the front.

"*The Book of Hastur*," Harley said. "I acquired it in India a month before my return to the States. I've spent months translating it, pouring over the language, and deducing the true meaning of the author. I wrapped it up lest it be damaged by our climate because each page is as precious as gold to me. More so even. Look upon its dreadful visage and be elevated to the ranks of an elite priesthood of mortals who have glimpsed the infinite."

My reaction was not what you expected. "Hastur? Really? Harley, you've been suckered. Again."

Harley narrowed his eyes. "I'm disappointed in your skepticism, Randolph. Why would you think so?"

I stared at him. "Hastur isn't real."

Harley frowned. "Your mind is not usually so prosaic."

"Ambrose Bierce first wrote about him as a god in *Haita the Shepherd* and he's the subject of Chalmers' writing in the *King in Yellow*," I replied. "I use *real* occult concepts in my writing. Names and concepts from the *Necronomicon* or the Black Book. Not this Hastur nonsense. Hastur is a literary homage nothing more."

"This is the same spiel you gave about Aleister Crowley's Thelemic pantheon," Harley replied.

"And I'm right about him too," I said, tapping the end of my pipe in an ashtray beside my typewriter. "Hastur isn't even a god outside of Bierce's work. Chalmers used him as a place. Your rival's writing doesn't make it clear what he is either, probably because it was just an homage to another horror writer."

"Hastur is…more," Harley said, almost reverentially.

"What does that even mean?" I asked, confused.

Harley furrowed his brow as if briefly broken from a spell. "It means the concepts of defining something in occult terms are not necessarily the best use of one's time. Is Hastur a place, a god, or an idea? Is Carcosa a planet, dimension, or kingdom? The Plateau of Leng and Hali are places but how do they relate? The King in Yellow is a personage but maybe it is a genius loci or personification like Columbia for America or Hypnos is of sleep."

"Please tell me you didn't just suggest America's symbol is a goddess." I rolled my eyes. "Cthulhu is a god. He lives in R'lyeh. He is worshiped by a bunch of degenerate Theosophists and weird Christian cult offshoots. Anthropologists try and link every squid god and fish man across Earth's mythology together under him. Either way, he's a god worth worshiping because he's one you can explain."

Harley stared at me like I was a small child talking nonsense. Which, given he was the occult expert who taught me most of what I knew about comparative mythology and the weird, was perhaps accurate. "The unknown is a major part of what makes gods worth worshiping. Why the Hebrew God presently reigns instead of Zeus. I also think you severely overstate just how much we know about Cthulhu. People conflate Cthulhu with all those gods because they're all descended from the same primal source."

"So you've claimed." Harley and I had spent the week in Innsmouth researching his theory before getting chased out of the town by the local fundamentalists. Harley was banned from our old Alma Mater, Miskatonic University, for much the same reason. Personally, I think they just grew sick of his lecturing. "You know I don't actually believe in this sort of stuff."

Which was a half-truth. Harley Warren had introduced me to a cornucopia of weird, surreal, and unnerving things. I'd attended seances with him, meetings with foul characters, and explored the most haunted locations from Kingsport to Ipswich.

Which wasn't a grand journey in terms of distance if you considered all of America but was larger than all of England. Oddly, it was Harley who was the quickest to believe in fraud and the most furious whenever the supernatural was not "actually" present in a medium or psychic's household. Personally, I could not often tell the difference between charlatan or soothsayer.

Frankly, some days it felt like I was following Harley along like Watson to his Holmes. As entertaining and congenial as I found Harley's company to be, it was often a demoralizing and unequal partnership. Yet the one time I suggested leaving for less arcane pursuits, he had positively revolted. 'You are a powerful dreamer, Randolph, and your destiny is to be far greater than mine. I rummage and scrape for scraps of knowledge, but you will bring life to worlds.' Which I'd assumed was referring to his appreciation for my short stories and novelettes. That had been ten years ago. Now? Now I wasn't so sure.

"A shame," Harley said, opening the book and looking over its contents. "This particular work provides more insight into Hastur, or the King in Yellow if you will, and the Yellow Sign than any other work I've yet read."

"Is he Cthulhu's half-brother?" I asked, sarcastically. "Some elemental spirit of the air?"

Harley glared at me, as if I was blaspheming. Which I suppose I was. "The things I have seen would turn your hair white, Randolph."

"Show it to me then," I said.

"You wouldn't understand the language," Harley replied. "It's written in a tongue that predates the human race."

That was a less than impressive response.

"Please tell me you didn't pay real money for this," I said, sighing. "Because that sounds very convenient for the seller."

"If it was a fraud, it was a very good one given the cipher used does translate to coherent passages," Harley replied, surprising me by arguing with logic rather than emotion. Harley was a good friend but something of a bully and if he'd been in a different mood, I expect he would have just yelled at me until I accepted his latest tome was a purchase of sublime genius.

I decided to indulge my friend. "A decoder ring can do the same thing. Still, what does it say?"

Harley's eyes seemed to bulge forward as if he was dealing with a concept too big for his brain to carry. He tapped the side of his skull with his forefinger three times. "Hastur is here."

"Uh huh," I replied.

Harley sighed. "The Yellow Sign, The King in Yellow, Carcosa, Leng, its satyr men, and Hali. All these things are related to the same prevailing concept. He is an entity or being or thing that you can touch through your art. The Muse of Madness or Grace of Chaos."

"You're not speaking sense, Harley," I said, now genuinely concerned for him. Harley was an intense man and frequently prone to obsession. Indeed, he was something of a bully even to his closest friends—myself included—and did not tolerate dissent.

"Exactly," Harley replied, as if he'd won an argument.

I sighed and got up from my seat. "I think I'm going to make myself dinner. Unless you want to go out?"

The storm was abating, and I suddenly felt my study had been invaded. If I was to listen to him claim yet another deity was secretly on the edge of human society, waiting to have the keys to their Olympus unlocked, I at least deserved a meal out of it. Harley would pick up the cheque and that was worth the price of listening.

"You're an artist, Randolph," Harley said, taking an almost conciliatory tone. "Of sorts."

I glared, taking him to be insulting of my profession. "Of sorts? Really?"

"No scorn is intended," Harley said, raising his hands in defense. "I find there is more value in a typical issue of *Arkham Scares* or *Outlandish Stories* than there is in any preacher's sermon. Had it larger print runs, I believe the combination of you and that Pickman fellow would have the entirety of the nation's men in rapt attention."

He was referring to the cover artist for a good number of Arkham's pulp magazines. Richard Pickman was not a gallery artist with his nightmarishly gory visages of otherworldly terror but had found an appreciative audience among the science fiction as well as horror fans of the genre magazine world.

Richard and I didn't always agree on content, and he often corrected me on how my monsters 'should' look but whenever I wrote from my dreams, I had his complete and undivided attention. He was, honestly, probably my only other close friend.

At least these days.

I'd lost contact with Etienne-Laurent de Marigny, who was every bit the occult obsessed madman that Harley was. Etienne had shown me the closest thing I'd ever come to the "true" occult in the crypts under Bayonne, New Jersey. He'd been less than pleased when I'd dismissed them as the products of mesmerism and no wilder than what I saw every night I went to sleep.

"I fear the average reader of both is more interested in the voluptuous naked forms being menaced by various creatures on the covers," I said, dryly.

I had been privately seeing a lovely young model for Richard's art from Innsmouth, her form absent that particular community's deformities save possibly unusually large eyes, when she'd suffered a dramatic change in personality as well as decided to no longer bare her skin for the cause of pulpish art.

It was a pity that Asenath had changed so much as some female companionship might have done both me and Harley good. Harley had no interest in such things, though, and I sometimes wondered if the intensity of his bond with me was serving as a substitute for it. I could not even say there was nothing sexual about it because the whole of that drive had been absorbed into his lust for the occult's power.

Harley gave a dismissive wave. "What I'm saying is that Hastur is a chance to open one's mind to a higher dimension beyond the sights and sounds of the common man. He is not a being who lives under the ocean or in the dark corners of the Earth but far beyond in the stars where reality merges with—"

"Dreams?" I finished for him. It was the one subject for which I believed I had a far greater authority than Harley. Neither Freud nor Jung had any insight that matched what my fantastical visions had bestowed me over the years.

"Yes," Harley said, staring down at this book with an almost lecherous gaze. "Imagine if inside this tome were the secrets to being able to connect our minds to the crossroads between inspiration as well as madness. Of dream with magic. Hastur is the key for that."

"I thought Yog-Sothoth was the Key and the Gate," I replied, referring to one of the imaginary gods of the *Necronomicon*.

Well, all gods were imaginary.

Harley gave me a withering glare. "No one likes a smartass, Randolph."

I snorted but decided to take his question seriously. "I suppose I think it would be truly amazing to encounter something unnamable. Indefinable. That would open one's mind to possibilities that would test the limit of what was conceivable. I'd very much like that, I think."

Harley snorted as if I'd said something very funny. "Perhaps you might very much like to touch the Yellow Sign. I suspect most minds would not. They would break under the strain of having not only their beliefs challenged but destroyed. The human mind is a fragile tower of building blocks constructed by a child. Remove any single one of them and the structure comes tumbling down, leaving only a gibbering wreck of shattered will."

I decided I did want to go out to eat. "I like that. Do you mind if I use it?"

"My verbiage would come off as purple to an audience of normal men," Harley said, self-deprecating.

"No more than mine and I get paid by the word," I replied, fetching my hat. "Are you coming? A good steak and some potatoes will do us both good."

"You need to get packing," Harley said, dismissing my concerns.

"What?" I asked. "Are we going somewhere?"

Harley had chosen not to take me across the globe last year, but he'd asked me to join him on many other excursions. Given I could write everywhere, it was not usually an inconvenience, but this still felt very sudden. Clearly, this so-called *Book of Hastur* had gotten deep into my friend's head and taken over. On the other hand, I couldn't help but feel a twinge of excitement at the possibility of yet another trip with my friends. Even the failed expeditions proved to be exciting and were ones I could never have afforded to undertake on my own.

"Big Cypress Swamp," Harley said. "I have already reserved our tickets on the train and paid for our lodgings. Gather your things, Randolph."

I stared at him. "You want us to go to Louisiana?"

I admitted, that was a location I'd long wanted to visit. New Orleans was a city with its own unique history, as old as that or the Puritans, and there were many occult leads to track down there. Supposedly, a Cthulhu cult had been founded among the Voodoo worshipers there by a renegade member of the tragedy afflicted Delapore clan. It had proven quite the scandal and was a worthy avenue to explore—assuming Harley hadn't found his own leads on his eternal quest for proof of the supernatural's veracity.

"I want us to go to Florida," Harley corrected, disappointing me. "To an ancient necropolis used once by the indigenous peoples and later by the Conquistadors. It is a graveyard that exists on no map but near the Gainesville Pike, preserved by local superstition as well as the remoteness of its location. However old it may be, it is older still as it was first a sacred place to a far elder people that predate humanity's arrival in the New World or perhaps even the world in general."

I was used to Harley Warren's fancies, but this was something else entirely. Or maybe I was just upset our trip wouldn't allow me to experience authentic Cajun cooking. "*The Book of Hastur* has led you to a flooded old tomb that you want us to visit? Really, Harley, at least New Orleans has hotels."

"Why do you say it's flooded?" Harley asked, focusing on the most irrelevant part of the question. "I have every reason to believe the tomb we seek will be guarded against all elements, earthly or otherwise."

"If it's in Florida and underground, it's flooded," I replied. Harley had a fascination with incorruptibility as a concept and of corpses that could spend centuries or even millennia without decaying. I had always dismissed that as a papist concept and Harley was as heathen as they came. Yet, the idea of him poking around a swamp for damp bones or rotted cloth seemed excessive even for him.

"The book, Randolph, the book," Harley said, tapping it. "The book describes so much in the margins. This is a volume of a people that no human tongue had spoken the language of, but I am not the first to read its contents or decipher its words. A Spanish missionary, brought there by tales of gold and pagan devil-worship, sought this place out. Inside, he discovered a doorway between this world and the next."

"And what happened to him?" I asked, suspecting how the religious fanatics of Spain would react to such an unconventional idea.

"It doesn't matter," Harley said, snorting his nostrils like a hog. "This location is a place between the worlds and a hole in the fabric of time. To pass through it will be the chance to finally prove all my theories and touch the fabric of the King in Yellow's robe. I have seen the Yellow Sign inside this book, and it has inspired me."

There was something disquieting about Harley's attitude, and I was no stranger to his uncomfortable moods and peculiar fixations. Like a modern-day Abdul Alhazred, Harley had ever wanted to be the prophet of the supernatural to a jaded blasphemous age. However, no secret seemed to be enough nor any revelation fully convincing.

Perhaps my friend had finally found the grail or Caliburn that he'd long desired inside this old volume's writing. I feared for my friend because if he put all of his faith into the least developed of the occult gods he'd so often spoken of then he was certainly setting himself up for further disappointing.

Still, that only made my determination to join Harley all the greater. After all, when and if we journeyed to this hidden tomb, I needed to be there for my friend. If he found nothing, as was likely, then he would need my counsel that all was not lost. If he did discover some secret *Key of Solomon* or *Book of Eibon*, well, then I wanted to be there for him as well. So that we might both unearth ourselves the secrets of time. Hastur was, at least in some of the writings I'd read, a god of hidden truths after all.

The horror followed me into my dreams.

I had not slept well, a status that had never afflicted me even during the direst of my circumstances, since that terrible night in Cypress Swamp. We'd found, much to my surprise, the tomb from Harley's book. It was an almost innocuous above ground stone mausoleum amidst other barely recognizable broken monuments. After removing a great stone slab, we'd both seen a set of stairs leading down-down into the proverbial rabbit hole of Charles Dodgson's Wonderland.

I'd stupidly, or perhaps prudently depending on one's perspective, allowed Harley to go forward into the chamber alone. We'd communicated via portable telephone throughout and I could still hear every one of Harley's final words spoken on that machine. I struggled not to think of that encounter but found it replaying endlessly in my mind.

"God! If you could see what I am seeing!"

"Carter, it's terrible—monstrous—unbelievable!"

"I can't tell you, Carter! It's too utterly beyond thought—I dare not tell you—no man could know it and live—Great God! I never dreamed of THIS!"

I could only imagine what amazing vistas and alien wonders my friend was privy to. There was true magic here and he had crossed the threshold between this world and the next. Had he journeyed like Orpheus between Earth and Hades? Or was he now on some grandiose other world or dimension? Perhaps a mythical underground kingdom like Burrough's Pellucidar. I wanted to join him that very moment but hung back due to some primal sense of wrong that froze me to my place. I had not even noticed it in my fevered conversation with Harley, but it had been there. Then? Then things had gone terribly wrong.

"Carter! for the love of God, put back the slab and get out of this if you can! Quick!—leave everything else and make for the outside—it's your only chance! Do as I say, and don't ask me to explain!"

But I'd needed more. Much more. I'd robbed Harley of precious seconds in my hesitation.

"Beat it! For God's sake, put back the slab and beat it, Carter!"

I'd wanted to help. Come down regardless of Harley's frantic bequest. To do… something! I'd called down, said I was coming to rescue him like some hero from lighter adventure fiction than the dark stories I'd always been compelled to write.

"Don't! You can't understand! It's too late—and my own fault. Put back the slab and run—there's nothing else you or anyone can do now!"

He had spoken with a desperation, urgency, and resignation I'd never heard from my friend. It had been the words of a man who had no hope for his own survival but only the desperate wish that I might escape. I'd stayed and begged for Harley to respond when he fell silent.

Right before hearing that awful-awful voice speak words burned into my brain, "YOU FOOL, WARREN IS DEAD!"

I had struggled to make my way to the nearest police station and give my statement, but the results had been less than gratifying. The police had not even charged me for Harley's murder but dismissed my story out of hand before releasing me. If they had bothered to investigate the cemetery, I knew they would find no body, but I suspect they had not even done that basic amount of detecting. Real life police were rarely Holmes or Dupin or even Lestrade. It was for the better, though, because the most merciful thing they might have found was death.

So, I had taken the next available train back to Arkham, Massachusetts where I had struggled to stay awake lest my dreams be infected by whatever fearsome horrors that he had met his doom at the hands of. Had he met Hastur? Was the place Hastur? Was the creature he had talked to the King in Yellow or one of its minions? Did it have any connection whatsoever to the concepts of that book other than a deranged monk's speculations leading Harley to his doom? I did not know and did not want to know.

When I reached home, only then did I finally feel a measure of safety. The events were like a terrible dream for me, and I had to admit a noxious moment of self-aggrandizement that I'd started writing in my notebooks feverishly on the train ride back. Some of my best work had born from my horrific encounter with Harley's killer. As awful as it would be to profit artistically from the death of a dear friend, I hoped that perhaps it would help exorcise the demons of my mind to put all my terrified tales to my typewriter.

Then I entered the study and saw *The Book of Hastur* was resting on my desk next to my typewriter. The book that Harley had most certainly had on his person when he had entered the awful tomb. A nightmarish conjuration of the most blasphemous sort yet innocuous in appearance. Walking with trepidation to it, I sat down and opened the book.

Its contents were hand-written, in English, and in Harley's hand. Except the scrawl had an undefinable sense of stiffness and forced strike to it. My friend was dead, yes, but I did not believe that had freed him from whatever horror he'd encountered down there. He was trapped in Hastur now, place or person or god or state of existence, and would never ever escape.

Like the King in Yellow, that place he now dwelled was a source of artistic inspiration for the contents of the book. A place or person that would inspire new dreams and tales of terror or pulpish heroism that seemed so childish yet was necessary to keep my sanity from crashing in on itself. The latter a delusion that was my only life preserver in a terrible storm. Had Harley sent this or his new dark master? Or had I summoned it from the Dreamlands through the power of a wish, reality now unmoored from my existence due to an encounter with the Yellow Sign? I had no idea.

So, I read.

Blood Eagle

By C. T. Phipps

I, *Harald Bjornson, would not die this day.*
   I, Harald Bjornson, would not die this day.
   I, Harald Bjornson, would not die this day.

It was a mantra I repeated as a prayer and a spell both against the hunger, cold, and exhaustion that would deny me Valhalla. Unfortunately, it seemed very likely that the magic in my words would do me little good as I stumbled through the woods with no idea where I was going nor really where I'd come from.

Njord, God of the Seas, curse me, what sort of navigator was I that I couldn't even figure out where I was on this island? It was like the woods had swallowed me whole and I'd been compelled to run through them from the moment I'd begun my shameful flight.

It had started so well too.

The Jarl had sent us on a mission of trade from their home port to their neighbors when Svend, my dear stupid older brother, had suggested they do some viking. There had been twelve of them and there was a fishing village on the coast full of fat Christians just waiting to be raided. Nordi, our leader, had objected. He'd married a Christian after his first wife had died and practiced the true faith while praying to their god whenever their traders arrived.

It was disgusting really.

How things had gotten so damned confused was an easy enough line to draw in the dirt. The storm had put them off course, they'd woken up adrift against this island that shouldn't be here, and a fight had broken out. In the old, proper days, it would have been settled one-on-one in a duel, but it seemed everybody had forgotten how honor was supposed to work.

Stupid Svend had declared Nordi unfit for captaincy, and I'd sided with him as a brother should. Hel, we should have read the crowds. They were Svend's men and the promise of raiding a bunch of the filthy kneelers like my grandfather and father had didn't appeal to them the same way it did us. They'd ganged up on my brother, beaten him to the ground, and put an ax in his forehead before I could do anything but reach for my sword.

Hel!

Still, I had no one to blame for what happened next. I'd run like a craven. Staying and dying against ten other men would have been foolish. Foolish but what honor demanded. I'd even now be feasting in Odin's halls alongside my grandfather and uncles had I charged them all. If I died here, I'd not only never reach Valhalla like my poor father (dying of the cough in his bed) but my brother would be unavenged.

Odin, he'd never let me hear the end of it and I bet he'd journey down to Hel just to taunt me about being an Einherjar. That was assuming I wasn't fully cast into Náströnd along with the oathbreakers, adulterers, cowards, and murderers. That would be horribly unfair. I'd killed fifteen men, three of them armed, and they should really judge these things in a context.

Eventually, I felt myself gain enough control to put myself up against the side of a tree. "Odin, I offer you this promise: if you can provide me with some food and a warm fire then I will kill a dozen Christians for you."

No answer. Well, obviously not. The gifts of the gods were rarely bestowed directly. Still, I needed to find a way back to the shore or some shelter against the elements. If my associates had left me on the island, which they might well have, and there was no one else then it would be a pitiful slow death. I needed to avoid that at all costs.

That was when I saw a burning fire in the night through the trees.

I arrived at the flames with a stumbling gait but the sight that greeted me was a welcome one, even if I suspected the man I found sitting at the fireside would not be happy once I took everything he possessed.

It was a Christian monk, sitting alone, on the top of a chopped down tree. His yellowed robes were old and ratty with an unpleasant smell radiating from them that I could not quite put into words. His skin was weathered like old leather with his eyes milky white, indicating that he was blind. I put his age between seventy and a hundred, somehow animate and still alive when time should have taken him.

There was a bag of food at his side, meat, and bread, with some fresh rabbit roasting over the fire. Sadly, I couldn't smell the deliciousness of the meat with the foul odor radiating from the man himself.

"Give me your wares, monk, and I won't gut you now," I said, pulling my knife instead of my sword. I did not know if he spoke my tongue and if he didn't, I was glad he was an invalid in the middle of the woods rather than someone who could fight back.

Much to my surprise, he spoke perfect Danish. "Everything that I own is something I am happy to share with you, Northman."

I blinked, staring at him. "How do you even know I'm a Northman, blind man?"

The old monk smiled a mouth of nasty yellow teeth. "I see more than you might guess. Either way, there is food, wine, and clean water. Drink and eat your fill."

"You act like you have a choice," I said, sitting down across from him on another log and tearing into his supplies while the fire warmed my spirit.

"Of course," the old monk said. "Tonight, is a fortuitous night for you, brother."

The fare was bland, but I didn't care, enjoying every bit of it. "My brother is dead, monk. The only reason I have not killed you yet is because I am too tired to do so, and you clearly have been left for dead by your people."

The old monk laughed as if the idea amused him. "My people have entrusted me with a mighty task. All is as the Lord wills it. My flock have been led astray by the words of false prophets and heathen blasphemers. This island belongs to the true followers of the Lord of Shepherds and not the foul liars who teach ruination. I had five soldiers with me, but they perished killing most of the heretics. Now, I have been sent a champion who might deliver us from the Great Beast's insanity."

I followed one in every third word in the old monk's ramble. Chewing between words, I stared at him. "I am a worshiper of Odin, Christian. As heathen and blasphemous as any on this Earth to your god of foolishness. I would kill you and your ilk if I could. I still might. I spit on any task that would do your god honor."

I'd already decided not to kill the monk. As repulsive as I found their religion, one that spread like disease via their preachers, it was bad luck to kill someone who offered you food at their table. Besides, it wasn't like I had anything to fear from a man older than my grandfather if he'd lived to today. Still, I wasn't going to allow him to spout his nonsense.

"Allow me to speak plainer then," the old monk replied. "Gold and a boat."

I stopped chewing. "You have my attention."

"These individuals are the followers of a god you will not have heard of called Dagon," the old monk said. "Throughout the lands of Wessex, they have spread a corrupted and foul version of Christianity that detracts from the worship of our lord. Their chief way of winning men over is gold trinkets and jewelry that they have much of. The ones here come every month to make an offering of a maiden to the sea to be ravished before collecting more gold. They proceed to bring it back and use it as currency to spread more heresy."

"How many?" I asked.

"Excuse me?" The old monk asked.

"How many men?" I asked, focused more on the practicalities than anything else. "I'm assuming you want me to kill them and take their boat with you on it. Presumably, one laden with gold as well as potentially one raped sacrifice."

"The sacrifice remains pure," the old monk replied. "She must be for the Day of Revelation."

"That is not my point," I replied.

"Eight," the old monk finally admitted.

I snorted in derision. "Madness. Far too many. I'm sorry but I may barter passage with these fools if it gets me off this island. Either that or I'll take you with me if you lead me to your boat. Surely you came here on one as well."

I was surprised I was apologizing to him, but it seemed Odin was set on denying me riches this trip. I did mean it that I would give him passage off this island, though.

"Madness? Perhaps not," the old monk said, reaching behind his log and pulling out a short bow. Much to my surprise, he notched it like a man in the prime of his life and fired the arrow past my head against the tree trunk behind me. It was done fast enough that I barely had time to react, and a little biscuit fell out of my mouth.

"Pretty good for an old man," I said.

"I am thirty-three," the old monk said.

I blinked. "You don't look it."

The old monk grunted. "My appearance is the result of an encounter with a fecund creature when I was a young man in the service of the church. It laid its touch on me and robbed me of what was a visage that Paris of Troy would have been proud of. My brother monks treated me, though, and my body still has the strength of three men."

I stared at him. "What kind of monk are you? I thought you all sat around praying and rutting sheep? Aren't you forbidden from killing?"

"Only humans. Not heretics."

I stupidly agreed to help kill the fish worshipers. Perhaps it was greed mixed with a bit of gratitude but a larger part of me believed this had to be a sign from Odin. A bizarre sign surreptitiously sent since I would be helping one group of Christians slaughter another since I couldn't tell the difference between their interpretations of their god. One called his god the Lord of Shepherds and the other called his the God of Fish.

Peasant gods.

Mind you, my own father had been a blacksmith, so I wasn't exactly a royal myself. Still, war had been good to my family and the prospect of returning with a boat load of gold back to the Jarl was an appealing one.

I could care for my brother's wife and child as well as wipe the stain of cowardice from my spirit. Hel, I could hire twenty men if there was more than a handful of gold and we could kill Nordi as well as his men before paying off the weirgild price to their families. And if I died? Well, that was better than the alternative of dying an old man. So why were my dreams nothing but nightmares?

Svend greeted me in my dream, his head caved in by an ax as his rotted corpse led me to the heart of our village's square where I saw Nordi suspended between two poles. The middle-aged captain was hanging there, the skin of his back flayed away and a pile of gore at his feet alongside what had previously been the contents of his bowels. Two men in black leather masks were working, tearing him apart like an old woman cleaning a fish.

"Blood eagle," Svend spoke.

"Gods," I said, disgusted. "Why?"

The Blood Eagle was the worst way a man could die, a man's ribs severed from their spine and their lungs pulled from their back to create wings. It was a ritualistic form of execution I'd heard of but never actually met a man who'd seen it. Well, any man who wasn't a drunken liar.

"Sacrifice," Svend said. "The winter will be harsh and food scarce. The Jarl will blame Nordi for his failure at the trading post."

"And us?" I asked.

Svend grinned, gore leaking out of the side of his head. "We do not trouble his conscience."

Of course not. As much as I hated Nordi, though, I found this far too much. It was far from a clean death. "Will he go to Valhalla?"

"Only if he did not scream before death," Svend replied.

"Did he?" I asked.

"Yes," Svend replied. "For hours."

I woke up to find the old monk making spirals in the dirt with the end of his staff. The morning mist had settled over us and the fire had long since died but I'd endured far chillier mornings. I did not feel particularly rested, but the exhaustion had mostly left my bones and my belly was full, which was more than I could say about most days.

"Did you sleep well?" The old monk asked.

I stared at him. "No."

"Pity," the old monk said.

I got up, relieved myself, and drank more of the old monk's wine. "You never did tell me your name."

"You never told me yours," the old monk said.

"Harald," I said. "Which means we're friends now, I suppose."

"Haïta," the old monk said. "Haïta the Shepherd."

"Uh huh," I said, shaking off the horrific imagery. "I don't suppose you have more food. I went through most of yours last night."

"I have enough for our journey," Haïta said. "We can reach their camp in a few hours."

I snorted. "You can't be serious. Why would you want to attack them during the day?"

"Day is when they are weakest," Haïta replied. "These are the mixed bloods who have at least one parent from the dark places of the ocean. They are not used to the sun, and it is when they are sluggish and weak."

I shook my head. "I do not believe in sea giants, Haïta."

"And yet your god teaches they are very real," Haïta said. "Just as mine teaches there are demons."

"Perhaps they're both foolish," I said, feeling particularly blasphemous. The dream of last night was a powerful omen and not a welcome one. It implied that I would never make it home to my brother's family.

"We should take out their sentries, there should be no more than three, and cut the throats of the rest while they sleep," Haïta said, ignoring my comment.

"That sounds less like a plan than a goal," I replied, sighing. "However, I have no better ideas."

My brother had always been the thinker between us and I'd seen where that had gotten him.

"Good," Haïta said. "Then you should get ready to travel. Once they are roused, they will perform the rite and summon their brethren from the sea. Then there will be no stopping them. They will have the aid of their dead god."

"Isn't your god dead?" I asked, only vaguely knowing anything about the Christians' religion. It seemed mostly nonsense about not seeking revenge and the poor being blessed, which was just silly by any right-thinking man's reckoning.

"My god lies dead until his resurrection too, yes," Haïta said. "Until the day he returns and destroys all of our enemies."

I really didn't need to get into a religious debate. Odin would provide and had up until this point. "How does one get to become a monk anyway?"

"I joined after I saw the horrible things out there," Haïta said, sounding more annoyed than anything else. As if he was explaining seamanship to a particularly easy to distract child. "Things that should not be and could only be fought by the power of my Lord."

"Uh huh," I said. "What does this Dagon have to say about it?"

"That there is only room for one god's faithful," Haïta replied.

Oh yes, this was going to be a lovely trek.

"Odin, that is one ugly son of a bitch," I said, wiping off my knife as I stared down at the dying Dagonite on the ground.

Sneaking up on the first of them keeping watch had been surprisingly easy, Haïta proving to be an able woodsman as well as every bit his claim as a hearty warrior despite his appearance. He wore a large backpack full of supplies, clothes, and his staff that plugged a hole in it. He also had a quiver and bow that, combined with the other materials, I would have struggled to carry half the distance we covered.

We were nearby the coast now with the forest growing right up toward its edge and too large for most groups to keep watch over. I'd gotten up behind the chainmail clad warrior and opened his throat with my knife.

Its blood was blacker than normal, though, and the man's appearance was obscene. He had eyes twice the size of a Northman's and a smooth face that seemed to sag off his cheek bones plus sacks bulging out of his neck. It reminded me of nothing so much as a frog mixed with a man. There was also a foul stench to the air that reminded me of rotting fish. His armor was good, though, and expensive too. I also saw his ax was fine steel, even if weirdly shaped with an eye-like design to the blade. The dead man wore rings of gold that I swiftly pulled off his fat fingers, already making this excursion worth it.

"It is an abomination," Haïta said, holding his bow steady as he surveyed our surroundings. "A product of man and not-man."

"If you say so," I replied, not willing to deny my senses but unconvinced as well that we were dealing with monsters. I'd seen what disease could do to a man and also encountered a wide variety of strange people when trading. None of them had been as repulsive to look at as this fellow but maybe he was a Pict. They supposedly married their sisters and ate the flesh of men according to my cousin.

Haïta cocked his bow and fired an arrow across the forest glade that struck another of the Dagonites in the throat. It was a supernaturally accurate shot, even for a man that didn't look like he was dug up from the ground a week after being buried. The figure choked in his own black blood before Haïta jogged toward him then drove the arrow deeper into his skull. It was a surprisingly brutal action, and I was starting to like the Christian.

"Two down," I replied. "So, that leaves six by your count."

"Yes," Haïta said. "We're nearby their camp. You should take his axe and smash in the heads of any that are still resting."

"That would not be honorable," I said, dryly. "I shall challenge them to combat open and honorably."

Haïta looked at me with a confused expression.

I grinned and let out a short laugh at the deliberate absurdity of my statement, going to check the second Dagonite body for more gold. This time, he had a little fish amulet that would buy me a shield when I made it back to my hometown.

"Your greed does not do you credit, Harald Bjornson. You can't take it with you," Haïta said, moving into the forest to look for more Dagonites.

"Then it's a good thing I intend to spend it in this life," I said, turning around to see no sign of my companion.

I also tried to remember when and if I'd ever told him my full name.

Calling it a camp was a misnomer as it was a single large Rus-style yurt erected on a hill overlooking the rocky shore. There were bedrolls gathered around it and a fire pit. It seemed an incredibly poorly chosen location for it as the tide would almost certainly wash over anyone sleeping around it.

Still, the wealth of my prey was impressive as I saw their longboat nearby and it was a genuinely masterful piece of craftsmanship, enough to have close to thirty men onboard and possessed a strange squid-like design on the masthead. If it had been fully loaded when Haïta's people had attacked, they must have been great warriors to kill so many. It also wasn't something I'd be able to man myself and Haïta would have known it.

Then again, the old monk had proven far from useless and between the two of us it would be possible to maybe direct it to inhabited lands if they were in Njord's and Odin's favor. That was never anything to count on when dealing with a bitch as capricious as the sea but there wasn't anything I could do about it now. It was also a prize that I'd look like a king bringing into the port and could hire a proper crew for at the nearest port.

Either way, I stayed low and saw only a single guard left awake. Taking the eye-shaped ax, I did my best to sneak up, but it didn't quite work out. Thankfully, the guard was lethargic and when he heard my movement, I was close enough to drive the ax into his neck. The man blubbered and reached for the blade even as he bled out from the enormous wound. I didn't give him a chance to go for it and drew my knife to stab him through the base of his chin. The fetid foul-smelling black blood made me gag but was still a welcome sight as it poured out over my hands. After all, it wasn't mine.

Five left.

Plus, the maiden they were going to sacrifice.

I hadn't given much thought to her, hadn't ever given much thought to women in my life, but noted that might be another bonus to this excursion. I preferred my women willing but provided I didn't have to argue too heavily with the monk, women slaves brought a high price at most of the markets I knew along these regions. The thought gave me pause and it occurred to me that I might just let her go with Haïta. He'd seemed oddly focused on her and she was probably a believer in his faith he wanted to rescue.

If so, I'd play the hero and let him take her back to her family or whatever monks did with women. This encounter was changing me, and I felt a better man for it. Not the least because the man on the ground had a pouch full of actual gold coins. At least twenty of them.

Odin be praised.

Clearing my head of any thought but the men around me, I found three sleeping the sleep of the dead in their bedrolls. There was a pot full of some sort of thick black liquor by the fire pit, I certainly recognized the smell of brew, and it amused me how much it was contributing to what I expected to be the easiest victory of my life. They were all as ugly and disgusting as the first one I killed. Destroying them would be a favor to themselves and whatever gods they worshiped. Most of all, though, it would be a favor to myself.

One head was easily caved in as he slept.

Two.

Then three.

It was bloody, gory, and entirely satisfying business, the Dagonite's own steel doing a better job than anything I'd ever wielded in my hands. With three more dead, I only had two to find and kill. Now, where were—

"*Dagon mftaghnah'pftyl! Muh'tah'ahh'zuul, Mother Hydra!*" A shout came from the yurt's tent folds as the two remaining warriors poured out with Moorish curved swords drawn. Clearly, these fish worshipers traveled as far as his people. Both had short, rounded shields too, something I could have desperately used right now. Both were even more frog-like than the others, but their fury was obvious as was their skill. Both charged forward, heedless of the danger but determined to avenge their slain comrades.

"Dammit," I muttered, holding the ax in both hands.

I had met many men who claimed they had struck down dozens of foes in battle. These men were all liars. The truth was that battle was often a matter of surprise, luck, and simple odds. Two well-armed men against one was almost always going to end in the death of the latter. A wiser man would have run but I'd already disgraced myself once.

Never again.

Instead, I surprised us both by charging forward with a curse on my tongue and no thought to my own safety. I slashed wildly and repeatedly, catching the first Dagonite off guard and cutting him to pieces before sheer chance allowed me to strike hard into the side of the second. It shouldn't have worked, mail existed for a reason, but the metal of the ax cut through it like linen. I had a feeling it wasn't steel but something much stronger and sharper. Either way, my next blow was enough to send it down. I kept cutting, though, and made a cruel sport of its form until it stopped moving. It looked like someone had poured an ink pot over his corpse.

"Ha-ha!" I said, as stunned as anyone by my triumph. "I piss on your god, Dagon! I piss on your language! I piss on your corpse!"

I was so relieved to be alive, I might have done so if not for the fact that I heard the tent flap of the yurt open again. This time, though, the sight that greeted me was far comelier. Her skin was as white as sea foam and her hair as dark as midnight with long lovely curls. The woman was clad in a white dress that was clean and tied to her waist by a well-tied rope. She moved with an ethereal grace toward me, her eyes a blue I'd never seen before.

I raised my hand. "You probably cannot understand me, but I am with the Christian monk. Cross? Friend? You don't have to die."

The woman showed no sign of understanding but still approached me, which made me wonder if she was simple. I had no idea how to respond but found myself strangely tongue-tied. That feeling swiftly left me as she opened her mouth and revealed two rows of teeth that were sharpened like knives, her jaw extending down like an eel's. Her mouth let forth an unearthly wail that caused me to drop my axe and cover my ears for fear of their insides bursting.

"Hel!" I shouted back, scared out of my mind and suddenly all too aware that Haïta hadn't been lying about them being giants.

That was when an arrow shot into the creature-woman's breast. A flower of clear liquid oozed from her injury instead of blood, smelling faintly of flowers like she'd been stuffed with plants instead of gore. Instead of dying, she screamed again, only to be shot again.

"Yield!" a familiar voice shouted to the creature-woman.

Haïta had finally made his appearance and calmly fired arrow after arrow into the creature-woman before me. She had six arrows in her before the clear ooze started to drip out of her mouth, her movements becoming sluggish as well as vulnerable. The sight compelled me to grab for the ax I'd dropped, climb to my feet, and swing around to decapitate the creature-woman in one easy motion.

"And stay down!" I shouted at her body, feeling quite proud of myself. I could now call myself Harald Giantslayer wherever warriors gathered to drink. Not that anyone would believe this story. I'd sound like the very drunks and braggarts I'd spent most of my life mocking.

"You destroyed the sacrifice," Haïta said, approaching me from behind. He tossed his bow on the ground and pulled his staff out of his backpack. I didn't know why he bothered with it since he clearly didn't need it to walk.

"Yes. She wasn't exactly pure, was she?" I made a half-terrified joke before sucking in my breath. "We make a pretty good pair, don't we monk?"

Haïta nodded. "Yes."

He then cracked me across the head with the side of his staff, sending me thundering to the ground.

Darkness claimed me with a second strike to the skull.

I woke up to the smell of burning flesh and rotting fish. My wrists were bound to a pair of poles set up before the shoreline. Night had fallen and my mouth was aching every bit as much as my head. My attempts to speak failed miserably because I discovered, to my horror, they'd been sewn shut with fishing line. Worse, my mouth had been stuffed full of some foul blackish substance that I could not taste but had a noxious texture.

Haïta was standing there with his shepherd's crook, in the center of a five-pointed star created by rocks combined that each ended in a strange dog-like skull that seemed more manlike than I was comfortable with. The bodies of the Dagonites were burning in a nearby pyre, sending forth black smoke into the night sky.

"*Catag'nh nergul Adonei Yog-Sothoth, Jehovah Azathoth Adzul, and Nyarlathotep Jibriel!* I call upon you, Lord of Hali, King of Carcosa, Lord of Leng, to come forth! Come forth and accept your gifts on this glorious day when the worlds merge! The heretics have been purged and the Dead God Who Lies Dreaming, your brother, lies sleeping still at the bottom of the dark underworld where your enemies have imprisoned him!"

"Mmmmph!" I struggled to speak.

"Come forth, Lord Hastur, Son of God, and bringer of the Revelation!" Haïta called up to the sky. "Come forth!"

I did not understand what had happened or who the names Haïta was calling upon were. He was like no other Christian I had ever met, and it occurred to me I was now dealing with something that I had absolutely no way of dealing with or escaping from. I struggled in my bonds but found them firmly tied.

That was when the sky cracked open and lights in colors I'd never seen before poured forth. They scintillated and danced in a rainbow of weird patterns before some THING began to crawl out from the rift that existed above me. It was indescribable and horrifying, causing fear in my heart that dwarfed anything I'd ever felt before.

I knew, though, I was its meal.

A sacrifice.

A Blood Eagle to appease the gods.

I tried to scream but could not because I realized that Haïta had taken my tongue.

La Compagnie Maudite

A Eugene Angove Adventure

By Tim Mendees

"God preserve us."

Eugene Angove looked down, his mud-caked boots tentatively nudging the shoulder of a fallen man. There was no response, no signs of life. He couldn't even tell if the deceased was one of theirs or belonged to the opposition, such was his pitiful condition. In the end, it didn't matter, this poor chap was merely grist to the mill of war. "What a blasted waste."

An explosion to his left knocked him off his feet and showered his Khaki uniform with debris and a wet substance that he prayed was mud. Glancing around, he couldn't see any of the men he'd recently climbed the trench ladders with. A warm stickiness trickled from his left ear, the concussion had blown his ear-drum. After a second or two of stunned immobility, he climbed unsteadily to his feet and shook his head in a futile attempt to clear out the cobwebs. Under the whistle in his right ear, he heard a tell-tale metallic *thunk* followed by a *hiss* as a thick yellow cloud started to billow around him.

"Gas," Captain Angove cried for anyone who might be listening as he pulled his trusty SBR gas mask over his head. His revolver shook like crazy as he pointed it impotently into the encroaching murk. "Sir? … Major Carrington, Sir? … Where are you, Sir?" His voice was muffled by the protective face-wear and drowned out by the nearby roar of machine-gun fire and boom of mortar shells. Even if Carrington had replied, it was unlikely that he would have heard him over the din.

Getting to his feet, unsure as to which way was North and which way was South, Eugene limped onwards, ever onwards. After all, this was his turn for the *big push*. Field Marshall Hague's grand offensive. The moment that top brass had been salivating over... and their troops dreading. Flinching at every noise, his body aching with every ragged breath, Eugene called out again. "Is anyone there?"

Without warning, the ground erupted in a plume of mud and a tangle of barbed wire. Eugene was knocked off his feet, landing hard on his back. The remaining breath in his body was forced from his lungs in a mucosal splutter. Convulsing and trembling, Eugene fought the urge to just lie back and allow himself to be buried alive by the constant churning hail of flying dirt and human mince. Would anybody know that he gave up? Would anybody care? At the end of the day, he was on course to becoming just another statistic in the endless tally of the dead.

Screaming into the charcoal filter of his mask, Eugene rolled onto his stomach and attempted to rise. Through his tear-smudged eyes, a shape appeared before him, making him yelp in alarm. It was sleek and black. Coming right for him. Did the Devil walk the fields of Gommecourt? Blinking to regain his focus, he finally became able to make out four legs. Four legs and a tail. What the hell was a cat doing in No-Man's-Land? Eugene got to his knees and pulled the feline to his side, running a gloved hand along its flank.

"You shouldn't be here, Puss... none of us should."

Meow...

Now, fully upright, Eugene watched as the unfazed moggy rubbed around his filth-encrusted legs before gazing up at him with its piercing emerald eyes. The warmth of the animal cutting through the icy chill of the mud was a jolt to the senses that served to clear the mists from between his ears. "Go on, get the hell out of here, you daft sod. I dunno how many of your lives you have left... but you are fixing to lose the rest of 'em in bally short order."

The cat moved off, away from the epicenter of the mustard gas before stopping and gazing back at Eugene. *Meow...*

"Go! Don't just bloody stand there!" Eugene's heated words fogged up the windows in his mask, making visibility even worse. All he could see as he peered into the smoke was two pinpricks of green as the cat implored him to follow.

Meow… The cat trotted back and repeated the process. When Eugene didn't follow, he repeated it again. Eugene had no idea how long he had been standing like a target in the middle of a war zone by the time something on his periphery finally shook him from the cat's spell. It was swift and violent, the deliberate slice of a swagger stick cutting through the miasma.

"Captain!" A voice boomed in his functional ear. It covered the meters between them as clear as a telegram. Eugene spun, nearly falling back to his knees. Instinctively, he pointed his revolver at the incoming figure before getting a hold of himself and snapping a perfect salute. Up as smooth as butter, then down like a sack of spanners. It was something he had perfected when he was barely able to walk. Being reared in an Army family will do that to a boy.

"Richard?" Eugene shook his head and quickly corrected himself. "Um, Major Carrington, Sir?" Eugene gabbled at the sturdy upright figure in the smoke. "Thank God, I thought I was the only one left."

"Dreaming again, Captain Angove?" Major Carrington snarled. The windows on his gas mask were two deep pools of black. Though it was hidden, Eugene *knew* that his SO's moustache was twitching impatiently.

"Um… No, Sir… Sorry, Sir." Fear radiated around his body. All the guns and bombs in the Somme had nothing on the terror instilled in him by Major Carrington. The man was nothing short of a Hellion when his dander was up. How his eldest sister had fallen for such a brute was nothing short of a mystery.

"Right, stop dithering and fall in!"

"Yes, Sir," Eugene saluted again, the middle finger of his flattened palm vibrating against his temple as his arm trembled violently. He took one step towards the Major and felt a sharp pain in his calf. Fearing that he had caught himself on the filthy barbed wire that littered the area, he looked down. Puzzlement creased his masked brow as he spotted the cat. "What the bloody hell are *you* doing?"

The cat had sunk the claws of one paw into his flesh and looked up at him with its dazzling eyes. Pleading. Imploring Eugene not to follow the other man, to take another path.

"Get a bloody move on, Soldier. I won't tell you again," Major Carrington snarled as he turned and marched into the gas cloud.

The cat detached itself from Eugene's leg, arched his back and hissed at the stern officer. Eugene tried one last time to shoo it away without any joy. It simply rubbed around his legs and mewled. Finally, Eugene raised his revolver to the sky and let off a round. The sharp *bang* startled the feline, sending it running for its life in the opposite direction. "Sorry, old chap... I must do my duty, for King and country." The words sounded alien on his lips. Eugene Angove had never wanted to join the Army. In fact, he would have done *anything* to avoid following in his father's footsteps. Then war broke out.

Turning, straightening his shoulders, and stiffening his upper lip, Eugene marched after the vanishing silhouette. Shrapnel, teeth and bullet casings crunched under his Army-issue boots. As more explosions shook the earth, thick black plumes of smoke joined the billowing clouds of mustard gas, stretching and writhing like spectral tentacles. "Sir, slow down, I can't see you."

The more he walked, the less he could see. More and more canisters of that hellish chemical weapon had been pumped onto the battlefield until all he could see was yellow. Yellow and black. Gas and smoke. Panic started to build, squeezing his lungs and constricting his throat. His breathing came in scratchy rasps as it made its way out of the gas mask's filter box, like someone scraping plaster off a stone wall with a rusty bayonet.

"*This way, on the double!*" The Major's booming voice, distorted and muffled by the dense atmosphere, urged him onwards. Smoke and gas quickly mingled into an impenetrable soup and the rattle of gunfire and *thump* of explosions had built into an almost mechanical rhythm. It was a noise akin to the clatter of the factories back home in North Cornwall. Timed perfectly with his footsteps and racing heartbeat, the infernal music of battle propelled him forwards. Not letting him stop. Not letting him get his bearings. Just keeping him marching like a good little soldier.

"Where are you, Sir? I can't see a bloody thing."

"*This way...*"

This time, the hollow-sounding voice seemed to come from behind. Eugene turned and called out again. When the response came, it seemed to come from his left. Eugene growled in frustration, picking a direction and walking. The cloud was so thick that he couldn't see anything below his waist. It was like floating in some vile-smelling liquid. It was only a matter of time before...

"Argh, bugger!" A loop of razor wire tangled around his shin, slicing through cloth and flesh alike. Pausing to untangle himself, he knelt down and put his hand on a damp skull. It was still warm. Eugene screamed and fell back onto his haunches. Lying next to the bloody cranium was a Captain's hat and a gas mask with *Angove* stenciled on the fabric.

"How can this be? ... Is this me?"

Halting his hyperventilation long enough to drag his bleeding leg free, Eugene scrambled to his feet and peered all around. It was no use. He was lost and alone. A lone island in a sea of filth and corpses. As despair took hold of his soul, he spotted furtive movement in the cloud. At first, he thought it was a fresh plume of gas, but it seemed to twist and writhe in unnatural ways. He stopped, temporarily mesmerized, as it was joined by another, and another.

The shadow-like tendrils squirmed and twisted in his direction. In the center of this strange display, an oily sepia blob started to coalesce. This was the epicenter. Those thrashing tentacles were coming from *whatever* the blob was. Eugene started to back away, horrified, as the entity continued to swell and bloat. It appeared to be composed of all the nightmare ingredients of battle. Mud, flesh, and pulverized bone... everything was being drawn into its bulk. Drawn in, assimilated, and dyed yellow by the mustard gas.

Eugene screamed as a monstrous eye formed of cinders and molten lead snapped open in its center. The tentacles lashed in his direction as he turned to flee. One caught his injured leg and tugged. Eugene was sent flying forwards... he felt the switch on the landmine depress with a slight *clunk* as he struck it with his chest.

Boom!

"Bugger me," Eugene shrieked, sitting bolt upright on his bunk. His vision swam. Taking in the sights around him... Sandbags... Rifles... Terrified faces... An angry red face with a twitching walrus moustache...

"On your feet, Soldier!" Major Carrington barked. The swagger-stick he had used to prod Eugene in the chest was just millimeters from the tip of the startled Captain's nose. It was so close he could have tickled his nostril hairs with it. "Up!"

Jumping off his thick woolen blanket and shakily performing a salute, Eugene tried to appear alert. The Major stared deep into his eyes before turning away. The hatred in them burned worse than any gas or incendiary. He didn't need to say any words, he'd said them all before. Disappointment... Disgrace... Degenerate... Lots of disparaging words beginning with D. There was nothing that the officer could say to him now that hadn't already been screamed in anger many times before. It didn't help matters that Major Carrington was his brother by marriage. Both he and his father never missed an opportunity to give him the needle.

Eugene had never wanted to follow in his father's footsteps in the first place. It wasn't that he didn't believe in the cause, Eugene just didn't have a regimented bone in his body. He was utterly convinced that he'd be able to do far more for his country if otherwise employed. He had even suggested that he join the newly minted Intelligence Corps, but his dad was having none of it. It was the front line or nothing. Anything less than rolling your sleeves up and getting bloody was seen as cowardice.

Up until that point, Eugene had been studying to become an archaeologist. When war was declared, his father had yanked him out of University quicker than you could say, 'God Save The King.' If the truth were told, he had been itching for an excuse for years. This wasn't helped by the fact that study was often the last thing on Eugene's mind. He far preferred employing his time in the pursuit of fine brandy and finer women. As soon as the first shots were fired, he was kitted out in khaki, handed his stripes and a sewing kit, then bundled off to the Somme under the care of his domineering brother-in-law. The poor sod never stood a chance.

"Today's the day, chaps!" The Major beamed as he paced the dugout. "A proud day to be British. Get up. Get kitted out… it's time to make history!"

The knot in Eugene's guts tightened. He knew what was coming… he just knew.

"It's time for us to give the Hun a damn good thrashing. It's finally time for the Great Push Forward!" If Carrington was expecting cheers, he would have been disappointed. All he got were a few involuntary gasps of acute terror. Undaunted and oblivious, the Major proceeded to rattle on for another five minutes, but Eugene didn't hear a single syllable. He kept replaying the dream over and over in his head. The wetness of the skull… the stench of his own burning flesh. That *thing*. Was it a premonition, or merely a heady combination of anxiety and dodgy trench cuisine?

Once the Major had finished spritzing the troops with jingoistic spittle, he had given a magnificent salute before finishing his sermon with a rousing cry. "You are all to become bally heroes today, every man-Jack of you…" He trailed off, levelling his swagger stick at Captain Angove. "Except you."

A hostile murmur spread around the low chamber and Eugene could feel the hatred in the other men's eyes as he had seemingly had his neck yanked from the noose at the last moment. Despite this gnawing sense of guilt, the relief was palpable. He'd have been lying if he had said he wasn't over-the-moon at the news. However, his jubilation was to be short-lived.

"Oh, don't you worry lads," Carrington grinned, sensing the growing animosity, "by the time he has finished, he will be wishing he was with you. Of that, I can guarantee. Follow me, Captain, the rest of you, get ready, we go at eighteen-hundred-hours, on the dot." With that order hanging in the air like the Sword of Damocles over the terrified regiment, Major Carrington strutted out of the barracks with his head high and his shoulders back.

"We, Sir?" Eugene asked when out of earshot of the troops. "Do I understand that you will be leading the push?"

"Don't be silly, Captain, I'm far too over-the-hill for that honor. Captain Richardson will be leading the men. He's a fine officer and has my fullest confidence. I think this shake up is best for all concerned. After all, this is a fine body of men that needs *competent* leadership, not the dithering of a dipsomaniac dilettante, if they are going to succeed." Carrington's pointed words struck Eugene between the eyes like a sniper's bullet.

Eugene was relieved. He despised his acquired sibling but didn't want him blown to Kingdom Come for his sister's sake, if nothing more. There was also their son, Thomas, to consider. Still, they were all dead men walking, at the end of the day. War had no regard for familial responsibilities or sentiment. Though, he'd have been lying to himself if he'd tried to deny that the thought of his untimely demise wasn't somewhat attractive.

"As for you," Carrington continued, "a driver is en route to collect you and take you to your new post. I think you'll like it. You always wanted to be an archaeologist, didn't you? I seem to recall my mother-in-law funding your ridiculous exploits."

Eugene wasn't sure where this was going. "Yes, Sir."

"Top-hole. Well, it has been decided to put you with the Royal Engineers Tunnelling Company so you can dig and wallow in mud to your heart's content. Let's see if you can bugger up digging trenches to your usual infuriating standard."

"You mean the moles, sir?"

"Spot on."

Eugene tried to hide his deflation. "Where am I being sent, Sir?"

"To the back of bloody beyond, from what I gather. An old farm complex or stately home kind of thing deep in the French countryside." Carrington took some papers from his inside pocket and thrust them into Eugene's hand.

"You mean a château?" Eugene couldn't help himself, his life had become a hollow existence filled with petty little victories, there was no way he was missing an opportunity to correct his CO. Once his pedantry had escaped his lips, he pocketed the papers and looked at the floor, the wooden supports, anywhere but the other man's eyes.

"Yes, well," Carrington sniffed after fixing him with a look that could have stripped the paint off a Mark I Tank at fifty paces. "Call it what you like, it's a run-down rat's-nest from what I hear. In any case, you will only be there until you and your grubby friends are redeployed to the front. Their previous CO, Captain Gillman, has turned deserter and disappeared without a trace. While you are there, try to find out what happened to the bounder," Carrington paused, a dark cloud occluding his features, "should you find him, your orders are to bring him in for court-martial. Though, between you, me, and the woodwork, I'd recommend you put a bullet between his eyes and save top brass a lot of bally paperwork. They have far better things to be doing than dealing with yellow-livered scoundrels like him. Am I understood?"

"Um… yes, Sir."

"Capital. You are to meet with the current senior officer, Second Lieutenant Hampton, he's holding the fort until you arrive. He will bring you up to speed, I'm sure. Now, do you have any questions?"

"Um…"

"Right then, time to press on, pack up, and push off, Captain Angove, your driver will be here within the hour. I'd like to say it has been a pleasure, but we both know that would be a lie. So, with that washing aired, Godspeed, Captain, I very much hope we don't meet again." Snapping off a salute and clattering his heels on the moldering wooden boards, Major Carrington left the trench with a sadistic grin plastered across his chops.

Eugene sighed, flipped him a defiant V-sign as he left, then muttered, "and bollocks to you too, Sir," under his breath. Turning back the way he had wandered, he let his shoulders sag and his chin drop. "Oh well, I don't suppose joining the moles can be all that bad. This next bit is going to be the worst, I imagine." The last thing he wanted to do under the circumstances was face the other men. Once again, he was left with Hobson's Choice. At least he wouldn't have to endure their silent disdain for long.

His feet dragged as he made his way back to the main domicile. The voices beyond were low and funereal. None of the men had any illusions concerning their fate. One man, a stout Scotsman, was cursing bitterly into his hat to muffle the noise. As Eugene crossed the threshold, the voices fell silent, and several pairs of haunted eyes snapped in his direction. Remembering that he was the ranking officer, he squared his shoulders and set his chin firm before starting towards his bunk.

Around halfway to his destination, a fruity Welsh voice sang out. "Can I have a minute of your time, Sir?" It was Private Brynn Williams, one of the very few people Eugene could have called more than a begrudging acquaintance. Both men were fond of a tipple… they became fast friends despite their disparate backgrounds.

Eugene sidled over to Williams' bunk with his pulse racing. The poor blighter in the adjacent bed had his scarred face buried in his hands as his shoulders heaved and shook. Everyone had heard the reports of the GPF attempts further down the line and they weren't encouraging. Many of the troops, Williams included had taken to calling it the Great Fuck Up.

"GPF?" Williams muttered as he hastily shoved what could prove to be his last letter home into a crumpled envelope and licked the gum. "GFU, more like…"

"You wanted to talk to me?" Eugene asked.

Williams banished the dark cloud from his face and stood. "I did, Sir. I wonder if you can do me a favor?"

"Anything."

"I wanted to get this letter to the BFPO before we went up those damn ladders, but it doesn't look like I'll have time. Could you drop it in on your way to wherever they are sending you?"

"I'll do my best, Lieutenant, though I haven't a blasted clue where I'm going. Some old château not far from the lines, is all I'm told. They've stuck me with the dratted Moles, their CO has done a bunk and left them up Shit Street without a map."

Williams furrowed his brow. "Captain Gillman?"

"Yeah. You've heard about it?"

"Haven't you, Sir?"

Eugene shook his head. "Not a Dickie-bird."

"'Ere, lads," Brynn called out, making Eugene flinch, "they've only gone and stuck the Captain with the *Cursed Company*." His words dispelled the harsh atmosphere in a trice. Instantly, the looks in the eyes of the assembled changed from one of hostility to one of pity.

Eugene swallowed. "Cursed Company?"

"Aye, Connolly told us all about it, didn't you, Willie?"

The swearing Scotsman paused in his steady release of invective long enough to nod.

Brynn continued. "He met up with a couple of them while on a detachment out North. They've got through four commanding officers in the space of three months. One shot himself, two went mad, and you know about Gillman. That's not all either. Several of the men have wound up dead or missing with no explanation. There's talk of a Hun curse…"

"Balderdash," Eugene snorted, desperately trying to sound unruffled, "no such blasted thing as curses." Though he spoke the words, he knew firsthand that this was a false assertion. Events back at his homestead a couple of years prior had proved that.

"Call it what you like, Sir, there's something bloody odd going on with that lot, and no messin' about. Willie reckons that Top Brass send their *problems* there to die," Williams caught himself and shuffled his feet awkwardly, "sorry, Sir."

"Aye, that's right," Connolly cut in, "like sweeping shit under a bush. You'd be better off goin' up the ladders wi' us, I'd wager. The

Frenchies 'ave told me some tales about that château that would curl ye hair an' turn it white."

Before Eugene could inquire further, Major Carrington's booming voice cut through the trenches like a blunt knife. "Angove, pull your ruddy finger out, on the double!" Almost inaudibly, he added, "I'll be damn glad to see the back of you."

"Whoops, better get kitted up, Sir," Brynn whispered, "I reckon it's nearly time for you to be off. If you could do your best with the letter, I'd be dashed grateful."

"I'll do my best."

"Thank you, Sir, oh," Williams paused and rummaged in his kit bag. After a moment, he pulled out a dented hip flask embossed with a Welsh dragon. "Here, take this, I reckon' you'll be needing a snifter."

"Oh, I couldn't possibly."

Brynn grinned and pulled out its twin. "It's fine, Sir, I have enough to see me up the ladder. Go on, take it, I filled it with the brandy we got from the Frenchies the other week."

Eugene laughed. "You sly old Taff, I thought that got depleted bloody quickly."

"You know me, I like to be prepared."

Eugene took the flask and shook his friend by the hand. "It's been a pleasure, Williams. Good luck out there."

"You too, Sir."

Nothing more could, or needed, to be said so Eugene turned and hurried to his bunk. He could hear Carrington's boots clip-clopping their way across the room. There was no time for delicacy so he simply stuffed his effects in his kit bag, holstered his revolver, and left before he could cop another earful. His mind was turning over the warnings of Brynn and Willie. It certainly sounded like something strange was afoot at his new posting. Making a mental note to question his driver, he made his way through the trenches and towards an uncertain future.

None of the rigors of training had prepared Eugene Angove for the discomfort of a lengthy journey in a repurposed ambulance through the French countryside. His buttocks were numb from sitting on a bare wooden plank as it rattled and shook its way over the pockmarked roads and scrubland. He had completely lost track of time and couldn't begin to recall how many times he'd been forced to leap out and crank the wheezing engine. The frigid night air had played havoc with the internal combustion engine. The entire experience had made him miss his horse and carriage back home at Angove Hall. He liked the idea of motor vehicles but, thus far, his experiences had been less than encouraging.

As he watched the shadows of trees and bushes recede through the flapping canvas at the rear, he once again turned over the little he knew about his situation in his mind. The driver, a taciturn Brummie named Gibbons, had little to add save that he knew Gillman and had never pegged him for a deserter. Quite the opposite, he had always struck him as the archetypical valiant Tommy who would give his all for the cause. He did mention that, on their last meeting, Gillman had seemed distant. Aside from that, their short conversation had little to offer. As a result of the mystery and the lurching suspension, Eugene's guts were in knots by the time they drew to a halt.

"Here you go, Sir," Gibbons grunted through the rectangular window separating the cab from the rest of the ambulance. "Mind how you go."

"Thank you, Gibbons," Eugene replied as he grabbed his bag and waddled to the exit, "are you not coming in for some refreshment?"

Gibbons let out a sharp laugh. "What, me, go in there… not on your Nelly. In any case, I'm needed back at Gommecourt."

Eugene didn't reply as he jumped down and planted his feet in the mud. Clearly, his driver had heard the same talk of curses that Connolly had. This was unsurprising, rumor and idle gossip spread through the ranks quicker than a dose of the pox in a brothel. Straightening his back and kicking his legs to get the blood flowing, he took a look at his surroundings as Gibbons turned the Ambulance around by driving up a grass verge, nearly toppling the wretched contraption over in the process. As it bounced and lurched upon reaching stable ground, Eugene couldn't help but smirk at the sounds of cursing that were audible over the thrum of the engine. He certainly seemed to be in a hurry to get out of the area. The dawning fact that Gibbons would much rather be in the trenches than there quickly wiped the smile from his face.

To the south a vast expanse of scrubland peppered with skeletal trees and jutting rocks tapered off towards the horizon. To the West was more of the same with a dirt road bisecting it as it climbed upwards towards a waxing moon hanging low in the sky. Back along the Eastern approach, the ambulance snaked along the road towards a small cluster of ruined farm outbuildings and twisted machinery left to rust amid tangles of weeds and debris. It was a lonely, unnerving place, but it was what sat to his North that made Eugene shiver. Just over a small rise, the turreted corner of a once grand château loomed above his position with a dark and unwelcoming forest beyond. Hefting his bag over his shoulder, he climbed the acclivity and peered at what was to be his temporary home.

"Where the bloody hell are the sentries," Eugene grumbled as he rubbed his gloved hands together to fight off the cold. Fashioned in the sixteenth century-style with a pointed turret at each corner, it was essentially the same size as Angove Hall, but had seen far better days. Ivy had all but claimed the northern half and the southern end looked to have been struck by a mortar shell. It looked utterly devoid of life save for a faint glow in one of the upper windows that could have been candlelight. A moat that had almost dried up fringed the property with its only access point being a stone bridge festooned with barbed wire and a roughly erected mesh gate on wooden posts. Just beyond was the sentry box… it was empty.

Taking out his hand-cranked torch and pulling the ripcord twice, Eugene shone the weak light on the ground ahead of him as he began walking towards the bridge. The harsh noise of the device startled something small and furtive in the undergrowth which, in turn, made Eugene flinch. "Sorry, old chap, didn't mean to startle you." Watching the foliage sway and buckle as the creature made its escape, he couldn't help but wish he could do the same. Continuing his course, Captain Angove had to pick his way carefully over jagged lumps of shattered stone and stray loops of barbed wire that had been discarded in what looked like a refuse pile. The Army couldn't half be an untidy lot when Top Brass weren't looking.

Upon reaching the bridge, Eugene was met by the sound of heavy boots racing along the stone. As he shone his light beyond the gate, a flushed-face Tommy no older than eighteen appeared out of the murk levelling his rifle. "H… halt, who goes there?"

Eugene shone the torch on himself to show his stripes and took his papers from his pocket. "At ease, private, I'm Captain Angove of the 46th… I guess that's *formerly* of the 46th. In any case, I'm your new CO. Here are my credentials." Stuffing the papers through a diamond-shaped hole in the fence, he put his shoulders back and waited for the inevitable salute. The shaken soldier peered at the compressed print before fumbling his rifle over his shoulder and snapping to attention.

"Private Jenkins, Sir, welcome to Le Château Dubois." Jangling a bunch of keys, he unlocked the padlock and let Eugene inside. His hands were trembling.

"Why weren't you on sentry, Jenkins?"

The young man looked sheepish. "I… I was taking a leak, Sir. Sorry, Sir. Won't happen again, Sir."

Eugene smiled. "Calm yourself, Private, we all have to answer a call of nature from time-to-time. Just bring a bloody bucket in future."

"Yes, Sir. I wasn't supposed to be on sentry, and I forgot."

"Where's the usual man?"

"Don't know, Sir, nobody does. Some of the men are looking for him now."

Eugene sighed. "Bugger me, this is a right rum setup. Where can I find Lieutenant Hampton?"

"In the main hall. Him and Gardener are trying to fix the radio."

The knot in Eugene's stomach tightened. *"Fix the radio? What's* wrong with the blessed thing?"

Jenkins shrugged and fussed with the keys as he returned the padlock. "Don't know, Sir. Sabotage, I reckon. It looks like someone thumped it with a hammer, if you ask me."

"Great, that's all we need. When did it happen?"

Again, Jenkins shrugged. "It were all right just before dusk. After that…"

"When did the sentry vanish?"

"Private Walsh? Um… must have been around dusk."

Eugene sighed. "Then, it doesn't take Sherlock bloody Holmes to work that one out, does it?"

"Um… No, Sir."

"Right, I'm off to find the Lieutenant. Stay on your post, you understand?"

Jenkins nodded.

"In future, if you need a slash… do it in the moat." Turning sharply, Captain Angove did his best officer strut, as it always paid to give a false impression of professionalism under these circumstances, and made his way towards the Château.

Beyond the bridge, a half-demolished wall spread around the perimeter. The gates had long gone and the wood repurposed in barring the ground-floor windows. In the center of a modest courtyard, a once-grand fountain towered over a cluster of tents housing shovels and other tools of the digging trade. It had long-since dried up and was now home to a sickly collection of invasive foliage. Again, there was nobody in sight. Eugene's boots crunched in the gravel as he skirted the ornamental feature. Glancing up, puzzlement creased his features as he noticed that the bare-breasted angel, which was the centerpiece of the fountain, was wearing a British Army issue gas mask. The juxtaposition would have made him chuckle on any other day. As it was, it made him shudder.

Two stout oak doors sat at the top of a small staircase and were topped by a shattered fan light. Its remaining panes were encrusted with grime and bird droppings. The doors were slightly ajar. As Eugene made his approach, a gust of wind made them slam together before creaking open once again. "Christ alive, this place looks like something dreamed up by M.R. James." Feeling a growing chill, he took out Brynn's hip flask and had a restorative nip. "Ah, that's better. Thanks, Taff."

Standing at the foot of the steps with his fists planted into his hips, Captain Angove cocked his head upon hearing a noise from inside. It sounded like a man screaming followed by several pairs of hurried boots pounding on the upper floor. Instinctively dropping his bag on the bottom step and unfastening the holster housing his trusty Webley, he began to creep upwards. The sounds above had died down but, the closer he got, he could hear raised voices coming from a room adjacent to the entrance hall. Reaching the doors, he took a breath and pushed them inward. Stepping inside, he took out his lamp and shone it around.

"Bugger James, this is more like something out of Poe!" He was standing in an airy chamber that stretched to the rafters. A wonky chandelier with most of its crystal embellishments cracked or missing hung over bare flagstones covered in muddy boot-prints, plaster dust, and other detritus. This was gothic enough, but it was the staircase snaking around the wall that gave him the willies. Lining its ascent were six portraits, evidently of previous owners. This much was to be expected, it was the unsettling fact that each one had its face scratched out that gave him pause. "Well, *somebody* isn't an art lover."

"*It's no good, Sir, he's made a right pig's arse of it!*" A voice raised in despair drew Eugene towards the door to his immediate left. Another man answered in level tones but was too quiet for him to hear. It looked like he'd found Hampton and Gardener. Checking that his buttons were done up and that his uniform was straight, he approached the door, knocked twice, then pushed it open.

A scruffy-looking private caked in grease leapt from his seat in front of a dining table cluttered with wires and bits of broken radio equipment. "Who the bloody hell are…"

The other man cut him off, placing a hand on his shoulder. "Good evening, Sir, I trust you had a pleasant journey?" Snapping to attention, the Second Lieutenant gave Eugene a salute.

Eugene returned the gesture. "At ease, Hampton, I presume?"

"Indeed, Sir. This is Sergeant Gardener, you'll have to excuse his manner, he's rather frayed at the moment."

"As I can see. What happened? I hear from your, *ahem*, sentry, that you have a missing man and suspected sabotage?"

"That's about the size of it, Sir. At around seventeen-hundred hours, Gardener came in here to relay a message to Top Brass acknowledging your pending arrival. Upon finding the smashed radio, he came to find me. I had the men fall in and discovered that Walsh was absent. He has been acting strangely ever since Captain Gillman absconded so, naturally, I assumed the two events were connected."

Eugene was somewhat taken aback by the man's unruffled state. Not once did his tone fluctuate and he was still standing to attention. "Thank you, Lieutenant. I did say you could be at ease."

This made Gardener snort. "He is at ease, Sir. Me and the boys reckon that the Lieutenant doesn't know how to relax."

Hampton rolled his eyes.

Eugene smiled. "Very well. I trust that everything is being done to find Walsh?"

"Indeed, Sir. I have the men split into two parties. One searching the house, the other the grounds."

"Speaking of which, I heard a cry from upstairs when I was outside." Now he thought about it, that wasn't the only odd thing he noted. If there was a party of men searching outside, where were they? The only soul he'd seen save the two before him was the weak-bladdered private on the gate. Before he could voice this concern, the door opened and another scruffy-looking private burst into the room panting for breath.

"What is it, Greene?" Hampton purred without a second's hesitation.

"It's Walsh, Sir… I think we've found him."

"You *think* you've found him?" Eugene asked. "You either have or you haven't."

"Um… it's 'ard to tell, Sir. Come an' 'ave a look."

"Where are you?" Hampton cut in.

"Guest bedroom, west-wing, Sir."

"Fine. Run along, Captain Angove and I will be along promptly."

"Thank you, Sir."

As Greene departed, Hampton turned to Eugene. "I think this explains your cry, Sir."

Eugene sighed deeply. "What the Devil is going on here, Hampton. The boys in the trenches are calling you lot the *Cursed Company*."

Hampton gave a wry smile. "I honestly couldn't say, Sir. There have been some strange things afoot since we came here. I'm not a superstitious man, but the run of bad luck we've been having I'd say that someone would have had to smash a cartload of mirrors to warrant it," he paused and motioned towards the door. "Shall we?"

Eugene nodded.

"Do you want me to come with ya?" Gardener asked, clearly wanting a break from the defunct radio.

"No," Eugene replied, dashing his hope of a reprieve. "Stay here and try and get that blasted thing working. I for one don't relish the thought of being stuck out here with no way of calling for help. This place puts the wind up me, and no mistake."

"Very good, Sir," Gardener grumbled before jabbing the back of the radio with a rusty screwdriver in frustration.

Hampton led the way towards the entrance hall, pausing to take a grimy paraffin lamp from the top of a moldering service cupboard below a dumbwaiter set into the north wall. Taking a box of Tison's matches from his inner pocket, he struck one and lit it before proceeding through the door and onto the foot of the stairs. Shadows flickered on the vandalized paintings, making them even more sinister than earlier.

"Did one of your lot do this, knacker the paintings, I mean?"

"No, Sir. They were like that when we got here. Le Château Dubois had been abandoned for many years prior to our arrival. Even the outlying farms and cottages had long since been left empty. I assume the vandalism was done by ruffians from the next village around two miles East."

Once again, Eugene was impressed by Hampton's delivery and demeanor. "I have to say, Hampton, your upper lip seems to be stiffer than most, under similar circumstances. Am I to take it your family was in service?"

"Of a sort. My father was a valet, and his before that. I too was in service to a young gentleman before war broke out. My employer joined up as soon as the bullets started flying. I saw it was my duty to try and protect him as best I could."

"I see. What happened to your employer?"

"He didn't make it, Sir."

"I'm sorry, Hampton."

"Thank you, Sir. As you know, one cannot simply leave the Army once one has joined up, so I decided to make the best of the situation."

"That's commendable. For my part, I had little say in the matter. I come from a long line of fighting men. I wanted to be an archaeologist, so it appears we are both somewhat reluctant soldiers."

"It would appear so, though, I would venture that most soldiers are reluctant, Sir. Show me an eager one, and I show you someone who should never be handed a loaded rifle."

"Ha, that's true enough, old chap," Hampton's quip made Eugene smile for the first time since he had arrived in that decrepit and sinister place. Reaching the landing, he took a look down both corridors to their respective wings before veering to the left. The walls were still adorned with grubby oil paintings of ruins and stormy seas. Halfway down stood a small table with a vase housing dead flowers wrapped in gossamer atop a mildewed doily. "It looks like the previous owner left in a damn hurry, Hampton, something of a moonlight flit, you could say. Is the rest of the place still fully furnished like some macabre hotel?"

"Indeed, Sir. When we first arrived, the larder was still stocked with rotted foodstuffs, most of it turned to humus by now. It stunk to high Heaven, so we had to clean it out. It is like the building is frozen in time, everything seems to be as it was left… aside from the portraits, of course. The wardrobes are full of clothing and the library is a sight to behold. Captain Gillman spent hours poring over the volumes."

As the duo reached the end of the corridor, a green-looking private burst from the end room holding a ceramic bedpan under his mouth. He proceeded to crumple in a corner, hunched over and retching.

"Well, that doesn't look encouraging," Eugene said as he pushed open the door and almost gagged on the sickly metallic odor that hung like a shroud over the grisly scene that met his gaze. They were standing in a guest bedroom lined with oak wainscoting and centered with a matching four-poster bed complete with yellow drapes. The rest of Hampton's indoor search party stood around it, looking pale and dumbstruck. On the bed lay a body, entirely naked aside from a pair of Army-issue boots and an ornate mask. His torso and extremities were a mass of lacerations, some of them looking to be crude symbols and lettering. The straight razor in the deceased's right hand told them that the injuries were self-inflicted. Above the bed, written in blood on the wall, were the words, 'HE WEARS NO MASK."

"God in Heaven," Hampton gasped, "what could have possessed the poor devil?"

"Possessed is right, Sir," Private Greene babbled, "I told Gardener he was actin' odd jus' this mornin'. It's this bloody place, the lot of us is cursed, everyone's going doolally!" He trailed off upon being elbowed in the ribs by the man standing next to him.

"Well, is it Walsh?" Eugene asked, choosing to ignore the man's words to keep his own anxiety from spiking.

Hampton moved around the bed. "No need to ask about the cause of death," he said, pointing to the gaping wound in the man's neck. It was so deep that the vertebrae were visible underneath the congealed blood. "I'll have to remove the mask to get a positive identification."

"I wouldn't do that if I were you, sir," Greene warned, "an' it won't do you no good."

"What do you mean?"

"He's... He's got no boat race, sir!" The young Cockney looked close to breaking down as he pointed to a tin helmet that had been placed over a bloody mass next to the bed.

Eugene turned away and drew out his hip flask. After a nip, he turned back to Hampton. "Do you think it's Walsh, or could it be Captain Gillman?"

"Too tall to be Gillman," Greene once again cut in, "and he has hair. Old Gillman was as bald as a baby's arse, sir."

Hampton rolled his eyes. "Thank you, Private Greene, that will be all. You men go down to the kitchens and put a pot of tea on, and check on Timms, the poor chap looked like he was about to turn himself inside out."

Gratefully, the men obeyed, leaving Eugene and Hampton alone with the cadaver.

Eugene pinched the bridge of his nose, "what would Carnacki do?"

"Pardon, sir?"

"Oh, nothing. I once met a man used to dealing with odd situations. Right, let's think about this logically. If we assume this is Walsh, what was he doing the last time anyone saw him alive?"

"That's easy, I was the last person to see him alive. He was in the library following up on Captain Gillman's research. I saw him take a book. I'd tasked him with going through the Captain's notes to try and glean some useful information that may lead to his location. He'd mostly been in the study next to the master bedroom."

"Then that is where we shall go. Let's get out of here before I bring up this morning's ration."

"Very good, sir. Before we do, what do you suppose this slogan daubed on the wall means?"

"I'm buggered if I know, Hampton. Probably just the ravings of a disordered mind. I'd wager it doesn't mean anything useful."

"Hmm," Hampton stroked his chin before following Eugene from the room. "The master bedroom is the one at the top of the stairs. The study can be accessed via the door on the other side of it."

As Eugene approached the study, a thought crossed his mind. "That mask, where in Hades did he get it?"

"Good question, sir. I'm afraid, I have no idea. There is a ballroom at the back of the building. Perhaps, it came from there?" Hampton thought for a moment. "The only mask I've seen like it before was on one of the two statues. I pegged it as a joke perpetrated by the same hooligans who defaced the portraits."

"Two statues?"

"Yes, one in the center of the hedge maze at the rear. You will have passed the other on your way in. Both had ornate masks on them when we arrived."

"The one at the front is now wearing a British Army gas mask."

"Good Lord, it must belong to who we assume is Walsh. I'll check the serial number once we are done here."

Reaching the study door, Eugene opened it and entered. It was a cramped space cluttered with generations-worth of journals, books, and assorted knick-knacks. A large mahogany desk took up most of the space and was piled high with reams of paper and general clutter. Another faceless portrait hung on the back wall while a moth-eaten taxidermy owl on the top of an antique bookcase presided over the scene. Its eyes had been gouged out.

"Looks like Gillman had been busy," Eugene sighed as he settled his rump in the wingback chair behind the desk.

"Not just Gillman, sir. Each Captain had taken this room, and each one became lost in study. There seemed to be some kind of mystery I wasn't privy to that consumed them."

Eugene gestured towards an empty bottle of absinthe sitting on the end of the desk. "I take it my predecessor was fond of smothering the parrot?"

"In latter days, I'm afraid so. I think he got it from the neighboring village. He said it helped him concentrate."

"Well, the blasted fellow could have left me a drop. Oh well, I'm assuming there is a stock of brandy?"

"Yes, Sir."

"Well, that will have to do. I fear I'm going to need it if I'm to wade through this lot." Taking a sheet of paper at random, Eugene squinted at the haphazard lines of increasingly frantic script. "Take a look at this, Hampton, your Captain Gillman appears to be as mad as a March hare!"

Hampton took the page and frowned. On it, repeated ad nauseam, was the line, *'Don't follow the shepherd.'* After a moment, he rummaged in the pile of notes and took out an earlier page. "I thought as much, this isn't Gillman's writing, Sir. I think Walsh wrote this."

Eugene took both pages and looked them over. "Well, Gillman looks to be equally disordered. This looks like a play, but it's in German. It looks like he was translating it. Hardly important military work, I'm sure you'd agree. I can't make head nor tail of it. Though, I'm sure it's a script of some sort, there are names down the side of the pages." Slamming both notes on the desk, he took out his flask and drained the last of Williams' purloined brandy. "Dash it all, I appear to be dry. Fetch me a bottle from supplies, would you, Hampton, there's a good chap?"

"Very good, Sir," Hampton purred, falling easily back into his valet role. Before turning, he pointed to a leather-bound book sitting next to the empty absinth bottle. "Oh, I believe that is the book I saw Walsh take from the library."

"Thank you, Hampton. Oh, do remember to check that gas mask for the serial number."

Hampton nodded and closed the door behind him as he left.

Picking up the book, Eugene ran his fingers over the gold embossed title. "*Le Roi en Jaune…*" Opening the first page, he looked upon what appeared to be a script for a play. Alas, it was entirely in French, so he didn't have a clue what any of it said aside from a few words here and there that he had picked up in the trenches. After a moment, he shut it and put it back on the desk. "No doubt a load of romantic tripe anyway." Turning his attention to a field notebook belonging to Gillman, he settled back into the chair and began to read. After a couple of minutes, the combination of the brandy, his long journey, and the lamplight made his eyelids sag. In the next breath, he was in the arms of Morpheus…

The roar of the men was infectious. Eugene bellowed his lungs raw as his feet touched down in the mud of No-Man's-Land. Instantly, the area was a chaos of explosions and gunfire. Slowing his pace, he looked around and surveyed the scene. Second Lieutenant Hampton was to his left, Privates Jenkins and Greene to his right. As the men scattered, he stuck to Hampton like glue, determined not to end up alone. A series of colossal explosions sent a geyser of mud and billowing smoke over the two men. Eugene paused and looked down. "God preserve us." There was a body below him. It was in terrible shape.

"I've seen this before… but it's different this time," Eugene paused, letting Hampton take the lead as he looked around for some kind of indication of which way he was heading. As his mind raced, the *thunk* of gas canisters striking the mud heralded the coming of the yellow miasma. Panicking as he fell into step with Hampton, he fumbled for his gas mask and realized, to his horror, that he had neglected to bring it. Frantically, he looked at the fallen men at his feet. Reaching down, he took the gas mask from one of the fallen, making a mental note of the serial number stenciled on the cloth at the back next to the sizing number and issue stamp as he did.

"This way, on the double!"

Hampton didn't hesitate, he followed the voice without hesitation.

Eugene quickly grabbed him by the shoulder. "Wait!"

"What are you doing, Sir? Major Carrington gave us an order."

Before Eugene could reply, a mortar shell exploded off to their left. Like before, he was showered with debris, and his ear was perforated, but he hadn't been showered in sticky wetness this time.

"Christ!" Hampton cried over the din, losing his clipped delivery for the first time. "You just saved my skin! Thank you, Sir."

"Move yourselves, men, I won't tell you again!"

"Come along, Sir," Hampton urged as the shadows of other men in the yellow cloud followed the commanding voice of Eugene's brother-in-law. "The Major will have us shot if we disobey a direct order."

Again Eugene hesitated. Something in the movement of the other men gave him pause. They were docile, like a flock of sheep. The scribbled note of Private Walsh flashed before his eyes as something warm touched his leg. Looking down, his eyes met those of a softly purring feline. "Don't follow the shepherd... Hampton, wait!"

It was too late, Hampton had heeded the call and had vanished from view.

"Blast it to buggery! Hampton, where are you, man?"

"This way, sir!"

Eugene was about to follow the voice when the cat sunk its claws into his leg. "Ow, you little sod!"

A fraction of a second later, the ground ahead erupted with a colossal bang.

"Hampton!" Eugene Angove called out as he jerked awake in that dusty wingback chair in the study of Le Château Dubois.

"Sir?" A voice to his left answered, nearly making Eugene scream like a babe-in-arms.

"Christ in lederhosen, Hampton, you nearly gave me a blasted coronary!"

"Apologies, Sir. I was just filling your flask. I tried not to disturb you when I saw that you were catching forty winks... sorry."

"No, it wasn't you, Hampton, you were as quiet as a church mouse. Dratted nightmare, that's all. I've been plagued with them since I was a boy. I used to take laudanum to keep them at bay. Alas, you can't get a regular supply out here."

"With reason, Sir," Hampton creased his brow in an attempt to look stern. "That stuff isn't good for anyone, especially an officer."

Eugene laughed, a short ejaculation that was closer to a bark than anything containing genuine mirth. "You sound like my mother. Anyway, did you have a look at the gas mask?"

"I did, it was..."

"Hold on a second." Eugene took a pencil stub from the desk and scribbled a series of numbers on Walsh's *shepherd* note. Once done, he held it up to Hampton. "Was this it?"

Hampton looked shocked. "That's uncanny. Where did you see that?"

"In my dream. I know it sounds preposterous, but I saw it in my dream."

"How odd," shaking the disbelieving look from his face, Hampton continued. "Anyway, I checked the number with his kit bag, and, yes, it belonged to Private Walsh."

"So, I think it's safe to assume that the man upstairs is Private Walsh. That still leaves Gillman unaccounted for. Have you seen or heard anything from the party you sent outside? That reminds me, I saw neither hide nor hair of them on my way in."

"That's perhaps not surprising, Sir. There are quite extensive gardens to the rear leading directly to a dense wood. I told them to check the hedge maze. Gillman had a strange fascination with the fountain at its center."

"Is it the same as the one in the courtyard?"

"Close, though there are subtle differences. They are fashioned after twin sisters, apparently..." Hampton was abruptly cut off by a commotion from downstairs. There were raised voices, one of which sounded like a hysterical Greene.

"What now?"

Hampton shrugged, returned the stopper to the decanter, and handed Eugene the flask.

"Thanks, I think I'm going to need it, come along, Hampton." Eugene rose from the desk, took a snifter, slipped Gillman's notebook into his pocket, and headed for the door. Fuzzy from the interrupted snooze and all the brandy, Eugene stumbled on the top step and had to steady himself on the banister. Turning to face the topmost painting, he noticed a detail that had thus far eluded him. The figure, a faceless woman in eighteenth-century dress, was clutching a book to her prominent bosoms. He squinted to get a better view, giving Hampton the wrong idea...

"Ahem, there will be time to *admire* the paintings later, Sir."

"What? No, I was looking at the book, not her... Anyway, I think it's that play from the study, *Le Roi en Jaune*." Moving down a couple of steps, he examined the next painting, then the next. "Here it is again. The damn thing is in each one."

"Do you think it's important?"

"Gillman certainly thought it was..."

"*Sirs, come quick, Greene's hysterical!*" Gardener's flat Northern vowels carried up the serpentine staircase, shaking Eugene from his reverie.

The two men hurried to the ground floor and headed North towards the servants' quarters and kitchens. They could hear raised voices, one low and stern, the other high and excitable. As they neared the two steps leading onto the bare flagstones of the sizable kitchen area, they caught the gist of the conversation.

"Pull yourself together, Greene," Sergeant Gardener grumbled, "why the chuffing Hell would they be stark bollock naked in the woods?"

"I'm telling ya' I saw 'em, plain as the nose on yer face. They were on their 'ands and knees, 'eadin' for the trees. It's this place, I bloody know it. I can feel it inside me 'ead... whisperin.'"

"Get a bloody grip, lad!"

"All right, Gardener," Hampton waded into the fray, "let us talk to the man, you get back to the radio."

"It's no use, Sir, the ruddy thing's knackered. We'd have better luck stringing tin cans to the sodding outpost."

"Great," Eugene sighed, taking out his flask yet again, "that's all we need."

"Keep trying, Gardener. If we can't fix it by daybreak, I'll send a party to the outpost to collect a new one." Hampton caught himself and turned to his new CO. "If that's agreeable to you, Sir?"

Eugene finished gulping brandy and wiped his mouth on the back of his sleeve. His eyes were beginning to glaze over and there was a distinct rosiness to his cheeks. "Fine by me, Hampton. Now, what's all this brouhaha about naked men trotting around the lawns on their hands and knees?"

"I told the Lieutenant, and I'll tell you, Sir, I saw 'em. It was Banks and the rest of 'em that the Lieutenant sent to search for Walsh. They went 'round the lawn in a circle then off into the trees. I think they were followin' someone, but I didn't get a look at who. This shithole 'as driven 'em barmy."

"Calm yourself, Private," Hampton purred as he wandered over to the window above a cracked and filthy sink and peered through the wooden boards affixed to the outside frame.

"Can't you 'ear it, Sir?"

"Hear what, Greene?" Eugene cocked an eyebrow.

"The voices, Sir."

"The only voice I can hear is yours."

"There's a man... and a couple of women, I think. I can hear them when I'm in the library..." Greene was wringing his hands, his eyes darting and lips quivering. This was a man on the edge. "They are babblin' on in French. I can't make sense of it, but it gets inside me 'ead somehow. Like a music hall tune you can't stop humming."

Eugene handed his flask to the distressed soldier. "Take a big gulp and try to catch your breath."

Greene did as instructed.

"Better?"

"Thank you, Sir. Sorry, Sir. I guess I'm a bit wound tight after findin' Walsh."

"Understandable, and no need to apologise. I'm a bit jittery myself. Now, you go and help Gardener with the radio. Maybe two heads may prevail where one has made a right hash of it, what?"

"Yes, Sir. Thank you, Sir." Greene gladly took his leave and hurried from the kitchen.

Hampton smiled. "I feel I have to say, you handled him jolly well, Sir."

"You can catch more flies with honey than vinegar, Hampton, remember that."

"Noted, Sir." As Hampton turned back to the window, he caught sight of a figure entering the overgrown hedge maze. "Sir, I think I just saw someone. It was just a fleeting glimpse, but I'm sure it was a person."

Eugene unstoppered his holster. "We should take a look, but be on your guard, Hampton. You saw what Walsh did to himself. I for one don't relish the thought of tangling with a naked man waving a razor around without my trusty Webley."

Hampton nodded in agreement and drew his sidearm. Making his way to the back door, he pushed it ajar allowing the chill night air to invade the room. Stepping out, Eugene couldn't help but smirk at the lawn. It stood in sharp contrast to the rose and herb gardens on the opposite side of the disheveled maze. Where they had been allowed to become engulfed by knots of invasive weeds and wildflowers, the lawn had been carefully rolled and manicured so that it was perfectly flat and each blade of regulation height. The boot-marks that marred its otherwise flawless appearance gave its usage as a makeshift parade-ground away.

The two men took the steps down to the path that led off to each area of the extensive gardens before veering right towards the maze.

"There should be a line here somewhere," Hampton grunted as he lifted handfuls of overgrown privet. "Ah, here we are. Gillman had a rope attached to the fountain so that he could find his way in the dark. It was necessary after Jenkins got lost when he went to take him his tea."

"Having met the lad, that I can believe." Eugene drew his revolver and motioned for Hampton to lead on. "Be bloody wary, Hampton. I'll make sure we don't have any nasty surprises from the rear."

It took them just over a minute at a brisk pace to reach the central fountain. Once they did, Eugene was forced to turn his back on the sight before them. Two men, naked aside from gas masks, were crammed into the fountain in a grisly parody of worship at the statue's feet. Both had opened their jugulars and attempted to fill the fountain with their blood.

"Good grief," Hampton whispered, "what in God's name is happening here."

"I don't know," Eugene replied, strengthening his resolve enough to face the horror. "Though, I'd wager God has little to do with it." He moved forward to inspect the fountain itself and not the contents. "I thought you said she was wearing a mask?"

"She was… Oh, no, please don't let this mean we have another atrocity like Walsh to look forward to." For the first time, Hampton looked genuinely shaken. Even the stiffest of upper lip's have their limit. If he wasn't a teetotaller, he'd have been troubling his superior for a nip of hard spirit. As it was, he took a deep breath and counted towards ten.

"What's this inscription at the base?"

"It's the name of the piece, Sir, *Cassilda's Song*. I think she is supposed to be singing. The one out the front, her twin, is called *Camilla's Lament*.

"Cassilda and Camilla? Now, where have I read that before?" As Hampton looked on with a puzzled expression, Eugene took out Gillman's notebook and started flicking through the dog-eared pages. "I bloody knew it, they are from that dratted play, *Le Roi en Jaune!*"

Before Hampton could respond, a rustle to his left nearly made him drop his revolver. The hedge parted to admit a feral-looking naked man in an ornate mask. He was brandishing a boning knife and bleeding from several cuts. "Follow Haïta. Follow the shepherd!"

"Hampton, look out!"

The crazed soldier pounced towards the Second Lieutenant, snarling, spitting, and swinging his blade. Hampton let out a sharp cry as he ducked left to avoid impact. He levelled his revolver, but the man lunged forward, knocking him backwards. A shot flashed from the gun's muzzle, but went skyward as the momentum sent Hampton sprawling onto his haunches.

"Iä Hastur!" Raising the knife in both hands, the attacker prepared to deliver a killing blow.

"No, you don't, you bounder," Eugene growled as he took a pace forward, placed the barrel of his gun to the man's head, and fired. The newly deceased dropped the knife and lurched forward, landing on top of Hampton. Quickly, Eugene grabbed one arm and rolled him off the now blood-spattered officer. "Hampton, are you alright?"

Using the edge of the fountain's foundation stone for support, Hampton rose and looked at his soiled uniform with disgust. "I'm fine, thank you, Sir."

"Don't mention it. Who the Hell was it?"

"Corporal Banks, he was in charge of the second search party. He was absolutely fine the last time I saw him. What could have broken his mind so?"

"I'm not sure I want to find out. One thing is for sure, Hampton, I think Greene was on to something when he said that it was this place doing it. There is a force here. It reminds me…"

"Sir?"

"Oh, nothing I will bore you with. There was an *incident* at my family home a few years ago. I'm afraid that I was under the influence for most of it so my memory is a tad hazy. Let us just say, strange things were going on and my father was forced to call in an *expert*."

"This Carnacki fellow that you mentioned earlier?"

"Quite so. You have a good memory, Hampton. Anyway, he was able to put the matter to rest. Alas, I don't believe we have any such expert on hand."

"Then the duty must be ours, Sir."

Eugene took out his flask. "I was afraid that you were going to say that. Come along, let's go back inside, old chap, we need to get you cleaned up. If Private Greene sees you covered in claret, I fear the poor blighter will lose what remains of his reason."

Hampton took out his handkerchief and started to dab at his soiled lapel. Before he could reply, he heard a voice on the breeze. He raised a finger and listened. "Speak of the devil. He sounds like he's got himself worked up again."

Cupping his hands around his mouth, Eugene called out in reply. "What is it, Private?"

Again, Greene's words were indistinct, but Eugene did catch the final syllable. "Well, I never," he huffed, "did that bloody meater just call me an ass?"

"Surely not, Sir… Say again, Private!"

This time, they heard the hard G…

"Gas! Quickly, Hampton, we have to get inside."

Taking off at pace, Hampton grabbed the guide rope and crashed through the maze with his superior hot on his heels. Overhanging tufts of foliage rustled and shook as their shoulders brushed them roughly aside. Reaching the exit, both men paused for a second to look at the dense yellow cloud creeping across the lawn.

"God in Heaven."

"Come on, Sir!"

Eugene followed Hampton's lead, musing aloud as he went. "Have you ever seen the like? It must be a new type cooked up by the Hun."

Hampton took the steps two at a time and reached the door. To his utter dismay, he found it locked. "What the Hell is the man playing at?" He grabbed the knob and gave it a twist but the door was unyielding. "It's locked, Sir!"

"Damn the fellow's eyes! Put your shoulder to it."

Hampton banged and cried out for Greene, but it was no use, the door simply would not open. "It's no good, Sir."

"Well," Eugene let his shoulders sag, "it's been nice knowing you, Hampton, if only briefly."

"We are not done for yet, sir," Hampton said as he started unbuckling his belt, "have you got a handkerchief?"

"What the Devil are you doing man?"

"Take out your hankie and, pardon the expression, widdle on it."

"You can't be serious?"

"Urine is supposed to ward off the gas for a while. It's the ammonia, or something. At least, that's what Sergeant Gardener reckons. It could be a soldier's myth but it's bally well worth a shot." Hampton turned his back and began to urinate on his handkerchief.

Eugene was about to follow suit when he realized that it was too late. They were fully engulfed in the miasma, yet it did not burn, and it didn't smell like gas. If anything, it had the gentle aroma of a summer's eve. Jasmine and honeysuckle mixed with a slight metallic taint to give it a perfume that was at once both alluring and sinister. He tapped Hampton on his shoulder to stop him putting the foully soaked fabric over his face.

"It's too late, I'm afraid but whatever this is, Hampton, it sure as death and taxes isn't mustard gas."

Hampton dropped his hankie. "It's almost pleasant. Could it be some new kind of weapon?"

"I really don't want to hang around and find out. Let's get this wretched door open and get inside." Shouldering Hampton aside, Eugene began hammering on the door with his fist. "Open up, blast it!"

Turning to gaze at the swirling yellow cloud, Hampton noticed several shapes moving in formation across the lawn. They were fully clothed, thankfully, but on their hands and knees like sheep, docile and obedient... good little soldiers. "Sir, I don't think anyone except Greene is inside."

"What?"

"It's Jenkins, Timms, and the others."

Eugene paused his kicking of the door for a moment and turned to look. "Where do they think they are going?"

Hampton's mouth opened, but before he could utter a response, a voice boomed from the dark outlines of the trees beyond the lawn. *"This way... on the double!"*

"Major Carrington? What are you doing here, Sir?" Hampton's feet started moving towards the steps, almost as though he were in a trance.

Eugene grabbed him and gave him a shake. "Stop. It can't be, he's at Gommecourt."

"Come on, you know what the Major's like, he'll have us shot for disobeying an order..."

"Oh, I know only too well what the Major's like, but that's not him, it can't be." Eugene paused as the penny dropped. "Wait, you know Major Carrington?"

Hampton said nothing, he just stared into the sepia fog.

Eugene shook him by the shoulders.

"What?" Hampton's eyes cleared as he snapped back to reality. "Sorry, Sir. I fear my mind took a bit of a stroll there for a moment."

"That's one word for it. You mentioned that you knew Major Carrington?"

"Did I?"

"Yes. Well, do you?

Hampton grimaced. "Unfortunately. I know it's wrong to speak ill of a superior officer, but I found him to be a contemptible man. It was him who sent us here after an *incident*."

"Like kicking shit under a bush..."

"Pardon, Sir?"

"Oh, nothing. Just something one of the men said to me before I left the trenches."

"Don't just stand there swinging the lead, move yourselves, on the double!"

One of Hampton's feet moved before he caught himself and rubbed his eyes. "It really does sound like him, doesn't it? I wonder why it has taken his voice. Assuming that we are dealing with an *it*, and not some kind of shared hallucination." Hampton trailed off when he realized that Eugene wasn't listening. His CO was looking down around his feet. "Sir?"

"Oh, sorry, Hampton, I was looking for a cat."

"A cat, whatever for?"

"I was hoping there would be a cat, then I'd know this was all a bad dream. Never mind, I'll explain later, if we get out of this alive. Let's focus on getting back inside. Is there another door on this side?"

"Yes, there is one..."

A heavy *click* silenced the Lieutenant as the key was turned in the lock. It opened to reveal Gardener's puzzled face. "What the chuffing Hell are you doing out there, Sirs?"

"Oh, Sergeant, am I glad to see you. That damn fool Greene locked us out when he saw the gas." Hampton beamed as he lurched to the threshold.

"He's gone completely off his rocker," Gardener scowled, "I had to..." The soldier went stiff, and his eyes rolled as the point of a bayonet, driven into the back of his neck, jutted from his windpipe, showering Hampton with yet more blood.

Quick as a flash, Hampton pushed past the dying man and landed a perfect right jab on the assailant's jaw, dropping him like a sack of flour. Shaking his fist, he turned to Gardener, but it was no use.

"What in blue blazes?"

"It was Greene, Sir. He…"

Eugene stepped over the corpse and went to check on Greene, kicking away the rifle as he did. "Nice punch, Hampton, you knocked him out cold."

"I was my regiment's champion during training. I've always had a knack for the pugilistic art. Not that it did Gardener much good."

"Look here, man. There is no way we could have done anything. It's not your fault."

"I suppose."

"Come on, pull yourself together. We'll have time to mourn him later. We need to shut out whatever that yellow stuff is and do something with Greene. Is there any rope inside, or a set of handcuffs?"

Hampton stood up from his crouched position. "There's some tools in the library. There should be a rope amongst them. I'll go and ferret it out."

"Splendid. I'll lock the door and keep an eye on matey here." Moving Gardener's leg out of the way of the door, he closed it, turned the key, and shot the bolts. "Well, no shepherd is getting in that way." As Hampton's footsteps receded through the house with a dull echo he contemplated giving Greene a kick for good measure. Eventually, he decided against it. Even in a time of war, a gentleman would never do such a thing. Instead, he took out Gillman's notebook and flicked to the front. Something had been bothering him about the whole thing.

"Where was it? Ah, there, I bloody knew it." In the very first entry, a detailed account of Gillman's hasty posting to the moles, there was mention of an *MC* having sent him there out of spite. "Major Carrington. The bounder." Flicking ahead, Gillman talked about his predecessors and their *great work*. According to him, there was a secret purpose for them being there, something Top Brass wanted to keep hush-hush. Eugene's brow furrowed as he continued flicking. The entries got more and more disjointed as they went on. He was witnessing Gillman's mind unravel as *something* started to twist reality around him. After a while, he seemed to believe that he was a French artist and the last living heir of Le Château Dubois.

"Well, clearly Captain Gillman was barking mad by the end. It's probably a good thing that he did a bunk." Reaching the final page, Eugene squinted as he tried to decipher the spider-like scrawl. What he was reading was part suicide note, part poem. It made little sense, but one line leapt out at him. "'The way to Carcosa is in the paintings.' What is he banging on about?" Checking that Greene was still out cold, he left the kitchen, bolting the door behind him. "You're not getting out of there in a hurry."

Moving through to the entrance hall, Eugene peered up at the paintings. "What could he mean?" He checked the plates affixed to the lowest three. Each painting depicted a member of a family named Castaigne and seemed to span generations with the oldest at the top of the stairs. "Name doesn't ring a bell. There must be something else." One more thing did strike him. It was the fact that the paintings were perfectly spaced leaving no room for any more portraits. Almost as though the family line was destined to end where it did.

Returning to the ground floor, he looked at each one in turn. They were all similarly posed against a backdrop of the night sky featuring a prominent star North-East of Orion's Belt. For the first time since joining up, Eugene got the opportunity to fall back on his classical education. "Hmm, my astronomy is a tad rusty but I think that is Aldebaran. Not sure how that helps us. Aside from the stars, the only common trait is that wretched play. It must have something to do with that."

As Eugene contemplated trotting up to the study to fetch *Le Roi en Jaune*, Hampton reappeared, minus a rope, and looking pale as milk. "Sir, I think you should come to the library. There's something dashed odd going on. I can hear voices like Greene mentioned."

Eugene's face gave away his alarm.

"Don't worry, Sir, I'm not ready for Bedlam just yet. At least, I don't think I am. It sounds like it is coming from behind one of the bookcases. I think there is a hidden room or passage. It sounds like there are people back there!"

Drawing his gun, Eugene followed Hampton along a short corridor lined with boarded up windows on one side and doors leading to a boot room and a small lounge on the other. A door at the far end opened onto a cavernous space with shelves cluttered with moldering tomes reaching from floor to ceiling. It was just the kind of place that he could have happily lost himself in under different circumstances.

"As you can see, we were using this room as a barracks, of sorts." Hampton gestured to the rows of makeshift bunks along the perimeter of the room. In the center was a cluster of chairs around an old gramophone. He spotted Eugene looking at the object. "We found it in the farmhouse down the lane. Captain Humphreys, our first CO, thought it would boost morale."

Eugene nodded then strained to listen. "I don't hear anything, Hampton. Where were you standing?"

"Over to the left next to the fireplace."

"This crest above the mantle," Eugene began as he made his way over to the indicated spot, "I assume it belongs to the family Castaigne?"

"I wouldn't know, Sir." Hampton paused and looked up at the crest. Its central feature was a curious symbol detailed in bright yellow. It looked somewhere between a question mark and the tail and legs of a scorpion. "An odd crest, don't you agree?"

"Dashed odd, just like everything else in this Gothic nightmare of a place. I still don't hear anything, Hampton, could you have been hearing things?"

"It's possible, I suppose. My nerves are a little frayed, after all, but I'm positive I heard both male and female voices."

Eugene planted his hands on his hips and regarded the bookcase. All the volumes were of poetry aside from a section that appeared to house plays. "That play, *Le Roi en Jaune*, you said you saw Private Walsh take it from here?"

"Yes, just where you are standing, Sir. Sixth shelf from the floor about halfway along."

"'*The answer is in the paintings*,' by Jove." Eugene reached his hand into the gap left by the play. After wiggling his fingers around for a second, he felt a small lever at the back. Coiling his index finger around it, he gave it a sharp tug. There was a satisfying *click* followed by a creak as the heavy bookcase opened on concealed hinges. "Voila, as the French would say!"

"Bravo, Sir. I feel like we are finally getting to the root of all this."

"One can only hope. Grab that lamp, would you," Eugene indicated a paraffin lamp next to the nearest bed. As he waited for Hampton to grab it, a thought occurred. "Is that Greene's bunk?"

"It is."

"That explains the voices he was hearing. They weren't in his head, after all. Presuming there are people inside, that is."

Lighting the lamp, Hampton pulled aside the hidden door and shone it inside. A narrow wood-paneled corridor led to a short flight of stairs to a previously hidden portion of the extensive cellars. It was festooned with cobwebs housing the bodies of deceased insects, yet there were recent footsteps in the blanket of dust beneath their feet. It smelt of a combination of damp and decay, yet that same perfume from outside was evident along with the coppery taint that may, or may not, have come from the stains on Hampton's uniform. As it was, it was enough to make them gag upon getting a lungful.

Another corridor greeted them at the bottom of the stairs. It was constructed of bare brick and led to another heavy wooden door. As Hampton reached out his hand to grip the knob, a female voice spoke from beyond. Snatching his hand away like he'd been bitten, he raised a finger to his lips and put his ear to the door. The voice was joined by another female voice, followed by one male. The two women sounded cultured and refined, the man sinister. His voice was a cavernous echo that sounded like it was the product of stage trickery. This, coupled with the scratchiness behind the voices, revealed the truth.

"I think it's a recording, Sir," Hampton whispered, "a wax cylinder, perhaps."

Eugene cocked the hammer on his revolver. "Open the door."

"Good grief," Hampton spluttered as he pushed open the door. The room was filled with that strange yellow miasma. It seemed to be emanating from a glowing symbol in a circle of purloined Army-issue paraffin lamps. Above it, an old stovepipe from a wood-burner, sucked the noxious cloud out into the French countryside. "I think we've found the source of this nasty stuff, Sir.

Adjacent to the symbol painted onto the flagstones, there stood a makeshift altar fashioned from an old kitchen table and a yellow velvet drape. On it sat the wax-cylinder player. It was rotating steadily as the voices poured forth from the speaker horn. Eugene stepped inside and switched it off. "That's quite enough of that, thank you very much." Next to the device were several metal canisters holding more cylinders. He picked up the lid from the open one and studied it. "'*Le Roi en Jaune, Deuxième acte. Première partie.*"

"*The King in Yellow*, act two, part one."

"Thank you, Hampton, my French is bloody abominable."

"Sir, look. The cloud, it has stopped."

"That's a mercy. What I want to know is, how the Devil was it coming out of a dratted yellow squiggle on the floor in the first place. I think it's the same daub from the crest above the fireplace. It's on the title page of that play as well."

"It's all connected," Hampton mused as he took in the rest of the room. They were standing in another study of sorts, complete with wooden wainscoting and a wing-back chair. Another desk piled high with jottings stood next to a partially completed portrait. He stepped over to the writing area and picked up a couple of sheets. They were transcripts of a scene from a play, one in French, the other in German. Both appeared to have been written by different hands. "Humphreys and Gillman. I think they were translating the play into German. Whatever for, do you suppose?"

"The *great work*," Eugene said darkly as he stepped over to the painting. "Does this ugly mug look familiar to you?"

"By Jingo, It's Major Carrington!"

Eugene touched the tip of his index finger to the walrus moustache then rubbed it against his thumb. "It's still damp. Whoever is working on this is still around… somewhere."

Hampton looked beyond the easel. On the wall behind it was the slogan, '*Haita wears no mask.*' It had been scrawled in yellow ochre. "I recognize the writing, I think it belongs to Captain Gillman."

A soft *click* followed by a creak startled both men into turning as a concealed door in the wainscoting opened to admit a hunched figure. He was shorter than average, bald, and clad in paint-splattered Baroque evening wear. His lace cravat was stained with blood. "Bonjour, Gentlemen," he beamed, his voice a disgusting gurgle. "Welcome to my humble abode."

"Captain Gillman, I presume?"

"In a former life. Gilles Castaigne, at your service." Gillman took an ostentatious bow. "Now, I don't believe I've had the pleasure, stranger. Hampton, I know, but you…"

"Captain Angove. I'd say it's a pleasure to meet you, but I've had far too much brandy to be able to lie convincingly."

Gillman chuckled. "What do you think of my work? A good effort, yes?" He pointed to the painting.

"You've captured the contemptible man quite nicely."

"I call it, *Haita the Shepherd*. So, I'm to assume that he sent you to complete the work?"

"I think I've already worked out the answer to this next question. What *work*?"

"I like to call it, *The Great Patronage*. It is our duty to translate *Le Roi en Jaune* so that the play can be performed to an entirely new audience."

"The Germans, you mean?"

"Just so." Gillman flounced over to the recorder and gently removed the cylinder from the arm and slipped it back into its canister. "An expeditionary group, under the command of Haita, happened upon this place and received an audience with The King himself! First, they found the play, then they *persuaded* some locals from the farms nearby to perform it. It was glorious! Since that day, The Shepherd has directed his flock to the stage so that they may all play their parts. I play mine, as you will now play yours. Once translated, the Word of Hastur will spread."

"As I suspected, the bounder wants to use it as a weapon." Eugene turned to Hampton. "I don't know how, but this play is linked to some kind of force or entity. It twists minds." He turned back to Gillman, his face flushing with rage. "It has killed good men, mere boys, some of them, and you intend on distributing it in the German trenches?"

"Trenches, cities, you get the idea. Not just German cities, either. French, Spanish, you name it. Captain Humphreys even did an admirable job of translating it into our own tongue. Think of it as deliverance," Gillman purred as he picked up a canister labelled, 'Le Roi en Jaune, Finale,' unscrewed the cap, and placed it on the rotator arm. "Once the flock has been swelled with participants, it will be time for the final performance and a new Imperial Dynasty will rise from the mud." As he reached for the needle, Eugene cocked the hammer on his weapon.

"Don't even think about switching that ruddy thing on."

Gillman's grin bisected his face and revealed rows of jagged teeth as he, slowly and deliberately, placed the needle at the start of the recording.

Eugene squeezed the trigger. The report of the firearm was deafening in that dank and confined space as a bullet thudded into Gillman's chest. To his astonishment, it had little visible effect other than to knock the target slightly off balance. "What in blazes?"

Gillman switched on the recording.

Snarling with rage, Eugene emptied his revolver into Gillman. The last bullet struck him in the center of his forehead, blowing out the back of his skull, and dropping him like a stone "Well, that worked." Eugene smiled as he began reloading. Cautiously moving over to the fallen man, he crouched and pulled down the blood-encrusted cravat. "I thought as much. It appears that Captain Gillman has been dead for quite some time. His throat has been cut from ear-to-ear."

"Dead? How? We saw him, he was alive!"

"I don't pretend to understand, but there is no way he could have been alive looking at this." Eugene paused as words began to spill from the recording device. Solemn and rhythmical, it was a chant of some sort. Instantly, wisps of sepia vapor began to emanate from the yellow squiggle on the floor. "Quickly, shut the blasted thing off!"

Hampton leapt into action, covering the cellar in a single bound. As he reached towards the device, a thick plume of yellow belched from the horn. The voices twisted and distorted, becoming a disturbing gabble of warped syllables and guttural barks. Silently mourning the loss of his handkerchief, he covered his mouth with his sleeve and tried again. This time, a dark shape in the billowing cloud lashed at his hand like a whip. He yelped and drew his hand back. "There's something in the cloud, Sir. I think it's a ten…"

Before he could finish, the clatter of boots followed by a frenzied cry of, "Iä Hastur!" announced the arrival of Private Greene. The deranged man had escaped from the kitchen and was now charging Second Lieutenant Hampton with his bayonet. Eugene twisted his body and loosed off two shots. The first went wide, striking the portrait of Major Carrington. The second, slammed into Greene's thigh. He spun and lurched forward, missing his target and crashing into the circle of lamps around the occult symbol. Greene screamed and writhed as his body was engulfed in flaming paraffin. The yellow fog swirled around him as his agonized cries mingled with the din coming from the recording.

"Quickly, Hampton, the lamp on the desk. Melt the wax cylinder!"

As the fire began to spread to the wainscoting and lick at the legs of the altar table, Hampton hopped back to his original position, grabbed the lamp, and tossed it at the wax cylinder player. Its glass shattered against the metal speaker horn, raining fire upon the wax cylinder. As it continued to spin, showering the rest of the equipment with burning oil, it began to melt. As the cloud began to recede, Eugene dashed over and pushed him towards the exit.

Taking out his hand-cranked torch, Eugene gave the cord a tug and shone it ahead. Black smoke was mingling with traces of yellow making it hard to see. Luckily, they didn't have far to stumble before they reached the steps up to the library. Already, the smoke had reached the ground floor, and they could hear the roar of flames beneath their feet as they raced towards the front door. Eugene turned the key as Hampton unfastened the bolts. Coughing and spluttering, they fell out into the fresh morning air and collapsed next to the fountain.

Smoke was starting to drift from between the gaps in the boards covering the ground-floor windows as the sun began to rise over the nearby trees. Soon, Le Château Dubois, and all the horrors it contained, would be gutted by flame. A thought that gave Eugene some comfort as he gasped for air. As his eyes followed the line of the building, he saw a small furry shape disappear around the corner. "I get it now, puss, you were trying to warn me about Carrington."

Hampton looked at him askew. "Pardon, Sir?"

"The cat in my dream, it was trying to warn me. Carnacki says I have a connection to another world. A land of dreams. Cats are guardians, or something. Whenever I see them in my nocturnal wanderings, something odd happens."

"Like some kind of premonition?"

"Something like that, I suppose," Eugene shrugged. "I don't even begin to understand."

"Probably for the best, Sir. Institutions all over the world are filled with people who tried to understand their dreams.

Eugene chuckled.

"Anyway, what will you do now?"

"I propose we hike to the outpost where I intend on getting as tight as a boiled owl at the first opportunity!"

Hampton rolled his eyes. "I meant about Major Carrington."

"I know what you meant. I confess, I haven't the first idea. It's not like I can just flat out accuse the rotter of dabbling in weird occult mumbo-jumbo. He'll have me shot, or carted off to Bedlam."

"That's true."

"Don't look so glum, Hampton, I don't intend on letting him get away with it. I just have to figure out a way to do it. I assure you, one way or another, there will be a reckoning for what he did here, you have my oath as a gentleman." Eugene rose and offered his hand to Hampton. "Come along, old chap, we have a good walk ahead of us. Might as well get started, what?"

Hampton took the offered paw and was hauled to his feet. Smoothing down his filthy uniform and doing up his top button, he squared his shoulders and nodded. "Very good, Sir."

To Play the King

A Captain Cross Adventure

By David Hambling

"Woe! Woe to you who are crowned with the crown of the King in Yellow!"

Robert Chambers, *The King in Yellow*

"No! I am not Prince Hamlet, nor was meant to be;
Am an attendant lord, one that will do
To swell a progress, start a scene or two,
Advise the prince; no doubt, an easy tool,
Deferential, glad to be of use,
Politic, cautious, and meticulous;
Full of high sentence, but a bit obtuse;
At times, indeed, almost ridiculous—
Almost, at times, the Fool."

TS Eliot, *The Love Song of J Alfred Prufrock*

London, 1928

Act 1: Finding Treasure

"Look, this is the secret compartment—isn't it thrilling?"

Cross smiled indulgently. There was no need for them to drag him up here to see this, but Cassie was so excited to show him the hiding place that he had not refused, despite those stairs.

"This piece slides away," she said, moving a section of wainscoting. "And here's the little cubbyhole where we found the books."

Tea chests filled most of the small room, under its sloping ceiling, and it was cramped with the three of them in it. Even with the skylight open it was oppressively hot.

"It was very dusty," said Milly. Cross had only just met Cassies' friend, but she had made a good impression. She wore owlish glasses and looked like a librarian. He liked librarians. "I—we—cleaned it up. Nobody has used the room for years."

"I agree they meant those books to stay hidden," said Cross. "Shall we make our way back down?"

Milly, closest to the narrow staircase, led the way. Cross, awkward on his prosthetic leg, leaned heavily on the handrail and took it step by step.

"And you're sure the contract of sale of the house included all the contents?" he asked.

"Quite sure," said Milly. "I kept a copy of the contract."

"Milly drove a hard bargain," said Cassie.

"And you're also sure the seller is the clear heir and successor of the previous owner?" said Cross. He had been involved in too many cases where ownership of a book had been unclear, unproven, or contestable, turning a valuable find into an expensive court case.

"I pestered the Estate Agent's solicitor until they confirmed it in writing," said Milly.

Milly was the meticulous type. Cassie needed a friend like that.

"An old man lived here for years and years," said Cassie from behind him. "It went to his great nephew, who let it out to some people, and when they left he sold it. I don't think he knew about the books."

They returned to the cottage's living room which took up most of the ground floor. It reminded Cross of a doll's house, a cheerfully disordered place with shelves crammed with books and knickknacks, a bowl of wax fruit, and a Votes For Women placard propped up in one corner. The gramophone player had its lid open, among a scatter of ragtime records in paper sleeves. French windows opened onto a patio where an easel supported a half-finished watercolour; brilliant floral colours suggested it was a study of the garden.

"Where have you hidden them?" asked Milly, going to the dining table and moving aside a book. It was a treatise on gardening by Vita-Sackville-West, Cross noted automatically. "Aha."

Underneath were two smaller volumes bound in matching red.

Cross inspected them in turn and identified them easily enough. Though one was in Latin and the other in German, both were illustrated, one with astrological diagrams and the other with pictures of gnarled, human-like creatures. They had been part of a private collection, all bound identically in burgundy leather, with a bookplate featuring a blindfolded angelic figure astride a chimera. Neither was rare, but both were worth something to the right buyer.

"I can't make any promises," he said, putting them aside. "It's a truism that any book is only worth what someone will pay for it. There's no such thing as a market value for this type of thing."

"But," said Cassie, a child convinced her pebbles were jewels, "but they *could* be valuable?"

Cassie's father, a major in Cross's regiment, had survived the war without a scratch, only to die in the 'flu epidemic of 1919. At the funeral, Cross and his brother officers had vowed to look after the widow and daughter. The awkward girl of almost a decade ago was now making a life for herself in London, and when Cassie found the cache of mysterious books, her honorary uncle was the first person she thought of.

"I'll go so far as to say it was worth my coming out here," said Cross.

"Wonderful," said Milly. "Anything we can get for the house kitty would be very welcome. Things are a little strained with the mortgage."

"You have a mortgage?" Cross had not heard that banks extended mortgages to single women.

"It's in my brother's name," said Milly. "He's in Ceylon. It's a sort of mortgage of convenience. Our combined meagre wages cover it, just about."

"Are you a teacher as well?"

"She's an administrative assistant at the BBC," said Cassie, patting her friend on the shoulder.

"Not that it pays any better."

"...but we don't mind putting ourselves in penury to get the garden, do we?"

Milly rolled her eyes.

"Heavens forbid we give up your dream garden just because we can't afford it! But a little more money would be useful."

"Don't get your hopes up," said Cross. "But I think you said there were three books?"

"There is another one," said Milly. Cassie shot her a look, but she went on.

"Cassie was reading it in the garden and one of the boys next door took it. Borrowed it, I suppose."

"It was a play," said Cassie. "In English. Well, actually, a masque rather than play, but I couldn't see the difference."

"A masque was a private production where the players mingled with the audience and at the end everyone danced together before unmasking," said Milly.

"Thank you, Professor."

That could only mean one thing.

"*The King in Yellow*," said Cross.

"Yes! I wondered what a play was doing in with those funny books. A gory Restoration tragedy."

"It is considered a work of occult lore," said Cross. "The writer included magical formulae in the text, as Shakespeare did with Macbeth, but more of them. And the *King in Yellow* is supposedly cursed—also like *Macbeth*, only more so."

The King in Yellow was supposed to drive actors, or even whole audiences mad. There were grisly stories about failed productions with grotesque suicides and on-stage murders. As with any legend, the stories outran the reality, but there was a kernel of truth in them.

"But is it valuable?" asked Milly.

"More valuable than these two at any rate. Some editions can fetch a decent price. You say somebody borrowed it?"

Cassie cleared her throat. "The bicycle factory owns the house next door, and their apprentices live there. A lot of rowdy lads." She tried to smile, did not quite succeed. "One of them took it as a sort of joke. They can be rather difficult, so...." She half shrugged.

"It would be so wonderful if you could go and ask for it back," said Milly with a winning smile.

There was clearly a great deal that Cross was not being told, but he could guess. A houseful of boisterous young men, living next door to two young single women. The 'borrowing' of a book sounded like a provocation to get some attention.

Both looked at him hopefully.

He was in the business of locating valuable arcane books. This seemed simpler than most.

"I doubt they'll be glad to see me," said Cross. He smoothed his moustache and picked up his hat. "I'll be back in a minute."

The little house was a Victorian suburban imitation of rural living. It had originally been a guest cottage or retreat in the grounds of the larger, uglier construction in dark brick next door. The cottage had retained most of the garden, while the house, now apparently little more than a dormitory, had only a yard.

Cross caught the strains of twangling music as he approached. There was no response to a knock at the door, so he sauntered around to the back, where several young men in shirtsleeves were idling on the steps and kitchen chairs. He counted seven of them, a habit learned from occasions when he had had to shoot his way out of places.

They were pale-skinned creatures, all hormones and acne, with wispy moustaches and traces of beard. Inevitably, they reminded Cross of his young platoon before they had shaped up into soldiers, with the same lively excess of energy, even after a long day's work. Wet clothes and hair suggested a vigorous water fight had been waged earlier.

These were the lucky ones. Securing an apprenticeship at the bicycle factory practically guaranteed work for years to come, while thousands of others were stuck on the dole with no prospects. The pay was bad, but the apprentices had silver in their pockets. They were young and healthy, and summer was blooming all around.

One of their number was strumming a ukulele. He struck a series of dramatic chords as Cross appeared, as though to announce the arrival of a significant new character in a melodrama. The tattoo on Cross's wrist tingled, a faint presentiment of something dangerous in the air. Cross hoped that meant the book was nearby.

"Good evening, gentlemen," said Cross, tipping his hat. "Sorry to bother you. I was wondering if you might be able to help me in the matter of a book borrowed from the ladies next door."

There were smiles and chuckles, and all eyes turned to the ukulele player.

"Oh no!" he said, in a comic voice, putting a hand to his face. "The overdue book! I'll be ruined!"

"Who are you, mister?" asked one of the apprentices, curious rather than rude.

"He's the blonde one's father," someone immediately replied, and someone else loudly disagreed.

"Captain Cross. I'm a friend of her family," said Cross. "Do I take it you are the book borrower?"

"Happen I am, and happen I'm not," said the one with the ukulele, this time in a comically-overdone Yorkshire accent. He stood up, a lanky figure, flicking back the long hair that flopped over his forehead. "That'd be 'twixt 't bonny lass and mi'sen. What's it to thee?"

He was a born performer, the type that was always acting up, always the centre of attention. He also looked to be the oldest of the group, the sort of apprentice whose certificate was withheld a year or two while he corrected his attitude to authority.

"'Appen she wants it back, lad—sharpish like," said Cross, in his own best Yorkshire, before resuming his normal voice. "If that's not too much to ask."

"Too much?" repeated the other, striding up and down. "What's too much? What's it worth to you?"

He held out a hand as if for money and the others tittered.

"Let me have it and I might be able to say," said Cross. "I'm in the book business."

To Cross's surprise, the youth picked up a burgundy-bound volume from a stool. He offered it to Cross but snatched it back as soon as Cross reached out, to general laughter. He opened it at random and declaimed: "…What shadow falls, in lonely halls 'neath castle walls, among the thralls, in Carcosa…"

This evoked a chorus of groans.

"Rubbish," called one of his friends.

"Not that again," said another.

"Put a sock in it."

"Best give that back and get yourself another script," said Cross, holding out his hand again.

"Arr matey," said the other, now a stage pirate. "If ye wants it, ye'll have to fight me for it, man to man!"

He stooped and picked up a rusty sickle from the grass and waved it like a cutlass, holding the book behind his back.

"A fight, eh?" said Cross, leaning on his stick.

"With cold steel," said the other, swishing the sickle close to Cross's face. "Defend yourself now!"

He was trying to goad Cross into raising his stick for a mock swordfight, one which would probably end with Cross falling over. It was the sort of intimidation which could be laughed off as nothing more than a joke. Then he would move on to the next prank, always keeping the book just out of reach. That was how bullies treated smaller boys who wanted their ball back.

The ukulele player grinned wolfishly, enjoying his role. Could he get a reaction from Cross? Could he make the small boy cry?

Cross knew how to deal with bullies.

He reached back quite casually and drew a revolver, thumbed back the hammer with a click, and aimed it between his would-be assailant's eyes.

"It seems to me, sir, you have pirated a valuable antique and are making threats," said Cross. "You oblige me to use reasonable force to recover the property. Your move."

The gun produced an immediate reaction among the company. Maybe they had seen these games get out of hand before, and with a firearm it could all go very wrong very quickly.

"Stop fooling with 'im, Mark," said one.

"Go easy, Mister, Chambers is only joking."

"Don't shoot him, he doesn't mean it."

Chambers, the one with the sickle and the book, gave a piratical cry and clutched his chest as though already shot.

"Arrr—'tis the Queen's Navee, I'm done for, lads!"

He fell backwards, dropping the sickle and tossing the book to one of his companions who caught it awkwardly. He flopped about on the grass like a landed fish, trembled and lay still.

"Bury me in the Sea of Demhe," he said.

"Take it, Mister," said the one with the book.

"Good performance," said Chambers, sitting up.

"The play's the thing," said Cross, not sure what direction this whimsical character would take next.

"I don't know why Cassie couldn't come round and collect it herself. Wouldn't have cost her more than a kiss—or two."

"I can give you a kiss," said Cross, pursing his lips, and the nervous tension of the group burst into laughter.

"Oo no, sir, what would people say?" Chambers squawked, putting his hands to his face and tittering.

As Cross went to leave, one of the other boys caught his eye.

"Friend of the family are you?" He asked. "You ought to put those two next door right."

"I beg your pardon?" said Cross.

"Do you know what those two are?"

"They're flappers," said Chambers, stretching the word out to three syllables—'fur-lapp-ers'—and making it sound obscene.

"Think they're better than men—taking men's jobs, smoking and drinking..."

"Being stand-offish."

"Dancing together without men."

"It's not proper," said another. "Someone should tell them what's what."

"Yeah, you tell 'em that, Mister. You're a gentleman. Tell 'em to act proper."

A murmur of agreement rose from the rest.

"You boys don't hold with modern ways then?" said Cross.

"Not when they're like that," said one sullenly. "They don't show us any respect."

"'These two houses, alike in dignity, are set against each other...'" said Chambers.

"Indeed. Good evening to you all," said Cross, touching his hat brim.

He did not hear what was said as he was going, but there was laughter, and the ukulele strummed quickly as a song started up.

He strolled back through the cottage garden with a modest air of triumph.

"Oh, well done, Captain!" said Cassie seeing the book in his hand. She came up and kissed him on the cheek. "I knew you'd do it."

Milly said nothing. Her expression suggested something like awe.

"It's a first edition from the London printing," he said, weighing the book in his hand. "It should fetch a few pounds, if anyone's buying."

"Gosh," said Cassie, taking it and running her fingers over the spine. "*The King in Yellow*. But who was the author?"

"That old favourite Anon," said Cross. "Or, if you believe it, the King in Yellow was also the playwright."

"How weird," said Cassie. "Still, it might be enough to get us a crust to go with our thin soup, maybe, Milly?"

"Is it safe?" asked Milly. "Should even we be touching it? You said it was cursed."

Cross suppressed a smile.

"Have you encountered Goethe's *The Sorrows of Young Werther*? It's the story of a doomed love triangle ending in suicide. That was supposed to be dangerous. They banned it for years because it drove so many young men to imitate the hero."

Cassie still held on to the book, but now looked at it as though it might explode.

"But you don't believe it," said Milly.

"Goethe is dull stuff these days," said Cross. "Young people don't read Young Werther for the thrill of mortal danger. Lots of books have dangerous ideas that might affect your mind—" he indicated their bookshelf, where Annie Besant, Marine Stopes and other radical tracts stood out—"and the *King in Yellow* is one of them. It can make you believe that the King is real and seeking vengeance on you."

"Gosh," said Cassie.

"Or, according to some, it actually summons him—but the effect is the same. As with the Goethe, it doesn't affect modern readers much."

In a sense it was dangerous, in the same way that a loaded gun was dangerous: perfectly harmless and sometimes useful in the hands of any responsible adult, but hazardous if used carelessly. It seemed unlikely that anyone these days would put in the necessary effort to unlock its secrets. The play could, perhaps, tip those who were already unbalanced over the edge into obsession. But Cassie was sensible enough, with no history of insanity in her family, and Milly seemed well-grounded. There was one point of concern though.

"Your neighbour, Mr Chambers, the one who took the book," said Cross. "Do you know him?"

"Sort of. He's the big wheel in the local amateur dramatic society," said Cassie, making a face.

"We tried it when we moved here but we didn't stay with it very long," said Milly. "They're not our type."

"He plays the lead in every production," Cassie added. "All the oldies love him. He gets his friends to be stagehands and everything."

It all fell into place. Chambers was not so much an apprentice, more an actor manqué, whose vocation was the stage but who would never earn a living by it. One day, he would grow out of his acting mania, but for now he was Peter Pan, eternally leading his pack of lost boys.

"He seems very interested in Cassie," said Cross. "But you don't have any connection with him?"

"None," said Milly. "And the less the better. He's odious."

That seemed a little strong. Milly seemed to be protective of her friend.

"We have a fence but we're growing a hedge," said Cassie. "As soon as that's high enough I hope never to see him, or the rest of the neighbours, ever again."

The man who Cross only ever referred to as The Turk posed on the terrace in Crystal Palace Park. One hand rested on the stone balustrade, the other raising a slim cigarette to his lips as he contemplated a statue in Eastern dress. Cross scanned the passers-by on the terrace, with their parasols and straw boaters, strolling and chatting as they admired the view, and soon found two heavyset men in shiny suits shadowing him at a discreet distance.

The Turk's bodyguards were pretending to ignore him.

Cross nodded to them. They had exchanged shots once, and one day might do so again, but today's meeting was conducted under a flag of truce. The Turk might be Cross's archenemy, but the world of esoteric books was a small one and there was business to be done. The two men had different networks of contacts; those who would talk to Cross would not talk to the Turk, and vice versa. Between them they spanned most of the collectors in England. On countless occasions they had been chasing down the same books; neither kept count of who won. All that mattered was the next round.

He was also one of the few Cross could talk to about esoteric books on equal terms.

"English summers are like spring in Heaven," opined The Turk, without looking round. He wore a lemon-coloured linen suit with a pale green tie, a Panama hat, and a fresh carnation in his buttonhole. Cross felt even shabbier than usual. "But sadly the autumn is like winter in Limbo, and the winter is the dampest, dullest circle of Hell."

Having experienced an August in Istanbul, Cross had his own ideas about what hell looked like.

"You need to include English spring for it to work as an aphorism," said Cross.

"It is a work in progress, as are we all," said the Turk. He had been shaped by an English public school, and Cross had to admit he was a passable imitation of a gentleman. He turned at last. "The King in Yellow is not an easy book to dispose of. It is neither particularly old nor especially rare, and those who wish to acquire it are rarely of sound mind. It is hardly worth my trouble."

"And yet here we are," said Cross holding out the book.

The two smiled. The necessary formalities had been concluded.

"Mint condition, the excellent 1783 London edition, in a collector's binding," said the Turk.

Some editions of esoteric works were bowdlerised and of no interest to students of the arcane. Even correcting a single supposed typographic error could ruin the effect, but this one retained all the potency of the original. Whatever his faults, the Turk knew his books.

"The collector is of course the late Baron Saint-Moury," the Turk said after a glance at the book plate.

It had taken Cross considerable effort to establish that the books came from the library of the eccentric de Saint-Moury, broken up when the man went spectacularly bankrupt in the 1860s. Creditors were paid off in books, and some had held on to them in the hope they would become valuable.

"With it were the *Book of Moons*, and *Uber die wahre Natur der Trolle*," said Cross, "also from the Saint-Moury library. I'm happy to throw those in as extras."

"Of course," said the Turk. "The King should have an entourage, even a modest one. Have you tried to sell them to your American book-burner?"

Dr. de Vere was a discriminating buyer of genuine arcane books. She did not pay 'top dollar,' but she would buy everything. In some cases, she really did destroy the books, those that could be destroyed. Her group took a puritanical view towards the uncanny, which was sometimes justified.

"She'll do as a fall-back," said Cross. "I was hoping for something better. I'm sure someone must be looking for this."

"Durston & McMullan will take it off your hands for a song," said the Turk.

The booksellers would file the play in their archives. It would be duly catalogued and circulated in the next season's list. They would certainly find a buyer and sell it for a profit, but it would probably take some months, more if they had a significant backlog. Things were quiet in the book trade at this time of year.

"I was hoping for something less musical and more profitable. The sellers could do with some cash, if we can set up a chain."

In this sector, deals most often involved exchanging books for other books. The market was sufficiently restricted that most books were not sold but traded for others of equal desirability. Only at the end of the chain would the least collectable works be cashed in: sold to someone who had nothing better to offer than money.

"I can pay your sellers today," said the Turk, weighing the book in his hand. "Pounds sterling, francs, marks, American dollars, or gold sovereigns. Name your price."

The Turk had inherited a good library, and improving it had been his life's work, which had incidentally made him into an important figure in this corner of the book trade. The Turk's interest lay mainly in works relating to Constantinople, Byzantium and Istanbul, and the doings of certain of the scholars, alchemists and magi of that city. He could only free the works he sought from other collectors by offering other works which they, with their own particular interests might value more greatly. *The King in Yellow* might help tip the balance of a deal, but it was clearly speculation.

Cross shook his head slightly. He had vowed never to sell a book to the Turk. The two of them still frequently found themselves working together, the two large fish in a small pond. He would get a better price if he could find a buyer who genuinely needed the book.

"You are at least principled," said the Turk, handing the play back. "Very well. I will set some enquiries in motion, and we will see where we find ourselves in a few days."

"Thank you," said Cross. His tattoo buzzed faintly as he held the book. "The finders are not scholars, and someone might be…susceptible."

"Ah," said the Turk, raising his eyebrows. "You think the King may make his entrance?"

"There are two young women and one young man in the case. No actual Signs, yet, but on days like this I feel that Carcosa is not far away."

"The unnatural experience of warm weather In London. You shed one or two of your layers and you feel inhibitions are dangerously loosened? Carnal lust overcoming English reserve when you see each other's enticingly pale skin exposed to the air." He smiled, showing his perfect teeth. "Or it is just that your leg troubles you in the heat?"

He glanced at Cross' prosthetic leg. It was true that it chafed badly in hot weather, and the Turk seemed to enjoy his discomfort.

"Better to lose a leg than a country," said Cross lightly, and by the look on the Turk's face he knew the barb had gone home. "But I have a sense for these things, and…"

"The King in Yellow can be troublesome," said the Turk. "A being who can write himself into existence solely for the purpose of revenge can do anything—and love triangles are dangerous."

Cross and the Turk knew that not all books were just lifeless wood pulp stamped with ink, but a repository for souls. Some of those souls were powerful, and not all of them were benign.

"You would have thought the King would have been outmoded in an age of radio drama and cinemas," said Cross. "Stage plays still seem to have an influence somehow."

"Sophocles, Euripides, and Aristophanes will never lose their power, even if they change form. Modern adepts no longer use eye of newt and toe of frog, but they still work their effects. The ancient forces retain their potency. You should know that."

"Are you praising ancient Greeks now?" asked Cross. "How unlike an Ottoman."

"They are properly included in our territory," said the Turk, with the certainty of an exile from an Empire which no longer existed, except in the books in his collection.

"Fortunately, the King in Yellow may be counteracted, as you undoubtedly know." This was a taunt, a challenge to Cross to admit his ignorance.

"Is that so? I'd be very grateful if you'd share the secret with me," he said.

"Perhaps when you have something I want badly enough, I will," said the Turk.

Cross had nothing to offer, and the Turk was enjoying his advantage—unless it was just a cruel bluff, which was equally possible.

"I would advise you to stay offstage for the performance," said the Turk. "You know how these things go. 'In the first act the stage is strewn with rushes, in the last act with corpses.'"

"I'll try not to get killed," said Cross. "I would not want to deprive you of your binding."

During a particularly heated argument, the Turk had once threatened to flay Cross and use his skin to bind a book. This threat had become a sort of joke between them, though the menace never completely went away.

"I'll get it one way or another," said the Turk. "Anyway, you have my advice, and our business is concluded." He made a gesture, not quite a bow, indicating that Cross should go in peace. "*Gorusmek usere.*"

"*Au revoir,*" said Cross, with an equally curt nod.

As Cross walked away, he waved to the bodyguards who were watching suspiciously. One of them made a pistol with his fingers to shoot at him. Cross paused, drew two imaginary revolvers, and fired back.

The three of them smiled. It was all very good natured, this time.

Act 2: Warning Shots

A week later the heatwave had risen to new levels. Sections of pavement became sticky with melted tar. The smell from bins and outhouses was oppressive. Everything was sluggish—even the London traffic seemed to slow to half speed. Houses normally firmly shut up stood with windows askew at random angles and curtains blowing in the faint breeze.

Every patch of grass was occupied as people moved *en masse* to occupy the parks and public spaces. Pubs and cafes moved tables and chairs outdoors, even on to the sidewalk as though this was Europe.

"If this is June, what will it be like in July?" had become a common refrain.

Walking even a short distance was hard work. By the time he reached the cottage, Cross had loosened his tie and undone his top button.

Cassie was kneeling in a flowerbed beside a wicker basket piled with weeds. She wore a broad-brimmed straw hat against the sun. Even her gardening clothes were stylish.

The sun was low, and the evening should have been cooler by now, but heat clung to London like a miasma. The occasional evening breezes were blissful sweetness when they wafted over.

"Good evening," Cross said, tipping his hat. "Everything in the garden looks lovely. Very distinctive."

"It's sort of Chinese," she said, scanning the brilliant flower beds and lush greenery which showed signs of wilting in the heat. "It's a miniature landscape—the rocks are mountains, the shrubs are forests, the ponds are supposed to be lakes…"

It really did look like a landscape, an enchanted little kingdom apart from the world. The herb garden might have been farmland, the tidy lawns prairies, one with a lonely well in its middle like a remote settlement.

"Very impressive," said Cross. "I've never seen anything quite like it."

Cross might have added that it did not much resemble classical Chinese gardens he had visited, and that Cassie should give herself more credit for originality.

"All Milly's work. I just have the ideas, but I would never have the determination to see them through. I'm too much of a butterfly. She's a rock."

"The two of you have worked wonders." He glanced towards the dark house, looming over the diminutive hedgerow. "But...your telegram mentioned a problem with the neighbours?"

"Let's go indoors," she said, standing up, with an odd glance over her shoulder.

Milly had opened the front door before they reached it.

"Hullo Captain! I'll put the kettle on."

Cross stayed with Milly in the kitchen while Cassie went to change out of her gardening clothes. He gave Milly a brief account of his meeting with the Turk while she moved about arranging the tea things.

"It might take a couple of weeks, but he knows all the right people," said Cross. "The Turk is a villain, but he's reliable when it comes to business. Word will go out on the bush telegraph, and if anyone is looking for a copy they'll hear about it."

They had worked similar arrangements many times before, on both sides. The Turk had a talent for nosing out valuable books, and the rivalry between them kept both men sharp. Nothing got Cross out of bed in the morning so much as the thought that the Turk might get to a book first, or the anticipation of being able to slide a book out of his case murmuring, "I think you were looking for this..."

"Could I be so crass as to ask about money?" she asked, placing saucers on the tea tray. "Cassie is vague, but I like numbers."

"The first English edition was limited to a few hundred copies. There is not much of a market for plays, and it mainly went to theatre groups. After it was staged—it was a notorious flop—it was banned by the Lord Chamberlain, so of course the edition sold out. A number of libraries took their copies off the shelves or destroyed them. Actors are a superstitious bunch and I doubt whether any of the rehearsal copies survived."

"So it's very rare?"

"Reasonably rare, and it has enough infamy to make it popular among a certain type of buyer. It all depends on who wants a copy and how badly, and how much money they happen to have."

"Let me ask another way," she said, with no hint of impatience. "How much have copies been sold for recently?"

Cross blew out his cheeks. He was loathe to over-simplify the business that was his life, and equally loathe to raise hopes. There were equal chances that the book would fetch a fortune and that there would not be any interest for months. The biggest risk was if other copies became available; the small market was easily glutted.

"If we can find a buyer—and that is by no means certain—then I would expect the sum returned would come to some hundreds. By all means get a second opinion on the valuation."

"I already did," said Milly. "Both the dealers I talked to referred me to you."

"I'm afraid it's rather a small world," said Cross.

Milly cocked her head at the sound of running water. It seemed Cassie would be a few minutes longer. She lowered her voice and looked earnest behind her glasses.

"About this trouble we're having. Cassie would never say it," she said. "She's afraid people think we are...you know. That one next door might think that we're too friendly with each other. And I wouldn't want you to think we are."

Cross was gathering his thoughts to respond, but Milly seemed to think he did not understand.

"We're not lesbians," she hissed, practically trembling with the effort.

"I've been to Lesbos, and I know something of the inhabitants," said Cross.

Milly made an exasperated gesture at his apparent obtuseness.

"I was on the trail of one of Sappho's lost works—the ones destroyed by the Church in the Tenth Century," Cross went on. The name of Sappho, the Tenth Muse, a poet who wrote paeans to the love between women, meant something to Milly. "It took a little time, but I finally managed to talk to some of the followers of her sect. They are not the twisted man-haters they are sometimes portrayed as being. Not at all."

He could still see the high priestess. The woman was said to be two hundred years old; Cross believed this was an underestimate. Her legs were useless, and she was held upright in the sacred cave by cords, like a living marionette.

One silent acolyte with a powdered-white face had held the point of a bronze spear to Cross's neck, while another stood ready with a silver castrating sickle. Males were not welcome there. Cross had been very careful indeed to avoid giving offence.

He had traded riddles with the high priestess in Attic Greek, testing each other's knowledge, drifting into a kind of literary discussion. Over the course of the long conversation the High Priestess gradually shifted from contempt to amusement to, perhaps, respect for her unusual visitor. As the conversation wore on, she increasingly reminded Cross of his favourite great aunt, a hearty woman who wore tweeds, bred Labrador retrievers, and terrorised generations of vicars at the village church committee.

Nothing would persuade the High Priestess to consider parting with the least of the scrolls hidden in the lower caves, or even showing them to Cross. But she did recite three precious verses of a lost poem no male had heard for more than a thousand years, and they were engraved forever in his memory.

Society might not approve of homosexuality, even if it was not technically illegal, at least among women. Cassie's father certainly would not have approved, but Cross had seen enough inhuman horrors to know how precious any love was in a hostile world.

"What I'm trying to say in my clumsy way, is that even if you were—which of course you're not—and whatever the world thinks of it—I'm on your side."

He forbore to mention that as one of the two bedrooms had been turned into a boxroom, visitors might draw their own conclusions about the women's relationship.

But Cross was also aware of how dangerous it was. It might not be illegal, but it would only take one anonymous letter to Cassie's headteacher to see her sacked on the spot. No school could tolerate having a teacher accused of living immorally. Sharing a house with a man would be bad enough, but the least whiff of homosexuality would throw the school authorities into fits. Nor would Milly's employers be any more sympathetic. Though young, the BBC was the embodiment of establishment value and already sensitive to charges that it was corrupting the nation's morals.

The least suspicion would see one or both losing their jobs—and their mortgage, their house, their life together.

Milly smiled and swallowed. "So, do you like our garden?"

"It's a regular Eden," he said, suppressing a smile. The English were always so anxious to change the subject and avoid making a scene.

"All Cassie's doing," said Milly. "She's the one with the imagination. I just push the wheelbarrow and do the spadework. It's an endless battle keeping the pests out."

"Some pests are more persistent than others," said Cassie, coming down the stairs. "The two-legged ones especially."

"So I gather," said Cross.

"They've got so much worse since the books," said Milly. "Whistles and catcalls and...looking."

She leaned to peer through the window at the big house. "Not right now, but we can't go into the garden without one of them popping up and saying something. Especially Chambers."

"Last night," said Cassie, "something woke me—I thought it was an owl. I looked out of the window and saw him standing by the big pond. The stars were so bright I could tell it was him."

"Every time I look up, I'm scared I'm going to see his face pressed against the window," said Milly.

"If he was in your garden that would be trespassing," said Cross. "You could tell the police, but on the whole, I don't think it would be advisable."

This was tactful understatement. It would be impossible to explain to a police officer, probably a young man himself, just why two single women would feel threatened by the innocent attentions of a neighbour when there was no hint of a threat. Everyone knew that boys would be boys.

"Has he done anything else?" asked Cross.

"He sends her love poems," said Milly.

"Ah," said Cross, sensing a change in the case. "Familiar poems … or ones with references to Carcosa, or the King in Yellow? Is he borrowing from the play?"

"I don't read them," said Cassie with reproving terseness. She paused.

"But…yes, there are. A lot. Things about Lake Hali and the Hyades and Aldebaran."

Cross nodded and stroked his moustache. He was not surprised that Chambers had been snared by the King in Yellow. That did not mean there was a threat to the two women though.

"You could talk to him," said Milly, placing a hand on his arm. "Tell him to stop bothering Cassie. Like her father would."

"Of course, I can try," said Cross. "But for one thing, it would alert him to just how rattled you are. For a second, my word doesn't carry much weight with those types. And thirdly, as soon as I walk away down that street, he'll be scratching at your door again."

"Can't we do anything?" pleaded Milly. "I just have such an awful sense of dread."

"You could just invent a fiancé," said Cross tentatively. "That usually puts men off. Have one of Milly's brother's friends come round with a bunch of flowers…"

"Never," hissed Milly, and Cassie shook her head.

They could not affirm their relationship. But neither, it seemed, were they prepared to lie about it. They were in a difficult position. So far there had been nothing overtly threatening. There was nothing to stop Chambers from standing at the window, or even coming inside if a door or window was left open. He might view it as a cheeky way of getting better acquainted.

There were far worse outcomes, especially if Chambers was rebuffed. Cross could all too easily see the worst case: late at night, after too many beers, the apprentices egged each other on to pay a visit to their neighbours. Teasing would become physical, would be met by resistance, and matters would escalate until the inevitable happened. Boys would be boys.

The worst of it was that, as two women living together, they would take the blame for it. Loose young women who were not decently married, nor even engaged, who smoked and listened to ragtime music would get no sympathy from the police, the newspapers or anyone else.

"It's a fine evening," said Cross. "Perhaps we can have a little target practice." He held up two revolvers.

They trooped out into the garden. At its end, the levelled area became a bank, with a hedge that separated the garden which backed on to theirs. Cross placed two cardboard boxes on front of this and set up the empty jars and bottles. It was not the worst firing range he had used. Most importantly, the neighbours would have an excellent view.

Walking them twenty feet back from the targets, Cross handed each of the girls a revolver. Today he had a matched pair of St Etienne 8mm, what he liked to call 'summer weight pistols.' They were perfect for the exercise. Both women looked slightly alarmed, as though he had given them live lobsters.

"The St. Etienne is a very forgiving weapon," he said, "but I would advise you hold it with both hands for today. And the first lesson, Milly, is never point it at anything you do not intend to shoot—barrel downwards if you please."

They listened attentively as he explained about grip and stance, the effects of recoil and the importance of coming up on the target as you aim. He told them about sighting and different opinions on whether it was helpful to close one eye.

All the while they were getting used to the weight and heft of the pistols. Cassie acted out everything as he described it, while Milly looked on with mute fascination. "That's about everything you need to know about theory," he said. "So, who would like to have first go?"

Of course it was Milly. She stood at a crouch as instructed, and, with a look of concentration, squeezed the trigger until a sharp crack sounded and the St Etienne threw out a puff of smoke.

Both women made small, startled sounds before laughing nervously. Cross noted that the bullet had struck about a yard from the target.

"Good show," he said. "Now you know what the kick feels like."

On her fourth shot, a chip of glass flew off one of the jars, which wobbled and then stood still.

"A hit," said Cross. "A palpable hit! You winged him."

"Gosh," said Milly wonderingly and lowering the gun. A new light shone in her eyes. "So that's how it's done. Come on Cassie, your turn."

Cassie stepped forward more hesitantly. She let out a little squeak when she fired, and Cross had no idea where the bullet went.

The disadvantage of a suburban upbringing, thought Cross. If she had grown up in a village she would at least have learned how to use a shotgun.

Milly made her fire twice more, and the results were slightly more successful, but she still seemed very glad to hand the St Etienne back to Cross.

"You see," he said, "there's nothing to be afraid of. Don't think about it too much, just aim and fire, all perfectly naturally."

He raised the revolver and fired three times, each shot producing a small explosion of shattered glass. Showing off was a vice, but at least there was some serious purpose here.

"Hold on to the St. Etienne," he told Cassie.

"We're not going to keep guns in the house," she said.

"The people next door don't need to know that. Give them back later."

Milly asked a few more questions and practised her firing stance. But she did not ask to do any more shooting.

Of course, the neighbours might guess that this was all for show. But as Cross knew, the main purpose of a gun is not to kill, but to persuade. If their little performance was enough to sow some doubts in the neighbour's minds and make them think twice, it would have served its purpose. In any case, he did not think it would be wise to leave a gun there. There was too high a risk of accidents or panic when held in inexperienced hands.

A few warning shots would be a good deterrent. It would take a bold prowler to risk creeping around the house, or even the garden, if there was a risk of getting shot. But there was a deeper risk, and Cross needed to tackle it.

"That may help matters a little," said Cross. "And for this evening, why don't I take you two girls out to dinner somewhere nice? Do you know a decent eatery hereabouts?"

"Anything other than fish paste sandwiches would be a gourmet feast for us," said Milly.

"At last," said Cassie. "Something we can dress up for."

Milly insisted on taking his arm as they walked back. Cross realised it was not for her benefit but his. Cassie took the other arm, and after the wine—something they had not been accustomed to—it was all quite jolly.

Normally he would have left them at the garden gate, but under the circumstances, with the shadow of the big house looking over the cottage, he felt it might be better to see that their return did not draw a reaction from the neighbours.

"All quiet, I think," said Cassie hopefully, looking up at the darkened house.

"No," said Milly. "There are candles lit in their common room."

The curtains had been left open, and the windows gaped wide. From their position on the garden path, they could just see the tops of three heads, nodding in rhythm. That was when Cross heard the sound, the low murmur of a chant or psalm,

"What are they doing?" Cassie asked in a whisper.

"Can you overlook that window from the box room?" Cross asked.

Milly nodded, and they let themselves into the cottage and went upstairs to where they could look down at the scene unfolding in the house next door.

A large dining table in the middle of the room had been cleared, and a pattern drawn on it with white powder. That would be salt, and Cross did not need to count the six bowls of water and the six flickering candles to know what was happening.

"It's the summoning scene," said Cassie. "From that play."

They watched with bated breath as the group of young men repeated the chant over and over. All of them were seated around the table, except for Chambers who they could see circling the table, anti-clockwise, waving his arms and making mystic gestures. Cross was shocked to recognise a Voorish Sign. Was that in the stage directions?

"It's a séance, isn't it," said Milly. "How ridiculous."

Her laugh was nervous, too loud and too brief.

"They're calling the ghost of the old King," said Cassie.

It was an act of blasphemous necromancy. Or just a group of young men having a bit of fun because one of their number told them he could show them something they had never seen before, something that would have cost them too much to see performed by a West End magician. Surely, they had no understanding of what they were doing.

Cross felt the tattooed stars on his wrist blaze, and a moment later the candles guttered and wavered in a sudden breeze, then blazed with dark yellow.

Someone or something was standing on the dining table now; they could only see from his knees down, but he seemed to be wearing a gown or shroud, and he gave a low, anguished groan.

Chambers spoke up, authoritative, commanding, but he was too far away for them to catch the actual words. He gave a short speech, and followed it with a question.

The ghost spoke just a few words, in a tortured voice. Again, they could not make out the words, but Cassie lowered her face and started sobbing. Milly cradled her at once.

"What is it? What's the matter?"

Chambers spoke again, and then the ghost. This time Cross caught it. Not the words, but the tone of the voice, one he had not heard for a decade.

It was his old comrade, Major Ward, Cassie's father, or at least it had the appearance of his spirit, dragged back unwillingly from the other world.

"...so that all may hear and know," Chambers said, his voice louder as he passed the window. "That you give your consent to this match. Speak!"

"I do," said the ghost, and as though released from its bonds, crumpled in on itself and disappeared downwards through the solid table.

The candles went out and the room opposite was silent for a second. Then there was a scattering of hand clapping, hoots and cheers as though they had just seen a rather impressive magic trick. A moment later an electric light came on and there was a buzz of excited chatter. Chamber's voice rose indistinctly above the rest.

"...told you I could..."

"Good god," said Cross to himself.

Chambers must have a talent that went far beyond normal acting skill. In another life he might have been an adept, one of the great ones exploring the Unknown World. But here he was, playing with it all unwittingly. That was the real danger, those who could channel the power without understanding any of it.

The scene was slightly different to that in *the King in Yellow*, but it would not take much to turn the scene to a different use. Plays were often copied and recopied, plagiarism was rife, and many unauthorised versions circulated. Some may have been improvements on the original. Shakespeare was not the first to write a play about Hamlet, Prince of Denmark, or Romeo and Juliet. What mattered was that the revenant had risen, and his words had driven the plot for revenge onwards.

Chambers has called up the ghost of Cassie's father to ask for her hand in marriage. And the tortured revenant, spirit-thing or phantom—more likely a psychic projection than an actual ghost, Cross was sure—had given its consent.

Cassie continued to sob, Milly hugged her and patted her back, looking mutely to Cross for an answer. Milly did not want to believe that it was real. She wanted it all to be trickery. But he had little consolation to offer them.

Cross arranged an assignation for the next evening. He had arrived early at the park bench, expecting to be kept waiting.

"Ill met by moonlight."

Startled, Cross looked up and saw Chambers saluting him. The orange moon, almost full, had indeed risen above the horizon. Cross had not been expecting the other man to be quite so prompt, and had assumed a casual attitude to appointments on his part.

But, of course, actors always had to be on their mark when the curtain went up.

Cross had settled on Norwood Park as neutral ground. Even this late at night it was not quite deserted, and there were more than a few couples walking hand in hand or sitting quietly under the trees, shadows merging.

"Don't get up," said Chambers, seating himself on the other end of the bench.

This was a calmer, more serious version of the man, his backstage self, without an audience to entertain. Or perhaps he had merely switched his dramatic mode from comedy to tragedy. Cross looked for signs that the King in Yellow was emerging.

"Thank you for coming," said Cross. "I wanted to tell you—in case you did not know—a man is dead."

"What man?"

"It was in the afternoon editions," said Cross. "The long and the short of it is that a man called Robin Wagner—your housemate, or should I say former housemate—checked into a cheap boarding house and cut his wrists with a straight razor. The police are not releasing details, but they believe the balance of his mind was disturbed."

"So," said Chambers, with a peculiar quiet satisfaction. "Robin made his quietus with a bare bodkin? He was a good fellow, but..."

Chambers' shrug said that if a man was not equal to the part, he had no time for him. "Is that all you have to say?"

"There was an argument, he packed his things and left," said Chambers.

"Wagner is dead," said Cross. "I take it he was upset after he realised that your séance was not just a bit of harmless fun."

"Sacrifices have to be made for our art."

Any doubt about Chambers' intentions were rapidly dissipating.

"That was a blasphemous piece of necromancy you carried out last night," said Cross.

"The scene went off without a hitch," said Chambers, with no little pride. "I knew it would."

"But it's all make-believe," said Cross. "You gained nothing. Her father would never really approve of someone like you. You could only command him by posing as the King in Yellow, who he could not refuse."

Chambers shook his head with a patronising smile.

"Have you heard of Stanislavsky and his Method? Too modern for you? Stanislavsky has reinvented acting. The actor doesn't just speak his lines, he inhabits the role, becomes the character. Stanislavsky has rediscovered the principle of the King in Yellow, the merging of worlds. With method, the King and I are one."

Chambers was calmer, more measured, as he settled into the role of the King—or the King was settling into him, taking possession. He must be a quick study. In a few days he had time to read, mark, learn and inwardly digest the play.

"Your Method sounds like madness. You will not use it to involve Miss Ward. You can keep her out of your theatrics."

"'She's beautiful, and therefore to be wooed; She is a woman, therefore to be won.'"

"You need to desist."

"If she doesn't like me, why won't she say so to my face?" asked the actor. "Why does it feel like this is nothing to do with her will? Back in the old days, you'd send a few of the stable hands to give me a horsewhipping for daring to address myself to the squire's daughter.

Times have changed. Any man is good enough for a woman. Isn't a gun enough to defend her against sonnets?"

Cross could not tell the actor that Cassie was terrified of what might happen if she turned him down flat, or that living next to an unruly gang of young men who might decide to come and visit was a frightening prospect.

"It is the content of those sonnets that worries me," said Cross. "As you know, I'm in the business of esoteric books—and you are playing with fire."

"Fire, the gift of Prometheus, the illuminating light," said Chambers.

"Obsession with *The King in Yellow* finishes acting careers. You already have one death on your hands."

"People die trying to swim across the Channel," said Chambers dismissively. "*The King in Yellow* is pure love, pure death, distilled and injected into your heart...Isn't that worth dying for?"

"Then die," said Cross. "But don't involve others."

"They want to be involved," said Chambers. "The girl teases and flirts; she never pushes me away. Her 'friend' Milly—she wants so much to be involved. Did she tell you she has written to me?" He reached into a pocket and waved a note in front of Cross with a flourish. "She says she has compromising letters that mean the two of them are bound together forever. What do you think of that piece of blackmail?"

Cross thought it was misjudged against someone who thrived on the promise of revelations.

"I think I'm more concerned about *The King in Yellow* and the fact one man is dead already."

"Can you remember life before you succumbed to middle-age?" Chambers asked pityingly. "Do you remember why young men race cars and motorcycles, risk their lives doing stupid things just to impress women? Did you never ride proudly to war, Captain, sabre by your side, unafraid of death, glorying in danger, and knowing what it felt like to be a man?"

Cross was unable to reply. That was exactly what he had been like in his younger days.

"Well, here's my war, my glory!"

Chambers stood up suddenly, spun on his heel, addressed Cross as though he was speaking an aside to the audience.

"Listen then, and I will let you into the shocking revelation of Act Two, the one that leads you to reappraise everything you thought you knew in Act One."

"At first Cassie was excited to have an affair with another woman. It was forbidden, exhilarating, different...." His voice became graver, slower, deeper. "Now that little vampire Milly has her hooks in. Milly persuaded her they should buy that cottage together. Now the trap is sprung, she's chained to that neurotic, frumpy little woman. She's young, she wants to taste all the pleasure of life. Now she's shut away in that place—have you seen that she's being walled in with hedges? Tell me how that's different from poor Princess Cassilda being forbidden to go outside the walls of Carcosa. She doesn't have the strength to get out on her own, she needs someone to help her: someone to cross the moat and send the towers crashing into the lake."

His face was alight with joy, and Cross could see the tumbling towers in his eyes, the temples desecrated, the palaces consumed in flames, the fleeing mobs.

"That's not true," said Cross. "Like every egotist, you only see reflections of your own desire. Your feelings for her would end with the next production, the next leading lady. A summer fling at most. She neither needs nor wants you to 'rescue' her. And she wants nothing at all to do with *The King in Yellow*."

"Excellently said," said Chambers, seemingly satisfied. "That means you will play your part just as you should. Good."

"Never mind my part, it's your part—The King in Yellow is an ill-fated role," Cross said slowly. "I once read a very short review in The Times about a production of Shakespeare. Just one line. It mentioned the name of a famous actor and said that he played Hamlet—and lost."

"Very witty."

"If you play the King in Yellow, you will not win."

"The show must go on," said Chambers. "I will see you on opening night, Captain. Be on your mark and ready for your cue. Good night."

He bowed and walked quickly off into the shadows.

Final Act: The King in Yellow

Two days later Cross was on his way to the cottage, another telegram from Milly in his pocket. She was a girl who believed in swift communication at any price when the situation demanded. Cross had stopped off on the way at a pub for some tactical advice.

The beer garden was crowded with perspiring men in their shirtsleeves. Cross and Stubbs shared their bench with two railwaymen, so deep in conversation about some technical issue that they were oblivious to the weird tale being spun next to them. The air was filled with the scent of warm beer, cigarette smoke, and sausages sizzling over an open grill.

"The boxing ring is also a stage, if you look at it in that way," said Stubbs. He should know: written on his battered features was a tale of glorious victories and ignominious defeats. He had played the victor and the vanquished, and like an actor, had risen again the next day, though often in worse physical shape than any thespian. "However, I should consider myself unqualified to take part in any dramatic production. A deficiency in the department of , what do you call it—"

"Spontaneous verbal fluency?"

"Exactly."

Stubbs, for all his size, lacked the self-confidence and stage presence of a born actor. He seemed worried he would not be able to think quickly enough on his feet, and his inability would be turned against him. Or against the Captain.

"I'm seeking your tactical wisdom, not your physical attendance," said Cross. "You have the clearest eye and the steadiest hand, even when dealing with things that turn anyone else into quivering wrecks."

"You mean I've been lucky and never had to fight above my weight," said Stubbs with a wry smile. The bench creaked slightly as he shifted weight.

Cross had to wait for a roar of triumph and laughter erupting from a game of quoits to die down before replying.

"I value your judgement. The King in Yellow is a tricky opponent and I believe I'll meet him tonight."

"This King—he's a fictional character?" Stubbs asked.

"He's the title character of a play which is apt to spill over into our world," said Cross. "It's revenge tragedy, a popular form in the seventeenth century, and like modern musical comedies or detective dramas, the form has a set of conventions: revenge with especially grotesque or bloody punishments, and three added ingredients. One, madness, either real or feigned; two, a supernatural element, such as the ghost of a murder victim calling for revenge; and three, meta-theatre—a play within a play."

"Sounds like *Hamlet*," said Stubbs.

"Yes, or *Titus Andronicus*," said Cross, "or many others of the type. Kyd, Middleton and Marston did it first, but Shakespeare is the master."

"No doubt," said Stubbs, raising a pint glass to his lips.

"In the masque within the masque—which is also confusingly called *the King in Yellow*—the Stranger steps out to become the King in Yellow, to general woe. When the King in Yellow unmasks he may enter our world—if we admit him."

"Hmm."

Stubbs looked at the wet circles on the table in front of him as he digested this. He was not a quick thinker outside the ring, but he was a thorough one. Cross paused before continuing, to a background of laughter from the quoits players.

"The King returns from exile to reclaim his stolen love and wreak revenge on his enemies. Some believe that his exile is to the land of death, which is why the return is so traumatic. His vengeance brings destruction to the entire kingdom. To my way of thinking, in the current situation there is little for the King to get hold of—no betrothed princess, just a pretty neighbour glimpsed over a garden hedge. Nothing for him to get traction on and haul himself into our world. But—I confess I'm worried."

As far as Cross could tell, Chambers had an egotist's overconfidence that he could win Cassie with the King in Yellow. But he could not help but feel there was more to it and, unlikely as it seemed, Chambers had some claim on Cassie.

"Yellow is the colour of jealousy," said Stubbs. "The actor is jealous of the women's relationship. Perhaps the second woman is also jealous of the attention the first is getting from the actor. Perhaps the first enjoys making her jealous?"

"I see what you're saying," said Cross. "Maybe there's enough there for a triangle even without attraction. Romance can be a tangled web."

"'For aught that I could ever tell, could ever read by tale or history, the course of true love never did run smooth'," Stubbs quoted, before taking another draught of ale.

"In the normal course of events I could pay this lad a visit and tell him he needs to behave himself. Act the older brother, standard procedure around here." Stubbs flexed a fist. He did not start many fights but knew how to end them. "I don't suppose that would help?"

"I'm sure you could go up against the lot of them and leave their battered bodies strewn all around the house and garden, if they were foolish enough to think they could take you on. And I'd pay to see that...but it wouldn't change things with the King in Yellow."

"But in the worst case—this actor, if he tries anything, he's mortal as the rest of us when it comes to lead?"

"If you shot him before the production, I suspect an understudy would step in," said Cross. "During the production...the King in Yellow has a special relationship with death."

Stubbs furrowed his brow.

"What does that mean in practical terms?"

"Well, in one famous production the King in Yellow uttered his last lines and collapsed stone dead," said Cross. "The coroner found Prussic acid in his stomach. Apparently, he'd been poisoned by a jealous actress. The funny thing was that the coroner also found he'd been dead for two hours."

"Is there some special ammunition for this type of contingency?" Stubbs asked, ever the pragmatist and unfazed even by corpse-actors.

Cross had spent an evening with an acquaintance who was a practising alchemist discussing this very matter. Much of the learned talk about yellow and colour correspondences had gone over his head; the alchemist wanted Cross to try different compositions and record the results. He had gone so far as casting a dozen bullets of a mercury compound but was highly doubtful of their efficacy.

"Firstly, it would be entirely experimental," said Cross. "I've never heard of such a thing being tried. Secondly, it is not wise to use force against the uncanny, it usually gets turned back on you. And thirdly, shooting an actor dead would be a difficult one to explain in court."

"Hmm," said Stubbs again, and rested his head on one enormous hand. He might have been the illustration from a fairytale about a troll in his cave.

"There may be some sort of counter," said Cross. "The Turk says there is some sort of protection from the King in Yellow, but I don't know if it's a charm, an amulet or some sort of formula. I can't find any references. He may just have been baiting me."

More likely the claim was genuine enough, but the Turk knew that Cross had little chance of finding the answer without his help.

"Paracelsus says that the doctrine of signatures is an infallible guide towards antidotes."

Stubbs was an enthusiast for Paracelsus, the old arch-alchemist, physician and mage. His course of self-education may not have given Stubbs depth, but he used Paracelsus as a ladder to get to anything otherwise out of his grasp. Cross, who had traded more of Paracelsus' works than Stubbs had read, was more temperate in his enthusiasm.

"Paracelsus was talking about herbs which resembled parts of the human body," said Cross. "Such as lungwort for lung conditions. He says they always occur in the same places as the sickness. The madness brought by the King in Yellow is a rather different beast."

"The ailment is an infectious madness contained in a masque, transmitted via a book," said Stubbs, proving that he had been paying attention. "Not your regular type of germ but nevertheless treatable, I should imagine, like every other malaise. A literary affliction should have a literary cure. A book, maybe another play?"

"Fair point," Cross conceded. The Turk, a bookman himself, may have found some other work which might counteract the King in Yellow. Cross had no idea where to even start, but the idea was sound.

"As to tactics, my advice would be to meet on middle ground—don't come out too quick from your corner, but don't let this King out into your space."

"You mean —"

"Would I be right in saying that if you join in the masque then he is constrained by its rules to play by the script?"

"Dangerous meeting him on his territory," said Cross. "But it's an interesting idea."

Stubbs was getting going, building up a head of steam now. He took it as granted that anything could be fought, even something which appeared to be a god. It was just a question of suitable tactics.

"Throw him off balance, hit him with whatever metaphysical weapons you have, and make him dance your way," said Stubbs. "But from what you say, according to his rules, he won't be able to land a punch—there's no revenge tragedy if there's nothing to revenge. Just a comedy of errors, perhaps. Or like that bloke whatsisname, the one in yellow, locked up for being mad when he declared his love for his mistress. Who happens to be in love with another woman, as I recall."

"*Twelfth Night*," said Cross. "Comedy rather than tragedy."

A burst of cheering announced that the quoits match had been won. The players were clapping one of their number on the back, before heading inside to the bar in a body. Still, it was light in the sky and more players were gathering to take over as the summer evening wore on.

"This is not a one-man show, so the rest of you get to say your pieces," said Stubbs. "Put a twist in his plot. Change the script."

"The play isn't exactly a summoning ritual that can be disrupted with one wrong word," said Cross.

"They do plays in different ways now," said Stubbs. "Even Shakespeare isn't sacred, so why not change *the King in Yellow*? You're part of the production. Surely you know more about how these things work than I do, Captain?"

"You think I could steal a scene or two?"

"Why not? If it's a question of bookwork, I'd put my money on Captain Cross to come out on top against any bad actor every time,"

Stubbs said, with conviction. "Just keep your guard up and your wits about you. Play it by ear and keep jabbing."

Cross did not hurry to the cottage. It was too hot for haste, and the curtain would not rise without him. The little house was lit up inside, but the larger property next door was dark and looked almost abandoned.

As he stepped over the threshold, Cassie pushed a card into his hand with trembling fingers.

It was a handmade invitation, cut out from card packaging. The yellow colouration would have been achieved by immersing it in weak tea and drying it out. The artwork and calligraphy were well-executed; perhaps someone had plenty of experience with playbills. A slender, ambiguous, crowned-and-cowled figure stood at one side, surmounted by clouds and moonlit peaks. The flamboyant script stated that the recipient was invited to the *Masque of the King in Yellow*. It gave no date, time or place.

"They've been so quiet the last two days," said Milly. "We thought...but then we got that card."

"Our actor friend has decided to take things the whole way, which is what we expected," he said.

He placed the invitation on the mantelpiece, in front of a card for a Summer Jamboree.

"Oh, sit down, sit down," said Cassie.

They had rearranged the living room. The furniture now faced towards the kitchen door, and two large pot plants and a net curtain blocked out most of the view towards the big house. Or rather, blocked anyone from the big house from seeing in. The French Window was closed, and it felt airless.

Cassie sat still, holding her hands in her lap, while Milly fussed about. Cross, noticing *The King in Yellow* on the coffee table, tried to calm things by telling them about the latest news from the Turk.

"There is a collector in North London who appears interested. He's an eccentric, but a wealthy one, and has recently taken an interest in Hastur. I'm hoping for a generous offer for your find."

"I wish we'd never found the wretched book," said Cassie. "I wish we'd never come here."

Cross fanned himself with his hat.

"So long as you keep your distance you need not be concerned," he said, sounding more confident than he felt.

"How do you mean 'keep our distance?'"

"He doesn't have any emotional hold on you. He's a magnet trying to draw a silver spoon. The King in Yellow is a shadow. Sit back and enjoy the show but don't get involved."

"We certainly won't be doing that," said Milly. "Will we?"

"However much he frets and struts, however much he promises or storms, he is as entirely unreal and as entirely harmless as Macbeth's witches or Caliban." Cross hoped that was true.

"But we don't have to stay for the performance though, do we?" asked Milly. "We could get the next night train to Dover and catch the dawn ferry, be in Paris by lunchtime tomorrow."

Cross could tell she knew the timetable.

"With no money? How long could we stay away? No," said Cassie, taking Milly's hand. "This is where we are strongest. This is where we stay."

"That may be wise," said Cross.

He suspected that wherever they fled, the King In Yellow would be able to find them.

"Is there anything we can do?"

Cross hesitated, not wanting to raise false hopes but hoping to strengthen their morale.

"A recent conversation reminded me about the theatrical superstition about *Macbeth*. Saying the name in a theatre is supposed to be unlucky. If you do it—"

"—You have to leave the room," said Milly. "And go out and turn around widdershins three times, and knock at the door to be let back in. "

"But there was an alternative way to avoid the curse. All you must do is speak any line from *Two Gentlemen of Verona*. The one play counteracts the other."

During the walk over Cross had convinced himself that Shakespeare was the answer. The Bard must have known about the King in Yellow, would not have been able to resist writing a reply to it somewhere in his own canon. Shakespeare, the master of words, would be a match for any.

"There may be an equal and opposite play to the *King in Yellow*. I was thinking of *The Tempest*…it's a good match for the revenge tragedy. Technically the only difference between Shakespearean tragedy and comedy is that nobody gets killed at the end, which is why the *Merchant of Venice* is classed as comedy. Comedies have weddings at the end instead of funerals."

"And why *The Tempest*?" asked Milly intently.

"It's a revenge story," said Cross. "With a royal court, and supernatural elements. And, crucially, a play within a play, and a happy ending of sorts," said Cross. "A small move to comedy, a shifting of the points to a different track."

"You can be Ariel," Cassie told Milly. "And the Captain, with his staff and his books, is Prospero. And he"—wrinkling her nose towards the big house—"is the vile, fishy Caliban who gets a good thrashing at the end."

"But I don't think it's quite that specific," said Cross. "Madness is the other important ingredient, and that doesn't feature in *The Tempest*."

"Oh," said Cassie, dismayed.

"But the idea is sound, I'm sure."

He sighed and looked outwards. The horizon was, he was slightly surprised to note, formed of trees. Norwood was a leafier suburb than most. Old oaks grew here and there in gardens, remnants of the Great North Wood. Perhaps there was still some lingering trace of the ancient woodland beings here, some old magic, but Cross knew it would never be enough to keep Carcosa at bay.

"What fools we mortals be," said Cross suddenly. "Look, may I suggest you two go into the garden? I have a few preparations I need to make. Don't worry, you'll be safe out there."

"You have a plan?" asked Cassie.

"Just a thought," he said.

When Cross emerged onto the patio he found the two women at the garden table, both smoking. Somehow the night seemed to have grown hotter rather than cooler.

"You know those awful dreams where you find yourself on stage in front of everyone and you don't know your lines," said Cassie. "That's just what this feels like: an awful dream."

"What's that?" asked Milly, seeing the brown paper bag he was carrying.

"A secret weapon," he said. "I had some last-minute ideas."

They had changed for the occasion. For some reason Milly was all in black, while Cassie had on a light, floral print dress and a tiara of woven artificial flowers, with matching bracelets.

The stone patio still radiated the heat of day, and the grass looked stiff and dry. A paper lantern sat on the table, next to three glasses, a pitcher of lemonade in which mint leaves drifted, and an overflowing ashtray.

The heat was debilitating, far more so than a temperature reading could tell. English winters had a peculiar damp coldness to them which the thermometer failed to describe. Cross had endured sub-zero conditions in the wastes of Norway, but had never experienced the kind of bone-chilling cold he had experienced in a boarding-house in Grimsby. Similarly, the summers might be no match for Borneo or West Africa according to the mercury, but his body told him otherwise.

The linen jacket was the lightest item of clothing in his wardrobe, and necessary to conceal the two holsters in the small of his back.

The circle of light was just enough to illuminate their three faces. Milly was tense, but Cassie seemed relaxed, almost tranquillised. Cross diagnosed fatalism. She was resigned to whatever was going to happen. Cassie stubbed out her cigarette and took a moment to breathe the air.

"Doesn't the garden smell delightful?" she said, closing her eyes. "The scents just waft over you. There, now, you can smell jasmine — and under it there's lavender."

A moth, pale, and huge, fluttered past in a zig-zag line, orbited the lantern and disappeared off stage left.

"At least out here, in the dark, I can't keep reading that play," said Milly.

From the big house, the sounds of drums, tambourines and cymbals, which had been playing softly for some time, became louder and changed their tempo.

The stars on Cross's wrist buzzed as though electrified.

"By the pricking of my thumbs, something wicked this way comes," he murmured.

He stuffed the paper bag into his coat pocket and ran a hand over his revolvers by reflex. He would curb his inclination to use them. This was, after all, just a play.

They came in procession, some bearing candles, some with crude torches, the robed figures moving with stately tread across the garden. As they came closer, Cross noted the robes were made from bedsheets, and all wore crude masks of cardboard with eyeholes scissored out. Each mask was different, some with glued-on noses or beards, some with grotesque mouths and eyebrows.

For an unrehearsed, unpractised cast, they put on an impressive show.

They represented the court of the King in Yellow. Most were attendant lords. There was also a herald with a cardboard tube for a trumpet, an archbishop with a mitre made from a tea cosy, two knights with broomsticks for spears, and an executioner with a cardboard axe covered in tin foil.

The court arranged itself in a tableau. There seemed to be more light than just their candles and lanterns could produce. They stopped playing but there was still faint music, as though there were string and woodwind sections playing far away.

From behind the others, the King In Yellow stepped into the centre of the tableau.

For a moment Cross thought the robed and cowled figure must be a visitor from another world, it was so majestic and baleful.

But then he saw through the illusion. The robes were a brilliant yellow bedspread woven with glittering threads; the edges had been scissored into tattered fingers. Cross could not make out a face under the cowl, just the hint of a pale visage, the fabled pallid mask.

The long yellow gloves were rubber gauntlets, the sort they used in the factory while mixing caustic chemicals, and the sparkling crown was a brass stage prop set with coloured glass gemstones. The sceptre looked like a stair-rod topped with a glass door handle.

Another actor might have looked ridiculous in that costume, but he was regal and intimidating, with all the presence of a sovereign ruler.

"The hour has come," said the King, his tones rich and resonant but carrying the hollow echo of a vast tomb. "The sun has rolled away and the kingdom of all-embracing night enfolds the land. The matters of the day are disappeared with the light, and the dark brings its own laws. The King is come, to call down vengeance on his enemies."

"Not on us, O King," said Cross lightly. "You have no issue with us."

The King did not seem to hear him, but turned to Cassie. He tilted his head and held out a gloved hand. As he did so the entire court bowed or stooped in unison.

"Princess. Your King bids you join the dance."

The garden seemed much larger by moonlight, the vegetation denser, the flowers swollen and merged. The two pools sparkled.

Here and there among the shrubs a faint yellow corpse-light glowed. The toadstools, Cross realised, must be some kind of luminescent fungus. The garden, which looked so perfect by daylight, had been stealthily infiltrated by the King in Yellow's footlights.

"You have no claim on her," said Milly. "Go back whence you came, foul dwimmerlaik."

"No claim? No claim? I have the strongest claim: the claim of love."

"Love unrequited, unsolicited and unreturned," said Milly. "Again: go!"

She spoke louder and more boldly. Cross admired her nerve. She showed the right spirit, but to enter this type of dialog was to challenge the King on his home territory.

"Love conquers time, distance and fate," replied the king, speaking more quietly. "A solemn vow is adamantine across millennia. I claim you from my heart, I claim you by your father's troth, and claim you by the vow you made. You will come and dance with me in Carcosa."

The surface of the nearer pond rippled, then dropped away to form a glass staircase spiralling down into darkness studded with deeper black stars. The garden pond had become one of the lakes which connect Carcosa with other worlds.

Cross exhaled slowly. Cassie and Milly gasped. Perhaps he should have warned them to expect the supernatural. He could forget that others were still surprised by such things. At least they must now know that they were truly in the masque.

"No!" said Cassie.

"I say again: I claim you from my own heart, from the words of her father—and by her own promise."

"That's a lie," said Milly.

"Of my love, the stars can attest. Of the vow given by the father, these good lords can give ample testimony. And your vow Princess - do you deny it?" he asked Cassie. "*Can* you deny it?"

Milly looked from one to the other.

"What are you talking about?" she asked. "Cassie, what is he talking about?"

The lantern guttered and the darkness gathered about them. The court stood motionless as statues, all fixed on Cassie.

"It was Victory Night," she said. "Everyone went a little mad that night."

Cross remembered the night of 11th November 1918, the day the Armistice was finally signed. The greatest war the world had ever known was over. Cross had lost a leg and his place commanding troops for a desk job on the colonel's staff. Millions of others had lost their lives including many of the men he had fought alongside. The celebration in the officer's mess had been noisy and very drunken, the bittersweet joy of a victory amid the memory of so many fallen comrades.

He had heard about the celebrations in London, a pressure cooker of exploding emotion. Spontaneous gatherings and parades, patriotic songs in the public squares, and drunken antics everywhere, with the police joining in.

"We met in the park," said the King. "There was a band. We danced and danced."

"I had never drunk wine before," said Cassie. "I was so young. Bottles kept being passed round and I just kept drinking."

"You were so beautiful and happy," said the King. "You danced on air."

"We both were," she said. "Everyone was so happy, it was like a golden cloud and nothing bad could ever happen again."

"The world was being reborn. We talked and talked about what we would do, the places we would go to now the war was over. Paris, Vienna, Capri…we made a pact."

"I could see all of it," she said. "The whole world was opened up again, and all for us. I wanted to see all of it and do everything, and there you were."

"You promised."

"I didn't know what I was saying," she said, wistful with nostalgia for a lost future.

"You promised," he said, with a harder edge. "You promised we would be married, and you would come anywhere with me."

"Maybe I did," she said.

"Cassie!" said Milly, outraged. "Is that true? Why didn't you tell me?"

"How could I tell you? How could I?" said Cassie, turning on her. "I was very young and very drunk, and it was a mad night. And I never saw Matt again. I never even knew his full name. I thought it was all past." She let out a sob. "What do you want? What could I tell you?"

"You could have told me *something*."

"Milly, I never lied to you!"

"But you never told me the truth!"

Both were breathing heavily. Neither seemed to want to speak next.

The silence was broken by the King in Yellow. "Princess, you gave me your heart."

Cassie looked stricken. For weeks she had been avoiding this moment. She had not confronted Chambers nor rejected him outright. Just as she had never stood up to proclaim herself to the world. She had hoped to remain unnoticed, living life on her own terms without being challenged on the details.

"I was young and drunk, and I didn't know any better," said Cassie, speaking as much to Milly as to the King.

"Even a girl who has not seen the change of fourteen years knows her heart," said the King.

"She knows her heart better now," said Milly. "And she loves me."

Cassie stood hesitant. She did not draw any closer to the King, but neither did she look at Milly. She had never declared herself in public, never told anyone. She did not seem able to speak up now.

"Your father granted me your hand in marriage," said the King. "Do you defy him?"

Cassie's eyes were fixed on the ground. She seemed to be in shock.

"Cassie," said Milly. "Tell him you don't love him. Send him away."

Cross gripped a pistol but hesitated. He wondered if a part of Cassie was still clinging to Chambers—not perhaps from love, but from the world Chambers represented as a possible male partner. He could give her the chance to lead a respectable life, have a big wedding, a family. With him she could be Mrs Someone and part of the community, instead of nervously clinging to the edges, hoping not to be found out, keeping her lover forever hidden.

"Shame on you," said Cross to the King. "You shared a beautiful dream, a memory you both could cherish forever about young lovers in a new world. And instead, you try to twist that dream into a golden chain to trap a girl on a drunken promise, to ruin her life and her partner's for your own pleasure. And you go further, you try to blackmail her with evil necromancy on the soul of her beloved father — my comrade."

Again the King ignored Cross, as though he had spoken his lines out of turn.

"I am King," he said extending a hand to Cassie. "You will dance with me."

"No!" said Milly. "She will not go with you."

The King in Yellow turned slowly to face her.

"You know the truth about the Princess and the King," he said. "Now it is time for you too to unmask, wench," said the King, turning on Milly. He pointed his sceptre at her. "Will you take off your mask?"

"I wear no mask," said Milly.

"Oh, but you do," he said slowly.

Cross saw Milly suddenly shivered under that cowled stare.

"I—" Milly said, but could speak no more.

"You show a brave mask to the world, and even to her. You pretend you are bold, fearless, that you are proud to be what you are. You cling to her because she is weaker than you and she makes you feel strong. But inside you are ashamed of what you are, scared, guilty—aren't you?"

"It's not true," said Milly.

"That's the true face you have never shown to anyone. The face of your shame. And now we will unmask you."

The entire court moved as one, as synchronised as dancers, surrounding Milly in threatening poses but not quite touching her.

"We will flay off that false covering and see the pretty white face behind it. We will reveal the clean bones and smiling teeth, your true self."

"No, no—" Milly said.

Cross reminded himself that this was all an act, that the court only had cardboard daggers, that they were not about to literally attack Milly.

"Shall we unmask her?" the King asked Cassie. "Do you want to see the maiden for what she really is?"

Cassie shook her head. The King had found her weakness, her inability to proclaim the relationship she had with Milly. Perhaps she was protecting herself, but perhaps she was more concerned about Milly. Wordlessly, and fearful, reluctant as a naughty child being taken home from a party early, Cassie raised her hand so the King could take it.

That was too much for Cross.

"You will not have her against her will," said Cross, drawing a pistol. "Not with threats against her friend, she will not go with you unless I hear from her own lips that she goes willingly and renounces this."

"Cassie, I love you," said Milly. "You know I love you. Don't do this."

The King moved back, pulling Cassie to her feet. She looked at Milly but said nothing.

"Let her go," said Cross. "She will go with you willingly or not at all. Let her speak."

"Her will is mine," said the King. "She is mine."

"Shoot him," said Milly. "Captain, shoot him now before he drags her away."

Cross should have explained to her earlier how futile attempting to shoot the King In Yellow would be. The gun was a signifier, a symbolic weapon.

"No, I don't want to dance with you," said Cassie at last, trying to pull her hand away, but the King held it firm. "I will not dance with you, in Carcosa or anywhere else."

"The lady says no," said Cross. "Even a king cannot command hearts."

The King drew himself up, impossibly tall and majestic, towering over them. He held Cassie's hand as if about to draw her into a waltz and raised the sceptre with his other. Ghostly music rose over the garden.

"The love of the King conquers all," he said. At least he seemed to notice Cross now. "No wall and no word can withstand it, no blade or bullet stop it, no hand, and no heart resist it. My love and I return to Carcosa."

Cross had not seen Milly move until he felt her jerk the second gun out of its holster at his back. She held the pistol in both hands just as Cross has shown her.

"You let her go now!" she ordered, the revolver trembling in her hands.

This was why Chambers—or the King, there was no telling them apart now—had wanted Cross in the masque. Not as an active player, simply as the bearer of firearms. Nothing good was going to happen now.

"She is mine," replied the King.

"I won't go," said Cassie, firmly.

"Mine forever," he said, more quietly but with menace.

Milly fired. The range was no more than ten feet, and her aim was good. Three sharp pistol cracks sounded, and an invisible finger seemed to tap at the King's chest each time.

He was quite unmoved.

"The King In Yellow is no mortal," he said, and pulled Cassie back another step. They were two paces from the staircase leading down into the dark.

"No," said Cassie.

"Can you hear the music?" he asked. "You will dance with me for eternity in Carcosa."

"I'd rather die than go with you! Milly, I love you," said Cassie, straining to get away from the King even as he pulled her closer to the head of the staircase between worlds. "I love you!"

Cassie had finally spoken those words out loud.

"I'd rather die than be with him!" Cassie repeated.

Her eyes met Milly's.

Cassie raised her head and threw her shoulders back to present the best target. Milly swallowed, aimed carefully at Cassie's heart, and pulled the trigger twice more.

Cassie fell. The King released her hand as she sank on to the lawn.

One chamber left, thought Cross, anticipating the inevitable. Milly placed the gun against her head. With a last look at Cassie she fired a final time, then slumped to the grass.

Silence spread across the garden.

With no hesitation, with no script, Cross came forwards. The stage was his.

"The King is deceived!" He let out a peal of forced laughter. It sounded crazed, but it was the best he could do. "Your court, O King, lacks a fool—that is, one who makes a fool of fools—so I am here to make up the want."

The King seemed lost for words, an actor who'd forgotten his lines, looking about him for the prompter to supply them. Cassie was still moving, feeling at the place she had been shot. Cross did not look at her. He was trying to capture the right stage-language, to force the King to heed him, to make sure he was in on the act.

"It is all play-acting! The fatal shots were merely blanks! False fire, noise and fury, passion without injury."

"But our play has exposed the lovers' true feelings for each other, a bond which defies tyranny. In like manner the King's heart was not pierced with cupid's dart, but perhaps only the pang of indigestion — another false fire—and now his folly is laid bare."

Now Milly groaned and raised a hand to her head.

"My love is not folly," said the King, but he seemed uncertain. That uncertainty thoroughly undermined the meaning: he sounded like a man with a growing awareness that he had made a terrible mistake and was about to be made to look ridiculous.

"It surely is," said Cross, growing in confidence as the ad libs came to him. "You danced with a girl in the park that night, and Cassie with a boy—but not with each other. You mistake her: your 'princess' was a girl called Carrie, not Cassie, and her boy was called Matt, not Mark. You would have known if you had compared your recollections. Instead, you saw only your own dreams. No, O King, you did but love a phantom, and you have no claim on this woman."

Cross tried to make it sound like a big joke. He was buying time as he crossed the distance to reach the King, who, he was pleased to see, looked stricken.

The King was the butt of a jest. It was in the finest tradition of restoration comedy, an important personage made to look ridiculous by their own actions.

"The wrong girl..." said one of the courtiers from behind his mask.

"All this time," said another.

"Imagination ran away with him again," said a third.

"Nothing between them after all."

The King looked around as though for someone to appeal to. He saw his court shaking their heads, Cassie staring at him in horror, and Cross advancing.

"I am sending you back to Carcosa—alone," Cross said.

Cross drew the item from his pocket, raising it backhanded, dagger-fashion as if to stab the King in the neck. The King raised his hands and blocked Cross's arm with his sceptre, then stopped as he saw Cross held not a thrice-enchanted silver blade, the point envenomed, but a curved yellow fruit.

"Have a banana," said Cross. "You'll want something for the long trip."

Tragedy had been upstaged by comedy; high drama turned into absurdity.

As the King, bemused, took the wax banana, Cross gave him a smart shove.

The King took half a step backwards and tripped on his tattered robes.

The King in Yellow was a creature of the theatre. He was bound by laws which were no less absolute here than the laws of physics. Tragedy and comedy both had their iron rules.

The King stood, arms windmilling for an impossibly long moment at the top of the spiral stairs, then tumbled majestically backwards down them into the infinite dark: as fine a pratfall as any clown ever executed, bouncing on every sixth stair on the way down.

The scene thus completed, the staircase collapsed in on itself, telescoping to become the surface of a garden pond once more. The music trailed off, disappearing with the wa-wa-wah of a phantom trombone.

The brass crown rolled across the grass and onto the patio.

Cross was still looking at the pond, as the yellow bedspread and gloves billowed to the surface. He waited to see if the drenched, bedraggled figure of Chambers would emerge after them.

"That's it, everyone, the show is over," said Cross, clapping his hands together loudly. He pulled the yellow bedspread out of the pond, but there was no sign of Chambers. "Now, perhaps some of you can give me a hand in getting your leader out."

The water could not have been more than a foot deep, but there was no sign of Chambers.

The members of the court were taking their masks off. As Cross hoped, they had woken at last from their sleep-walking or whatever hypnotic hold the King in Yellow had over them. They did not look dazed and befuddled so much as resentful, as though they had all been dragged unwillingly from a beautiful dream to a Monday morning, a cold bath and a week's work.

"He's gone," said one, his voice dulled by psychic exhaustion.

"They buried him yesterday," said a second.

"He walked into a swing beam in the loading yard," said another.

"Hit him right on the head."

"Crowned him. Dead on the spot."

"Everyone knows you have to stay out of the yard when they're using the cranes."

"But he just walked into the beam. And the last thing he said…"

"The last thing he said…"

All of them spoke in chorus.

"'Hey everyone, watch this.'"

One by one they turned away, and, with faces downcast, walked slowly back towards their house.

Milly's scalp was bleeding, as scalp injuries often did in Cross's experience, but she was not seriously hurt. There was a scorched circle of hair the size of a half-crown, but the damage all seemed superficial. He made a compress from his handkerchief and had her hold it against the wound.

"Milly, look at me," he said. "Can you speak?"

"Yes, yes, I'm fine. No, I'm not fine."

"You might have a concussion," he said. "It isn't safe firing blanks at close range, it's like being hit with a hammer. I used a very reduced charge, but still…"

A larger-calibre weapon with a full charge would have cracked her skull. Maybe the St Etienne would have done so too if the scene had been played for tragedy rather than comedy.

"My ear is ringing," she said. "Where are my glasses?"

She felt for them on the grass beside her with her free hand and put them on. They were undamaged.

"If I had thought of it earlier, I would have acquired some prop stage pistols," said Cross. "Those are safe. But I did what I could."

"You tricked him," said Cassie, slowly getting to her feet. "And me! I thought I'd been shot."

"Suggestion is a powerful thing," said Cross. "The whole art of theatre, you might say."

"But it felt like…" said Cassie, feeling her chest again and finding no injury. She still seemed more stunned than Milly.

"A practical joke," said Cross. "Not a very funny one, but no worse than the ones in *A Midsummer Night's Dream*."

"I don't know it," said Milly.

That play had been the key. Tomorrow morning, for his own satisfaction, Cross was going to go through the listings of the late Baron Saint-Moury's library to see if it mentioned any plays other than *The King in Yellow*. And when he found the Shakespeare in there, he would kick himself for being a bloody fool, and award himself a bottle of good claret for working it out in time. He would share the bottle with Stubbs, who would protest that he was not a wine drinker while downing glass after glass.

"So, there was an antidote?"

"A rather obvious one, in hindsight," said Cross ruefully. "*Dream* has a revenge plot, plenty of supernatural elements, a play within a play, and madness, and it is set in a royal court. Mainly though, it involves a practical joke in which an immortal monarch is made the butt of a joke involving loving the wrong person."

"You didn't tell us," said Cassie, with the mildest of reproof.

"I wanted everyone else to play it straight so I could upend it all by surprise at the last minute. Playing a Joker after he played the King, so to speak."

Cross had assumed that he would be the one to be shot with his own gun, and that he would then be able to get up and laugh at them, and maybe trip up the King with a banana skin.

"I'm not really hurt," said Milly, struggling to her feet. "I have a thick skull."

The two women looked at each other. Cross wished he could quietly disappear as easily as Puck, a spirit melting into thin air. Perhaps he did, because they fell into each other's arms and kissed as though he had vanished.

"Cassie! I thought I'd lost you."

"I thought I was lost," said Cassie, laughing and sobbing at the same time.

"Well, well , well, "said Cross after a suitable interval. "Tragedy is averted and you get your happy ending. A wedding is called for."

"That would take more than stage magic," said Cassie ruefully.

"As matter of fact I know a High Priestess who can arrange a ceremony for you," said Cross with a smile. "But I'm afraid you'll have to go to the Greek islands for it."

"It's a lovely thought," said Milly with a laugh. "But I'm afraid Greece is out of our price range."

"I just told you," said Cross, his smile widening. "It's a happy ending. I'll be exceedingly surprised if I don't get a substantial bid for your copy of *The King in Yellow* in the morning post. And given that we can now offer the antidote—and an actual crown worn by the King in Yellow himself into the bargain—you can expect a tidy sum."

"I suppose we shall have to sell the cottage and go and live in Paris," said Cassie. She sounded resigned. "We can't stay here after this."

"I don't care where we go so long as we can be together," said Milly, gazing fondly at her. "But if we can make it through that, we can survive anything."

"Oh Milly! Can you forgive me for not telling you about him?"

"There's nothing to forgive," said Milly. "He was never real anyway."

CURTAIN

Andrew Doran and the Masks of Flesh

By Matthew Davenport

Chapter One

My panting and the feeling of my feet pounding against the dirt floor were what I noticed first.

Floor to where, I had no recollection. I also had no idea why I was running.

Not knowing why I was running or what I was running from, I decided to gauge my surroundings before slowing down. While jarring, what went from nothingness to seemingly waking up mid-sprint in an unknown area, this was the type of daily occurrence that I was more than accustomed to at this point. In a world of the fantastic, even the insane can begin to normalize.

I was in a hallway with barely any lighting. I saw no light sources, but I could see well enough that continuing forward was not a problem. The walls were wood boards, as was the ceiling. It all gave the impression that I was in a basement. The illusion was destroyed however by the sheer length of the hall.

I risked a glance over my shoulder, still unsure if I was running from something or not. The hall ended in the distance in complete darkness. In front of me was only more of the same.

Slowing only enough to investigate further, I pulled open my satchel. Inside were a few of my tools, including my .38 pistol and several vials of various chemicals and concoctions. One of them was empty and there was a hastily scribbled note on my notepad.

In the last two years, I had gone from a practicing academic in the field of archaeology, to the Dean of Miskatonic University, to something akin to a wizard, and then, almost all at once, back to being the practicing academic. Unfortunately, that meant I needed a few tricks up my sleeves for the things that I ran into that my long-gone magic couldn't do for me anymore. That's why the vials and the notepad.

Five of the vials were … were …

I couldn't remember. That was odd.

Scooping up the notepad, I stopped and looked at the note.

SAW THE YELLOW SIGN. ACTORS ARE AFTER YOU. HIDE. FORGET. GO HOME.

It was my handwriting.

Pieces came back to me. The vials had powder in them collected from the Dream Lands. It wasn't easy to come across but, when consumed, it could make a person forget everything for the last few hours.

Except that it was not an exact science.

In my studies of the occult over the years, I had come across some things that were dangerous to the mind. Full-blown madness was a very real hazard. As a precaution, I had worked out the Dream Land Dust for erasing one's memory. In a pinch, it worked great, basically making you forget that mind-melting thing stuck in your brain.

I had never used it before and had yet to run into a situation that required it.

If I had seen the Yellow Sign, though …

Well, that explained why I wasn't recognizing my surroundings.

Shouts of alarm, or murder, or generally angry voices rose up from behind me.

Suddenly, the previous day's events cut through the fog of my mind except for the last few hours and real fear began to sink in.

I was in Carcosa.

Damn.

―――――

Yesterday

The small get-together before the winter break was meant to be social and light, but there was an unspoken rule that all of the faculty needed to be present.

I could have skipped, but the last few years, both as the university dean, and then as the person who everyone blamed for a semester of nightmares meant that I had to show my face even when I didn't want to. Otherwise, the eye of the board would find it suspicious, and I didn't need them looking any deeper into my life.

That was why I was wearing my nicest suit, which wasn't that great, and already finishing a whiskey-ditch surrounded by the stuffiest people I had ever known.

To my credit, I had lasted an entire five minutes without rushing to the door. That was likely because one of the least boring people, Dr. Ruth Dodgson of the Theatrical Department, had seen me from across the room and rushed over with a drink. She tended to be one of the few people who didn't make me want to summon Icthosthau as soon as these things started.

"I'm glad I caught you before James could," Ruth said as she approached. I took the glass and had half of it down before she continued. "He's under the impression that a cat is stalking him, and we both know that it isn't some creature from beyond so much as he needs to stop keeping bacon in his pockets."

Well, she was only half right. The cats were stalking Professor Herrod, but it wasn't entirely about a bicycle accident he and a calico experienced last summer. It was also the bacon.

"And what plagues you?" I asked Ruth, entirely expecting her to turn the conversation to the weird. My reputation among the staff was mixed at best. Most of them chose to ignore me, but a handful either thought I was crazy and didn't understand how I still had a job, or the rest, like Ruth, thought I was the real deal and were looking to find some sort of occult edge to make their lives better.

To Ruth's credit, she was more of the curious sort, interested in the weird for the weird's sake. Unfortunately, the kind of weird that I dealt with tended to be the kind that would melt your mind.

"Can't a friend say hello?" Ruth smirked, and we both knew well enough that she wasn't seeking me out just to say hello.

"Alright, Ruth," I said to her while indicating the drink she brought me. "You've bought me for an evening if you can keep these coming. How are you on this miserable occasion?"

"Dr. Andrew Doran," she giggled. "You're always so much fun."

Don't get the wrong idea here. Ruth Dodgson was attractive to those interested in the mature, academic type, but neither Ruth nor myself wanted more from our discussions than fun conversation. Besides, my most recent romantic interest had fallen through a portal into another world and that had left me sour on the entire idea of love.

"What odd mystery have you brought to me today?" I pressed her as I grabbed a handful of crackers and cheese as the caterer went past. Before the United States had joined the war, this would have been something more like shrimp, or at least a French cheese.

Ruth's eyes lit up as if she had been waiting all day for this conversation. Knowing her, she likely had been.

"A play. A play with a torrid past." She leaned in conspiratorially. "Do you know of The King in Yellow?"

It was my turn to chuckle. "The stuff of myths and legends." I took a deep breath before continuing. "Until recently, it was believed to be written in the 19th century, but letters discovered last year of correspondence between Shakespeare and a German acquaintance push that date back to the mid-17th century." A memory surfaced in the back of my mind, and I was suddenly excited to make the connection. "Actually, a Dr. Stephen Marquesee, at one of the New York schools just submitted a paper on Roman writings that led him to the conclusion that, at the very least, the myth might date back to at least 100 B.C." Ruth's attention was almost a physical presence around me. She was waiting for me to speak about something specific. "You're curious about the curse that follows the play, aren't you? The curse of the Yellow Sign?"

"A play with such a … checkered past would certainly draw quite the crowd, don't you think?"

There it was. Everything she usually asked me was about how to use the occult to bring about fortune and glory. She never acted on any of it, but that was the appeal of the supernatural, wasn't it? How could we use magic to better our lives? Unfortunately, I saw the supernatural as something else. I knew it as a tool for the machinations of beings much smarter than us to bring about their own betterment in their lives. We were the rats collecting the magical scraps of beings that could devour gods.

And those scraps came at a high cost that we mere humans were forced to pay.

"If any of those patrons were intelligent, it would drive them away. The curse isn't some bedtime story that people go running to find. The play, the story, or the myth behind it anyway, acts as a sort of summons to the King in Yellow. Many believe the King to be the physical manifestation of Hastur in our reality. The story says that anytime the play is performed madness, death, and possibly worse afflicts all who witness it before the second act has finished."

Ruth scoffed at me. "Like you said, Andrew, myths. That kind of story builds intrigue. The ticket sales would be through the roof."

I wasn't ignorant to the fact that the board had been discussing cutting funding to the Arts. Specifically, the Theatrical Department. I could see Ruth's mind trying to cut through her excitement to ask the questions she had prepared.

"What were you saying about the Yellow Sign?" Ruth pressed.

I sighed. Forewarned was forearmed and I saw no reason not to try and scare her away with the truth.

"The play and Hastur himself are about creating portals between worlds. Hastur doesn't just want to drive people mad. I have heard so many different stories about why and what he wants that I don't know what is true, but I do know what he's supposed to be doing." I took a sip of my drink and savored the burn before continuing. "I think that the way he creates portals is inside of us." I poked my temple. "First he has to rewire our brains. To do that, he has the play, preparing us for the journey, but also taking this crude hardware and adjusting it so that our minds become the machines that create the portals. Then he needs us to trigger it. That's where the curse comes in. The play designs the door, but the sign is the key that unlocks it. Once the people who have experienced the play begin to lose their minds, they start seeing the Yellow Sign. Once they start seeing the sign, it is only hours before they are whisked away to Carcosa."

The light in her eyes didn't change. If anything, Ruth looked more excited by the concept of going mad and being kidnapped to another world than upset about the idea that people would likely die.

To emphasize the point, I said, "Madness, death, stolen to a faraway place, and then driven madder to the point of losing your sense of self. That's what happens when this play is read."

Ruth smirked at me. "Myth and legend, though." She shrugged and leaned in a bit. "Imagine if they didn't see the sign, though. Theoretically, without the sign, it's just a play that summons the Yellow King. Do you know of any other myths or legends that might stop the sign from being seen? A sort of inoculation?"

I held up my hand. She was using my cautionary tale as an instruction manual. "Either you aren't taking this as seriously as I am saying that you should," I said, "or you are purposefully being ignorant of the potential dangers represented by that manuscript."

She scoffed at me, and I noticed the scent of whiskey on her breath being stronger than I had expected.

"Even if I believed you, that doesn't change the fact it would take an act of God," she grinned and in her inebriated state it looked almost crazy, "or King in Yellow, to save the theater department this year."

"Dead is dead," I countered. "If you could find the play," and with her level of desire, I had no doubts that the play was already seeking her out, as those types of possessed tomes were known to do, "and the hype brought in the acclaim and money that you needed to save the department, would the loss of those lives, either in a gory death or as victims of another world, be worth all of that?"

The look on her face said that it possibly would be.

"No," she lied. "Of course not, but I'm desperate, Andrew." The line of questioning seemed to be over with her saying that, but after a long pause she asked a different and perhaps more telling question.

"A world of artists and actors." Ruth sighed. "Doesn't that sound just heavenly?"

Now.

I saw an alcove, a break in the tunnel walls, ahead and on the right. I ducked into it. I could hear the things in the distance and couldn't tell how far away they were. Even so, I was exhausted and had no idea how long I had been running.

Candlelight dimly lit the area from sconces every few feet. As I stepped into the alcove, I found that it wasn't very deep at all. Leaning against the nearest wall, I crouched to catch my breath.

Collecting my thoughts was useless. Until my memories returned, talking to Ruth was all that I could remember. The vials in my bag were for memory loss, except that the dosage had been measured out to only erase about an hour of recall.

Something had gone wrong, as I was having a hard time believing that the faculty party had only been an hour ago.

I also knew that I wouldn't have used the potions without it being my very last option. I was averse to things mucking about in my mind, even if I was one of those things. My mind had been invaded before and it was not a pleasant experience. Perhaps the potion was the only inoculation that I could come up with after Ruth's queries.

I squatted lower and scooped up the dirt I had been running on.

Rubbing it between my fingers, I spit on it and continued to rub it together. Staring at it told me nothing, as the lighting wasn't anywhere near good enough. The feel told me a little, though.

There was no grit in the soil, and it was very smooth, becoming sticky when I added my spit. In the dim lighting, I could see a sheen and my fingerprint left an impression. I rolled it into a ball and noticed that it was staining my fingers a dark color.

That was enough to know that this dirt was a silty clay loam. Nowhere near the school would have soil like this. Perhaps closer to the river. Definitely south of Arkham, anyway.

A buzzing thought in the back of my brain broke through, then.

If I was still in Arkham.

The thing that was chasing me was getting closer. It sounded like many things, scurrying like large rats.

I dropped the dirt and noticed that where I had picked it up was a much lighter color. I reached down and grabbed at it. Finding it solid, I began digging it up.

I held up my discovery to examine it closer. Through the dirt streaked across it, it was a plain and white mask. Smooth, like half of a large egg, with an exaggerated expression cut into it. There were eyeholes with painted tears under one of the eyes. The mouth was turned down, with the curve above the points.

The eggshell thought floated to the forefront of my mind as I turned the sad mask over. Veins and wet flesh were tightly stretched and covered the inside. Through the dirt I could see that the veins were moving. Blood was pumping. This thing was in some sort of living state.

Something in me was demanding that I put on the mask. If I hadn't been me, as versed in the strange attractants of the world and its horrors, I would have put it on.

Instead, I set it back down on the ground and stood up.

The scurrying grew louder and the things were getting closer.

I looked down at the mask again and then to my bag. Whether or not it would be useful, it was part of this and everything crashing down on me. Scooping it back up, I dropped it into my satchel and waited to see who my pursuers were.

Chapter Two

My gun was in my hand as I pressed my back further into the alcove. I didn't remember grabbing it but was happy for its presence. Whatever was running my way had the sound of scurrying without the sounds of mice or rats. The only sounds accompanying the scratching and thudding of hundreds of feet was a grunting akin to a pig or horse stampede.

Then they burst past me.

They moved fast, but I was able to make out several distinct features that only left me more confused. They were completely naked and seemed to have no sex organs. They also had no hair anywhere on their bodies. Their complete nudity left little to the imagination, but there was already too little to imagine about them. If anything, they looked like a type of human, but with no discerning features. Everything that would make them individual was scrubbed away. Their faces were entirely blank, except for two small holes where their eyes should have been and a small hole for a mouth. They were pale, as well. No distinctive colors that would normally associate them with the human race. Instead, they were the same milky gray color as the moon.

They were running and panting on all fours as they hunted for, presumably, me.

And there were at least fifty of them racing down the crowded dirt and wood hall. It was a lot to take in. If I was, as I assumed, in Carcosa, I didn't know what these things could be. Even knowing how little I knew told me nothing. While well-versed in the horrid monsters of our world, even I laid no claim to knowing all of them.

Either way, if this was Carcosa, then I was no longer on my world.

All of them made it by me without looking in my direction. I waited a moment before relaxing and peering around the corner toward where they had gone.

I should have looked the way they had come first.

When my head pivoted to the left, the direction they had chased me from, I saw a lone creature meandering down the hall. The slow movements of its approach halted once it noticed me before it propelled itself into a gallop toward me.

My pistol was firing before I could stop myself. No doubt the monsters that had just left would hear it, but I was more concerned with survival in that moment than ten minutes from now.

Bullets had no effect on the thing. I couldn't tell if they were absorbed into the thing's flesh or if they were even hitting it. I fired and the monster did not flinch or slow down.

I dove back into the alcove as the thing came up on me. It slid past in the loose dirt but gained enough traction to leap back toward me as I scrambled for anything in my bag. As I dropped the pistol, my hand fell on the fleshy mask. Grabbing it, I slapped it onto the blank face of the creature as it lunged for me.

It was a dumb idea at the time and all I can assume is that somewhere, deep in the erased memories of my previous hour or more there I had formulated some inkling of an idea around what these masks were. The echo of that memory was still present enough that pressing the fleshy mask onto the thing's face felt like the right idea.

The thing clutched at its face, clawing and groping at the edges. It fell away from me as I watched the mask take change. It took on more specific characteristics. A mole near the hairline, a nose filling out, full lips, and eyes. Then the beast itself began to change. It sprouted ears, a short, cropped bit of brown hair on its head, and then, oddly enough, genitalia.

Then it stopped moving and slumped against the wall opposite me.

Sitting across from me was a naked man. Nothing stood out about him and if I hadn't just seen the transformation, I wouldn't doubt this being's humanity.

Since I had seen his transformation, I brought my pistol back up and aimed it at him.

"What the hell is this?" I demanded.

Yesterday

"What the hell is this?" I demanded.

Ruth's smile wavered. "This, Andy, is a copy of the script for *The King in Yellow.*"

"I told you not to do this, and now you're parading your ignoring of my advice in front of me?"

After the party, Ruth had invited me to her office to show me something she had discovered. The math had been simple to figure out before we arrived. Her excitement over the prospect of finding the play had been the only thing occupying her mind. I had assumed she had combed through the campus museum or archives and found a clue to the whereabouts of such a document. When she pulled out a wooden box wrapped in a leather strap I was curious. When she opened it, I was furious.

"Stop thinking like all this magic stuff is real," Ruth scoffed at my reaction. "We both know that most of what you have been forced to deal with is crazies wanting to make deals with devils for shinier jewelry." She touched the manuscript and I flinched. "This is a book. A play. It is meant to be presented to the masses, not locked away as some cursed relic."

I could have said something about the nightmares that wrecked campus last year or how no one knew the whereabouts of the former dean, Brandon Smythe, or the number of times faculty had gone missing in the history of this school, but instead I clenched my jaw and stared at her.

"You're being a child," Ruth said. I almost lost the last remaining bits of my restraint.

Taking a slow breath, I said, "Ruth, this play attracts the same types of crazies that you're saying I have to deal with regularly. Even if nothing I have tried to warn you about is true, there will be people desperate enough to believe that it is and they will come here. They will not come to watch your play, they will come to be consumed by it, or worse."

She laughed, not even looking at me as she started to thumb through the manuscript. "Worse? Worse than thousands of adoring fans pouring their money into our arts department?"

"No," I answered. "Worse than those fans hoping to be devoured by the earthly presence of Hastur. If I'm wrong, it would be likely that they would, instead, be the ones doing the devouring. Those crazies you pretend aren't a threat, are as much a threat as the monsters that I claim do exist."

"Can I use the play or not?" Ruth closed it and turned back to me.

"What?" I was confused by her question. "Are you asking permission?"

"Of course." She found her glass and took another sip. "You're the most senior member of the anthropology department. I can't borrow the play without your signing off on it."

"I'm not the department head. That's Professor Reynolds. Was this the only reason you even approached me today?"

"You're not the head of the department, but you're the former dean. If anyone can grant me access to this, it's you."

"Then no, I don't give you permission. That belongs back in the museum." I wanted to say that it belonged back in the armory, locked away, but I was already expecting resistance.

Now

The man seemed to wake up a moment or two after I aimed the gun at him. His eyes fluttered open and he stared at me, then the gun, then back to me before gently holding his hands up.

"Please," he said in a whisper, "don't shoot."

"Then I need you to start talking," I countered. "Who are you and what is going on?"

"You are in danger," he said. "That's what's going on." He looked around at where he was sitting and the walls before returning his gaze to me. "Are we still in Carcosa?"

I nodded, assuming his asking of that question only verified my own assumptions about the place.

"Then, yes, you are in grave danger." He eyed my clothes. "You aren't like me?"

"Like you, how?" I asked. The gun hadn't moved from where I aimed at his chest.

"An artist, an actor." He sighed when he saw that I didn't understand. "You aren't a faceless thing wearing a mask?"

I shook my head.

"Good," he said. "Then there's still time for you."

"If you don't say something that starts explaining what's going on here, I will shoot you."

He nodded, seeming to understand. "Carcosa is a place of artists and actors. A place where the creative mind is free to be anything that it wants to be, but to be anything, you must first remove everything. My body, before I put on this mask, or …" he paused as if the memory wasn't as easy for him to recall, "… when you put the mask on me. That body was an actor, someone who had been stripped of all that made them who they were. Once stripped of the roles of life we are forced to wear our masks." He ran a finger along his face. "We are free to put on any mask, play any role, and be anything that the story demands of us. Or, even better, anything that we desire to be at any moment."

"Who are you now?" I demanded.

"The role is still asserting itself, but I believe that I'm a man named Edgar McDougal. A sad story, this one. A farmer turned writer who couldn't make it big. His family left him and he sought to find solace in the bottle. Wonderful, I haven't been a drinker in several scenes, this will be fun."

"Fun?" I asked. "You're wearing someone else's face."

"Someone who gave up everything to come here. Everyone who is here chose to open the play. The sign claimed them and gave them everything that it promised." He squinted at me. "Except you, it would seem."

"I am not sure why I am here, yet." I pointed in the direction of this 'actor's' comrades. "That's what those faceless things are? People who were drawn here by the Yellow Sign?"

'Edgar' nodded. "Actors looking for more. They gave up their faces to become anyone. Today, I wear one of them, but tomorrow I might wear another."

This acknowledgement of knowing what he was and being who he wasn't was a dichotomy that was leading me toward mistrust. "Who am I dealing with, right now? Are you the Actor-thing, or are you Edgar, the drunk?"

"It is everyone's dream here to be the role they wear. You have blessed me with a mask, so I must honor that with the best portrayal of Mr. McDougal that I can create." He gave a slight bow and said, "I am Edgar McDougal, playwright and drunkard, at your service."

I lowered the gun but didn't put it away.

"Alright, Edgar, here's the scene: I'm not supposed to be here. I have amnesia, possibly to erase the Yellow sign from my mind. I think I looked at the Yellow Sign so that I could find a friend of mine and bring them home. Your part is to assist me in locating my friend and getting back to my world."

Edgar nodded and closed his eyes. I wasn't sure what was happening until his shoulders sagged and his head started to sway.

"Yeah, ok, s-s-sure." His words were slurred. He had gotten into character. "I'll help you, but what's in it for me?"

Great, Edgar wasn't an altruist. Just my luck.

"What's in it for you is that you can go home, too," I said.

Edgar shook his head and it came across more like a rag doll lolling its head about.

"Actors can never leave. Masks are tied to this … here." He waved his hand about and I assumed he meant Carcosa.

An idea struck me then. This was a scene, so perhaps the things I offered didn't have to exist if I imagined they existed.

Reaching into my satchel, I mimed pulling a large bottle from it. "Well, then perhaps you would be interested in this fifty-year-old scotch I managed to bring with me. The seal is broken, but I have only had a swig. It's mostly full."

Edgar scrambled across the dirt floor so quickly that he kicked up a dust cloud. He grabbed the imaginary bottle, put the imaginary cork between his lips, pulled and spit before tipping it back.

Sitting in an infinite basement on an alien world and being hunted by monster actors I found that I could still be surprised. As Edgar tipped the bottle back, scotch sloshed from his mouth as the sloppy drunk almost missed his face.

Scotch that hadn't existed was just mimed into reality for the benefit of this 'play.'

I had to get out of here.

Chapter Three

Yesterday

I tried taking the manuscript with me, but it was clear Ruth wasn't going to part with it until her mind was clearer. I went back to my hole-in-the-wall office and paced in anger and confusion for what felt like hours. A glance at the clock showed me that barely one hour had passed but my frustration was far from abated.

So many questions flooded my mind, starting with how did I not know that we had a copy of the most dangerous manuscript in existence on campus? In hindsight, it was obvious that we were the ones who had it. Miskatonic University seemed to attract anything with the title "most dangerous" on it.

My next question was if she had read it already. She obviously hadn't finished it or Ruth would be gone or dead. Or worse; she could be right, and the play is more hype than fact. I doubted that, again, because this was Miskatonic University. If she had read it, it would explain her manic desire for approval. The script was said to create an obsession with the play, and Ruth's behavior, although excited and drunk, could be interpreted as manic obsession.

Either way, if she hadn't read it, she would soon. She was probably scribbling down a copy of it as quickly as she could, just in case I decided to force the script from her.

That was when I decided that I was going to do just that. Just in case, I grabbed my satchel and several vials of a Dream Land Dust I knew could erase my memory if I came into contact with the Yellow Sign or some other mind-altering pathogen that might escape from the book. I didn't want insanity, but I didn't want my friend succumbing to it either.

And yes, my pistol was in the satchel as well. The bullets of my pistol had a destructive influence on things not of this world and if that playbook could actually summon the King in Yellow I wanted to have a fighting chance at putting down the otherworldly deity.

I stomped back down the hall, preparing myself for confrontation, as I returned to Ruth's office.

The door was shut, but that didn't stop me from turning the handle and walking in.

One hour. That was how long I had been away from her office and in that time everything had changed.

Now

The actor wearing the Edgar mask led me, naked as the day he was born, as we wound through the tunnels back the way that his kind had been chasing me from.

On the one hand, this seemed like an entirely bad idea. The masks seemed to possess their wearers, but he had managed to keep his awareness of his real situation. He simply pushed what he was to the back of his mind so that this Edgar personality could be in control. It left me with a lot of questions, with the first being whether or not I could trust this character.

The actors were obviously after me for some reason. It was likely related to why I hadn't turned into one of them yet or Ruth's current situation. They wanted me, but Edgar seemed to want to help me. Did they desperately want to be part of the role they were given to the extent that previous orders or wants were driven from their minds? I found that hard to believe, but the same could be said about every aspect of my current scenario. The actor wanted me but the mask wanted to help me. Or at least seemed to. It was a Russian Doll of questions. I didn't know the actor's motivations and I didn't know Edgar's motivations. The actor might be some mindless animal that would bide its time until it had a mask, or a clever monster trying to use the power of the mask to lure me into a false sense of security. If the latter was true, it was just me versus a monster again. If the monster actually was trying to be their character, then more questions came into play. What kind of person was Edgar? Did Edgar want to help me, or did he see our meeting up as an opportunity that he could exploit?

That didn't change the fact that when I had returned to consciousness, I had been running away from the direction that Edgar was leading me down. If there was anyone that I should be trusting, it should be me and I had left a note stating that I needed to keep running. Nothing felt right about any of this.

I had a sudden idea that might help, but I was still grasping at straws.

"Hey Edgar," I asked during his next drunken stumble, "what kind of scene is this? Are we in a tragedy, a comedy, or an adventure?"

Edgar looked over his shoulder and smirked at me. "Maybe a romance, even?"

"Or that," I played along hoping to get some sort of information from him that I could trust.

He let out a slow sigh that ended in a burp. "Unfortunately, I have yet to read any script. We are in uncharted territory. My improvisational skills are being exercised today."

That was not the answer that I had been hoping for.

"A promise made is a promise kept, though," Edgar continued. "Edgar McDougal is a man of his word. I said I would get you out of these catacombs and I have."

Up ahead a light could be seen. Even Edgar started running toward it. We came out and onto a cobblestone street in bright daylight.

It took a moment for my eyes to adjust, but as they did, I took in what I saw.

The road was slanted, as if I had come out onto a street that was on the slope of a hill. Buildings rose up all around me with barely any sidewalk and only minimal room for the streets. The tightly packed buildings were made of stone and gold and looked to be a range of architectures that I both recognized and had never seen before. English architecture clashed with Italian designs and rural American housing. It was as if a different building from every time and location on Earth had been transported here and shoved between an already tightly packed city. Even the simple wooden housing and other structures seemed to only match the surrounding city by having golden elements built into them. One house had every shingle painted in gold. While another had any metal, such as stair-railings and windowsills, replaced with gold.

Then there were the people. They were everywhere. No vehicles were being driven in the streets, but people filled the streets, the sidewalks, and every nook and cranny of every building entryway.

The creepiest thing of it all was how normal everyone looked. They all had different styles of clothes, from entirely different time periods, but they mingled and talked as if they were all old friends who belonged where they were. At first, I was elated to see normal people, and then I saw what they all walked around.

Faces. The ground was littered with faces.

Closer inspection subsided my horror by only a minor amount. They weren't faces, they were masks. The ground was littered with masks just like the Edgar one that the actor I was traveling with was wearing. These were not normal people, at all. They were actors wearing the flesh faces of the people that Carcosa had collected.

That Hastur had stolen from Earth.

Every eye seemed to be watching me and my naked companion as we stood there, at the wooden entrance to the surprisingly large basement we had just escaped. They kept talking but they couldn't stop looking at me. That was when I realized why they didn't stop talking.

The show must go on.

This entire world was a play being put on for the audience of one. The torturer on the marquis; the King in Yellow. As long as the play continued uninterrupted, I assumed that I would stay safe. That's why the actors were chasing me and it wasn't anyone with an actual mask. The actors were cleaning the mess while the show continued above. I would need to be more careful in the daylight.

"How do we find my friend?" I asked.

YESTERDAY

Ruth was hunched over her desk, her drink long ago emptied, reading the manuscript and doing exactly what I thought she would be doing. She was scribbling furiously into a notepad on her desk to copy the play down before I could take it away.

I was too late.

If the fact that she was reading the play wasn't enough to alarm me to her precarious situation, the looming dark figure in golden robes behind her was a dead giveaway.

The King stood behind Ruth with his hands on her shoulders. He stood at least 9 feet tall with long flowing robes that weren't of any material on this plane of existence. They flowed like cloth in water while wisps of the robes seemed to dissipate into the air like smoke. They were as yellow as a dandelion's petals but exuded anxiety that my mind was more than willing to drink up.

Of his flesh, all I could see was his hands. He wore a hood that kept his face in the shadows. His hands were a dark obsidian color and jointed like something from an insect. A carapace that clicked together as he massaged his newest victim.

From this epicenter of calm, chaos emanated. The room had black flames in each of the corners. They didn't seem to affect their surroundings yet, but I could feel the heat and a dread filling my bones. These weren't normal flames and were instead extensions of the King's power. Possibly even of his body. As they flickered and licked at the walls, I couldn't help but get the sense that these dark fires were tentacles of a kind, reaching out and away from the god-like thing before me.

The flames worked, too. They did not burn, but they etched something into the walls. Years of dealing with the dark side of this and other worlds made me look away from the etchings before I understood what they were. My quick reaction was the only reason that I wasn't carted away to Arkham Asylum or straight to Carcosa. I knew what this thing drew while Ruth transcribed her punishment into the notepad. He was covering her office with the Yellow Sign.

My hesitation went entirely unnoticed by Ruth and the dreaded patriarch. My attention snapped back into place, and I did the only sane thing someone could do in that situation. I drew my pistol and fired into the yellow and black mass of the otherworldly regent.

It could have been the atmosphere being created by the beast, the shaking of my sanity by looking at it, or some demonstration of power on his part, but while my bullets exited the gun, I did not hear the gunshots.

The bullets made holes in the thing's yellow robes. Black smoke leaked out but the King didn't react at all to my attack. That was disconcerting. I needed the connection to be broken and my weapon had no effect on the monster. That left Ruth.

I ran forward and slapped her across the face before reaching for the manuscript. The world spun as I touched it. It wasn't the play. I had finally gotten the King's attention. He grabbed my wrist and pulled me closer. I heard no words as the idea to drop the manuscript filled my brain.

As I fought to resist, a new idea filled my head.

If I would not listen to the King, perhaps I could join him in Carcosa.

It was a threat sent to my mind as if the idea had been entirely my own. I bucked and kicked to get out of his grasp but suddenly his hand was on the back of my neck and his alien strength was twisting me around to face the wall and the carvings.

The Yellow Sign.

Thanks to the magic of the Dream Land potion, I didn't actually recall the Sign or much of the following events.

The only thing that still stands out from my encounter with the King in Yellow was him standing over Ruth. She laid on her desk and for whatever reason I was frozen and incapable of moving toward her. One long and sharp finger was running along the side of her face, blood spilling as he circled her features before he began to pull at the edges of his newest mask.

Chapter Four

NOW

Heads twisted to follow us as we moved through the streets. I kept telling myself that it was because of Edgar's nudity, but that was obviously not the case.

The only thing that continued to stop them from mobbing me was that they refused to break from their roles. That led me to believe that I needed to be more careful than I previously believed. They would have no problem attacking me if I did something to break the scene.

"Where are you taking me?" I whispered to Edgar.

"You wanted to save your friend and escape," he answered without whispering. "I am taking you to the place where you can do that."

"And where would that be?" Edgar the drunk or the actor or whatever wasn't the most direct and it was starting to wear on me.

"The understudy wing of the Grand Theater."

He said it in a way that implied that not only should I already know that, but I should also be excited by the prospect of getting a chance to visit it.

I was not. The truth was closer to the opposite, actually. In a world of malicious actors hunting for new faces to wear, going to a place called the 'Grand Theater' seemed like the last thing that I would want to do.

"The Understudy Wing?" I asked. "Is that where people, like me, learn to become actors?"

Edgar twisted a bit to give me an exaggerated wink. "You catch on quick."

"You're aware that I have no personal interest in being an actor, right?"

Edgar shrugged and kept moving through the streets and people. I did everything in my power not to bump anyone and flinched every time that it could not be avoided.

"We're all actors," he said. "From the moment we are born we start putting on masks to communicate how we feel, what we want, and what we need. Does a baby need to cry to tell us that it needs a breast? No, but crying gets the fastest reaction. So, the baby puts on the mask of sadness and the moment it gets what it wants, that mask evaporates like it was never there. What masks do you wear, sir?" He stopped and turned again, frowning as he did. "What is your name, by the way? I didn't catch it." He held up the imaginary bottle and wiggled it around. "Or perhaps I forgot."

I hadn't told him my name for a litany of reasons. We were no longer on my planet, but even on Earth names held power and my name was slightly more dangerous than the rest. Ruth came to me to wax poetic about what she believed to be fictions regarding magic and the occult, but everything I ever gave her was fact. My job was to be a professor of archaeology, but my hobbies were slightly more hazardous. I hunted down the creatures and nightmares that haunt humanity, much like this damned play that had been weaponized against me. Many of the monsters and demons that I found myself standing against tended to be intelligent and liked to warn others about me.

So, I gave Edgar a real name, but not my own. Instead, he got the name of a long-passed friend of mine.

"Leo," I answered. "Leo DuBois."

For all intents and purposes, Leo was dead and I knew he wouldn't care.

"A man of French descent?" Edgar smiled. "Parlez vous Français?"

I smiled and shook my head. "Non," I lied.

If Edgar saw through my lies, he didn't say and I held no guilt over lying to him. Edgar wasn't this thing's real name either and at least my face was still my own.

The road narrowed and curved downward. There was a sensation that this entire city was on a giant hill as everything seemed to curve away from where I stood as if I was always standing at the apex of a hill. That, or this planet was much smaller than Earth. The base of the hill ended in a set of double doors as if a large mechanic's shop or fire department was at the bottom. Above the door was a large sign that read "Grand Theater."

As we approached, I tried to calculate how much ammunition I had in my satchel. I doubted it would do me much good, if whatever these actors had become was anything like their king, but I would be damned if I didn't try to defend myself if it came to that.

Edgar approached the double doors and pounded his open palm against it before taking another swig from the imaginary whiskey bottle.

The large door creaked open on the right and I jumped, grasping at the gun in my satchel before realizing that I needed to calm down.

I had fought invisible monsters while surrounded by the entire German army, this shouldn't have me as on edge, but it did. Something about being removed from your home without your memories intact tended to make a scenario more terrifying than not.

A blonde-haired woman stuck her head out. She was wearing thick actor's makeup and a dingy green ball gown.

"Edgar?" her voice was shrill. "Edgar! It is you. Where have you been? I have not seen you in ages."

Edgar shrugged. "Passed out in the tunnels and was left for the land of the forgotten, but my good friend," he waggled his imaginary bottle again in my direction, "Mr. DuBois, liberated me from my imprisonment and I am here to return the favor."

The woman pushed the door open wider to take me in before thrusting her hand into mine and shaking vigorously.

"Well, I do thank you, Mr. DuBois. Yes, I do. Edgar is a role that many here hope to try out. He's one of the few writers we get and with his predilection for the bottle he is also one of the more fun people to be."

I suppressed a shiver at how normal they treated this shifting of identities.

"It was my pleasure," I answered. "Edgar has been most helpful in figuring out where to go."

"And where is it that you are trying to go?" the woman asked.

"I'm sorry," I needed more information. "I didn't catch your name."

She stepped back, giving me a minimal view behind her as she held her dress and curtsied. "My apologies," she said. "I am Anne Palance. My mask is that of the proprietor of this establishment. I am in charge of helping the newest actors let go of themselves so that they can more properly take on new characters."

'Anne' helped the victims erase their humanity. That's what she meant. If I had any extra time before I left, I would make an effort to destroy that mask.

"Perhaps you can assist me then," I said. "My friend would have arrived within the last day, although I don't know when. I am looking for her and a way to leave back to my own world."

Anne's face turned serious. "Leave? No one leaves."

Edgar shrugged. "I think I said as much."

"No, Edgar," I said. "You did not. You said that the actors cannot leave. You said nothing about myself."

"Everyone here is an actor," Anne said. "We all wear masks. Have you had yours on too long, Mr. DuBois?"

Edgar shook his head. "Leo isn't an actor. Not yet. He somehow made it here without going through the Grand Theater." He took another swig and hiccuped.

Anne's eyes widened as if I had just sprouted a duckbill.

"How is that possible?" her voice was only a whisper.

"I'm just special, I guess," was all that I could think to say. My hand was inside my satchel and around the handle of my pistol. Anne and Edgar both didn't seem to notice.

Anne shook her head. "One thing at a time, I suppose. Who are you looking for?"

"A teacher," I answered. "Professor Ruth Dodgson."

Anne nodded. "We did get a teacher here about three days ago. From Miskatonic University. Everyone can't stop talking about her. She has an energy and excitement to her that makes us all excited for the chance to be her."

Three days. My Dream Land potions were not an exact science, but they were never off by days. At worst they only erased a few hours. With only one vial emptied, I shouldn't have entire days missing from my memory. Either Anne was lying or time worked differently here. Either was a viable option at this point.

"Can you take me to her?" I asked, still with my hand on the gun.

Anne nodded. "Certainly. Edgar, you can come with us. I am sure many here will be looking forward to having you among us again."

Anne stepped aside and Edgar went in. I followed behind him.

While I could see almost nothing from outside, once I stepped across the threshold the entire place lit up. I was in a large auditorium with costumes and clothing and those flesh masks scattered all over the place. All around me was a bustle of motion as actors swapped masks and various masked actors were in every stage of dress.

People were shouting lines, singing songs, and expressing every emotion. The floor was made of some sort of polished stone. The walls were covered in lit sconces creating an ethereal glow that seemed to reach every crevice of the place while not adequately lighting anything. On the far side of the room was a stage. On the stage was a throne made of gold and surrounded by black wisps of smoke.

The King in Yellow sat on that throne.

I did not want to attract his attention. I was concerned that I already had.

Anne bid me to stay put for a moment while she gathered Edgar and went in search of Ruth. I stood still expanding my awareness as far as I was capable. I needed to be gathering information if I planned on making it out of this with my face still attached to my body. I had no reason to believe that these things were going to let me or Ruth go, and was only waiting for the double-cross to happen.

The clothing and accents that I picked up were from everywhere that I could think of, and plenty that I had never heard of before. The majority of the beings here were human, or were at least the masks of humans, but I saw a few that were decidedly from an entirely different species and planet. Humans didn't own the market on visual entertainment, but we seemed to be the ones most likely to read dangerous scripts.

The entire time that I waited, I felt like the King was staring at me.

"Excuse me," a voice that I felt more than heard, said from behind me.

I spun around and gasped when I saw that it was the King. Somehow, as only evil deities could, he had appeared directly behind me while I had been staring at him on the stage.

"Dr. Doran," the thing said. I would not look at him. "How is it that, in my eternity of hosting the Great Show, I have never met anyone with the ability to avoid my gifts as thoroughly as you?"

I shrugged and did what I always do when confronted with something that could devour my very essence as easily as I blink.

I was a jerk.

"You know what they say about that third eternity, once the omnipotence starts to go it's all downhill from there."

He let out a low chuckle. "Perhaps. Or perhaps you are a special project. Perhaps you demand special attention."

"Perhaps I am more trouble than I am worth," I said. "You know my name which means that you either know of me or can see into my mind. Either way, you know the kind of fiery hell that I bring down on those of your kind. Return Ruth to me, show me the door, and I will avoid everything to do with you and yours for the rest of my natural life."

"Dear Doctor," his voice reverberated through my bones, "you may have spoken to the messenger and been promised to the destroyer, but you have never met my kind before."

I nodded. "You certainly have more theatrics than the rest of them." I looked over my shoulder. Everything I could do to keep any piece of this monster's body out of my field of vision was in my best interest. I could feel his will trying to worm its way through my own.

"You are correct, though," the King said. "I think that you could be more trouble than I care to deal with, but nothing comes for free."

Chapter Five

That was when I noticed that every actor or mask or whatever they were was staring at us while we spoke.

"The journey is simple," the King in Yellow said to me. "Once your friend is returned to you, you will exit out the same door you came in. Then you must run to the sea. Throwing yourself into the waves of this world will return you to your own."

"But?" I asked. This was obviously not going to be that simple.

"The play is never ending and my people do not want you to leave." His voice was vibrating my bones at this point. I felt his words more than I could hear them. "You can leave, but they won't let you. Then there's the problem of Hastur."

"Him? I thought you were him?" I didn't want to say the name for fear of summoning some sort of eldritch wrath. Names had power and more so when in the presence of those who also had power.

"That is a complicated concept for human minds and yours is already cracking from our conversation."

I could hear a river roaring in the back of my mind. It felt like it was crashing through the dams of my mind and clearing entire cities before the residents knew they were even in trouble. It was my tentative grasp on reality breaking. My grasp was better than most but insanity came to us all when we lifted the veils of reality and saw what was really hidden in the shadows.

"Andy?" a voice that I only distantly recognized came to me from the crowd of actors staring at us.

I turned at the sound of the name before I even realized that it was my own. "Ruth?" I saw her pushing her way through the crowd. She was wearing the same thing that I had last seen her in the evening before.

Was it only last night?

My hand was on something small and solid. I looked down at it and saw that I was holding another of the Dream Land potions I had made up for forgetting. Obviously, the rational piece of my mind had realized that if I didn't want to go insane I would need to take this soon.

Except, if I did take it, I wouldn't ever leave. If I forgot the last hour, or however long the Dream Potion's effects lasted in Carcosa, I would forget how to escape and possibly even why I came here in the first place.

If the choices were to save my sanity or save Ruth, then I knew what I had to do.

I grabbed her by the hand and we ran out of the Grand Theater.

"What are we doing?" Ruth demanded. "Andy, where are you taking me?"

I stopped, but only briefly.

"This is Carcosa," I said. "This is what I warned you about. They want to steal your face and make you live here as a nameless actor, constantly changing roles and always being part of the King's play. This is a prison for artists and I am going to get us back home."

"They were being good to me," Ruth protested. "Why would I want to leave this? A prison for artists sounds almost perfect."

"Why did you want this?" I demanded. "Was it for your own glory? A day at the fair without all the hassle of responsibilities? Or was it because you thought it would save the department and your job?"

"Well," she hesitated, trying to parse through what I had said, what she had experienced, and probably the shock of how real this was all turning out to be, "the … the department, of course. I'm a teacher. Without the department, who am I teaching? Without the arts, what are we? Are we even people?"

"Exactly," I agreed. "Without art, history, and the fanciful stories of the past, how can humanity grow and learn? I am on your side," I said. "While this looks good today, in ten years, it will grow stale, your students will have forgotten that they once took a class with Ruth Dodgson, and you will be a faceless memory drinking from an imaginary bottle of scotch."

"That is," she paused again, "oddly specific."

"You're not the only one who's had an odd day."

The oddities did not stop.

As we exited the Grand Theater, it was obvious that, somehow, everyone had been informed about our flight from the city. Heads slowly turned to watch us as we started our march toward the sea. It was clear that they were not going to make this easy, but they also did not seem to be in any hurry to come after us yet. They either knew something that we didn't, or they were biding their time.

Grabbing Ruth's hand, I dragged her along as we ran down the cobbled roads. From my memories of what I had heard of Carcosa, I knew it to be an island surrounded by ocean. We only needed to pick a direction and we should hit the water. Assuming the city itself didn't block our paths while the monsters masquerading as people chased us, it should be a piece of cake.

That was when I heard the clatter of a lot of something solid hitting the cobble steps. I didn't recognize the noise, so I turned to look at where it was coming from. It seemed to be increasing in volume, like eggshells raining down on stone.

It was their masks. Every person that I could see was slowly pulling off their masks, returning to their blank actor state, and shifting their stances. As the transformation back into what they were finished, it was clear that these were no longer the people that they had been portraying.

These were predators.

This play, whatever the premise was, had turned into a horror story, and we were the victims.

I grasped Ruth's hand tighter and took off in a sprint.

She didn't fight me, but she wasn't nearly as fast. I found myself slowing just so I didn't lose my colleague.

A lot of what I thought I knew of Carcosa was turning out to be wrong, or maybe I was misinterpreting the myth. Carcosa was supposed to be in perpetual night. The buildings were supposed to be domes, monolithic spires, and towers with jagged edges. This looked more like a cross between ancient Rome and Egypt, all blended together. The sun burned overhead, and light seemed to permeate everything. It felt like...

That was when I think I began to understand. Everything in this world was play-acting, or part of the script. An art world for artists. Or, more appropriately, a show for actors.

Because the sun felt more like a spotlight than a sun and in that moment, I knew that it was.

"It's all a show," I huffed as we ran around another corner. If any of the myths were true, we should be surrounded by some sort of ocean, but I still wasn't seeing it. I spared a glance back at Ruth. "You wanted a world of art for artists, and you found it. This place is entirely fake. A show to feed his ego."

We turned another corner and almost crashed into several of the actors. The small holes they had for mouths stretched open to reveal a gaping tube of teeth as they reached for us.

My pistol was up and two of them had new holes in their heads.

We spun away and ran, but not before I almost crashed into Ruth and noticed something.

No.

A perfect line along her forehead showed that her face was beginning to slip.

She was already an actor; this body probably wasn't even hers.

"Damn it," I shouted.

I wasn't sure what to do next, but the rules were clear. If I got Ruth to the water, they would let me go home. I still wasn't sure what to do with her, but the plan remained the same.

And if Edgar the drunk's time with me had shown me anything, it was that as long as this actor wore the mask, she would at least act like my friend.

I couldn't afford to lose an ally at this point, so I gritted my teeth and we continued to run from the now hordes of actors chasing us.

The nature of this play seemed to also be keeping us alive for the big climax. I felt that at any time these things could have overtaken us but instead continued to only barely get close enough for us to continue running.

We were being driven somewhere.

"What are they doing?" Ruth seemed to catch on as well.

"They are pushing us toward something," I answered.

"What?" She asked again. "What are they pushing us toward?"

I had no idea, but she might.

"I don't know, but do you?" I tried to make it sound as casual as two people being chased by faceless monsters might. "You were in their company for a while. Did you happen to see a script or a plan?"

We turned another corner and back onto a main road and I looked ahead. I still felt like I was on the crest of a hill, but this time it came with an advantage.

"There," I pointed. "The water."

The ground rocked as if reacting from a huge explosion nearby. We almost fell over, but Ruth helped me keep my balance.

"A script? You said this all feels like a show. Do you really think that?" Ruth pressed instead of answering. It made me suspicious. What did she know?

Then I had a fun idea. It would likely get me killed, but it had the potential to subvert the plot. It might help me cut the strings that were dragging me along on this Punch and Judy skit.

"I mean, it's a horrible play, if that's what it is," I shrugged, glancing behind me to see the creatures had stopped. They were all keeping to the shadows of the buildings, waiting to see what I did next.

"They have almost killed us at least a hundred times. If this is a show," Ruth said, "it is surprisingly effective."

"Almost killing me isn't effective." Now was the time to test my theory. Here's mud in your eye.

"Nyarlathotep has done more to effectively ruin my life by doing nothing than Hastur has with me locked in his cage."

Ruth stopped and stared at me with barely contained rage. The actors all took a step forward, their mouth holes stretching wider.

I smirked. I hadn't expected them all to have minor reactions, but it was a bonus. I was waiting for something else.

When it didn't come, I decided to add some more gas to the fire. Ruth and I hadn't moved since the ocean had come into view, but it seemed our audience wanted to see where this was headed and had paused all of their aggression.

I let go of Ruth's hand and turned to face her.

"Those stories the campus tells, they aren't the work of fiction," I explained to her. "Shoggoths have made me bleed. A dream god from another world tried to kill me." I shook my head, "Well, he did kill me, but it didn't stick. Monsters bleed into our world all of the time, and I have had more problems dealing with a man-faced rat that lives in the crawl space above my apartment than I have had here." I pointed at the actors behind her. "They're just actors. What good are they? Anyone can pretend to do something, but it takes moxie to actually do the deed." I turned and started, slowly, toward the water. "We were never in any real danger. It was all pretend."

The world shook again. This time it knocked me to my knees with its violence. Buildings rocked, stones fell and crashed onto the ground.

Bingo.

That was when I turned back to Ruth and was hit with the force of a football tackle. I had always been a baseball guy, so the hit took me down and onto the cobble road quicker than I cared to admit.

With a clatter, the Ruth mask hit the ground next to me and reverted back to a plane mask, eggshell white, with no defining features.

The actor that had been wearing Ruth's mask was pawing and slapping at my face and chest with enough force to have me worried.

Through the attack, I could see the other actors slowly encroaching on us.

I put one hand up to block the attacks from the Ruth-actor while my other hand, still clutched around the bottle I had removed from my satchel while I was talking to Ruth, worked at the stopper. When I felt it pop out, I put all of my weight into beating this thing off of me before jumping on top of it. I punched it once and then shoved the entirety of the Dream Land memory potion into its mouth hole.

I slammed my hand over the gaping maw and did what I could to not get bit. It didn't go well, but when the Ruth-actor relaxed, I let up. Whatever happened next, at least this one was knocked out.

I scooped up Ruth's mask, slid it into my bag, and slung the actor over my shoulder. It was lighter than a normal human and I briefly wondered if that was somehow a reference from this reality that this person had been stripped of everything that made them who they were.

Relieved of the weight of humanity.

I sprinted down the hill toward the water. It wasn't until I was at a full run that the actors behind me took up the chase. The shaking only continued, but it was subdued from its earlier excitement.

I made it most of the way down the hill when I noticed the ground beneath my feet was changing. The previously well-kept cobblestone road was losing its sheen and becoming patchy. I stopped when the cobble turned completely to a dirt path. The edge of the island that dropped off and into the water was only about ten feet ahead of me.

I checked the actor on my shoulder. They were still awake. I laid it down and pulled the mask from my bag.

Haste was in order, as the other actors hadn't stopped chasing me.

The mask merged with the actor's unconscious face and within seconds I was standing over an unconscious Ruth again.

A violent shake of the entire world reminded me that this wasn't over and I turned to see what the actors were doing.

They had stopped, only about thirty feet behind me and were staring past me. I feared to look, but at this point it was either turn and go to the water or stand here and die.

So, I looked.

The cliff-face that led to the ocean had become a barrier of sorts. On this side was the play. Bright lights, shiny buildings, and all of the actors doing as they were told.

The other side was something else entirely. Darkness and stars filled the sky. The glimmer from an unseen moon reflected from the water as a mass, larger than the city itself, writhed just beneath the surface.

Hastur? Likely.

Something shot from the mass and came toward the shore at incredible speed, riding under the water and creating a spray behind it.

When it reached the cliff it fell out of sight before launching up in front of us and landing on the edge of the land.

My surprise at the speed of it knocked me back to the ground, but I righted myself and pulled my pistol, aiming at its center mass.

What stood in front of me was nothing short of complete terror. My mind threatened to buckle under the weight of what I was seeing.

At first, my mind tried to rationalize what it was by assigning it the moniker of some sort of Cthulhu spawn. A face similar to that of a human skull, but with tentacles bursting out from where the mandible should have been. The rest of its body was a multitude of many grasping and stretching tentacles, with speckled dark skin. A seam in the center of what should have been its face peeled open, only a little, to show hundreds of teeth.

Its voice offended my humanity.

"Why do you seek to subvert our will?"

I grabbed at my head from the pain of the thing's voice but tried to focus and talk through my gritted teeth.

"I want to go home." I could taste blood in my mouth. The King hadn't done this to me when he spoke. This was intentional. "What are you?"

"We are the Watchers in the Water, Guardians of the Court. You cannot be allowed to leave. None who have seen the sign can leave."

The pressure was letting up, if only barely. I straightened and spit blood on the ground.

"I have lost too many people," my voice was strained. The exhaustion and the pain were catching up to me. "Hast-"

A boom of noise pummeled me back to the ground and I vomited.

"You are not worthy to say the name of He Who Is Not To Be Named."

When the pain let up, I wiped my mouth and continued. "He Who Is Not To Be Named promised me safe passage if I made it to the water."

"You have not made it to the water."

Chapter Six

I wanted to scream.

I wanted to hurt this thing that was just another barrier in this quest that I was shanghaied into being a part of. If Ruth had just listened to me. If I had just taken her more seriously.

It was a frustrating thing to know that in the past you had been capable of making creatures from other worlds shiver with fear at the prospect of what I was capable of and now I was standing next to creatures and gods on an alien world that was likely not to be part of my original reality.

All because this thing wanted people to be in its play.

I was fed up.

No more.

Still gritting my teeth from being in the mere presence of this thing, I asked, "Watcher, is your master plan to honor his bargain with me?"

It didn't move, but I got the impression that it was doing the telepathic equivalent of raising an eyebrow.

"If you make it to the water, you are free to leave," the voice that felt like every sunburn I have ever experienced searing itself into my brain said. "He did not say that it would be easy. If you make it to the lake, he will let you return to your home."

"Are you going to stop me?"

"Myself and many more."

"Then the deal was made in bad faith," I said.

"How is that so? He made a deal that you blindly agreed to," the Watcher countered. "It is not the responsibility of the King to outline every potential limitation before you. If you are capable of beating myself and my many kin, you may make it into the water. If that happens, the King shall honor his agreement."

"Except that no mortal man can best a legion of the King's Guardians of the Court," I mumbled.

The thing heard me anyway and gave a slight nod of its tentacled skull.

I had a thought then. "Is it me that he's trying to keep here or the mask?"

The guardian didn't move as it answered. "I am not here to answer your every question. If you intend to advance, I am here to stop you. That is my purpose. None may breach the seas."

Whatever pain the voice of the Watcher was causing me seemed to be subsiding and that concerned me. Over-exposure to things not meant for the human mind can destroy it. I had already danced too closely to that flame more than once. If the Watcher's voice was no longer hurting my frail human mind, it was not because I was getting familiar with the creature. It was because we had moved beyond pain and it would only be minutes before my brain melted out of my ears.

I turned away from the minion of the ancient alien lover of the theater and decided to check on Ruth. Kneeling beside her unconscious form, I felt for a pulse. I was not surprised to find it.

My actual intention was to get my fingers under the Ruth-mask.

With a fast tearing, I yanked the mask off of the actor and threw it like a discus toward the shoreline, and about thirty yards away to the monster's left.

The entirety of reality trembled. A bulge in the black ocean lifted, never breaking the surface, but obviously examining what was happening.

Hastur was paying attention.

It was about damned time.

"Hastur!" I yelled the only thing I was not supposed to say toward the ocean as the Guardian darted after the mask. The world shook more. Buildings within the artistic theatrical world threatened to topple, while outside the fictional paradise, ruins fell into the obsidian sea. The land-based actors fell to their knees as they tried to grab anything that could keep them on their feet.

I fell too, but I was scrambling for the edge of the water.

Over the rolling rage of the ancient deity, I continued to yell.

"Let me reach the water and I will offer you a show like no other." I was only feet away. Glancing toward the Guardian, I saw it looking for the mask while also looking up at the swelling mass in the water before returning my glance. It didn't know what to do.

Good. When in doubt, always try to be the craziest entity on whatever plane of existence you find yourself on.

I had just reached the edge when the rocking got so bad that I couldn't stand anymore. I fell to my hands and knees and looked back at the actor who had once worn Ruth's mask. I said a silent apology and then rolled off the cliff.

It wasn't a straight drop into the water and that wasn't something that crossed my mind until it was too late. With hazards such as the bodyguards of Hastur, defleshed humans that wanted only to act and eat my flesh, and the odd nature of the illusion around all of Carcosa, gravity and jagged rocks hadn't even crossed my mind.

If this had been my home reality, I would have been unconscious on the first bounce and likely dead by the second.

As the first rock, enshrined by the evening's void that somehow failed to penetrate the well-lit illusion of Carcosa, touched the side of my head, I was somewhere else.

Balls of energy swam around me in a myriad of colors. They left trails of reality in their wake. Emotions chased after red and orange lights, while plant life and crustaceans chased after purples and blues. It was both beautiful and maddening.

From one of these orbs of light, two soft leather chairs fell toward me and situated themselves on a plane of reality that I could not see. The lights moved faster, gaining speed until the flashing and strobing was so much that I had to close my eyes. Once I did, there was a movement of air on my face. I opened my eyes to see what had caused it and was greeted by an entirely new environment.

I was in an office that looked like something directly lifted from Miskatonic University's registrar's building. The only indication that I had been in some other place entirely only moments previously were the chairs, now situated on opposite sides of a desk. I stood by the one closest to me. It faced the desk where a name plate read "King H." Underneath that was a smaller description of the role 'King H.' was responsible for: "Administration."

The door to the office opened and I spun, slapping my hand at my side for the satchel with my pistol in it. My hand came away empty.

My satchel was gone. Reacting purely on irrational thought, I grabbed the next nearest thing to me in this conjured reality and raised a coffee mug above my head, prepared to throw it.

The absurdity of the situation turned me to stone. I could not throw the cup, I only stood there, frozen, as this random individual who I had never seen before came into the office.

The man was portly, but not so much as to slow him. He moved with the pace of fanaticism. He was dressed in a suit, still wearing the jacket, and had dark black hair at his temples with nothing on top of his head. He looked like a car salesman or the type of person who would be trying to shove his foot in your door to convince you to buy a vacuum cleaner.

He darted past me and behind the desk where he more fell into the chair than sat in it.

"Andy, I got to say, you just don't pull the crowds like you used to." His voice was deep and he spoke quickly. I couldn't place his accent. As he spoke, his hands moved constantly. "I am going to need you to mix things up, add some spice, if you want to make it in this business."

My brain was as frozen as I was holding the cup. I couldn't be more confused if one of my poor dead friends had walked in here and tried to sell me a chicken for my as-of-yet non-existent children.

"Business?" I think that I asked, but I didn't hear any words and was still frozen holding the cup. Lowering it, but not letting it go, I added, "What is going on?"

The look from the car salesman was perplexed. He looked as if he was trying to decide if I was pulling a prank on him.

"Wake up, Andy," he said with a smirk on his face. He opened a drawer in his desk and began pulling out thick piles of bound paper and slapping them onto the desk. It wasn't until the third one came out that I realized they were film scripts.

"I'm talking about the movies, kid. Look," his tone dropped to something milder, "you've been to Berlin and bloodied the nose on the Traum Kult real good, and that thing in Antarctica with the proto-shoggoth was drama in spades. You filled the house with that one." He leaned in and reached across to slap the desk, emphasizing his next point. "That Nancy and Itchy-whats-his-name," he pulled his hands together and brought them to his chest, over his heart, "even I cried, and we both know how heartless I can be."

When I saw his hands on his chest, that was when I began to pull things together. Perhaps he made that entire movement just to assist me in catching up with what was going on. Whatever the reasoning behind this charade, the pin on his chest told me almost everything.

On the lapel of his suit was a golden pin in the shape of the crown.

This 'man' was the King in Yellow. Did I summon him?

Or, perhaps given the situation, he summoned me.

The King liked his theatrics. That offered up at least some explanation of the office and this talk about movies and scripts. I still needed information, so I leaned into the weird.

"What are you trying to say... boss?"

The King leaned back, his volume rising again with his animated nature.

"What I'm saying is 'what's next for our adventurer?' When was the last time you left Arkham?" He jabbed a finger in my direction. "Nobody likes watching a sad man pining over the loss of his likely dead girlfriend. What are you going to do to bring in the crowds?"

The room grew a shade darker as he said that last bit. Darker, and notably yellower as well.

"Andy," his voice was deeper, menacing, and somehow entirely unchanged, "what are you going to do to entertain me?"

There it was.

Veiled in theatrics and delivered as a show, the offer.

So many monsters and deities had found me more of a problem than not and Hastur was not a fool at the worst of times. I had learned to counter his Yellow Sign and was showing myself to be persistent enough in escape that he was having to reallocate resources, likely the actors and who knew what else, away from the things he found more entertaining.

Although even he knew that I could not face down a god and survive, he still wanted to cut his losses before the war.

If he could do that and still be thoroughly entertained, then all the better.

This was the truce table. I could get what I wanted, a free trip home, but I had to promise something as well.

A movie pitch.

He was asking me to make him some sort of promise of the future that even the great Hastur himself couldn't ignore from an adjacent universe.

Or I would forever stay in Carcosa. Even with my powders, I wouldn't last longer than another day or two before I saw the Yellow Sign and began to lose myself.

Until I became an actor.

Never in my over three decades of life would I have considered myself any kind of artist or actor. My interests had always centered on history, the occult, and baseball. I am a simple man, driven toward understanding more than creation. At the best of times, I have been known to poorly con my way out of a situation, but that was an entirely different skill set than providing entertainment. Especially to something as unknowable as a deity.

My first thought in response to this offer was, "don't."

In every situation, every fight, where the rules were being dictated by someone opposed to me, that was always my first response. Be contrary. If they set the rules, break them, or don't play. Don't be mistaken, this was a fight. The battlefield was an office in Carcosa, and the fight was between me and a movie producer.

My usual play would not work here. The enemy hadn't just defined the rules, he defined this reality, of which, my continued existence was at his whim.

He had given me clues to what he was looking for. He liked the drama. He cried when Nancy had been taken from me. He lived for violence and emotional scarring.

Everything about my life was one mind-shattering tragedy after another in this pointless battle against the alien threats of our world. All I wanted was to get home, and if Ruth could still...

An idea was beginning to metastasize.

I straightened my back and tried to emulate his animation.

"You're right, boss, and when you're right, you're right," I said. "I've been working on something, though. Something big. Rule breaking big." I stood up and kicked the chair behind me. I was fast. Any mortal man would have flinched or leaned back. The King didn't move. "Do you want crowds? Do you want to be entertained? Well, your adventurer," I hated that word, "wants to take some of Carcosa back to Earth."

The King was entirely impossible to read.

After what felt like forever, the King finally spoke.

"I like your spark, kid, but the script, the sign, heck even the big man himself already visits that world. If that's all you've got, then I don't know that our time together will be much longer."

I poured every ounce of my non-existent acting skill into being annoyingly cocky. Ignoring that he was literally a god, I dismissed his words with a flippant wave of my hand.

"You haven't seen anything like this before," I said. "Imagine this: An alien beast of ravenous intent, stripped of their humanity, their empathy, and let loose in Arkham." My eyes lit up as if a better idea had come to me in that moment. "No, better yet, the creature is running havoc on the campus at Miskatonic University. The only thing between humanity and complete destruction directly from the shores of Carcosa is the beaten and tired former dean. Down and lost because of his failures with his companions, his love locked away on another world, his friends all dead, and tasked with making certain that this monster kills no one. The sheer weight of that failure might kill him."

On the inside, I was a ball of emotions. Feelings that I had burned away and buried with as much booze as I could find resurfaced and demanded my attention. Not here, though. I couldn't show weakness now.

The King was frowning.

"Hero punches the monster. That's old, even for you."

I shook my head. "Hero disguises the monster," I corrected. "The hero feels responsible for escaping Carcosa with a violent alien and how many more deaths could be laid at his feet. As both a punishment and, perhaps, a form of too little redemption, he brought a mask back as well. So, he forces the alien to wear the mask, to keep the mask on, knowing that if that lie ever slips, death and destruction will come to Miskatonic and the former dean." Time to bring it home. "The threat of discovery, of horrible tragedy, looms over him like the," I let the emotion come through and choked up a little bit as I continued, "shadows of his fallen friends."

I took a deep breath and saw that the King was still chewing over his response.

"Our hero might find new purpose or a renewal of his depleted spirit with his new charge of protector. He might find his drive. Heroes punch monsters every day. What happens to the hero when he has to learn to live with one?"

The King's eyes were staring into an unknown dimension somewhere while his eyes were aimed at his desk. I had nothing more to add and was waiting to hear if I was going home or not for minutes, moments, hours, or years, I couldn't say. Just in case, and entirely out of habit at this point, my mind hunted ferociously for an alternative means to escape this place when my pitch ultimately failed.

I had nothing. There was no plan or trick that would get me out of a reality completely controlled by this thing more powerful than anything man can concoct. If I knew how to traverse realities, I would have done it by now. In the past, I knew the methods of generating portals that could deliver me, but that ability had been stripped from my toolbox.

I was entirely at the King in Yellow's mercy.

The King's voice, when he finally spoke, startled me.

"On the one hand, your pitch was solid. Good job." Shit, I was in trouble. My eyes darted around for the mug again. "People go to your shows for the monster killing and the Nazi punching. That stuff, though not new, pulls in the crowds." He paused again, likely for dramatic effect, but it felt like he was thinking through his words carefully. "This project of yours sounds like a longer one. Normally, we prefer the quick shows. We get the story, get the cash and move onto the next project. This sounds like a longer project, perhaps a serialized fiction." He held up a hand to some unseen objection he imagined I was having while I slowly inched closer to the mug. "That's not a bad thing, but something to consider. Bold of you to come to us and suggest a concept." He turned his chair to face the window, mumbling as he thought out loud. I snatched up the cup and prepared to strike him. It would be a fart in a hurricane, but I was not about to go down without at least fighting back.

That was when he snapped his fingers and I started. The cup was in my hand, but again, I was frozen in panic.

"That's it! The will-they/won't-they of it all. The suspense. Oh, yes, this might be it." His chair spun back to me, holding the cup and standing in front of his desk. "They really like it when you punch Nazis. Do you think we can work that in?"

I shrugged. "As long as the war is still going, that shouldn't be a problem."

The King barked a laugh, dismissing the idea. "That won't be a problem. You have a few more years on that one."

Everything about where I was, why I was there, what I was doing, and getting home fell through the floor with my heart.

"Years?" was all that I could make myself say.

The King laughed some more. "Wow, kid! You're good." He held up his thumbs and index fingers in a box, as if framing me in a camera shot. "Drama." He chuckled to himself and then began putting the manuscripts back into the drawer. "You're green-lit. Take the mask," he pulled Ruth's mask from another drawer and slid it in front of me, "but I do have some notes on who should play the part of the theater teacher."

The lights went out after he told me his suggestion that was clearly not a suggestion.

I woke up at my desk in my office. Drool poured from my mouth. The satchel laid on the floor by the door, its contents scattered. I could see the empty vials, confirming that it had all been real.

In a flash, I was down the hall and in Ruth's office. She was waking up as well, but otherwise seemed normal.

"Andy?" she frowned at me, blinking the sleep from her eyes. "I just had the weirdest dream about you."

This wasn't Ruth. It was a Watcher of the Waters, a tentacled monster with only the barest resemblance to a person. With Ruth's mask, the illusion was perfect.

I don't know if the deal that I made was right. I worry about how self-serving it was. Did I save a friend by bringing back the mask? It was everything that she was, her entire identity, but it wasn't her underneath. Am I really so exhausted with losing the people that I care about that even a mirage was better than another loss?

Or maybe the mask, her identity was her soul, and I had saved at least one of my friends.

That's what I tell myself when the booze won't help me sleep.

A Required Sacrifice

By Andrea Pearson

Travis flipped the shovel over, dumpin' the last bit of manure into the wheelbarrow from the stall he'd been muckin' for the last two hours. Two hours!

Truth be told, it woulda only taken half an hour if he hadn't spent most of the time daydreamin' 'bout Cassilda.

Cassilda …

A different name for a different kinda girl. Cassilda was a blonde bombshell with long legs and long eyelashes, and who sent him long glances whenever they were in the same room. He'd guessed fast that she had a thing for him, and his suspicions was confirmed when she said yes to bein' his girlfriend. Their next date was set to happen that evenin', and he couldn't wait.

Travis propped his shovel against the barn wall so he could admire his arms. They were finally startin' to show muscles. 'Bout time, too– he'd worked hard on the family farm for years, and bein' scrawny had gotten old. Real old. He'd started wearin' his flannel shirts with the arms cut off just to show the amazin' guns he'd developed, along with that deep gold tan.

Not everybody was lucky enough to have a body like this, and no way in heck was he gonna hide it.

Cassilda had recognized him for the beautiful specimen he was right away. She said she woulda liked him scrawny too, and he believed her. She was that awesome.

Somethin' caught Travis's attention, and he straightened, the hairs on his arms risin'. A feelin' like he was bein' watched crossed over him, makin' his palms sweat and his ears buzz.

"It's just yer imagination," he whispered.

It had been a long time since he'd had that feelin'. They lived way out in the boonies and didn't git visitors often, so the only thing that ever watched him was the animals.

"Pay that no mind," he muttered, "and git back to work."

He couldn't help it, though. He looked out the window of the stall, his eyes rovin' the landscape. Nothin' was there.

"See? Got yerself all scared for no reason."

But just then, Travis saw somethin' that made his stomach do a flip–a man headin' into the forest, comin' from the direction of the family graveyard. He held somethin' in his hands.

Travis stared long and hard at the man, tryin' to make out his features. He wore a long black cloak with a hood that shielded most of his face, so all Travis could see was his nose and a cheekbone. Goosebumps erupted again as Travis wondered where he'd come from and why he was there. And had *he* been watchin' Travis? Was that where the feelin' came from?

The man glanced up, and Travis stepped to the side, his heart poundin' all heavy-like again.

"Trav?" Ma's voice called from somewhere not too close, makin' him jump. "Travis, git yer skinny butt out here now!"

Travis glanced toward the forest–the man wasn't there no more. Knowin' he shouldn't make Ma wait–not when she used that tone–Travis pushed the man from his mind, scurried out of the barn, and raced toward the trailer where he and his parents lived.

"Yeah, Ma?"

"That darn chicken's been cluckin' at the door for over an hour! She needs to lay, and you've made her wait too long!"

Dang it! He couldn't believe he'd forgotten. "Sorry, Ma. I'll git to it now."

"And one last thing–did you mess in my stuff? The drawers of my bureau all was opened this mornin' when I got up. And I know I didn't leave 'em that way last night."

"No, Ma, I didn't." His parents weren't young no more, that was for sure, and their memory wasn't super fresh.

She harrumphed, goin' back into the trailer, and Travis hurried around the side of the dilapidated buildin', findin' Sally near the kitchen window. She clucked with excitement when she saw him and immediately raced off to the coop with him hot on her tail feathers.

Sally turned to see if he was still followin', then hopped into the coop and entered her favorite nestin' box. The moment he was in sight again, she promptly laid an egg, then clucked and cooed and sang proudly. Travis went through the usual routine of pattin' her head, cheerin' her efforts, and pointin' at the egg. Then he took the warm egg into the trailer where Ma stood over the stove, cookin'.

"That's gittin' real old, Ma," Travis said. "Can't we turn her into chicken soup yet?"

Ma turned a scandalized look on him. "Sally's ma favorite chicken! Ain't no way I'm eatin' her."

Travis grumbled. "I never shoulda watched her lay her first egg. I just thought she'd git over the excitement by now. But she ain't. And I'm tired-a doin' it." An idea popped into his head. "Maybe we could hire someone to watch her lay for us." He wasn't sure if'n they could train Sally to lay for someone else, not when she wouldn't lay for no one but Travis, but maybe Sally just didn't like Ma or Pa.

"Ain't no one gonna be willin' to drive all the way out here just to watch a chicken lay an egg, Trav."

She was right, and he knew it. "Worth a shot." He thought about bringin' up the man. "Has Pa hired any help lately?"

"No. Why?"

He hesitated, then said, "Just wonderin'. We sure could use some help out here. I'll keep watchin' Sally lay, but there's other stuff that needs doin'." He glanced at the time on his phone, tuckin' it back into his pocket. "Well, I should hurry an' finish my chores so I can git ready for my date."

Ma nodded. "By the way, Alice's pig got loose again. If'n you see him, grab him and take him back, would ya?"

Travis nodded. Alice was their nearest neighbor and Ma's best friend. Her darn pig kept escapin', and instead of goin' back home, it came here, to Pa's farm. It drove Travis nuts. He didn't mind havin' to take the pig back, but he hated the mess it caused in Ma's garden.

He was about to head back to the barn, but thought better of it, instead grabbin' his rifle when Ma turned her attention back to what she was doin'. He'd check them trees out first. Ain't no way he could focus on his chores when a stranger was there.

Travis strode across the field toward the forest where he'd seen the man go in. When he arrived, though, ain't no one was there. He scanned the trees, only enterin' a little way. Even though they didn't creep him out near as much anymore as they did when he was a little kid, he still hated bein' there. But the place was empty as empty could be.

Still, Travis stood, holdin' his rifle with both hands, feelin' the gentle breeze tickle his face. Somethin' felt disturbed there, like there'd been a presence not too long ago. He watched the sunlight filter down through the trees and how it played across the undergrowth, tryin' to spot anythin'. But nothin' looked out of the ordinary.

Had he imagined it all? Maybe. Maybe that was the case.

But then, Travis glanced down and saw boot tracks in the dirt. And they was fresh. The man *hadn't* been his imagination!

He tipped his hat to the side and stared at the tracks, keepin' a hold of his gun, then started forward, followin' them through the trees. He didn't git far, though, before comin' across a smolderin' fire that was on its way out. Who in tarnation would build a fire right in the middle of a forest? Only an idiot!

The smell of meat was in the air, and Travis's stomach dropped as he stared real hard at somethin' big on top of them coals. He took half a step closer, afraid he would see Alice's pig there. It sure looked like it had been pig.

The wind shifted, and the acrid smell of smoke drifted across his nose. Travis's eyes blurred, and he blinked several times, tryin' to clear them. But they didn't clear. He gasped when he realized it wasn't his eyes, but his surroundin's that was goin' crazy. The trees shimmered, gettin' blurrier and blurrier until they weren't there no more. Instead, ruins of buildin's and walls appeared around him. A cobblestoned street was underneath his boots. That street was littered with all sorts of bricks and stones from walls that had collapsed.

How had he come to be in a city? And where was his trees?

Travis heard a familiar scream from somewhere ahead of him. Ma! Throwin' caution out the door, he dashed forward, followin' them screams, his brain barely registerin' a new, different kinda smoke smell. He rounded a corner of the street and saw her tied to a bunch of branches and logs. Flames was lickin' up around her legs and sides. Her mouth was open in agony as she continued screamin'. Her legs was bright red.

"Ma!" he yelled, continuin' toward her. He'd only taken a few steps, though, when she and the fire disappeared completely. He stumbled, frozen in place. The city walls dissolved back into trees and his forest surrounded him again. The silence pounded against his ears. He looked around for a moment, disoriented.

"Ma?" Had he imagined it all? Was she okay?

Travis turned and raced as fast as he could, ignorin' as branches whipped his face and chest. His feet pounded the ground, the sound gettin' swallowed up by the springy underbrush. He burst out of the forest and ran across the field, past the barn, and to the trailer. He yanked the door open and dashed inside, callin' out for Ma.

"I'm back here, son," she said from her room.

Travis hurried in to see her. She was sittin' on her bed, starin' at her bureau.

He almost collapsed with relief. "You're here. You're okay."

"'Course I am. What's the matter with ya? You look like you seen a ghost."

He could only shake his head in response, starin' at her, tryin' to see if she was harmed in any way. "Nothin'. Just my crazy imagination." Ain't no way he was gonna tell her what he'd seen.

And luckily, seein' her now made it hard for him to picture her back there, in them flames.

"Okay, well, I need to finish supper. I had to lay down for a rest, but I'm ready to git at it again." She glanced back at her bureau, then scowled at him. "You sure you ain't been messin' in my stuff? I'm missin' my brooch."

"I swear I ain't done anythin'. And why would I? I don't want nothin' to do with your clothes and stuff."

She relaxed a smidgeon. "Yer right, son. Ain't no way you'd go diggin' around in my drawers."

"No way at all."

"I must have dropped it behind the bureau, then. I'll need yer help pullin' it out later."

"Sure, Ma."

They walked back to the kitchen, Travis's heart still poundin' from his experience in the forest. Though, this time, try as he might, he couldn't quite picture anythin' but them city ruins.

Good riddance. Ain't no way he wanted to remember what he'd seen.

But what if it had been a vision? A warnin' of somethin' to come?

Travis pushed that thought from his mind. He didn't believe in superstitious stuff like that. If God wanted to warn him, He would.

Realizin' there wasn't anythin' else he could do for his ma right then, Travis headed back to the barn to finish his chores. He found it easier and easier to shift his thoughts to his upcomin' date and to forgit his experience in that other, faraway place. What other place was it anyway? Had he even *gone* to another place? His memory sure was foggy now. Somethin' 'bout a city in ruins?

But the campfire in his forest. He remembered *that* clear as day. What idiot would start cookin' in a place like that? Travis grumbled. There wasn't anything he could do 'bout the fire until the mornin'. He didn't want to upset Alice prematurely until he had a chance to have a looksee, and investigatin' would have to wait. He couldn't afford to be late for his date with his girlfriend.

Cassilda had invited him over for dinner with her family. It would be the first time he met her folks, and he really wanted to make a good impression.

He grabbed the shovel and tossed it in the wheelbarrow, then took up the handles and pushed the wheelbarrow out of the barn and to the compost, where he dumped the manure. He'd be spreadin' that stuff in Ma's garden soon enough, but they needed a place for it to stay until summer ended.

And with that, his chores were done and it was time to git ready for the evenin'. Cassilda had told him to wear his best clothes. Apparently, her folks liked people to fancy up, and he'd bought a brand-new shirt just for them. He hoped they'd like it–he'd used the last of his savin's on it.

Travis put his rifle up, showered real quick, and threw on the clothes, then found Ma and Pa sittin' at the little table in the trailer. He couldn't leave without warnin' them 'bout someone trespassin' on the property.

"I saw someone in the forest while I was doin' my chores," he said. "Ma, that's why I asked if'n Pa had hired someone."

Ma's eyes widened. "Who was it?"

Travis shook his head. "Don't know. They were gone when I went to check. Keep yer gun handy, though, and I'll check them trees every day from now on." Maybe he should mention he'd seen the man walkin' from the family graveyard, but he didn't want Pa checkin' things out without some backup. No, that too would have to wait until the mornin'.

"Good thinkin', son," Pa said. "Might be time to hire more hands just to help Ma feel safer."

Ma nodded gratefully, and Travis said goodbye and hopped into his truck. Now that Pa knew, he'd be on extra alert, and Ma would be okay. Travis could go on his date without feelin' bad.

He punched Cassilda's address into his phone–he'd only been there once before and wanted to make sure he didn't take a wrong turn. The last time he'd been there, it was nighttime, and he hadn't gotten a good look at the house. He did now, though. The thing was massive–two stories with a huge front porch and a second-story balcony with big ol' pillars supportin' both. A windin' sidewalk led from the half-circle drive to the double front doors. Little bushes lined that sidewalk. It sure was purdy.

When Cassilda's ma–Lucinda–answered the door, Travis was glad he'd worn that new red flannel shirt. Cassilda hadn't been exaggeratin' when she said her parents liked to dress up for supper. Lucinda was decked out in a long dress with a plungin' neckline, fancy high heels, and large, sparkly earrings.

"Travis! You're just in time." Lucinda stepped back, openin' the door farther. "Henry and Cassilda are waiting in the dining room. Come along."

He followed her down a large, elaborate hallway and into a big room with a massive table and many chairs. He tried not to stare at the lavish furniture and decorations. He'd never been inside the house, and he didn't want them to think he was beneath them or nothin' like that. It was best to act like he saw tables that seated twelve people on the regular.

Cassilda squealed with glee and rushed to his side, interlacin' her fingers with his and leadin' him to the table. She sat on her father's left side, across from Lucinda, and invited Travis to sit next to her.

Henry–Cassilda's father–nodded at Travis. "Glad you made it, son. How are your parents?"

"Them's good. They send their best."

Henry smiled. "Excellent to hear." He cleared his throat, then nodded, and a man and woman brought in plates of steamin' food.

Travis dug in immediately. "Oh, this is heavenly. Did you cook it, ma'am?" he asked Cassilda's ma.

She tilted her head, starin' at him for a moment. "No, Travis, I didn't."

Had he said somethin' wrong? Better try to smooth things over. "I never thought I'd find someone who cooked as good as Ma, but this comes real close. Whoever fixed it up did a real good job."

"I'll be sure to tell Mrs. Smith," Lucinda said.

Cassilda put her hand on Travis's leg, sendin' him a smile. "Mrs. Smith has been with us for years. She started out as just a housekeeper, but one day, our old cook got sick, and Mrs. Smith took over for a few days. When we tasted her food, Mother knew the lady was gifted and needed to do it for us from then on. Luckily, Mrs. Smith loved the idea, and she's been our cook *and* housekeeper ever since."

Travis had a hard time payin' attention to Cassilda's words because he'd gotten distracted by her lips. He pulled his thoughts away from memories of kissin' her and allowed what she'd said to sink in.

"Ma always said she wanted a housekeeper, but Pa never allowed it. Probably cuz they cost so darn much." He looked around the lavish dinin' room and whistled. "I can tell money ain't no problem for y'all, though." He looked at Henry. "What do you do for work?"

Henry cleared his throat, glancin' at Lucinda. "What should we tell him, Lu?"

"It's up to you, dear," she responded. "I'm fine with whatever you want."

Just how many jobs did Henry have? Or was he in the Mafia? With all the money they obviously had, Travis would believe pretty much anythin'.

Henry nodded. "I'm an attorney for a group of Hastur followers."

Travis nodded. "Interestin'. A lawyer, huh? Yeah, lawyers make plenty a' money." What was it that Henry said about Hastur? What was a Hastur?

Henry half-smiled. "Indeed." He nodded to his daughter. "Cassilda, would you please pass the rolls?"

Cassilda handed them over, and Travis watched her for a moment. "Where'd the name Cassilda come from, anyhow?" he asked.

Henry's smile deepened. "Her mother and I watched a play years ago where the main character was named Cassilda. Another big character was named Camilla. The play made quite an impact on us, and we named our daughters after the women."

Travis tilted his head. Daughters? "Cassilda ain't an only child?"

Cassilda shook her head. "No, I'm actually a twin. My sister, Camilla, died years ago."

"Oh, sad," Travis said. "I'm sorry to hear that."

Lucinda nodded, her expression mournful. "Such sweet little girls. They were identical. The only difference was a mole on Camilla's forehead. We still miss her, of course, but we're grateful her oblation was accepted."

Oblation? What in the heck did that mean? "I'm glad," Travis said. It was the only answer he could think of.

"Father?" Cassilda started. "I've been thinking about inviting Travis to our next chapter meeting. Would that be all right with you and Mother?"

Henry and Lucinda made eye contact before Henry looked back to Cassilda. "If you think that's wise, yes, that would be fine. And if he's ready for it."

"Oh, I'm ready for it!" Travis said. He had no idea what they were talkin' 'bout, but if it meant more time with Cassilda, he was down.

Cassilda nodded. "And if he's not, I'll help him get there." Her eyes lit up. "Oh! Father! Travis has a goat with two tails!"

Henry's eyes widened. "That would be perfect, Cassilda. Excellent suggestion. We still haven't found an animal to immolate." His eyes started sparklin' and an excited expression crossed his face. He looked at Travis. "Make sure you bring it."

Travis glanced at Cassilda, confused about what his goat and this event had to do with each other. And why would they want to emulate a *goat*, for cryin' out loud? "Are you gonna fix Ronnie? He's perfectly healthy, aside from them two tails. If you can fix him, that'd be great. The big tail is fine, but the little one gits infected sometimes. The skin don't always want ta stay closed over the bone."

"Oh, yes," Henry said, "immolating always puts animals in a better place after."

Cassilda gasped. "Father!"

"Cassilda, we know they're happier."

"Yes, but still. I can't believe you'd say that."

Travis looked back and forth between Henry and Cassilda, knowin' he wasn't catchin' the punchline. "Well … I'm just glad ta hear there's hope for him."

"There's definitely hope," Henry said. "There's always hope."

That made Travis feel better. They fell into silence, each eatin' their own food, and Travis tryin' to figure out what to say next while still processin' the weird conversations they'd already had. After a moment, Travis asked, "So, what brought ya to our town?"

Henry waved him off. "Just looking for someone who used to live here years and years ago."

Travis straightened. "Tell me their name. I'm real good with names–anyone who's lived here, I for sure know them or at least their kin."

"Unfortunately, I can't reveal that information. Client-attorney privileges, you understand. But I can tell you I'm investigating that family for one of my clients. Someone who lived a long time ago left a lot of valuable things–valuable and dangerous. I'm trying to discover how many descendants that person had and what has happened with those descendants *and* the items." He leaned forward. "See, Travis, over a hundred years ago, this man stole valuable knowledge from the Celaeno library, and the task has fallen on my shoulders to find out where that knowledge is and how much his descendants know about it."

Travis nodded as if he totally understood what Henry was talkin' 'bout. Somethin' 'bout books from a library or somethin', but it had been years since Travis had been to the library, so he couldn't help there. He used to love the place when he was in grade school, but duties on the farm had kept him away for a long time. Maybe someday he'd git the chance to go back again.

Henry continued. "In other words, work brought me, but when we found out your area doesn't have a Hastur branch, we decided to relocate here and start one up. We're pretty excited about all the possibilities."

Lucinda nodded. "Are you really interested in coming to our next event?"

"Come," Cassilda said, trailin' her hand down Travis's arm. "I'd seriously love it if you joined us."

Travis found himself gittin' lost in her eyes. "Anythin' you want, darlin'. I'll go anywhere you do."

Cassilda's cheeks reddened, and she glanced at her plate bashfully. "Thank you, Travis," she said quietly.

An urge to take her into his arms nearly overwhelmed him. Instead, he dug into the plate of cake that a maid had just placed in front of him.

Conversation drifted on to other topics–Cassilda's college applications, what Henry wanted to do the rest of the year, and Lucinda's favorite places to shop–and Travis kept up only enough not to look dumb.

He couldn't believe how lucky he'd gotten with Cassilda. Boy, she was one heck of a gal!

The moment Travis walked through the door of his trailer, Ma and Pa was ready for him.

"I don't like you datin' that girl," Pa said immediately.

"Why not?" Travis asked. "She ain't related to me or nothin'. I checked and double-checked."

"It ain't that, son," Ma said. "We just don't like her family. There's somethin' off 'bout them."

"What do you think is wrong?" Travis asked.

Pa shook his head. "That's just it. We can't tell."

Travis had learned to trust his parents' intuition, but this time, he just couldn't see what was bad about Cassilda. She and her folks were good people. Instead of arguin', though, he decided to turn in for the night.

As he was gettin' ready for bed, though, he heard his parents talkin', and stood real quietlike next to his slightly open door.

"Maybe you should just go right out an' ask 'em," Pa was sayin'. "Maybe a blunt approach would work."

"Nah–I don't wanna scare 'em off."

"Well, we need ta tell him to break up with her."

Travis's heart clenched at the thought. He knew he should obey his parents, but to break up with Cassilda? He couldn't even think that without achin'.

Luckily, Ma seemed to agree. "He still ain't recovered from his last heartbreak."

Pa sighed. "I know, I know."

Pa mumbled somethin' else, and Travis heard what sounded like kissin'. Not wantin' to listen to that, he quietly shut his door and went to bed.

The conversation left him unsettled, though, and he couldn't drift off. He spent an hour at least tossin' and turnin'. Finally, he sat up. "Ain't no way I'm gonna be caught off guard," he muttered to himself. If'n his parents thought somethin' was off with Cassilda and her kin, he'd just have to prove them wrong. But how?

He needed to try somethin' Cassilda had showed him—he needed to write a pros and cons list.

Travis flipped his lamp on, then sat at the small desk in his room and pulled out a notepad and pen. He wrote a big PROS across one side, then CONS on the other, and divided 'em down the middle with a fat line. Then he got to work.

He hadn't known Henry and Lucinda for long, so neither list ended up bein' too big.

Starin' at what he'd written, Travis chewed on the tip of his pen, thinkin' over his conversation with them earlier that evenin'. What was it they'd said about bein' believers? They followed someone named Hastur, right?

Travis blinked, realizin' that name was familiar. Hadn't he read it somewhere in one of his great-grandfather's journals? Grandpa Algernon Blackwood wasn't the best folk out there, but he'd been super smart and connected with other smart folk. Travis had gone over his journals a lot recently, and while a bunch of the stuff freaked him out, some of it was good info to have.

A glance at the clock on his phone let him know Pa and Ma would be asleep by now, givin' him a chance to find what he was lookin' for cuz now he was *sure* he'd seen the name Hastur in Grandpa Blackwood's journals.

Travis grabbed a black hoodie and slung his arms through the sleeves, zippin' it up. Then, with phone in one hand and rifle in the other, he snuck out of the trailer and headed to the main house. The clapboard shutters, blue sidin', and white trim all needed to be repainted, but still, it was a beautiful house in the bright moonlight. Travis was constantly embarrassed that his folks lived in a rusty ol' trailer when they had a perfectly good house on the property.

'Course, "perfectly good" was a bit misleadin'. Pa had started too many projects that he hadn't finished, and the stove and sink were still out back from when he'd gutted the kitchen.

Travis opened the door, turnin' on the flashlight on his phone, glad his parents had never started lockin' up. Any burglar who came would change his mind real quick after enterin'. The place was full of old yard stuff and broken decorations, car tires, cinder blocks, and toilets–old ones gittin' ready to be tossed, and new ones ready to be installed.

Travis had offered to help Pa put the place back together a few times, but Pa had refused, sayin' he didn't need no help, and besides, Travis had to focus on his schoolin' and chores around the farm.

Travis realized that meant the house would never git done because the farm alone needed more hands than just his and Pa's, but Pa still refused.

A sound at the back of the house caught his attention, and Travis froze, then headed that way, hopin' no one was there. He pointed his phone flashlight around, pausin' in the kitchen, eyes rovin' the place.

"Hello?" he called out quietly.

Nothin' happened. Travis stood there for several moments, feelin' the hair on his arms risin'. A feelin' that he was bein' watched crossed over him like earlier, and he swung around, shinin' his light back down the hall he'd just come through before shinin' it in the kitchen again.

But once more, nothin' was there. Had he imagined things?

After waitin' a moment longer, grip tight on his gun and thoughts on the man who'd been watchin' from the forest earlier, Travis made his way up to the attic. He hated goin' in there–the feelin's in the room were awful. The place was creepy, dusty, and felt like some bad spirit lived there. But at least it didn't feel like someone was watchin' him, like downstairs.

He stepped to the far side of the big room and knelt in front of a couple of cardboard boxes, tryin' to relax so he could focus. Travis shifted through the boxes, settlin' back on his butt, not mindin' the dust gettin' on his pajama pants. Then, cell phone flashlight in hand, he started flippin' through the pages of the journals he'd found in the boxes.

"Hastur, Hastur, Hastur," he mumbled to hisself, keepin' his mind focused on the task. He could spend hours in them journals if'n he wasn't careful.

A mention of a city in ruins drew his attention, and he paused on that page. *City in ruins ...* why was that so familiar? And why did it make his hands all clammy-like? It drew images of a cobblestoned-street with bricks and stones fallen all around and even the acrid smell of smoke. Travis shook his head, mesmerized from what felt like a memory but was probably just deja vu. It was so vivid.

A headache began formin' at his forehead from all the thinkin' he was doin', tryin' to remember why the mention of some dumb ol' ruins would catch his attention like that. He took in several deep breaths, forcin' himself to get back on task, and started flippin' pages again.

See? He'd gotten distracted yet again from Grandpa Algernon's journals.

Finally, he found somethin'. It wasn't a lot. Just the name Hastur, followed by the words,

King in yellow. A sign. Be wary of his coming.

A prickle of excitement crossed Travis. His great-grandfather was a bad man, and if he disapproved of Hastur, that was sure to mean Hastur was good.

The journal entry continued on the next page.

I have found and include here a knowledge spell. Do not waste it on pointless information, as it can only be used once. T'would be wise to use it to learn when Hastur will come.

Then Algernon indented the followin' paragraph.

He who seeks knowledge, whether past, present, or future, eject sputum onto your thumb, press your thumb against your forehead, and speak these words—

Knowledge Guardian, I seek enlightenment.

Then ask your question. The answer will come to your mind.

Travis knew what the word "eject" meant, and he gave a nervous chuckle, wishin' he was with his buddies, who'd have a good laugh with him. But what was sputum? That part didn't make no sense.

A quick Google search told him it was a fancy word for "spit."

"Gross," Travis muttered. Still, spit was better than blood, and it was worth a try.

Travis spit on his thumb, pressed it to his forehead, and said, "Knowledge Guardian, I seek enlightenment." He paused, wonderin' if he had someone's attention. He didn't feel no presence or being in his thoughts, and he decided to continue anyway. "Are Henry and Lucinda good folk?"

Nothin' happened, and Travis slumped down with disappointment.

But then, a deep, throaty voice entered his mind, and Travis sprang backwards, bangin' into an old table of his ma's.

They are good, for I have approved of them.

Was that *God's* voice? Travis trembled, so shocked he'd heard anythin' at all. Deep down, he hadn't expected anythin' to happen.

It probably wasn't God. And maybe Travis shouldn't trust the answer. He hesitated for a moment, thinkin' on that. Great-Grandpa Algernon was evil. He'd done some pretty awful things durin' his lifetime that Ma was only just tellin' Travis about. And he disapproved of Hastur. Therefore, the voice *had* to be tellin' the truth. Henry and Lucinda were *good*.

Yes, that was right. Travis knew it cuz his heart started to get all warm and fuzzy. 'Course, that could have to do with the fact that if Cassilda's parents were good, he wouldn't need to break up with Cassilda. Travis refused to follow that train of thought. No, he'd believe the voice. Henry and Lucinda were good.

Now, to prove it to his parents.

A footstep sounded on the stairs behind him, and Travis whirled, scramblin' to his knees. He saw the top of a black hoodie just as whoever wore it disappeared down the stairs.

"Who's there?" he called out.

He lurched to his feet, slamming into the corner of the table as he did so.

"Ouch! Crap. Ma, yer dang table."

Travis grabbed his rifle, then raced across the attic to the stairs. They were empty. He'd taken too long to git a move on!

"Yeah, you'd better run!" he yelled down. "I'm comin' for you now!"

Travis raced down the stairs, takin' them two at a time. The sounds of feet poundin' below him echoed up the staircase. Whoever had been watchin' him was on the stairs headin' to the first floor. Travis leaned over the railin', aimin' down with his rifle, but he couldn't spot 'em with how dark it was inside the house.

He continued, racin' as quickly as he could. By the time he reached the first floor, though, stumblin' past broken garden gnomes and stupid huge flamingos, the man—he was positive it was the same dude—had long since gotten out of the house.

How'd he done that so fast? Travis glared as he raced across the first floor of the farmhouse. The man must've been there before. But why? What was he lookin' for? Probably Ma's antiques up in the attic. Well, that was the last time the guy would go up there.

Travis burst through the front door, gittin' his rifle ready as he flew across the porch and down the steps. The man was roundin' the corner of the trailer, racin' for the forest.

"Git off my property!" Travis screamed. He dashed around the trailer and watched as the man entered the forest.

Travis shot the rifle into the sky, hopin' the man would take it for the warnin' it was. "Never come back!" he screamed at the recedin' figure. "Ya hear me? *Never come back!* I'll shoot you, if'n you do!"

Pa and Ma stumbled outside of the trailer, Pa carryin' his shotgun.

"Did you see the man again?" Ma asked.

"Yes. He was ... he was just standin' there, watchin' me."

Neither parent asked why Travis was awake and out of the trailer, and fer that, he was grateful.

"That's the last straw," Pa said. "I'm gonna hire someone."

"To work on the farm?" Ma asked. "Or to stay here overnight? Cuz it's night."

"Heck, woman, I don't know the right answer," Pa said.

Travis did. "Hire someone to help durin' the day, and I'll grab some motion-detectin' lights to set up all over the place for the night. We'll put out 'No trespassin' signs. And we'll all sleep with our drapes open. Them lights'll wake us up, and Pa, you and me will keep our guns beside us and we'll run out and shoot anyone who trespasses."

"I have a gun too," Ma said with irritation.

"That's right, Ma, but it's Pa's and my job to protect you."

She beamed at him, pullin' him close for a hug. "I'm so proud of the man yer becomin', Trav."

He felt his cheeks redden under the praise, and he squeezed her in return.

Ain't no way he was gonna let harm come to his family.

First thing the next mornin', Travis drove into town and bought everythin' he could git his hands on. Then he and Pa set it all up, lacin' extension cords all over the property. Travis hammered in some "No trespassin'" signs too, along with "Trespassers will be shot" ones.

That man wouldn't know what hit him if'n he ever came back again. Literally.

Once everythin' was done and Pa and Ma was both happy, Travis turned to Pa. "There's somethin' else. Yesterday, when I first saw the man, I went to investigate and found he'd started a campfire in the middle of the forest."

Ma startled. "You didn't go into them woods, did ya?"

"I had to, Ma." He looked back and forth between his parents. "Here's the thing. I smelled meat on the air when I got into the forest, and when I found the campfire, there was a big lump of somethin' cookin' on it." He took off his hat, turnin' it around and around in his hands. "I'm afraid it was Alice's pig."

Ma gasped. "No."

Travis nodded, lookin' at Pa. "We should go investigate, just to be sure."

"Yes, we should," Pa said. "Let's do that now."

"Should I come with?" Ma asked.

"No. Stay here and keep an eye on the property while we're gone."

Ma cocked her gun and gripped it tight. "Got it."

And Travis knew she did.

He and Pa headed across the field, neither talkin'. When they got to the forest, Travis only hesitated a moment before enterin'. He still didn't like bein' there.

"Where now, son?"

"This way," Travis said, headin' in the right direction.

They reached the campfire–long dead now–and Pa stood over it, starin' down at what was left of Alice's pig. It was obvious what the animal had been. Travis had seen many-a cooked pig before.

"How we gonna tell Alice?" Travis asked.

Pa shook his head all slow-like. "Not sure. It might not even be hers."

"We don't have any missin' pigs right now, though," Travis said.

"I know."

"And we live too far away from other neighbors to have it be anyone else's."

"I know," Pa said again.

"We should call her," Travis said.

"Yer right," Pa said. He pulled out his cell and dialed, holdin' the phone to his ear. "Hello, Alice?"

Travis stopped listenin' to Pa when somethin' caught his attention in the fire. He squatted next to the coals, shiftin' through them, tryin' to grab at the glintin' metal he'd seen. It was caught on somethin' underneath the pig. He dropped to his butt, needin' to get a better grasp on the thing. The pig was sticky–the meat hadn't all finished cookin'–

and the bones had been partially picked over durin' the night by wild animals. They didn't have no large predators in the area, so it didn't surprise him that nothin' had carried it off yet.

Shiftin' his grasp on the metal thing, only able to grab a part of it, he yanked real hard. Still, it didn't come out. He was gonna have to move the pig to release it.

With a grimace, Travis got to his feet and heaved the huge, partially burned animal away from the coal and logs.

He did *not* expect what he saw.

A human hand–a skeleton hand–was encircled around *Ma's brooch*. What in the world?

Travis stepped back from the campfire, bumpin' into Pa.

"What are you doin,?" Pa asked, tuckin' his phone into his pocket, call now done.

Travis could only point at the hand in response.

Pa's eyes got wider than the full moon. He approached the hand cautiously. "What on earth is this?"

"Ma's brooch," Travis said. "Bein' held by a human hand."

Pa squatted down by the old fire. "That's what it looks like."

Travis couldn't ask what was on his mind, though. Who did the hand belong to, and where was the rest of that poor person?

"What do we do?"

"Call the coppers."

Travis nodded. Definitely. But he'd remembered somethin' just then. "I might know where it came from."

Travis led his pa to the family graveyard. They'd left the hand in the fire, knowin' the police would want to see it regardless of where the rest of the body was found.

"And you say he was walkin' away from them graves?" Pa asked.

"Yup. Ain't no other reason for him to be comin' from that direction. 'Specially not when the highway's on the other side of the farm."

"Good point."

Travis opened the little gate to the plots, already knowin' exactly where to walk because the earth over a particular grave had been freshly stirred up. Unlike in the movies, though, whoever had been diggin' had replaced all the dirt.

Pa stopped in front of the grave. "That the one?"

"Must be."

"I hate diggin'."

Travis shook his head. "We don't need to. The cops'll have to do it. Grave robbin' is a crime, even from private graveyards, and we'll need to leave everythin' how we seen it just now."

Pa put a hand on Travis's shoulder. "I'm right proud of you, boy. Them books you used to read sure did you a lot of good."

"Thank you, Pa." He turned. "Anyway. Looks like we know what happened to Ma's brooch."

Pa nodded. "And this is your grandma's grave on your ma's side. The daughter of Algernon Blackwood."

"Why'd they dig her up?"

"Well, son, I been thinkin' on that. The brooch is Ma's, and the hand belonged to her grandma. I hate to say it, but it seems like someone is targetin' Ma and her family."

Travis gripped his rifle tighter. "I think you're right."

"What time does yer event start? I know you don't wanna be late for it. I'll call the cops. You run back home and tell Ma what we found, then head to your event. I know they'll want to talk to you, but you can do that later."

Travis nodded. "You can have Alice's husband and her boys help out while I'm gone too."

Pa shook his head. "They can't help out–least not right away. Seems Alice has an event to attend tonight too."

"Well, see if'n Tom and the boys can come anyway."

"Fine. Now, git. You got a lot to do still."

Travis nodded. He'd done his chores early that mornin'–the ones that couldn't wait–but he still had several more to do. Plus changin' and showerin' and gettin' Ronnie ready.

What a busy day it had turned out to be.

Travis hooked a leash to the collar around Ronnie's neck. "Come on, boy, we gonna git you fixed." Ronnie bleated, and Travis chuckled. "Not *that* kinda fixed. Y'all're my favorite stud–you know that. Them parts'll still work."

Ronnie bleated again, and Travis led him up the ramp to the bed of the pickup truck and then into the large dog kennel, which he secured shut. He patted the roof, and Ronnie lay down and started munchin' on the snacks Travis had left him.

"There, there. Get all comfy, okay? It's gonna be a long drive."

For some reason, the meetin' had been set to happen in a place the town over, despite there bein' plenty of big enough places nearby. Cassilda had been quiet about the reasons, and he had a feelin' she wanted to surprise him.

Travis hopped in his truck and headed to Cassilda's house. She'd be takin' the trip with him, and he couldn't wait to spend time with her.

The cops had shown up while he was doin' his chores, and he still couldn't believe all they'd found. They'd dug up the grave and discovered that yes, the hand had come from his grandma's body. But that wasn't the only body part missin'–she also was missin' her other hand and both feet.

Only the hand holdin' the brooch had been discovered.

Where was the rest of them body parts? Travis had an unsettled feelin' in the pit of his stomach, thinkin' about an old lady's body bein' treated like that. It was so disrespectful and disturbin'.

Ma had been delighted to learn her brooch had been found, but not so delighted by where it'd been discovered. She declared she'd never look at the thing the same after that.

With all the motion-detectin' lights set up, everyone would sleep better that night. At least, Travis hoped so. He hadn't gotten one wink of sleep when he'd returned to his bed the night before, and he knew he was gonna start draggin' soon.

One more reason to be glad Cassilda was takin' the trip with him. She'd keep him awake.

Travis jogged up to the massive white double doors of her house and rang the bell. Cassilda answered, steppin' out onto the porch. She looked lovely in a light pink dress with her hair done up all fancy. Travis gave a low whistle and she blushed, twistin' away from him slightly in a ladylike way, hands clasped in front of her.

"Do I look good?" she asked.

"Good? You look *great*."

He stepped to kiss her, but she grinned and ducked away, headin' to the truck.

"I don't want to smudge my makeup," she said. "You can kiss me all you want tonight once the event is over."

Travis chuckled, then opened her door, shuttin' it behind her. He hopped in behind the wheel, then smiled when Cassilda scooted across the bench to sit right next to him.

"That's better," he said.

A bleatin' sound came from the back of the truck, and Cassilda looked behind them. "Oh!" She paused for a moment. "I'm surprised you were brave enough to bring him."

Travis's heart clenched. "You don't think I'm brave?"

"I didn't have reason to doubt before, but I truly don't now." She turned her big brown eyes to him. "You're going to fit in so perfectly, Trav. I can't wait for the others to meet you."

The clenchin' feelin' subsided, replaced with warmth, and Travis gave Cassilda's knee a squeeze. "Good."

He pulled away from the mansion and got onto the highway, headin' to the next town. Conversation with Cassilda flowed smoothly and perfectly, as it always did. She fascinated him with her experiences travelin' the world and meetin' all sorts of people. He could listen to her for hours.

"Are you gonna tell me what to expect tonight?" he asked when the conversation lulled.

She glanced at him. "Oh, you know, the usual rites and such."

He nodded, actin' like he had a clue what she was talkin' bout. "Great." He hesitated. "But what does that mean?"

Cassilda laughed and swatted his arm. "You tease."

He wasn't teasin', but he did enjoy her flirtin' with him.

Cassilda sighed, snugglin' up next to him. "I hope you like my part." She faced him more fully, and Travis had a hard time keepin' his eyes on the road. "Okay, I'm going to tell you what I'll be doing. You know I was named after someone in a play, right?"

"And there was a gal named Camilla in it too, right?"

"Right. Well, the play is hugely important. Anyone who watches it gets converted."

He didn't like how that sounded. "Converted to what?"

"Hasturism." Her eyes practically glowed, makin' her face shine with excitement.

That didn't sound so bad. Least it was somethin' his evil great-grandpa would frown upon. "That's awesome," he said, though he still wasn't super sure.

"It really is. And guess what?"

"What?"

"We've officially been invited to put that play on here, for you and other people."

"That's cool. Have you done it before, or is this like openin' night or somethin'?"

"This is technically opening night, though I've seen the play countless times at other events. I've had it memorized from start to finish for years."

"Wow." He cleared his throat, thinkin' through the implications. "So it's like, your favorite show, then?" He knew people who had a certain level of obsession for movies like *Star Wars* and *Twilight*. He needed to be careful and not say nothin' to hurt Cassilda's feelins'. He just didn't feel passion like that for entertainment.

"It goes beyond favorite, Travis," she said lightly. "It's a belief system. A way of life."

Travis swallowed. "Tell me about this way of life."

She shook her head. "I can't. Not until you see the play. Specifically, the *end* of it."

"What's so special about the end? 'Sides from it bein' the part that ties the whole story up."

"It's when people *get* it. When they truly understand. When they *join* us." She traced figures on his free hand. "I haven't yet met someone who hasn't gone completely mad for our cause after watching the play. I'm so excited for you to understand too. I know all this is new to you and probably overwhelming and even a little bit weird, but I promise it'll all make sense by the end of the evening."

Travis took in a deep breath and let it out slowly, thinkin' over his words carefully. "I'm not sure how I feel 'bout all this, but if it's so important to you, I'll give it a go–an honest effort."

Cassilda squealed, threadin' her arms through his and leanin' her head on his shoulder. "Oh, Trav. I knew you'd be just perfect. Perfect for me and what we're trying to do here."

Travis allowed a small smile to cross his lips. He didn't know what Cassilda's group was tryin' to do, but he loved how her words made him feel. That he was *perfect* for her.

More like they were perfect for each other.

They finally arrived at their destination–an old theater. Travis parked the truck, and Cassilda gave him a quick kiss, bein' careful not to smudge her lipstick.

"I have to head backstage," she said, arms around him.

He nodded. "Where am I takin' Ronnie? Is there a vet nearby?"

"Just bring him inside. Someone will help you know what to do."

Take the goat inside the theater? That was silly. Maybe the vet was there, though.

Cassilda skipped off, her pink dress flutterin' in the breeze, and Travis watched her go, grinnin'. She sure was a beauty.

He opened the bed of the truck, pulled out the wooden slat to make a ramp for Ronnie, then hopped up and undid the door on the dog kennel. "All right, boy, let's git you inside." He stooped and gave the goat a hug. "You're gonna be all better soon. I can't wait."

Once the goat was out of the truck, Travis put the board back into the bed, shut the tailgate, and led Ronnie inside.

A man sat at a table just inside the buildin'. His eyes landed on Ronnie. He tilted his head and said with awe, "Is that the goat Henry promised for the immolation?"

Travis nodded, feelin' a sense of pride. "It sure is."

"Bring it here," the man said. "It looks pretty healthy, though—what imperfection does it have?"

"Imperfection?" Travis asked. "Oh! Right. It has two tails." He turned Ronnie around and showed the man.

The guy's eyes lit up. "That's so wonderful. Hastur will be deeply satisfied."

"Good." Travis still didn't understand what Ronnie and Hastur had to do with each other, but that sense of pride continued glowin' in his chest. It sure felt good to be needed like this, to be contributin'.

The man took Ronnie's leash, handin' it to another man who led Ronnie away. "He'll have his part in the performance pretty early on, but we'll take great care of him in the meantime."

"Thank you," Travis said. He glanced around. "Is there a program or an agenda for the meetin'?"

"Yes, over on that table." The man pointed to the other side of the room, where a table stood next to a door. "I need to check you in first, though. What's your name?"

"Travis Blackwood."

The man's eyes shot up from his clipboard, and he dropped his pen. "*You're* Travis Blackwood." It wasn't a question. He slowly rose to his feet, reachin' for Travis's hand, which he shook with both of his. "It's an honor to meet you."

Travis sensed it as his face flushed. "I don't see why–I'm nothin' but a country boy."

"Your great-grandfather … he was a lunatic. A madman."

That, Travis could agree with.

The man continued. "But he was also one of the smartest people to roam the earth. I've heard of his writings." He sent a hopeful glance to Travis's hands. "Did you happen to bring any of them with you?"

"I … I uh …" Travis said, stammerin'. How'd the man know about his grandpa's writin's? This conversation was makin' him real uncomfortable. "I'm sure we can chat later 'bout them."

"I'd be honored."

The man ushered Travis past the checkpoint, tellin' him to go through the door by the table, and Travis picked up the agenda and opened that door. Inside was the auditorium and stage. The large room was dimly lit and mostly empty, but Travis and Cassilda had arrived pretty early so she could get ready for her part. Accordin' to the program, the event wouldn't be startin' for another half hour.

Forty-five minutes later, it still hadn't begun, and Travis started growin' real restless. His phone battery was almost dead from all the games he'd been playin'. He decided to stretch his legs, find the bathroom, and see if there was snacks somewhere. He got to his feet, surprised to see people he knew there, also waitin' for the event to start.

"Travis, is that you?" Alice said from halfway back.

Oh, so *this* was the event she had to attend. Small world. Travis approached her. "Hello, ma'am," he said, tippin' his hat to her.

"Thank you for findin' my pig. Even if it wasn't in the best condition." She sniffed, her eyes wellin' up with tears.

Travis cleared his throat and nodded. "Ain't no big deal, ma'am."

"It was to me. I sure 'preciate you." She cleared her throat and dabbed at her eyes with a tissue. "Do you know anythin' 'bout what we're doin' here?"

He shook his head. "Nothin'. I was gonna go find out why it ain't started yet."

"Good. Let us know," she said.

Several other people nodded. Mission accepted, Travis left the auditorium with determination. He was surprised to find the front of the buildin' empty. Where had everyone gone? There was now a sign on the check-in table that read, *We'll begin shortly. Please take a seat in the auditorium.*

Not one to skirt an assignment, Travis wandered down the hall that led to the left of the auditorium. Surely this would take him backstage and to someone who could tell him what was goin' on.

And maybe he'd catch a glimpse of Cassilda.

The smell of smoke wafted around him, and he stepped faster, hopin' the buildin' wasn't about to burn down.

At the end of the hall, Travis entered a large room with several vanities with mirrors and lights, lined with lots of racks of costumes. Fans littered the room too. An acrid smoke wafted past Travis, smellin' of BBQ. In the middle of the room, on the cement floor, was a fire with somethin' biggish burnin' on it. Why hadn't the fire alarms gone off?

Encirclin' the fire was a group of people holdin' hands and lookin' up, their faces slack, mouths open. Henry, Lucinda, and Cassilda were part of that circle.

Travis stared at the fire. "Where's Ronnie?" he asked.

The people startled, and Henry glanced over. "Oh, Travis. Are you ready for the play?"

"Where's my goat?" he asked again.

Henry, Cassilda, and Lucinda approached him. "He's great," Henry said. "Content. Happy. The immolation was successful–he's been accepted."

"I'm glad to hear that. I want to take him home now." Travis couldn't shake the dark feelin' that entered his soul. Somethin' was off. Had his parents been right? Were these folks *not* good people? He tried to muster some trust for the voice that had entered his head earlier, but it was hard. And somethin' about that fire reminded him of the one in his forest. He couldn't focus on that, though–couldn't even think about it.

"His immolation was honorable," Lucinda said. "We'll … help you take him home after the play is over."

"I don't think he knows what 'immolate' means," Cassilda said, compassion on her face. "But Mother is right. The play needs to start, Trav. I'm sorry I can't explain it to you now, but I'll fill you in and answer all of your questions the minute the show is over." She reached out to him, takin' his hand. "I promise, everything will make sense. Trust me."

Travis looked deeply into her eyes. They were wide, open, honest, and he felt himself relaxin'. "Okay." He took in a deep breath and let it out slowly. "Okay."

Henry looked at his watch. "While the interruption wasn't welcome, I'm glad you came. We weren't aware of the time–that happens sometimes at these events. We get so wrapped up in the visions that enter our minds that we forget what's going on around us."

"Yes, we're glad you came," Lucinda said. "Please return to your seat and let our other guests know the show is about to start. We'll be along shortly. Well, Henry will–Cassilda and I will be on stage."

Travis nodded. "Sounds good."

Heart still unsettled, Travis sent another glance toward the fire, hopin' that everythin' would soon make sense like Cassilda had promised. He headed back to the auditorium and strode down the middle aisle to the front. He turned and faced the crowd of ten to fifteen people.

"Ladies and gentlemen," he said, "they told me to tell you the show is about to start."

"'Bout time," a man called out.

"Thank goodness," a woman said.

"For cryin' out loud," came another man's voice. "I didn't expect my whole evenin' to be spent waitin' for an event I don't know nothin' about."

Henry entered the room just then. "You won't be waiting much longer," he said, rubbing his hands together, an excited expression on his face. He pointed. "Look! The curtains are opening."

Sure enough, the stage was now visible, and Cassilda and Lucinda were there, on it.

Henry placed a hand on Travis's shoulder. "You're the guest of honor," he whispered. "We want you in the best seat in the house."

Travis followed Henry a little closer to the stage, where Henry removed a "reserved" sign from two seats. Travis took one, and Henry the other, then they turned their attention to the stage.

Lucinda spoke first. "The play you're about to watch has been banned in most states and in countries across the world. Copies of it have been burned, it has been denounced from pulpits, and it has been censured by even the highest literary acumen. Years and years ago, our original New Jerseyian chapter of Hastur followers found an old French copy. We cleaned it up and translated it, and now we perform it in every location where we hope to begin a new chapter."

Lucinda drew herself up, lookin' authoritarian. "Prepare to be awed, amazed, and even dumbstruck at times. Above all else, this event will have more impact on you than anything you'll ever experience. We look forward to you joining our chapter at the conclusion."

Travis raised his eyebrows. They sure had a high opinion of this thing. Well, he'd just have to see what *he* thought.

The lights in the auditorium dimmed, and Cassilda and Lucinda exited. Fog billowed across the stage.

Travis watched, head tilted, and mouth open as the first act began with a vengeance. People dashed and danced across the stage, shoutin' and callin' words he'd never heard before. They screamed, attackin' each other with wooden swords.

"They're enacting the final days of a kingdom on a far-off planet," Henry whispered.

Travis nodded. "Thanks," he whispered back.

Henry patted his arm. "Sorry. I'll let you enjoy it now."

The actors crowned someone king, then the next scene, that new king was murdered and a huge revolution started. Words like Carcosa, Cthulhu, and Alar were tossed back and forth, along with Hastur. At least Travis recognized that one. He blinked, tryin' to keep up with the plot. Cassilda came on stage with Lucinda actin' as Camilla. Cassilda was apparently the damsel in distress who kept gettin' saved over and over again by all sorts of fellows.

Things got more and more complex durin' the second act as the stage filled with masked dancers who sang and twirled, shoutin' and singin' unintelligible words. Scenes blended together, and Travis could no longer grasp a single plot line that connected anythin'. Cassilda and Lucinda were there, giratin' around with the other actors.

A weird sensation crossed over Travis, and he felt himself stand. What on earth? Was he bein' emotionally impacted by the scenes in front of him?

But no—he glanced around—the other attendees was all standin' now too. And instead of the walls of the auditorium, they was surrounded by ruins. Tall buildin's half crumbled, bricks and stones litterin' a cobblestone street. The dancin' and screamin' actors continued, though now, they was doin' it all around Travis and the other attendees in the middle of the street.

Travis fixated on them ruined walls. It was like a dystopian scene—like somethin' from a movie. But above all was the feelin' he'd been there before. Them walls was so familiar. But *why*? And how? He couldn't remember where he'd seen them before.

The flurry of action got more and more intense, and Travis fisted his hands, eyes wide, unable to look away from the colors flashin' around him. Robes, dresses, ribbons braided into long hair, flags, banners—all of it flowed together as the actors spun faster and faster.

Discordant music boomed from somewhere, the rhythms poundin' so hard against Travis's chest, it was almost impossible to breathe.

Travis felt an urge to walk forward, and the dancers and actors followed. He was vaguely aware of Henry grinnin' next to him, watchin' him closely. They rounded a corner in the city of ruins and there, before them, was a massive pile of logs, branches, and sticks, formin' a huge unlit campfire that pointed toward the sky. In the middle of it, barely visible, was a stone slab. Somethin' was on that stone.

Travis squinted, tryin' to get his eyes to focus. Why couldn't he see? Oh, because they was still surrounded by the fog that had billowed across the stage at the start of the play. Where was it comin' from now?

The frenzy suddenly stopped, the actors freezin' in place. Five breaths later, when the silence had become so deafenin' Travis thought he'd lost his mind, they dropped their arms and bowed their heads, slowly shufflin' together until they formed a group near the logs. Then the group parted, turnin' to face each other, and a tall, yellow-robed man glided through.

The man held somethin' in his hands. He wore a yellow mask with only holes for the eyes. He turned to face the members of the audience who stood near Travis, lookin' just as confused, and held up the thing for all to see.

The actors gasped and fell to the ground around the man, bowin' to him.

Travis stared at the symbol, unable to make sense of it. Somethin' told him it was important, judgin' by how the actors reacted, but he couldn't figure out why.

That symbol … like the city walls, it was both familiar and foreign. Travis couldn't quite make out the shape of it, and he didn't know why. No way would he be able to describe it.

A gush of wind rolled over the group and the fog dissipated. A greenish yellow light from the sun shone through, brightenin' the scene, and the actors got to their feet and stared at *him*–at *Travis*–waitin' for his reaction. The man still held up the sign. Travis looked around– everyone else seemed just as uncomfortable as he felt. What in the crap just happened? Where were they? And what was the importance of what they'd just seen?

Henry turned to Travis, waitin' expectantly.

Travis looked back at the group of actors and the man, sensin' that this was an important moment, that his reaction would dictate his entire future. He wasn't sure what led him to believe that, but he knew it was true as strongly as he knew his name was Travis.

Only, he wasn't sure what everyone was waitin' for.

He took off his hat and twisted it around and around. "I don't get it."

Cassilda crumpled to the ground, sobbin', and Travis knew he'd said the wrong thing. "I'm ... I'm sorry." What could he do to make things better? "Do you want to show me again? Maybe 'splain things as we watch?" He knew that was a ridiculous request, but he didn't know what else to say.

Cassilda didn't answer, and Henry, who still stood near him, shook his head in disappointment.

"I'm serious," Travis said. "Someone help me understand."

Cassilda stopped cryin', lookin' up at him with hope on her face. Travis loved that expression–he really wanted her approval. He didn't want to disappoint her no more.

Henry stared at Travis, still shakin' his head. "You missed the entire point," he said. "I've never seen anyone *not* get the point of this play."

Travis motioned to the fire. "Why didn't we light it? I kinda sorta felt that was part of the event."

"It *would* have been. We would have had *you* light it. But you missed ... you missed *everything*."

Cassilda gathered her skirts and dashed to Travis's side, takin' him by the arm. "But we can help him understand. Can't we? Maybe we could do the performance again, like he suggested?"

Henry pointed at Travis, lookin' at Cassilda. "No. You can't date him, Cassilda. He's too stupid for Hastur. If he didn't catch it the first time, he never will."

Travis felt his mouth drop open. *Stupid?* He was too *stupid?* He almost slugged the man, but Cassilda's reaction to her father's words stopped him. Her face crumpled, and she started cryin' again. Travis tried to pull her in for a hug–hopin' maybe to comfort her—but she pushed away, turnin' to her father instead.

That hurt more than the "stupid" comment. If'n he could convince Cassilda that her kin was the dumb ones, not him, their relationship might still work out. But no, she was choosin' her parents and that dumb, weird play over him. He looked around, tryin' to figure out how to git back to the theater, but the only thing that surrounded him was them stupid ruins.

Just then, the man holdin' the sign shook and shivered, his hands tremblin'. He doubled over, droppin' the symbol, wrappin' his arms around his stomach. Then he froze for several seconds before straightenin', appearin' taller now than he was before. His robes swelled and billowed. Travis stared at those robes. Somethin' was twistin' in them, causin' the fabric to roil and shift grotesquely. What was behind them robes?

A deep, raspy voice boomed from behind the mask, echoein' off the ruins, and Henry and Cassilda dropped to the ground, bowin'.

"The people of this region are simpletons," the tall man said, "too dim to join my followers. Henry, I warned you of this."

The man stepped to inspect the logs and whatever was on top of that stone slab. The other play attendees called out, offended, but Travis didn't pay no attention to them. His eyes had widened at the sound of the voice. It came from the same bein' who'd told him that Henry and Lucinda were good!

"Yes, my lord," Henry said. "But I've been watching Travis. I thought he was worthy."

That caught Travis's attention. "It was *you*?" Travis said, aware of the other members of the audience callin' to go back home. "*You* were the one comin' on my property? I almost shot you last night!" He balled his hands into fists. "You killed Alice's pig! And … and you're a grave robber! You took my grandma's body parts! Where's her hand and feet, Henry? You give them back, now!"

Henry's eyes brightened. "I have a mission to accomplish, Travis." He motioned to the yellow-robed man who was still inspectin' the wood. "I was called by Hastur himself to destroy the writings your great-grandfather recorded while studying in the library of Celaeno. The journals you were reading last night in your attic." He paused for a moment, and Travis glanced at the tall man, suspectin' he was the real danger there. He saw movement behind the robes again as the man glided behind the logs, inspectin' things from that side.

Henry continued. "I must destroy all of Algernon's descendants. But Travis. The moment I saw you sitting there, reading the journals, I realized I couldn't destroy you. Not yet. Not until I'd given you a chance to accept Hasturism. I foolishly believed you were young and impressionable enough to be swayed to see our point of view." He glared at Travis. "It never occurred to me you were too stupid to understand any of it."

"You assume too much, Henry," the deep voice said from behind the woodpile, with a tone of boredom. "I never commanded you to do any of that. You took it upon yourself."

Henry swallowed, noddin'. But he didn't respond to the man. He continued talkin' to Travis. "Algernon Blackwood is an enemy of Hastur, and he obtained his incredible wealth of knowledge illegally. His family can't live–no one who has read those words can. And the writings must be destroyed. I have taken it upon myself to do it." His eyes widened, excitement crossin' his face.

Travis tilted his head, studyin' Henry. "You want to keep them journals for yerself."

Henry sputtered. "What? No. Not at all. I want to destroy them." He slid a glance to Hastur who had just come around this side of the log pile.

"Henry, Henry, Henry," Hastur said, his voice still soundin' bored. "You can lie to the boy, but you can't lie to me."

A movement on the slab of stone caught Travis's attention. "There's a person tied up there!" he said, pointin'.

"Of course there is," Henry said. "And I can't even begin to tell you how difficult it was to get all of this put together after you interrupted my earlier efforts."

"We gotta get them down!" Realizin' Henry wasn't gonna help, Travis rushed across the cobblestoned road. They were gonna burn a *person*? Were they *crazy*?

He nearly fell in surprise when he saw just who was tied up on that slab. "Ma!" he said, tryin' to climb the logs. "Ma! What are you doin' here?"

A gag covered her mouth and thick rope bound her legs and hands. She looked at him, dazed, confused. Hastur paused his inspections, watchin', and Travis felt his gaze on him. It creeped him out, but the guy wasn't doin' anythin' to stop Travis, so he ignored him.

He continued tryin' to climb the logs. Why'd they have to make the pile so big? He didn't git far, though, before an actor grabbed him and pulled him back. Travis shook the man off, turnin' to Ma again. Before he could do anythin', though, several more people grabbed at him, pullin' him away.

"She's needed for the immolation," one of them said. "Hastur requires a sacrifice."

Hastur gave a slow nod, then turned his attention to Henry, who'd approached with head bowed.

"Not of my ma, he don't," Travis said. "I don't care who he is."

But the people held tight to him and continued draggin' him away.

"Someone help me!" Travis called, strugglin' against the many hands on him. Then he noticed the other attendees was all bein' held back too.

Lucinda approached the logs with a gas can. "You might want to keep your distance, Travis," she said. "It's about to get hot."

"Please, Lucinda," Travis said. "Please. It's my ma. You can't burn her."

Lucinda stared at him, eyebrows up. "I burned my own daughter. What makes you think I'd hesitate for a stranger?"

Travis's mouth fell open, and for a moment he was too shocked to even think. In his surprise, his arms fell slack, and the men holdin' him relaxed their grips just a bit. She'd *burned* her *daughter*? She killed Camilla? What kinda mother was she? Travis couldn't even comprehend someone that evil, that cruel.

He gritted his teeth, forcin' himself to concentrate. Before the actors could stop him, he burst through their weak holds and grabbed the can of gas from Lucinda. He tossed it as hard and as far away as he could, then, adrenaline pumpin' through his system, he scaled the logs up to his ma.

Travis grabbed at the ropes, tryin' to untie them, wonderin' why ain't no one was stoppin' him now. But a quick glance told him his neighbors was fightin' the actors. Travis felt a sense of pride build up in his chest as he watched for a second or two. Ain't one of them actors as strong as his neighbors. Not with how much hard labor him and his people did every day. Them city folk just wasn't a match.

Not wantin' to get distracted again, Travis turned to the ropes, very aware of how closely he was surrounded by logs and branches, tied together, formin' a loose pyramid shape around him and the stone slab. If'n someone grabbed that can of gas again, he and his ma would be toast. Literally.

Luckily, Travis was an Eagle Scout. And he knew knots. It didn't take him long to get the ones on Ma's hands and wrists loose. He glanced at the action, knowin' he had to hurry. Lucinda had retrieved the gas can and was approachin' with it, a look of pure evil in her eyes. Henry was arguin' with Hastur, his body language showin' frustration. And them actors was still gittin' their butts whooped. Most of them was down now.

Alice, now free of the lady she'd been fightin', raced at Lucinda, knockin' the gas can to the ground. Travis worked on the ropes tied around Ma's feet. She was actin' all sluggish.

"Can you sit, up, Ma?" he asked her. "It would make me feel better 'bout you if'n you could."

She tried to do so, but failed, her actions too sluggish and slow. She did manage to shift her position enough to show she was lyin' on top of somethin', though. Travis gasped in horror. The remains of a goat was there ... along with a skeletal hand wrapped around one of Ma's necklaces. Travis knew where the goat had come from. And the parts of the skeleton. But why? Why were they there?

Tears filled Travis's eyes as he continued workin' on the knots that held Ma's feet bound, thinkin' 'bout his poor goat.

"I can't stop her no more!" Alice shrieked.

Travis looked up. Ma's best friend lay on the cobblestoned road, her face bleedin' and startin' to swell. Lucinda stood over her triumphantly, holdin' the gas can. The evil woman kicked Alice in the side before turnin' to the pile of logs.

"Come on, Ma," Travis said. "We gotta go. We really gotta go."

Lucinda started sloshin' gasoline all over the logs, and Travis pulled on Ma's arm, tryin' to git her to move. She was dead weight, though. Why was she so tired?

"The spell makes her like that," Henry said from where he stood next to Hastur. Both were facin' the woodpile. "The one I used to get her to the fire." He laughed at Travis. "You can thank your great-grandfather for that one, boy."

Hastur abruptly turned to Henry, his robes shiftin' to follow. "How much power have you borrowed?" He grabbed Henry, placin' a hand on his head. "Those powers weren't yours to use, Henry."

Hastur raised his voice, sayin' somethin' that sounded like gibberish. His deep voice boomed over the commotion, and everyone fell silent. The actors fell to the ground, bowin' to Hastur, Lucinda with her fist still wrapped around the handle of the gas can.

"For you, my lord," Henry said, still standin', but avertin' his gaze. "I did it all for you."

"I see your thoughts, Henry. You can't hide them from me anymore. You don't seek this knowledge to grow my followers, you seek it to grow your fame and your own power."

Hastur had bought Travis more time. With a mighty heave, Travis pulled Ma up again, slingin' her arm over his shoulder. He was surprised when Alice joined him, helpin' by loopin' Ma's other arm over her own shoulders. Together, they started slowly makin' their way down the woodpile. Ma tried to walk as best she could, but they ended up mostly draggin' her. It was rough goin'. Travis hated to think of how Ma's legs would look.

"You were my most faithful follower," Hastur continued. "But at some point, the temptation must have become too much. You seek powers that no mere human can possess. You're jealous of my strength and wisdom."

Travis, Ma, and Alice finally reached the cobblestone road, but Travis gasped, eyes on Hastur. A massive tentacle roiled out from under the robe, snakin' its way around Henry's legs.

Henry stared down at the tentacle, revulsion and fear coverin' his face. "I can make it up to you, my lord. I promise."

"You can't," Hastur said. "I don't forgive unfaithfulness." He chuckled, a deep and gratin' sound. "I do require a sacrifice to be made, though, and since *your* offering has escaped ..."

Henry only had a moment to make eye contact with Travis before the tentacle yanked him off his feet, his body slammin' into the cobblestones. Henry screamed, writhin' and clawin' at the tentacle, tryin' to free himself. Several more tentacles slid out from under the robe and hefted Henry, carryin' him to the slab.

"Lucinda," Hastur said. "Light the fire."

Lucinda cried out, pressin' her face against the stone. She made no move to obey.

"Lucinda ..." Hastur said, patiently, while Henry screamed, still tryin' to free himself.

Not wantin' to stick around and see what happened, Travis and Alice continued helpin' Ma walk, headin' down the cobblestone street. She was barely able to move, and Travis was startin' to lose his grip on her arm. And if'n he was strugglin', Alice was too.

"Lord," Henry screamed from the woodpile. "Travis and his mother are getting away!"

Hastur didn't respond. He was still facin' Lucinda. "Would you like to join your husband on the slab and have your daughter complete the sacrifice instead?"

Cassilda ... Travis almost looked, but instead forced himself to continue walkin'. Ma was his first priority. And gittin' the heck outta that place. But Cassilda. Ugh.

"Let me help," a man said near Travis, startlin' him.

Travis nearly slumped in relief. "Thank you." Ma wasn't a big woman, but she wasn't tiny neither, and Travis was grateful to know he and Alice had help. In fact, all of the attendees was there, many injured, all surroundin' Travis.

"Where are we goin'?" one of the women asked.

Travis chewed on his lip, starin' down the cobblestone street at more and more ruined buildin's. He'd hoped that by walkin' away from the woodpile, they'd return to the auditorium, but that ain't happened yet. He scanned the ruins around them, tryin' to figure out what to do. Now what?

He turned to see if'n the auditorium had appeared that way, but no–the wood pile was still there. Travis's heart sank when he realized they'd only gone about twenty feet. It felt like so much more than that. Lucinda stood near the woodpile, holdin' a lit match. Tears poured down her face as she stared at her husband, the empty gas can lyin' on its side at her feet.

Henry screamed from on top of the stone slab. Hastur held him in place, facin' Lucinda.

And Cassilda. Cassilda looked at neither of them. She was starin' at Travis, an intense expression on her face. Travis met her gaze, tryin' to figure out what she was sayin' with that expression.

"Come with me, Cassilda," he said.

She opened her mouth as if to respond, but waved instead.

Travis thought she was wavin' goodbye to him, and he raised his hand to wave back, but before he could, the walls of the ruins disappeared, replaced with the walls of the auditorium. Cassilda must've released them from the vision.

Except, it hadn't been a vision. Alice's face was still busted up. Ma was still slung between Travis and the man. And Ronnie … Ronnie was still dead, back on that stone slab. Travis felt tears prick the back of his eyes again, but he knew just how lucky they'd been to get out alive.

The only ones who'd returned with him were the other townsfolk. Travis breathed a sigh of relief, but didn't relax. He had to git these people taken care of. Because of the fight that had happened, and whatever spell had crossed over Ma, he was the only able-bodied person there.

His phone had long since died, so he borrowed one from another person and called nine-one-one, askin' for help. Luckily, the town they'd ended up in had a fire station, so they wouldn't need to wait too long.

Paramedics soon rushed into the buildin', and while they were checkin' everyone out, Travis called Pa.

"Who's this?" Pa barked on the other line.

"It's me—Travis."

"Oh, thank goodness," Pa's voice held a note of panic. "Son, yer ma disappeared. She was sittin' there, eatin', when all of a sudden-like, she got real tired and slumped over. I helped her to her bed. I went to get her a drink, but when I got back, she was gone. I looked all over the place for her and I can't find her nowhere. I was 'bout to call the cops when you phoned."

"She's here," Travis said, "with me."

"What? How in tarnation did she git all the way over there?"

"It was dark magic, Pa. Real dark. But she's gonna be okay—the paramedics say so."

"*Paramedics?* Son, what in the heck is goin' on?"

"I'll fill you in when we git home. For now, just know we're all okay. Alice too."

"*Alice?*"

Travis bit his lips. He needed to stop talkin'. He was too tired, and when he got tired, he couldn't keep words from fallin' out of his mouth. He was just causin' Pa unnecessary stress by lettin' little details slip.

"Don't worry. Like I said, I'll fill you in when we git home."

"Okay, son. Okay. 'Bout how long do you think it'll be?"

"Not sure. My phone's dead, though. So, I won't even be able to tell you when we've left."

"You can borrow my phone," Alice said. "I'm comin' home with you and yer ma. Me and Tom will come get my truck tomorrow. I don't feel well enough to drive."

"Okay. Pa, I'll have Alice's phone. Call that number if'n you need anthin'. We're gonna come as soon as we can—promise."

The rest of the night was a blur. Cops and paramedics asked all sorts of questions and re-asked those questions. It was obvious they was disturbed by the answers they got. Travis could tell they was tryin' to decide if'n they should put everyone in the mental hospital, but Pa showed up and told them about all the weird things that had happened on the farm. Havin' someone's testimony who hadn't been in the theater seemed to help, and rather than institutionalize everyone, the cops decided to chalk it up to another unsolved mystery. 'Sides, it was apparent none of the people there was at fault for any crime. The doors to the auditorium was unlocked, and there wasn't no evidence of damage.

Not even charred logs existed still in that back room. Travis was surprised to find that when he went lookin' for Ronnie's body. Henry's magic must've been real dark to pull everythin' to that city in ruins.

Travis drove his truck home with Ma and Alice on the bench next to him and Pa followin' behind them in his own truck. The whole way, Travis couldn't stop thinkin' about the empty dog kennel in the back of his truck.

He ain't never had a goat like Ronnie before, and he knew he wasn't ever gonna have another one.

But at least he had Ma still. And Alice. He glanced at the two of them. They was snoozin', their mouths open slightly. Alice's face was pressed against the glass, bandages coverin' a bunch of it, and Ma's head was restin' on Alice's shoulder. Pride welled up in Travis's heart over the fact that both women trusted him enough to sleep while he drove.

And he had plenty of time to think 'bout what all had happened. He couldn't believe he'd almost seen his ma get burned alive. And the evilness and vileness of the people there. Who could be okay with sacrificin' their own child? Or husband? Travis knew Lucinda hadn't wanted to burn Henry alive, but she held that match in her hand and somethin' told him she'd done it.

A part of him felt pity toward her. She probably didn't think she had a choice.

"There's always a choice," Travis muttered.

He'd rather be dead with his ma and pa than to ever burn 'em alive. But people did crazy things when they believed in somethin'. And maybe–just maybe–bein' a Hastur follower was all they said it was.

Travis didn't care, though. He didn't care one bit. He was happy with his simple house and simple family. With the *simpletons* who lived around him.

They dropped Alice off at her place first, then drove to the farm. When they pulled up next to the trailer, Pa rushed to the truck to help Ma inside. Travis followed. His heart hurt from the events of the night, and he knew it would for a long time.

They got Ma all situated on the couch, wrapped in a blanket, a cup of hot chocolate on the side table by her. Travis sat next to her, exhausted, and Pa paced the carpet in front of them.

"I knew that event was gonna be trouble," Pa said. "I knew that *family* was gonna be trouble."

Ma nodded, rubbin' Travis's arm. "I'm so sorry, son," she murmured. "But I'm glad to hear you didn't fall for it. And Alice, neither." She took in a deep breath and let it out slowly. "And I'm glad you was there to rescue me."

"Ain't no way nothin's gonna happen to you, Ma, if'n I have a say 'bout it."

"And I can't believe how they treated you, son," Pa said, still enraged. "They called you stupid? They're the stupid ones. Idiots."

Pa eventually calmed down, and after makin' sure Ma really was okay, Travis turned in for the night.

The next day, after Cassilda hadn't answered any texts or phone calls, he drove to her house. He couldn't understand why she was ignorin' him. For some reason, his recollection of their date the night before was off–he couldn't quite remember what they'd done–but had it been all that bad? A sinkin' feelin' hit him in the stomach. He definitely remembered disappointin' her. What had he done to do that, though? And was it somethin' he could fix?

He was dismayed to see a for sale sign out front. The place looked deserted. He knocked on the door anyway, and then walked around the place, peerin' in all the windows. The entire house was empty–a shell of what it'd been just a couple a nights earlier. How'd they vacated it that quickly? They must've had a whole army to help.

Heart somewhere near his feet, Travis headed back to his truck and hopped in, bucklin' up. Then he hit his steerin' wheel real hard. "Dang it!"

Despite knowin' the night hadn't gone how Cassilda had wanted it to he'd still hoped beyond hope he might have a chance with her. But no–she'd obviously left with her parents.

Either way, Travis was back to square one in the datin' arena.

He dropped his head to his steerin' wheel and closed his eyes.

"Aw, man. I gotta find a new girlfriend."

The Stranger

By Eric Malikyte

OEI Archive Serial Number: LGAI1601
Date: 09/06/2007
Audio Transcript: Interview with Subject 1601
Time: 19:00:45

This audio file is for internal use of the Office of Extra-dimensional Intelligence only.

By listening to this file, you confirm that you have an Omega level clearance.

Punishment for agents without the proper clearance will be severe.

My name is Doctor Webber, I am the Director of the OEI.
The following is our final interview with Subject 1601, who was discovered wandering naked on Montana Interstate 90 by a Wildlife Officer, fifteen miles from the city of Missoula.

Initial interviews revealed that the subject presented no memory of his identity. He appears to be of Caucasian descent, in his early fifties, overweight, and balding. The Wildlife Officer had Subject 1601 admitted to Second Winds, a mental health facility in Missoula.

When he was found, Subject 1601 was covered in a foul-smelling black substance. Unfortunately, due to our late arrival on the scene, we were unable to run tests on this substance. The local authorities had already allowed Subject 1601 the use of the shower, writing it off as fecal matter from a septic system and washing all potential evidence away. I'm told the Police Department in Missoula has been reprimanded and will follow CDC guidelines more closely in the future.

Our initial interviews yielded little to no information about him. At least not in regard to his origin, his personal history, or even his name. The subject was talkative, however, and seemed to have a large knowledge of home improvement, sports trivia, and paleontology. In particular, he appeared to have a professional level of knowledge of dinosaur species from the late Triassic, Jurassic, and Cretaceous periods of Earth's history.

Doctor Patton suggested we bring in a specialist and put Subject 1601 under hypnosis, thinking whatever happened to him may have been traumatic enough to have caused him to block the events out.

Doctor Arden Livingston arrived earlier this morning via helicopter and was immediately brought to the underground facility where the research subjects are kept.

We set up in Interview Chamber 5, since it's on the eastern wing of the facility and closest to the surface lift, should anything go wrong.

Once Doctor Livingston was ready, we retrieved Subject 1601 from his cell.

He was docile when he arrived.

We had no need to restrain him, but Doctor Patton felt it best if we chained him to the floor, considering we had no idea what might happen once the trance was induced.

Once the subject was secured, I turned on the audio recorder and had Doctor Livingston perform the hypnotism.

What follows is one of the strangest cases I have ever witnessed in all my years leading this organization.

Date: 09/06/2007
Time: 06:00:30

"Tell me, what is your name?" Doctor Livingston asks.

"I... I don't know," Subject 1601 responds.

"How long have you been here?"

Rustling sounds echo over the mic. Subject 1601 is looking around at his surroundings. I note that the subject seems unfocused. Listless even.

"A few days, maybe? Why?" Subject 1601 says.

"Do you mind if I refer to you as 1601? Subject just seems so, inhumane."

The Subject glances around the room again, a blank look on his face. "I guess not."

"Very well. 1601, I've been asked to come here to perform hypnosis on you. Do you know what hypnosis is?"

"Yeah, guess so."

"And do you consent to this procedure?"

"Sure."

Rustling sounds echo through the interview chamber. Doctor Livingston produces a black and gold watch. I note that Subject 1601 is intently focused on the watch. The subject's brow is furrowed. He scratches at the collar of his coveralls.

"I have in my hand a pocket watch," Doctor Livingston says. "Old fashioned, I know. It's a family heirloom. My grandfather gave it to me."

"That's nice. I don't remember my grandpa."

"Well, let's see if we can't jog some of those memories for you. Are you ready?"

The subject's eyes open wide. Sweat dots his brow.

"Guess so," Subject 1601 says.

"I will swing my pocket watch like a pendulum. I need you to devote all your focus to this watch and listen to my voice as I count down from ten to one. When I finish counting down and snap my fingers, you are to close your eyes. Is that understood?"

"Sure, Doctor."

"Keep your eyes on the pocket watch. Watch as it swings back and forth. Back and forth. Ignore everything else in the room. And imagine yourself back in your home, wherever that might be. Imagine the sights. The sounds. The smells. And listen only to my voice as I count from ten, nine, eight, seven, six, five, four, three, two, one."

Doctor Livingston snaps her fingers; the sounds ricochet off the walls.

I note that Subject 1601's body language has become far less rigid. His eyes are closed. He is once again docile.

"1601. I want you to tell me where you are."

"I'm...I'm at home."

"Good. What does your home look like?"

"Langville, Montana's a mountain town. We got a view of Ch-paa-qn peak. It snows all year long sometimes."

"Are you outside?"

"Yeah. Been doin' repairs on the siding and roof of my house before the next storms roll on through. Don't want it getting any more damaged than it already is."

"What is Langville like?"

"It's small. Got a grocery, a hardware store, and a diner, but not much else besides my neighbors."

"And what are your neighbors like?"

"Most of them are real friendly, but it's a small town so everyone knows everybody. Few folks keep to themselves."

"Are your neighbors far from you?"

"Not real close, but close enough I can see two of em across the way from my living room."

"So, not a suburb."

"No."

"Can you tell me your name?"

"My name is Doctor Eli Jones."

"Eli, can you tell me how you ended up wandering along Interstate 90 in the middle of the night, where the Wildlife Officer found you? Why you were naked. Why you were covered in that strange black substance. Can you do this for me?"

"I..."

I note that Subject 1601 appears to be grasping for his throat. Whimpering sounds come from within.

"This is a safe place. You can tell me anything."

This seems to calm the subject somewhat. His hand falls from his throat.

"Are you okay, Eli?"

"Yes, ma'am."

"Can you tell me what you remember?"

I note that the subject's demeanor has changed again. His fingers writhe, tensing up like he's attempting to type something on a non-existent keyboard.

"I…remember everything."

"Can you tell me."

"Yes." The subject's voice changes. His lips twist into a smile. "Yes, I can tell you."

Doctor Livingston glances at the two way mirror. I note her unease in my journal. The orderly tells her to continue.

"Please tell me everything you know, Eli."

It starts innocently enough.

The familiar static and chatter of the morning news spills into my home. Sometimes I wonder why Langville, Montana doesn't have its own local news program.

Before I remember why I settled down in the middle of nowhere in the first place.

Nothing happens here. It's a blessing and a curse.

My home smells like dust and mold. The smells common to all those widowers out there left unable to fend for themselves.

I fell asleep in my chair again.

The all too cheery tones of the KLEZ-TV's news anchors—their smiling, ruby lips, their lush, Hollywood perfect hair, their expensive clothes—bore me.

I crave a thrill.

I crave excitement.

And I don't particularly care where it comes from anymore.

I pry my aging body from my chair and drag myself into my cluttered kitchen, dancing around dishes and pots with beans and rice combinations that are days and weeks old.

The smell. I'm accustomed to it.

Briefly, I think about how much easier things would be if I'd just clean up.

But the thought is insurmountable. An overwhelming weight.

I kick the Lazy Susan open and grab the can of coffee from the top shelf. I dump a mountain of grinds into the coffee maker and fill it with water from the sink.

While the coffee's brewing—the smell, slowly combating the stench I've come to fester in—I shuffle into the den and turn on my computer.

It's an old box of a thing, with a white, dust covered keyboard. The serial number on the back is mostly scratched up, but when I got the thing, I could make out the year 1993 printed on it.

A dial-up connection screeches and chirps through my home.

Black-green bands flicker across my screen.

I smack the monitor and call it a piece of junk to get it to stop.

The forums are active today. Most of us are Montana locals, spread out from different towns. We spend our time talking about the things no one else will mention in polite conversation.

How strange it can feel living in the middle of nowhere, with nothing more than the hum of my aging TV set and the Milky Way drifting quietly over our sleepy little mountain town.

Lots of posts about people claiming to have seen strange lights in the sky, weird shapes roaming the Montana wilderness. I often tell myself most of them are probably full of it as I lie awake in my bed, afraid of the shapes that might come crawling past my window.

I never used to believe in this mumbo jumbo. Before I retired, I was a respected paleontologist. A real bone hunter. Archaeology was a hobby of mine, too, thanks to my late wife.

Usually, when I visit these forums, I'm just reading post after post about UFO abductions and how the government's gonna turn us all into mindless zombies.

I don't believe in that crap, but I've always been a fan of a good ghost story.

But...

This visit to the forums is different.

TRAVELING SALESMAN, OR MAN IN BLACK?

The title of the thread caught my eye.

I tell myself it's okay.

It's daytime.

The shadows can't hurt me.

Like an addict, I click on it.

The post reads: *I saw a man in a black suit walk up to my neighbor's house today. The weird thing is the guy was just standing in front of the door. Like, for hours. I went back into my kitchen to make myself a midnight snack and sat down to watch the monster movie marathon on KLEZ-TV. But when I walked by the window, the guy was still there, talking to my neighbor. When I asked my neighbor why the guy was there, she told me he was trying to sell her a computer of all things. For those of you who don't live in Langville, we don't even have DSL. She told him she didn't need one and wasn't interested. He claimed the computer would open up her mind to the universe of all things.*

I asked her what she thought of it, and she just shrugged.

I thought it was weird, but I went on with my week.

Last night, I saw him again. Or someone just like him. It was midnight, and he was standing in front of her next-door neighbor's house. Same suit. Same weird, stiff posture.

And here's the weirdest thing. I saw his car parked across the street, and I kid you not, it looked like it came right out of the 1930s.

I guess I'll have to ask my other neighbor about this tomorrow. I'll update when I get the chance.

End post.

The replies to the post are all from anonymous users. Most of them claim that the user is a hoaxster trying to "troll" the forum.

A few replies stand out.

Anonymous User: The computers he's offering are mind control devices. Do not buy them from him.

Anonymous User: You saw a MAN IN BLACK. Did your neighbor smell sulfur, did the guy have a hat and no eyebrows? These aliens have a contract with the US Government to let them abduct us out here in the middle of nowhere. They don't care about us, we're just expendable livestock to them.

Anonymous User: Ask your neighbor if they got anal probed.

Anonymous User: Ha. Ha. Real original.

Anonymous User: Have you seen the Yellow Sign?

The coffee pot goes off.

I've had enough forum time for now.

I get up and go to the kitchen. Grab an extra-large mug and pour myself a generous amount and try to shake off the fatigue that's resulted from too many sleepless nights, watching my TV set burning away into the late hours.

I set about doing my daily chores.

I'm in the long process of repairing odds and ends around the house. It's a Rancher, and a lot of the siding has been damaged in the last ten years. We get a lot of snowstorms, so I've only got a short time to finish the repairs before the first big storm of the season hits.

The siding is old, not the UV resistant stuff they just got in at Joe's Hardware last month. The old stuff's hard to find out here. But I manage just fine on my own.

With the tasks for the day done, I wipe my forehead with a rag and make my way back inside. I set my tools down on the old wooden floor and take my clothes off.

The shower somewhat refreshes me before my stomach demands dinner.

I can see the sun setting outside my living room window. The clouds set against the blackened outline of Ch-paa-qn Peak look yellow. For a moment, I feel almost as though something is slithering up my leg.

But when I look away from the sunset, the feeling fades away.

The TV's going on about hell and damnation. Religious programming from some bygone era. Probably an old Billy Graham sermon or something.

Langville loves Billy Graham.

I don't know what I love anymore.

Used to be, I'd spend my days poring over old dinosaur reconstructions from my glory days as a bone hunter. But now, I can't seem to bring myself to do it. Seems like a young man's game now, with all the new data and toys they've been working with.

Besides, the public doesn't seem to care about dinosaurs unless they're trying to eat Jeff Goldblum.

I retreat into the kitchen and grab the one pot that ain't filthy with moldering bits of beans and rice and make more beans and rice.

Dinner is a quiet, lonely thing on a dusty table. I don't even bother adding Tabasco sauce anymore.

No reason to enjoy food if there's no one to share it with.

I can't help but look up at her picture, hanging crooked and collecting dust on my eat-in-kitchen wall.

Used to be, I'd pray before dinner.

Mostly out of habit.

Now I don't see the point.

After dinner, I sit before the TV once again, only to find that paid programming has started.

I sigh, disappointed. And try to enjoy the traffic camera feeds. Most towns, at least the ones near civilization, get infomercials, or home shopping stuff. But not us. We're not important enough. Too remote. Instead, we get camera after camera of traffic views, for hours on end. But traffic is a bit of an oxymoron because there isn't any. Not with barely fifteen hundred residents here. The feeds show nothing but empty roads most of the time, or the odd traveler stopping at the lone gas station off the Interstate.

Soon we won't even be a town, the way things have been going.

Whoever thought that traffic feed thing was a good idea should be shot.

The residents of Langville are like the forgotten children left behind in orphanages all over this great country's cities. Out here, we get the world's hand-me-downs.

Like ghosts stuck on repeat, we argue philosophical points from decades prior, call our neighbors with rotary phones, and listen to the frightening, all-encompassing darkness that permeates the Montana wilderness after the sun sets.

Ironically, as I'm dozing off in my chair, the phone rings.

It's 12:30am.

I groan, rub my eyes, and I drift into the kitchen to pick up the phone.

When I say hello, there's no one there. Just a crackling line.

I sigh and hang the phone up.

The TV's still playing the same boring traffic feeds.

I sit down at the computer and bring up the forum.

My eyes scan over the threads. The others barely register when I see that TRAVELING SALESMAN, OR MAN IN BLACK? has been updated.

The ball and track inside my mouse squeaks and squeals as I coax the cursor over and click on it.

Anonymous User: Update: My neighbor tells me that Apple Picker came back to sell her the computer. Tells me he wouldn't take no for an answer, gives her this sad song and dance about being a traveling salesman. So, y'all, she bought one. Says the kids were jumping for joy in the morning when they woke up to see the box in the living room. But the weirdest thing is, when I asked her how much she paid for the thing, she gets this confused look on her face. Tells me she can't remember paying for anything. Then she runs back into her house to grab her purse, and when she comes back, she's holding a wad of rolled up bills. Says that's all the cash she's had on her since she went to the bank the other day.

I can't stop wondering... If not cash, what did she use to pay for it?

It's been a week since then. I've come back to write this post a bunch of times, but more stuff keeps happening. Now she's telling me her kids are glued to the damn thing like zombies. They won't even touch their video games.

And get this. She tells me her neighbor, the one I told y'all about last time also bought one of them machines. And she says she hasn't seen him leave the house in days.

Anyone else here from Langville, Montana seeing this guy?

Anonymous User: I told you to warn your neighbor about this. Those kids are being mind controlled. No doubt in my mind.

Anonymous User: Don't listen to this hoaxster. They just listened to the late-night radio too much.

Anonymous User: Have you seen the Yellow Sign?

Anonymous User: Bet you there isn't even a Langville, MT. Probably some Yank trying to scare us.

Anonymous User: I'm from Langville, MT. I ain't seen this guy, but I do watch the public access traffic cams every night before I go to bed (I put on the oldies station while I watch. It soothes me, what can I say?). I can count on one hand how many headlights I seen watchin' it in all the years since they started it. But the other night, I seen a car, an old thing like what OP described, driving off the Interstate. I don't know if it's just a coincidence, but I ain't been able to sleep since.

*Anonymous User: Yeah right, if that's true, what's the name of the Interstate, huh? Bet you can't ****ing answer that.*

Anonymous User: WTF, why can't I swear here?

Anonymous User: You should tell your neighbor to check her kids for weird bumps under their skin. My husband got abducted by a UFO and they put a little metal device inside his neck. The doctor had to remove it, but they don't know what it is.

I rub my eyes and check the time.

It's almost 3:00 AM.

I decide that's enough computer time for the night and get up to turn things off.

But when I bend down to turn the knob on my TV set, something catches my eye. Headlights outside my window.

I panic, dropping to my old knees. When I crawl over to the window, I see a fella in a black suit with a fedora approaching an old vehicle. Maybe the same one from the forum post.

When he turns around toward the floodlight coming off my neighbor's house, I get the strangest sensation. Like I recognize him...

Then he gets in the car and drives away.

I'm about to back away from the window, to close the blinds and check every lock in the house when I see my neighbor across the street. Even with an out-of-date prescription, I can tell there's something wrong. He's just standing with the door open, holding a black box with a blank expression on his face.

I manage to get the blinds closed and check all the door locks. I grab my .22 rifle and park my butt in my recliner.

I wake screaming, firing my .22 at the wall.

When I see I'm okay, daylight filtering through the living room blinds, I sigh in relief.

I'm sweating, clutching the .22 close to my chest.

I'm at the computer in seconds.

The screen's flickering black and green again. I slap the side of the box over and over until it starts working right.

Stupid thing. Should have never trusted Peabody's word that it was "like bran' new."

I'm about to jump into the forum when my stomach grumbles.

Next thing I know, I'm in the kitchen making more beans and rice.

The phone rings.

My eyes drift to its surface. Its yellowing plastic. And I begin to shake once more.

I don't want to answer it.

I'm scared. No. I'm terrified of what might be on the other end.

But the next thing I know, I'm standing there in front of it, my hands on the receiver, and I'm picking it up.

I don't remember walking over to it.

I say hello with a shaky voice that'd make my father ashamed to call me his.

"Mr. Jones?" my next-door neighbor says. "I'm your neighbor, Mrs. Johnson."

"Hello, Mrs. Johnson. What can I do for you?"

"Well, first let me say how sorry I am for your loss. We wanted so badly to come and pay our respects when we heard about Linda's passing."

I don't know how to respond to that. So, I don't.

"Anyway...I had a strange question for you."

"Shoot."

"We heard a loud bang this morning, like a gunshot. And that got us thinking about something that happened recently."

"Yeah. I'm sorry. I was cleaning my .22 this morning and I forgot to check the barrel. Put a hole in my ceiling."

Mrs. Johnson's quiet for a moment. I don't think she believes me.

"Anyway. A couple nights ago, we had a visitor. A salesman, Jerry thinks. He showed up at our door in the middle of the night and just kept knocking. Wouldn't stop till we answered the door. When Jerry answered, the man just stared at him. Personally, I would have slammed the door in his face, the fella smelled something awful. Like he'd rolled around in spoiled oranges or something. You ever smelled a spoiled orange? Smells like death itself, I tell you."

I'm nodding, repeating "Uh huh" over and over again, but I'm shaking something fierce, and my knees feel like they're gonna buckle.

"Anyway. Jerry was finally about to close the damn door in his face when the man starts mumbling, trying to sell him a new computer of all things. In his own way, he says it's the fastest one ever made, that it'll change his life. Jerry tells him he ain't interested a thousand times, I swear, but the salesman ain't havin' it."

"He didn't buy it, did he?"

She's quiet for a second. "He bought one just to shut him up."

"Can I talk to Jerry?"

"That's the thing. Ordinarily, I wouldn't call like this. Jerry's old fashioned, don't like me talkin' to other men. But since he bought that damn thing, all he does is sit in front of it. Even when it ain't on."

"What's…" I swallow the lump that's been festering in my throat. "What's on the screen?"

"I ain't looked too hard. I never believed in watching or playing with those things when a good book'll do just fine for entertainment. Rot your brains, that's what I always said they'd do. Course Jerry loves his television set, despite how I feel about it. Maybe I'm worrying for nothing. You know men and their toys."

"Mrs. Johnson. Can you go check on your husband, and tell me what's on the screen?"

"I suppose I can do that. One moment. I'll be right back."

I hear a click, most likely from the receiver being placed on Mrs. Johnson's kitchen counter. I hear muffled sounds in the background. I can't quite make them out over the phone. Sounds like Mrs. Johnson's voice.

Minutes pass. Many of them.

I'm about to hang up when she comes back to the phone.

"Hello?" I ask.

"Hello," Mrs. Johnson says. "Who is this?"

"It's your neighbor, Eli Jones."

"Did you call here for a reason, Mr. Jones?"

"You called me."

She's quiet, sighing in what I can only presume is frustration.

"Now I don't rightly appreciate you trying to scare me," she says.

I'm afraid she's gonna hang up, so I just come out and say it. "Ma'am, I asked you to check on your husband, to tell me what was on his computer screen."

"We don't own one of those infernal contraptions, and we never will. Don't call here again!"

The phone clicks.

I'm wondering what's wrong with Mrs. Johnson's memory, trying not to allow my imagination to run wild.

I grab my beans and rice and take a seat at my computer again.

I see the topic's updated, and I can't help but forget all about Mrs. Johnson's memory problems as I catch myself up.

Anonymous User: I'm a resident of Langville, MT. And I just saw that guy you described. He was walking away from Charles' house, wore a black suit and a fedora, and I swear he drove a car right out of the 1930s. I was scared ****less. All I wanted to do was close my blinds and check my door locks, but then I noticed Charles standing in his doorway. He was holding a black box, just staring like nobody was home.

I managed to get the blinds closed and made sure my house was locked up tight. I grabbed my rifle, and I sat in the living room, damn sure I wasn't gonna sleep.

But I did sleep. Holy hell, I did.

I don't remember when exactly it happened. My head still feels fuzzy. But I remember I had a terrible nightmare. I was in this city made of glass, with black domes, under a ghost white sky peppered with what I can only describe as black stars.

Everywhere I went, I felt like I was being watched...like I was being hunted or something.

Those glass buildings made my head hurt. I've done lots of repairs to my house over the years, seen the seven wonders of the world with my own eyes, and I've never seen buildings like this. The way they twisted in on themselves... Yet, I was afraid to look at my feet.

I could feel something slithering up my leg.

When I finally found the courage to look down, I was yanked right off my feet. I screamed and screamed and screamed as I was dragged toward a black dome in the distance. The closer I got to it, the slower everything felt. I thought I could see glass reflecting on the edges of the thing as it drew near. It looked like it was made to resemble one of those fun house mirrors you see on TV.

No matter how hard I screamed, my voice didn't carry.

The...things wrapping around my feet. They were long, writhing, twisting shapes. I didn't have the heart to look at them for too long.

Finally, after the skin on my back was totally stripped, the black dome encompassed my entire field of view.

I had this feeling, like being plunged into the ocean. A burning, seething pain in my lungs that felt like it would never end.

I was drowning.

Silica filling the empty spaces in my bones.

My body went stiff, and I had no further need to breathe. The pain finally subsided. And I was glad.

Finally, I was a fossil.

All I could see was a yellow light.

And it was drawing closer.

Getting bigger.

Until I could make out its details.

The shapes that twisted around my legs flowed all the way back to the figure. At first, I thought it was wearing some kind of yellow cloak. It seemed to be moving on what I can only describe to you as black and yellow snakes.

Those snakelike shapes all funneled up into a mask, capped by a crown of withered spikes.

When it stared at me, I felt like it knew me. Like it had always known me.

I couldn't scream anymore.

I couldn't move.

I could only stare at the mask as it drew upon me. I noticed, as I stared, that it must have been made from some kind of stone. Ancient, as though it was older than the Earth itself. Cracks seemed to form and seal themselves up.

Moments stretching beyond Earth's entire cosmic history.

It had two black pits for eyes. No mouth. No nose. But as it drew closer, I could see it breathing.

Through tiny, ageless holes, I could see them opening and closing. Like pores. As if it were made of something rock hard, yet simultaneously alive.

I felt like I was having a stroke.

A strange thing for a fossil.

It came so close it swelled to the size of a house.

It bent down and pierced my soul.

And I stared into its blackened pits.

And I saw no humanity in its eyes.

If it even had eyes.

I realized I had my .22 in hand and I took aim down the iron sights right between those black pits and I pulled the damn trigger…only to realize I'd put a hole in my ceiling.

I'm sitting here shaking.

Staring at the last few lines…

I can't believe what I've read.
I don't remember the dream.
I don't remember the mask.
And I...
My seat is wet.
I'm sweating, and I'm shaking, and I've just peed myself.
The post is clearly mine. But I don't remember writing it.

I've been up for days.

It's dark. I'm not sure when the sun went down.

The TV is still running in the background. I don't know what's playing. Part of me doesn't want to know.

I haven't been able to tear my eyes off the computer.

The screen has shorted out three times today...but it seems to be working fine now.

I've been looking up information on the Men in Black on the forum. There's lots of posts about them with links to other websites.

Apparently, they smell like sulfur, or brimstone, and they always appear wearing older formal wear. Suits and fedoras right out of an old gangster movie. The cars are always old, too.

Their mannerisms aren't normal. They can behave like robots. The simplest things can fascinate them, such as a pen or a paperweight.

The websites tell me they've been around since the Roswell crash in the Sixties.

The reports are always threatening, but never fatal.

I don't take much comfort in that.

A few details don't quite match up with their description, but at this point, I'm not sure what else to believe.

I keep checking the forum to see if there's an update to TRAVELING SALESMAN, OR MAN IN BLACK?

My eyes feel heavy.

It's started snowing.

I never finished repairing the siding.

It doesn't feel like it matters now, for some reason.

Sleep pulls at my eyelids.

I refresh the screen one last time before I head for my recliner.

My eyes open wide.

The post has updated!

I open it.

Anonymous User:

Update: False alarm. Everything is fine. We are all fine. Sorry to scare all of you.

I can't believe what I'm reading.

It reminds me of how Mrs. Johnson acted when she came back to the phone.

Anonymous User: Told you it was a hoaxster.

Anonymous User: They got to him.

Anonymous User: How do you know it's a him? Maybe it's a woman?

Anonymous User: She has found the Yellow Sign.

My eyes hover over that last reply.

I scroll up. There were several other replies just like it after the original post and updates, only, they were asking if the original poster had *seen* the Yellow Sign...

At first, I thought it was someone making a crude joke, but now?

All I can think of is the post I made. The nightmare I can't remember.

And that strange feeling I had when I stared at the salesman's face...

A part deep inside of me claws its way to the surface.

I think about the way the morning light filtered off the dust in the air.

Her eyes open. Staring at nothing.

Her chest, completely still.

No.

I swore I would never relive that day or the long, torturous months that preceded it.

I distract myself by asking the forum where I might find more information about the Yellow Sign. Someone tells me to use this new thing called a search engine, so I do.

I get a bunch of links to some writers named Ambrose Bierce and Robert W. Chambers. Some websites telling me to download their books.

I don't see the point.

Linda was absolutely obsessed with them. She'd read those stories over and over again and then tell me about all the minute details.

Especially The Yellow Sign.

A few websites mention a guy named H.P. Lovecraft and Aleister Crowley. The site claims they were in communion with dark forces when they wrote their works.

Another claims those same people made deals with the devil himself for forbidden knowledge.

Another changes the details to aliens instead.

One page in particular stands out to me.

It's a blog, made by someone that calls herself Yellow Sign Seeker 49. Years of posts run together...like someone opened their skull and let the contents pour out.

Yellow Sign Seeker49:
1/24/97

The King in Yellow is capable of exerting His will upon those who have seen the Yellow Sign. His emissaries reach out across the lands of this world, spreading His influence.

Those that interact with these emissaries, and are gifted the Yellow Sign, do not live long.

Or, at least, that is how the story goes.

It is easy to write off the King in Yellow as fiction. The personification of the loss of innocence, the spreading corruption of death, and forbidden knowledge.

But all fictions have a basis in fact, do they not?

Or at the very least, they draw from our collective unconscious and the nightmares that fester in the depths of it.

Some have called me crazy for my obsession with the King in Yellow. The first time I read Robert W. Chambers' work, I must admit I was captivated. Mesmerized even.

I did not find the work scary in the least, but something at the back of my mind felt like I had heard of a similar figure in mythology. And I set out to discover if that feeling held any merit.

The ancient Egyptians for example, held the belief that the skin of their gods was yellow, or gold. They used gold extensively in their tombs. Rome follows them in this trend, as their gods are often represented as having golden skin.

It might surprise you, dear reader, to find out that I've partaken in many archaeological digs. I can't say much more than that, as it could cost me my career.

But my travels and studies have offered me a unique vision of our world.

My colleagues in the archaeological and academic community would never understand this unique obsession.

They do not share my perspective.

I doubt even my husband would understand.

Yellow Sign Seeker49:
3/17/98

In my research, I have found many similarities between The King in Yellow's attributes and those of ancient myth. Indeed, He has many similarities with the Olympian god of wine, pleasure, agriculture, and of course, madness and wild frenzy, Dionysus.

I would be a fool not to mention the various gods of death such as Hades and Anubis, or the god of fear and panic in Greek mythology, Phobos.

I have long held the belief that many of the deities of the ancient world, and perhaps many in the modern one, are simply new names for much older beings.

Things beyond our comprehension.

In the time of the renaissance, a newly uncovered account describes a particularly harrowing event witnessed by Catholic clergymen who were charged with preventing peasants infected with the black death from entering their cathedral. These clergymen described strange, limping figures roaming about their walls. Figures who wore the garb and personal artifacts of plague *doctors whose bodies had been added to the death pits outside their cathedral mere hours earlier.*

Many townships during the 17th century vanished in those days under what I would call mysterious circumstances. Stories that are quite like the account summarized above.

My colleagues disagree, of course. The plague doctor is a common figure in renaissance history.

However, they have not seen what I have seen.

I have scoured the world for its forbidden histories.

Books that were once thought to be pure fiction.

Such as the Kitab Aljini, otherwise known as the Arabic Book of the Djinn. *It is a pre-Islamic text, one that carries strict penalties for those who read it.*

At first, I thought the man who sold it to me was referring to the book's banned status. But I was gravely mistaken.

The book describes the hierarchy of Djinn. Many of them appear to the author as snakes or lizards and are considered to be mortal, like humans.

Most pre-Islamic Arabs believed that the majority of Djinn were mortal beings with incredible power. However, other scholars have noted that the only distinction between the Djinn and other gods of the time was the fact that they were worshipped in private.

Once the Islamic religion began to take hold of the Arab world, however, they were re-written to be subject to Allah's judgment just like humankind.

But the Kitab Aljini tells a different tale. That the Djinn are the servants of greater forces. Kings. And those kings inform the nature of the Djinn and their duties.

One of the book's entries described one such king, a being who lives beyond the throne of Earth. An evil force that siphons the very life and soul of our world to sustain itself and its king.

Al'asfar.

The Yellow One.

Or, perhaps, put more aptly, the Yellow King.

It tells of many civilizations that have fallen thanks to His influence.

In my visions, I have seen these places turned inside out by His spreading corruption. Their peoples rotting from within, their souls snatched up and devoured by His great, insatiable hunger.

I believe these visions aren't just dreams, but the collective unconscious of the human spirit trying to tell me something important.

The King in Yellow is real.

My colleagues might balk at this notion. They might call for me to be committed, even threatening behind my back to alert my husband to the poor condition of my mental faculties.

But He IS real.

Yellow Sign Seeker49:
10/10/99

His influence dates back even further in history than that of Rome, all the way back to Sumer and into the depths of unrecorded history, those mad oral traditions that spoke of a primordial world, ruled by beings from on high.

From the stars.

Upon reflection, I cannot help but notice that He shares many similarities with Nergal, the Mesopotamian ruler of the underworld. Or, in other terms, the god of inflicted death.

Perhaps there is some connection between the days of the black plague and the cult of Nergal, which is thought to have survived the Sumerian Empire?

Outbreaks of the black death have been recorded in 541, 1347, and 1894 CE. But it's entirely possible that this illness dates back much further, perhaps reaching into the depths of prehistory.

Though I once thought the various printings of the Necronomicon as nothing more than Satanic fluff written for gullible teens, its pages do mention how the Yellow King and the realm of Hastur feed off of our living realms. The eerie similarity to the description found in the Kitab Aljini has given me pause to reconsider that notion.

Perhaps the authors of these two works, separated by hundreds of years, were touched by some other force?

Perhaps the same can be said of Robert W. Chambers, Giger, Crowley, and Lovecraft?

All these men died under what I would certainly consider mysterious circumstances.

Lovecraft famously suffered in silence from stomach cancer. A rot from within.

Chambers died after receiving intestinal surgery three days prior, though I could find no record of the procedure.

Crowley succumbed to what his personal attendants swore was Chronic Bronchitis. But the texts of his attending physicians tell a different tale. The man was coughing up a strange black substance. Something they swore moved with a will of its own.

The Kitab Aljini describes something quite similar to this in its pages. That the blood of the living is replaced with His blood so that the newly risen servant may be guided by His hand.

In previous posts, I have talked about the eerie similarity between the symptoms described in that forbidden text and how people described the black death in the 14th and 17th centuries. It is true that much of those outbreaks can be attributed to Yersinia pestis, a bacterium that is often transmitted by fleas. Despite what my detractors say, I am not trying to claim that the black death as a whole was some form of black magic.

I am a woman of science first.

The symptoms are quite uniform: Fever, chills, weakness, and headache. Before long, the infection spreads to the lymph nodes, and they swell. These are called "buboes."

If the illness is left untreated, the patient will likely die of sepsis. The illness can also take different forms depending on where Y. pestis is introduced into the body.

Since Bubonic plague, or the black death, is caused by a bacterium, antibiotics are quite effective at treating it.

But something I found curious about reports in crude medical journals from the 17th century is that not all descriptions for symptoms of this illness were uniform.

Some carried additional *symptoms.*

Such as the graying of skin, the growth of bulging tumorous masses on the body, and the vomiting of a foul-smelling black substance.

In fact, the illness still exists to this day but is largely confined to rural areas here in the United States.

Curious. Isn't it?

It makes me wonder if the cases we find here in my homeland are all indeed caused by Yersinia pestis...

Or something else.

More research is needed.

Yellow Sign Seeker49:
11/13/99

Looking over cases of Bubonic plague in the United States has revealed some intriguing parallels. Most of the confirmed cases do happen in rural areas but are stopped easily with antibiotics.

However, through cross-referencing symptoms, I've noticed something strange.

And it's connected to an alarming number of ghost towns in this country.

Ardmore, South Dakota was founded in 1889 and was a frequent stop for steam trains. The local creek was too acidic for human consumption, so the town became a popular stop for those trains to refuel at the creek and drop off fresh water for citizens to drink.

The invention of the combustion engine made the steam locomotive a thing of the past, and Ardmore's population dwindled.

All that remains of the town are decaying buildings.

Officially, the town's population all left for greener pastures. However, last week I was contacted by a person who works for the Bureau of Land Management with information regarding many so-called ghost towns just like Ardmore.

My source would like to remain anonymous.

But he has provided me with a large package of information regarding various ghost towns much like Ardmore.

Concerning Ardmore, the package contains many newspaper clippings, journals, and the diaries of several of the town's last remaining residents that detail the town's decline.

The journals tell of a suspected outbreak of plague. Many of the entries speak of strange dreams, the most common one being of a place with a white sky filled with black stars. These entries always seem to precede ones detailing plague symptoms.

The symptoms are familiar as well, beginning with graying skin and a gradual degradation in motor function and mental faculties.

The final symptom before death appears to have been the vomiting of black viscous fluid.

Moving on from Ardmore. A headline from Cairo, Illinois reads: "The Black Death Returns?" The article itself speaks of familiar symptoms.

Similar artifacts in the package came from Garnet, Montana, and Thistle, Utah.

To me, this is a clear pattern. But I must gather more evidence.

I must see for myself.

Yellow Sign Seeker49:
1/13/00

My dreams have been strange since beginning this research.

My husband worries about my health. Keeps insisting that I refrain from traveling for work.

As if I could resist the call.

The invitation to participate in what could become the most historic dig of our time.

I will not be left out of this discovery. Not after all of my hard work. Not after I have sought so long for someone who believes as I do.

I will travel to Thistle, Utah.

Yellow Sign Seeker49:
1/24/00

I've found it.

It was late. The only time when we would be able to conduct our investigation without interruption.

My colleague was waiting for me in a beat up 1984 Toyota Camry off the side of Highway 89. Moonlight caressed his raggedy clothes.

The ghost town of Thistle, Utah, is buried in a watery grave. From the road, under the watchful eye of a gibbous moon, I could see telephone poles and wooden rooftops poking above the surface.

I asked my anonymous friend what we could possibly do to search the area. He smiled. Pointed toward the water.

It was clear he didn't want us to speak. I couldn't help but think about the house I saw off the side of the road, not far from this small ruin. In these dried out hills the faintest sounds travel miles uninterrupted.

My colleague led me to the trunk of his car, where he was keeping a set of scuba diving gear.

In the dark, I remember him pointing at me.

It was for me to do.

And only me.

When I was suited up, he led me to the water's edge.

He stood there and watched, stiff as a board, as I dove beneath the surface.

The town of Thistle was founded in 1883. It was a mining settlement. By all accounts, it should have remained a flourishing ranching community.

In 1984, a mere hundred years after the town's founding, one of the most expensive landslides in US history dammed two creeks and flooded the town.

But is that the whole story?

I wondered, dear reader.

My suit was equipped with a light, but it did little to illuminate my surroundings.

I remember seeing a pair of rotted baby shoes floating by me in the black, and wondering how many were able to get out before the town was completely submerged.

After a time, though, my eyes seemed to adjust. And, perhaps only because of the moon's brilliance, I was able to see the ghostly outlines of the submerged buildings in the dark.

I don't remember how I found the path.

Even with the moon as my guide, something else seemed to be leading me forward.

I remember a great void of light. A tunnel, perhaps. The moon's faint glow vanished, and my light gave little indication of where I was.

At times, I wondered if my air would run out down there.

My eyes played tricks on me. Sometimes, I swore I could see eels writhing just beyond my peripheral vision.

It felt like hours passed before I caught the faintest glimmer of metal.

A golden gleaming thing in the dark.

Somehow, I knew.

I just knew.

I cradled what felt like a small chest in my arms and retreated.

My air was nearly depleted by the time I emerged from the blackened deep of lake Thistle.

My colleague and his car were gone.

I told myself he must have gotten spooked by the landowner and hurried to get back into my own clothes.

I got in my car, and I made the long drive home.

Yellow Sign Seeker49:
1/25/00

I used a pair of bolt cutters to get inside the chest.

The contents were surprisingly dry.

Inside, I found a leatherbound notebook and a small black and gold trinket with a symbol I don't recognize engraved in its surface.

Whoever wrote the journal had a somewhat uneasy hand, but its contents are a revelation if true!

The journal's author, one Noah Anderson, spends many entries talking about a traveling merchant. These entries range from 1977 to 1982, and the penmanship seems to degrade over time.

Noah believed wholeheartedly that this stranger was a snake oil salesman. The man is described as wearing a black suit, with a black tie. He would only come at night.

The item this man seemed to be offering was an oil that could be added to soil or feed. The claim being that it would double the size of any crop or livestock that consumed it.

The ranching community in Thistle was apparently unenthused by this. Save for one man, Joe Jensen. To him it was a bona fide get-rich-quick scheme, a once-in-a-lifetime opportunity he could not pass up. Joe bought as many of the black vials as he could from the salesman and immediately began adding the stuff to the food supply his livestock would graze on.

Instead of growing twice the size of his competition, however, his cattle and chickens grew sick.

The symptoms should be familiar to you, dear reader.

Graying skin.

Slowed vitals and motor functions.

And black, viscous vomit.

Noah describes waking in the dead of night from the screams of his neighbor. When he peered out his bedroom window, he saw Joe Jensen yelling at the salesman.

Noah claims that the stranger in the suit and tie said nothing as Joe let him have a piece of his mind.

At least, until Joe Jensen ran out of steam.

Noah remembers the only words spoken by the salesman that night.

"Have you seen the Yellow Sign?"

They haunt the remainder of the man's feverish entries until the town's demise in 1983.

By the summer of 1978, Joe Jensen had to sell his ranch. But the new owners would not find success with their livestock. No, they too would wake in the dead of night to strange sounds coming from their stables and fields. To the sight of cattle vomiting black rivers into the Earth.

Until that fateful day in 1983, when the Earth shook and the waters devoured the town of Thistle, the ranch changed hands at least five times.

From 1978 to 1983, Noah grows increasingly certain that whatever sickness is coming out of the livestock in Thistle, is still inside the Earth. He claims that the black substance is festering, growing, weeding its way into the shallow cracks and crevices of the land.

Noah's entries reach a fever pitch in early 1983. He confesses to breaking into a home, scouring, and scrounging in the owner's things.

And he finds a black and gold talisman. The same one in the chest. A round object with a strange symbol in the middle. I have sketched it in my diary, but something tells me I should not allow you to see it, dear reader.

I've attempted to cross reference the symbol with all of the known languages, and it doesn't seem to match any of them.

I don't remember being lost in its curves and lines…

Yellow Sign Seeker49:
6/13/00

> *Dear reader, my career appears to be at an end.*
> *My husband is none the wiser.*
> *But through email correspondence with those few who will still openly talk to me, I've been told my reputation is in tatters now.*
> *Someone told them.*
> *Told them I was obsessed. Mad even!*
> *I am an outcast.*
> *Only you, dear reader, understand me now.*
> *My experiences from Thistle, Utah have not left me.*

Yellow Sign Seeker49:
6/14/00

> *I will not stop my work.*
> *And I'm certain I'm onto something big here.*
> *None of the news reports I dug up from 1983 mention the famine and sickness in Thistle. Not one.*
> *I believe they wanted to keep it quiet.*
> *To let the true cause for the landslide that claimed the town remain shrouded in secrecy.*
> *But to this day, geologists are left scratching their heads as to the cause of the landslide.*
> *We know the truth, though.*
> *Don't we, dear reader?*

Yellow Sign Seeker49:
7/13/00

> *My home of Montana is no stranger to ghost towns. Places that were once bustling with human life, many of whose populations vanished overnight.*

I can't help but think about those medieval plague towns I discovered in my earlier research. The sickened livestock of Thistle.

The black vomit in Cairo, in Ardmore, and Garnet.

How eerily similar they all are.

The Internet has opened up a new avenue for research.

I've been seeing rumors about strange men in suits visiting small towns all across the northernmost parts of the country.

According to the rumors, their suits are often old, covered in grime and rot, and they are reported to be seen driving older cars, some as old as the Model T.

The reports suggest these strangers come knocking door to door in the dead of night.

People telling these so-called tall tales remember being compelled to plug their noses at the presence of an awful odor accompanying these individuals.

The smell of death itself.

I can't help but be reminded of Noah's words and of the countless medical journals provided by my now silent anonymous source.

The smell of rot. Of death and decay.

And once again I turn to the **Book of the Djinn** *and its description of the Yellow One.*

I can't help but wonder as I caress my precious talisman. As I hold it close to my heart.

Could the Yellow King and the realm of Hastur be one and the same? Could they be feeding off of our world, like some kind of cancerous thing, existing outside of our known dimensions?

I do not know.

Yellow Sign Seeker49:
10/13/00

I feel weak today.

The cough is getting worse.

My husband thinks it's just a cold that's overstayed its welcome. But I know better.

Death itself flows from my mouth.

My time is running out.

Dear reader, I must travel one last time.

I have to find more evidence. I have to prove my theory true!

Though my anonymous source will not return my emails or calls, I believe I have the perfect destination in mind.

I've already bought my train tickets.

I leave tomorrow.

Yellow Sign Seeker49:
11/13/00

My journey cost me my legs. I'm now confined to my wheelchair. My husband has been seeing to my needs well enough, and he's insisted I stay away from my work.

The doctors can't figure out what's wrong with me.

My husband thinks it's just old age and too many excavations spent on my hands and knees finally catching up with me.

He tells me I'm retired. That I've been retired for years.

I do not believe him.

I must tell you about my trip before he returns from the hardware store.

My journey took me out to Centralia, Pennsylvania. A ghost town with a unique story.

The tour guide was unaware of my previous work in academia and insisted I stay with the group.

Damn these men for thinking I'm so frail!

But I found a way to give them the slip when we got near the old mineshaft.

My departure went unnoticed, and I sank into the mine's depths.

I traveled its long, burned-out tunnels and down its rickety old ladders.

The mine is supposed to be off limits to tourists due to structural instability in the wake of the fire.

Those who frequent ghost towns will remember the story of Centralia well. A town once home to over two-thousand people suffered a horrific accident when one of its mine shafts caught fire. The fire produced temperatures in excess of one-thousand degrees Fahrenheit and left the air toxic and unsafe for residents.

To this day, the origins of the fire are unknown.

Until now. At least.

In the depths of the mine shaft, where the fire appeared to start, I found something intensely familiar to me.

A black and gold medallion, with a strange curvilinear hieroglyph etched in the center.

Though the carrier of the Yellow Sign had changed, it was unmistakable to me what had happened to the mining town.

A fate similar to Thistle, Utah. Yes.

Now, it makes all too much sense to me.

The scattered reports from residents of a strange man in a black suit and fedora knocking on their doors in the dead of night. Reports that have all been discredited by mainstream news outlets.

Even now, as I hold the Yellow Signs in my hand, I can feel it.

The sickness that has taken hold of me is no mere cold.

My husband will soon be a widower.

And I will go to the grave clutching these gifts from the stars.

They are mine alone.

MINE!

I stare in disbelief at what I've read.

Why did she never tell me about this obsession?

My memory is clear. Her many departures and returns. How she smelled of dust and decay, her voice and body losing more and more of its strength with each passing day.

How she kept to herself most hours of the day, toiling away on her computer or poring over decades-old research notes.

My eyes track to the back hallway, tracing the shadows to the foot of her office door.

I wonder what I might find if I look through her things.

My body feels like it's got a mind of its own.

Next thing I know, I'm at the precipice of the hallway, gazing into its shadows.

How they twist and wrap and point to the doorway.

Creaks and pops echo through the house.

My heart strums in my chest.

The cool touch of metal on my skin sends a jolt through me as I twist the doorknob.

And I open my wife's office door for the first time in weeks.

Her desk and filing cabinets are all covered in white sheets. The other side of the room has become my emergency water storage. Crystal blue jugs of water are stacked up in the closet.

I take one step into her space.

It feels like I'm trespassing.

She never liked me interrupting her work.

Trembling fingers grasp the sheet over her desk.

I take a deep breath and pull.

The thing is just as she left it.

I don't even know how long it's been now. The march of time feels so…strange.

A cruel nightmare that I will soon wake from.

My Linda will come walking through that door with a scowl painted on her face, ready to chastise me for digging in her things.

But that's not going to happen now.

Linda's dead.

Worms crawling in and out of her eyes.

My eyes focus on her computer. I run my fingers over the cracks in the screen.

I can still remember it.

The screams.

I'm watching a program on the new Tyrannosaurus reconstructions when I hear her. I get up from my chair and ran as fast as this old body will allow. I find her smashing the thing with a hammer.

Struggling to keep her wheelchair from rolling backward, to hold the hammer upright. The curses that flew from her mouth are a distant memory.

I see them.

Like flashes in my mind's eye.

Blackened spittle flying with each frenzied swing of the hammer. With every scream.

Draping off her lips like frayed curtains.

I never saw what was on the screen. The thing that drove her to it.

I shake my head. Rub my eyes.

Right. The filing cabinets.

I'm on my knees poring through them. She had cabinets stacked on top of each other, all full of research notes, diaries from her travels, and photographs she took while on site.

I can't stop staring at one of the photographs. A trinket resting on a table with five other artifacts.

I can still remember the estate lawyer running through her documents, finding out that she'd had them redone without my knowledge.

The only change: she wanted to be buried with two golden trinkets. Each with the same, familiar hieroglyph.

Its curvilinear shapes, twisting and twisting like snakes.

The rest of my search is a blur.

At the end of it, I come back to myself. Sitting in the middle of a room holding a thick, crudely bound bundle of papers and notes.

The cover reads in bold scratchy letters: KITAB ALJINI.

I can hardly contain myself. My dread, totally eclipsed by a sudden, burning need.

There are sticky notes protruding from the papers. I pull at one.

And open it to a page.

It's Linda's translation.

> *Al'asfar.*
> ~~*The Yellow One.*~~
> *The Yellow King.*

The entry is hard to read. Linda's notes are all over the place, the earliest markings are clear, but the last ones…they resemble her handwriting right up until that fateful morning.

One of the translations reads:

> The Yellow ~~One~~ King commands his ~~emissaries~~ vessels from his ~~throne home~~ world. Across the divide ~~between~~ inside stars and dreams.

He reaches, offering gifts to the chosen.
The Chosen are reborn. They belong to The Yellow King. They
spread His will, His gifts.
Glorious is the Yellow ~~Sigil~~ Sign. Glorious is His gaze.
This world will be for the taking, for the feeding of His throne.
Through Him, we die. Through Him we are reborn. Through Him,
our enemies whither.

I slam the book closed and toss it away. The pages tear and scatter from their loose binding.

My eyes find an illustration made by my wife's own hand.

And I can't look away.

Most of the page is black, but at its center is a thing with a mask and horns like a crown, and from that crown flows the familiar, twisting form of snakes.

As my eyes follow their twisting arcing forms, I notice that some of them end wrapped around other shapes. Human silhouettes.

What did you get yourself into, Linda?

I'm at the computer again. My fingers hovering over the keyboard. I can't bring myself to write the post, to tell everyone what I've found.

After all, who would believe me?

My eyes drift to my eat-in-kitchen, to Linda's crooked picture on the wall.

Why did I let her go so far astray?

Why did I never ask what she was doing up late all those nights, typing away in her office?

Why was I so stubborn in my belief that she would recover from her illness?

Even when I saw the crawling black residue on the toilet seat.

How it oozed from her lips the day of the wake.

Clawing for life.

A sound echoes through my home. A groaning thing that seems almost alien to me by the time it reaches my ears.

My hands cradle my head.

It's my voice. I'm in pain.

I struggle from my seat, limping into the kitchen, tossing empty and expired pill bottles from the medicine cabinet.

I take two pain killers with freezing water from the sink.

I rub my eyes again.

When I open them, I'm staring at the yellowing plastic of the phone.

My thoughts drift back to the phone call with my neighbor. Her complaints about the salesman's stench.

The rivers of ichor that flowed from *her* lips.

The many nights spent alone in bed.

Eyes always fixed on the windows.

The shadows.

Knowing something was out there.

Feeling His gaze.

I find myself at the windows, shaking with fear as I peer through closed blinds at my snow-covered street. My neighbors' homes.

At this hour, the street should be dark.

Not tonight.

Their living rooms burn away with eerie yellow light.

I move into my bedroom to get another look.

I can see something through the cracks in the fence. That same sickly yellow. It bleeds across acres and acres. Spread across Langville like a lattice of decay and rot.

The kitchen is similar. The neighbors behind me are on over an acre of land. I'd have to go over the fence into their yard to check…

I look at the back door. The doorknob.

I'm too scared. I can't bring myself to do it.

I take a deep breath.

I tell myself it's okay.

That I should just go to bed.

I've been up long enough.

I'm just being paranoid.

My wife died of natural causes. That's what the doctor said. He swore through blackened, rotting teeth.

There is no King in Yellow.

There is no King in Yellow.

There is no King in Yellow.

Three knocks rap at my door.

My heart stops.

I check the time.

It's 12:30AM.

The same time I saw the figure standing in front of my neighbor's door...

The knocking.

It echoes through the house, bouncing off the walls like nothing I've ever heard.

Strangely, part of me feels compelled to move toward the door.

My weight presses on the floorboards with each careful step. Each and every squeak and crack and pop in them makes me want to scream.

Makes my heart pound and ache and writhe.

My hand presses up against the door. It doesn't ease my shaking. My eye peers through the peephole.

And I see him.

He's exactly as I remember him being the other night. Wearing a black suit and a fedora and... His skin...beneath his hat, it looks so pale...

It's almost wet in its appearance. I can't make out any other features other than his chin, but I spot black veins creeping up his neck.

In the fish-eye lens of the peephole, I can see that his puffy, pale hands are wrapped around a black box with no clear markings.

And...just as it did the other night when he turned into the light, the sensation strikes.

Familiarity.

Somewhere before I have seen those puffy, pale, engorged features.

I almost lose my composure when his closed fist reaches up to the door.

The knocking sounds vibrate within my eye socket.

I breathe a sigh of relief when his fist goes back to his side.

He doesn't know I'm here.

It's only my imagination.

He stands there for a long time, repeating the motions again and again.

I swear to myself I'll never answer the door.

I check my watch repeatedly.

The hours tick on, until at last, 3:00AM comes around and I...

My eyes...

They drift down to the doorknob.

My hands feel like they've been grabbed, or wrapped up in something...

Ropes or...or *snakes!*

And I watch in horror as they move to touch the doorknob.

I whimper, and I hyperventilate, and I scream for it to stop when I feel the brush of cold metal against my skin.

The doorknob twists...

And it twists...

I wake up to the sounds of the Emergency Broadcast System screaming through my house.

The text scroll at the bottom tells me it isn't a test.

A blizzard is headed our way.

They urge Langville and neighboring communities to find shelter.

I rub my eyes, cursing my nightmares.

Cursing my obsession...

My eyes lock on my computer in the corner of the living room, sitting on the sagging picnic table Linda picked out so many years ago.

Only, it's not my computer.

It's black, gold, and brand new.

The life of a retired Paleontologist is never glamourous.

On my social security and my savings, I'd never be able to afford something like that.

I can't help but think about the stranger. The salesman from my nightmare last night.

Was it really a dream?

I don't even remember falling asleep.

The computer.

I decide I won't turn it on.

I won't—

The TV shuts off, silencing the emergency tones. The light switches won't work either.

Power might be out for the whole town.

I find myself at the blinds.

I open them.

My window's completely buried in snow.

They weren't lying…

Next thing I know, I've got a flashlight in my mouth and I'm rummaging through my cupboards, assessing my situation.

I've only got a few cans of beans left, and my rice is running low.

My freezer's practically empty. The refrigerator is even worse…smells like something died in there.

Since Linda's passing, I haven't had the will to leave the house. To replenish.

I'm at the sink next, twisting the handles.

The pipes are totally frozen.

I remember the water jugs in Linda's office.

I move to the back of the house, ignoring the sight of the black and yellow machine in my living room as best I can.

When I get to the back room, the one that used to be Linda's office, my heart jumps into my throat.

The jugs…they're all…black.

I approach slowly, shining my flashlight through them.

It looks like some kind of liquid. Something thick.

Memories come flooding back. Flashes I'd long since pushed to the deepest, darkest parts of my aging mind.

The lights off. Linda sitting at the dinner table beneath her picture. Crying. In the dark, silhouetted saliva hangs from her lips like strings.

Her eyes glisten in the dark as I move closer.

The bowl on the table. The strands, silhouettes, whatever they are, all flow into it.

Like rivers.

She tells me not to turn on the lights.

Against my better judgment, I open one of the jugs.

I reel back, gagging at the smell before I slam the cap back down on the jug.

Five gallons of water. All ruined.

Somehow, I doubt boiling it will do much good.

Okay, I'm trying not to panic.

I've got next to no food. No water.

And the power's out…

My eyes drift to the scattered pages on the floor, the images of the symbol and the trinkets she took to her grave.

I wonder if this is the rot she warned of. His influence.

Is there any escape?

It's then I hear it.

At first, I think I've finally lost my marbles.

It sounds like some kind of music.

The same few off-key notes.

Repeating over and over and over.

And it's coming from my living room.

I check the light switch nearest to me.

Nope. Power's still out.

I move toward the door.

The flashlight flickers.

I give it a few smacks. The flickering stops and I move into the hallway.

And then it dies.

I'm left in the dark.

I try not to think about the fact the whole house is buried in snow. That I'm all alone.

The sound...that eerie music...like a chorus of violins and dead men echoing through the ninth circle of hell.

I don't want to move.

Not in the dark.

Not with that music permeating every inch of my house.

Then, as if in reply to my thoughts, I see a dim yellow light cascade through my house, emanating from my living room.

It's the same light I thought I saw in the windows across the street.

Just like in my nightmare, my legs move with a will of their own.

Slowly.

Each footstep sending creaking, bending sounds through the whole of the house. Alerting whoever is in there with me that I am coming.

When I emerge from the hallway, I see it at last.

The box burning with that familiar, sickly yellow light.

And on the screen, that portal to hell. Something familiar at its center.

A symbol.

That eons old hieroglyph.

The Yellow Sign.

A gift from the space behind stars and dreams.

I can't stop myself. It's as if some other force has taken hold of my legs.

I am a puppet.

And He is the puppeteer, pulling on blackened membranous strings.

I'm hyperventilating.

Watching the screen grow larger and larger.

My eyes dart from my recliner to my TV, to the kitchen, to the front door, hunting for anything I might use to free myself.

Putrid yellow light gleams off of my .22 rifle.

It's lying next to my chair.

I can't think of a way I might reach it.

I do the only thing that makes sense to me.

I still seem to be able to use my arms, so I throw my weight forward until I fall flat on my gut.

Splinters stab into my flesh as He pulls tight on the strings.

My hands scrape and dig into the floorboards.

I pull myself toward my .22.

But the more I pull, the further it seems to be from me, as if the floor is a desert. Longer still.

It feels hopeless.

I should give up.

If He is what took her, then at least we will be together.

But then I remember the salesman. I remember his puffy face and the awful smell wafting from his dirty suit. And I wonder if that's what I'm going to become.

If that is what *she* became.

I glance back at the machine.

It's almost upon me.

I can feel His snakes tightening around my ankles, squeezing the life out of them.

Twisting and pulling and yanking.

My legs hang on nothing, draped before the Yellow Sign's hungry light.

I don't want to go!

Desperation burns my lungs as I scream. With bloody fingers I scrape, and I claw once more at the floorboards. My hands gush, leaving great crimson streaks across the floor.

Every time I gain ground, He pulls me back.

A never-ending tug of war.

Until I feel like I can finally reach the stock of my .22.

With bloody hands I reach for it, stretching, stretching, stretching.

But still He pulls.

Still the rifle remains out of reach.

My body tells me to give up.

Slowly, I watch myself drift across the floor. The scattered, bloody trails leading across its impossible length.

I watch the rifle fall further and further away.

I feel my feet go first.

Like being plunged into the same tar pits that claimed so many of the dinosaurs I've spent my life digging up.

I don't dare look back.

Something tells me if I do, I might never be the same again. Just like Mrs. Johnson and her husband and…Linda.

All I can do is sob rivers of blackened blood.

I cry for Langville, my neighbors, and…my wife.

My rivers of tears join His snakes, His strings. My legs are swallowed up whole. As my torso sinks into the depths of an impossible ocean.

Yellow light burns at my eyes, and I scream.

I scream because I can see the screen—that hellish portal to Carcosa—eating me alive.

My bloody hands clutch the black edges of the machine.

A new, fearful strength fills my tired muscles and I hold on for dear life as He plunges my head into the black.

Into the dark.

The ocean is not cold or hot. Its alien sensation equalizes, until it feels as though my body has no beginning and no end.

Minutes stretch on for eons and slowly my lack of air becomes apparent.

I'm going to die!

I'm going to die and it's all I can do to hold on to the outside.

Memory surges within me.

I remember the salesman at my door.

Again and again, he comes.

Every time I tell him to go away.

Every time he drones on and on about the Yellow Sign. About the machine that will make the stars right.

And every time I notice the thing draped from his neck.

And I rack my mind as to where I've seen him before.

Where I have seen the Yellow Sign.

Then, I remember. It's the same one my Linda insisted she be buried with.

Surely, I would remember someone hanging around Linda's grave?

I cannot tear my eyes from the trinket around the stranger's putrid neck.

My rage intensifies.

How dare this man steal from my dead wife!

I finally snap, and I claw for it, struggling with the stranger. His grip is slippery, his whole body is covered in rancid slime.

His mouth opens, and he bares rotted, blackened teeth at me.

Inside his mouth, I can see black things twisting and writhing. Snakes. Just like the ones I saw comprising the yellow figure in my nightmare.

The Yellow King.

I remember reaching for the trinket and snapping it off.

Then laughter.

Sickening, wheezing laughter. As if the man's lungs are full of puss.

And I look into his eyes as his mouth closes.

A lipstick-stained smile twisting.

Cracking, decaying flesh.

My Linda's milky stare.

And then, she drifts away.

Stiff as a board standing at the end of the walkway in the dark.

I can't see her legs move.

But I see the yellow light burning away from my neighbor's windows.

Like lamps in the dead of night.

I remember picking myself up off my floor and chasing after her. Calling her name. My bare feet sink in the snow as I wander aimlessly. Relentlessly searching Langville's snow covered streets like those few dinosaurs who survived the asteroid to find their lands covered in ash and their skies on fire.

House after house after house with that same evil yellow light in their windows.

The storm ridden sky writhing above.

I suspect there isn't a single house in Langville that's dark. Not a one without an infernal gateway to Carcosa.

His Yellow Sign burning away, pulling them all in.

A feast for a King.

I remember waking up the next morning, not remembering the salesman. My Linda's decaying, rotting face. Not remembering the trinket, burning in my hands as I rest against my wall, unable to look away as I trace its curves and lines.

As I lose myself in the Yellow Sign.

I open my eyes in the black.

I can see a yellow light in the distance. Just like in my nightmare.

I'm about to let go.

She's here after all.

Won't Carcosa be better with her?

When I remember Linda's face. Not as she was in the suit she insisted she be buried in…but as she was when I found her.

I wake up to the sight of sunlight leaking through the blinds. I crawl out of bed, making coffee, bacon and eggs. Chewy and over hard respectively, just the way she likes 'em.

I bring the tray into the room and call her name.

Only, she doesn't answer.

The tray falls from my hands.

I pull the covers away only to see she stopped breathing in the night.

Blackened rivers oozing from her mouth.

Just like that. She's gone.

And I'm alone.

The doctor says it had to be pneumonia of some kind. Though, he doesn't sound so sure.

I should be happy to die.

I should be happy to join her.

But then I remember her rotted, milky gaze.

How I tore after her into the night.

How I called into the abyss.

How she didn't answer.

As I look into His blackened stare.

I realize the truth. I will never see her again.

I belong to Him.

In Him I will cease to be, rotting away as my body is forced to wander this world, spreading His influence.

A new panic seizes upon me.

And I do not release my grip.

I pull like I've never pulled before.

I drag myself out of that blackened pit gasping for stale, moldy air, and I claw my way across my bloody floor naked as the day I was born.

And I reach, one last time for my .22.

And I grab the stock.

And I take aim.

And I fire.

And at last, I'm left in the dark.

I lay there, clutching my rifle for days. Waiting in the dark for the death that comes from within.

But it never comes.

Eventually, I get the bright idea to find my flashlight and look at the remains of the machine. It's in bits and pieces. Inside I see something gleaming black and gold. A thing just like the trinket I snatched from Linda's cold, dead neck.

The sight renews a panic in me and I move without thinking.

I run to the front door, and I pull it open.

An avalanche of snow fills my doorway, but the cold biting at my naked body does not deter me.

I scrape and I dig, and I tunnel until the flesh tears from my fingers.

But eventually, I find my way out.

Above the snow, above the houses, the town of Langville is no more.

The moon tracks overhead, through the Milky Way.

And I follow it.

I follow it for days and nights on end.

But even as I leave Langville behind, I always feel Him watching.

I always know the King in Yellow is one step behind me.

Once He knows you, there is no escape.

One day I will die and go to live forever trapped in Carcosa. Forever in the thrall of Hastur. Forever to be devoured by the Yellow One.

Time: 07:20:45

I note that Subject 1601's mouth is hanging open, his eyes focusing on Doctor Livingston's swinging watch.

Hands writhing. Grasping.

"Eli? Are you okay?" Doctor Livingston asks.

Subject 1601 does not answer. He cannot look away from the watch.

"Doctor Eli Jones. Please answer the question."

The subject's limbs have become rigid. A choking, gurgling sound echoes from his lips.

His eyes open.

The lights flicker.

And the words that spill forth from his lips have the quality of a disembodied voice. They fill the Interview chamber as if his mouth is the conveyance for some otherworldly device.

A speaker from beyond the stars.

"*I have seen the Yellow Sign,*" he says.

The subject grabs for the watch.

"*You will give it to me!*"

The chains rattle. Doctor Livingston backs away, screaming.

"*Give it to me!*"

The orderlies step forward, ready with sedatives. I hold my hand up, telling them to stop.

I want to see where this is going.

When he is denied the watch, Subject 1601 grows frustrated, screaming and yanking at his chains. Strip by strip, he tears his coveralls from his body, and beneath, his flesh is covered in blackened veins that stretch and snake from his neck to his feet.

"A rot from within…a rot from within!"

I'm surprised, Subject 1601 appears to be looking at me through the two way mirror.

"Have you seen the Yellow Sign?"

Subject 1601 falls face first on the concrete floor, where his vitals flat line.

After Subject 1601's death, we sent teams of agents to survey the Montana wilderness, where he claimed the small town was located.

Despite months of searching, we could find no sign of a town North of Interstate 90. Even when the snow was finally washed away from the mountain and its surrounding foothills, all we could find were empty forests and plains.

Tests on the mysterious substance that flowed from Subject 1601's mouth could not be conducted, as the corpse of 1601 and our samples vanished, as if they were pulled through cracks opened up in the fabric of physical reality.

Even with our resources and access to top-secret information, we could find nothing to indicate that the town of Langville, Montana ever existed.

END TRANSCRIPT

The Feller in Yeller

An Old Mill, NC story featuring Cletus J. Diggs

By David Niall Wilson

One

Randy Hemphill ran the only sheep farm in Perquimans County, North Carolina, and there was a reason. There wasn't much of a market for mutton near Old Mill, where his farm was located. He didn't have enough sheep to provide wool to make a mitten. There was, in fact, no simple way to make a business out of his sheep, other than sending a few to county fairs or lending them out to petting zoos. Randy didn't care. His sheep were neither for sale, nor loan.

His family had owned the land he lived on since British governors had overseen the state. They had always had sheep, because that was what they'd raised across the pond, but thankfully for Randy, that was only a tiny part of the operation, and the rest of it was profitable beyond reason. There were a lot of poor families in the county. There were a few rich families as well. Then there was old money. The Hemphills were old money, and if Randy wanted to raise sheep as pets, nothing was preventing it.

It wasn't like that, though. Not really.

Near the center of the property, surrounded by fields sown with soybeans and corn, cotton and potatoes, was a grove of trees. You had to go deep into the Hemphill property to find it, and all that land was posted, fenced, and protected.

The grove hadn't always been there. Once the family had staked their claim and begun building their new world fortune, they also began importing things from the old country. A ship with a cargo of soil. Carefully packed and preserved saplings and cuttings from trees. Stones and some small idols. All delivered discreetly. All handled only by the closest family members. The grove was deeply rooted, strange, and absolutely did not belong within a country mile of Old Mill, North Carolina. Yet, there it was.

There was a small cottage just beyond the grove. Despite his wealth, Randy Hemphill wasn't directly involved in the day-to-day affairs of the family or their business. He had pulled back, slowly, once his father had died, preferring to spend as much time as possible near the grove, tending the small flock of sheep. Randy and his father, Ethan, had been close, and the grove had been their shared passion, as it had been for all the generations of their family, before and after setting sail for the new country.

The rest of those who lived in the area, though, he had little use for. His grandmother, Elspeth, was the eldest. She oversaw much of the day-to-day business, but her interests lay deeper, and darker. She approved of Randy's tending to the grove because there had to be someone doing it, and it had to be a Hemphill. There were reasons. Randy both agreed and disagreed with those reasons, depending on which family member's perspective they were viewed through.

There was an arched gate at the grove's entrance. It was formed of wrought iron, and among the intricate designs at its peak it was possible to make out the name Haita. It was written in English because Randy had never been to the old country. He was generations past his family's emigration. He'd had it translated. He knew the family secrets and he had studied the lore.

He tended the sheep, watched them in a field on a rolling hill just beyond the grove and drove them back to their pen at night. They had a warm barn and plenty to eat. There was a dog, a grey and white border collie named Ambrose—Bro for short—who helped keep them in line.

But none of that was important. In the evening, Randy sat back in his Adirondack chair, a cold beer open on the wooden table he kept on the porch, and he watched. The only light was provided by a single candle in an iron lantern that hung from a hook beside the table. Towns and roads were far distant; only the grove had a voice, and it spoke in the tongues of whispering leaves and chittering insects.

Before he sat down each evening, he went to a small altar beside the porch, carefully constructed of rocks gathered from the banks of the nearby Perquimans River. Each night he left a small cup of wine, a bouquet of flowers gathered from the fields, a coin, and a small tuft of fleece from one of the sheep, gathered that same day. He knelt in the soft grass beside that altar, but he didn't pray. Old Mill, the closest town to his farm and his grove, was lined with so many churches it was hard to believe the population could sustain them. He had seen and participated briefly in the act of prayer, and it left him empty.

Instead, he talked to the altar as if it were a deity, listening intently. He told it about the flock, the day's work, the crops. He shared his genuine love of his work. In the morning, the offering shifted to small handfuls of grain from the sheep's pen. Randy was a very patient man. Bro came and lay patiently at his side as he spoke, ears perked as if he heard, and understood.

The night everything changed, the two were just rising from the altar when something flickered at the edge of the grove. Randy turned slowly, fighting the urge to run to the trees, and watched. The second time he saw the motion in the trees, it was clearer, like a flash of white cloth trailing behind a slowly moving form. He stood and he waited, but that was it. He thought he might have seen a dim light, deep in the grove, but he couldn't be sure.

Bro whined. His ears tilted forward, but he didn't leave Randy's side. Then, as if something had shifted, or disappeared, the dog sat, thumped his tail, and grew silent. Randy stared at the trees for a long time, and then, without a sound, turned and returned to his chair. He pulled a beer out of the cooler and popped the top.

"Guess it's near, boy," he said softly.

Bro woofed lightly in response. Randy glanced down at the dog and narrowed his eyes. The sense the animal understood him had never been so strong. He lifted the beer and tipped it toward Bro, who only watched, tongue lolling and eyes bright.

Two

"I seen it, Cletus," Jasper said. "Wasn't just Bubba this time. Aliens, some sort of government hoo ha, whatever. There was something strange as hell happening out across them fields."

Cletus J. Diggs glanced up from his desk, where he'd been reworking an article for the *Globe* about a three-headed goat that had been born out by Raccoon Creek—and lived. The owner, a guy named Simmons, said he was raising it to guard against things crossing the river. Something about faces in the waves. The old guy was as crazy as a fruit bat, but it was just the kind of story the *Globe*'s clientele loved. The goat was named Cerberus.

"I'm going to need a bit more than that, Jaz," he said. "Something strange hardly differentiates Tuesday from Friday around here. Exactly what kind of strange are we talking? Giant grasshoppers? Flocks of birds falling dead from the sky? Talking Alpacas?"

Before he answered, Jasper glanced down to the floor beside the desk, where Cletus' constant companion Dog was listening intently. "You might want to reconsider calling that last one strange, all things considered," he said.

Cletus laughed. He leaned over and scratched Dog between the ears. It had been a little over a year since they'd met, Dog wandering in from the road and sitting down like he owned the place, but Jasper wasn't wrong. Cletus wasn't sure how he felt about it, but he and Dog had bonded well beyond man and best friend. His friend, Donovan, had called the animal his "familiar," and that sounded right, but at the same time like something out of a weird fantasy book Cletus would never have read. If he hadn't seen and experienced all the things he had over the past few years he'd have dismissed it and said Dog was just really smart, but that tractor had turned down a different field.

"Fair enough. So, what happened? You've seen some things yourself, so I guess when you say it's weird, I better listen."

"It's that Hemphill place," Jasper said. "The fields on the other side butt up against Lenny McMullan's place. Nothing but soybeans in there this year, so you can see clean through to that weird little forest way out in the middle.

"I ran into Lenny at the Cotton Gin the other night. Thought we might play some pool, but when I sat down, he didn't even look up. You know me, can't let a loose thread hang, so I poked him on the shoulder. He looked up, but not like he was scared, or mad, more like I woke him up.

"Asked him what was wrong, and he just started talking. Not to me, though. He was staring at his drink, and I'm pretty sure if I'd walked away, he'd have gone right on telling his story to nobody, or maybe someone I couldn't see."

"That doesn't sound like Lenny," Cletus said. "He's kind of intense most of the time. Funny, but…"

"Right? That's why I listened."

"That's the first part that threw me," Cletus said. "You were in a conversation but someone else was talking."

"You want to know what he said, or not?" Jasper asked. He didn't wait for an answer.

"At first, he was just talking about the fields, and the trees. Not like a farmer would, but weird shit, like plowing the fertile earth, and curatin' the trees. Like it was some sort of religious thing. That was weird enough, but then he started talking about lights. He saw them in the trees, saw them floating over the trees. He heard whispers, not anything he could understand, but that's when he looked at me."

"Not English," he said. "I could hear it. I knew there were words and they made me feel warm, like I might melt into the ground I was standing on, but I couldn't understand. I couldn't reach them."

"Reach who?" Cletus asked.

"That's the thing," Jasper said. "I asked him that same question, great minds and all, and he said… the sheep."

"So, it *is* about talking alpacas."

"I said sheep."

"Right."

"That wasn't the whole of it, Cletus. He walked out into that field, posting and trespassing be damned. Said he had to. Said they were calling to him."

"The sheep?"

"Nah, the trees. There were things moving in that little grove, dancing in and out of sight. There were lights, but they didn't stay still like a lantern or a flashlight. He walked out into that field, but he stopped, and he watched, because, get this, the trees wouldn't let him in. Said he stood there, tears runnin' down his cheeks, and watched, but there was some sort of wall in the air, something he couldn't cross.

"Then he woke up, but he was still standing. Right there in the double-D goddam field, Cletus. It was morning. He went home, took a shower, and went to work, and then I found him at the Gin. He was afraid to go home. He was still there when I left, and I don't know what happened, but I thought, maybe, you and me might check out that field."

"What if the trees won't let us in?"

"You think it's funny," Jasper said. "You didn't see Lenny. I don't want to go to those trees. I got me another idea, though. Funny you mentioned Bubba. Saw him at the Gin too, and he has a new toy. Says he's going to use it to watch for alien landings. Got him one of them drones with the hi-res camera, good for a couple of miles."

"Bubba must have hit the lottery then," Cletus said. "Those aren't cheap—at least the ones that actually work."

"I asked him if he was up for a little practice with it, and he's all in. Seems he didn't really think through how to aim that camera up where the aliens would be and was having a hard time figuring out where to scan for abductions."

"Thinking isn't his strong suit."

Cletus glanced down at Dog, who was watching them curiously. "What do *you* think?"

Dog gave a short woof, rose slowly, and stretched the full length of his body, then headed for the door.

"Guess that's that, then," Cletus said. "We can swing by and pick up Bubba and be out to Lenny's before sunset. He know you're doing this?"

Jasper nodded. "Even if we don't find anything, he'll be glad to see us. Never seen that guy so spooked. I mean, he's built like a tank."

"Let's just hope he didn't go back into that field between then and now. If what he told you was true, he could be standing there, might have been ever since. And that wall he ran into? That sounds too much like what happened with Donovan and that bird of his last year. Feller can put protection like that around a bunch of trees isn't someone to mess with."

They walked out into the drive. Jasper stopped for a minute and stared up at the old plantation house directly across from Cletus' trailer. It sported freshly painted wrap-around porch shutters, a new roof, and still you couldn't help but feel the age, and the strange aura it exuded.

"Still don't know why you don't' stay in there," Jasper said, glancing back at the trailer. "Sure, it's spooky, but man! And that bar…"

"You try going to bed in 2024 and waking up in 1962 a couple of times and see how restful it is," Cletus said. "I spend plenty of time in that library, and I go there when I need a bottle of something different, but that is Donovan's place, and I'm just happy to share the real estate. Hell of a lot better than the end of that dirt road."

Jasper glanced wistfully up at the old home, shook his head, and turned toward his truck.

"I'll follow you into town," Cletus said. "Meet you at the Quick Stop and we can call Bubba from there."

Jasper gave a sloppy salute, and the two climbed into separate trucks, Dog hopping up to ride shotgun with Cletus. The sun had just started to dip toward the trees, and the sun was bright and warm. Perfect night for a drone-surveillance of a haunted forest. At least, that's how it seemed to Cletus.

He turned his truck and followed Jasper out toward Highway 17, shaking his head. Dog stared at the road ahead and let out another soft woof!

Three

Randy had just finished his ritual at the small altar when Bro let out a short bark and stood up, staring into the trees. Or through them? There was something in the air, something Randy couldn't quite put his finger on. He followed Bro's gaze and was certain he saw something white flash between two of the trees.

"What is it boy?" he asked.

He stood and turned, moving toward the grove, and as he did a woman stepped into sight. She wasn't dressed like anyone from Old Mill. She wasn't dressed like anyone from 2024 for that matter. She wore a long flowing white dress. He couldn't be certain, but she didn't seem to be wearing shoes. Her hair was long and dark and glistened as it spilled over her shoulders. Her eyes, though, captured his gaze and held it without effort.

Randy didn't speak. He stepped closer as the woman came fully into view. She was beautiful. Her smile danced all the way from her lips to the sparkle in her eyes, and at that moment, the oddest thing happened. The sheep, safely bedded down for the night, bleated softly, all of them, in unison.

At the sound, the woman cocked her head and smiled, and Randy felt his knees grow weak. He started to rise, but at that moment a sudden sound, a whirring vibration, rose. It grew louder and nearer, coming from just above the trees. He glanced up.

A drone circled the grove slowly, spiraling toward the center. Randy returned his gaze to where the woman had stood, but she was gone. It was as if she'd never been there at all. He let out a wail. As he did, the drone passed directly overhead, then turned and shot over the trees and out of sight.

Bro sidled up beside him, confused by the strange sounds. The dog licked his cheek gently, and Randy leaned to the side, hugging him. Then he rose, gave the grove a last, longing look, and turned away, heading to his cottage.

While Bubba worked the controls, steering the drone back toward Lenny's farm, Cletus and Jasper hunched over an iPad, staring at the input from the camera. There were shapes moving in and out of the shadows and wandering among the trees. Some of them were small and white, as if the sheep had broken free and wandered into the grove. It was impossible to make out details through the dense foliage.

As the drone crossed into the small farm, another figure appeared on the screen, but something had interfered with the video. A bright ball of light moved from the trees into Hemphill's—yard? The glowing thing had been vaguely human in appearance, but—again—impossible to make out.

Hemphill had fallen to his knees when it appeared.

"What the hell was that thing?" Jasper said.

"No idea. When the drone was on the way back, there were no sheep, or whatever those were in the trees either. It was all dark. Sort of like someone snuffed something out."

"You think he knows we were watchin'?"

"He knows that someone was. I'd say it would be a good time for us to get the hell out of here. Lenny, you want to stay over at my place? It's a little tight, but I can clear the couch."

"Lenny still stood staring out at the trees. He didn't speak, and it seemed as if he was leaning closer to the field, like he was thinking about walking out there.

"You help Bubba get that drone packed away," Cletus said. "I'll get Lenny.

Jasper nodded. Bubba was already tucking the drone into a large, foam-lined case. Cletus stepped into the field, purposefully not looking at the grove of trees. Whatever it was that had caught hold of Lenny was still out there, and he didn't trust it. He grabbed the big man gently by the elbow and tugged. At first, it didn't seem like Lenny would come, but then Dog nuzzled his leg and pushed. There was a small spark of—something—between Cletus and Dog, and in that moment, Lenny shook his head and took a step backward.

Cletus turned him slowly, and the three made their way back to his truck. Jasper and Bubba were already in Jasper's old Ford with the engine running. A few moments later, both vehicles rolled slowly out the long drive from Lenny's place toward highway 17.

Four

Since there were four of them, and the trailer was small, Cletus led Lenny, Bubba, and Jasper up the steps onto the porch of the old Pope Plantation, and inside. For once, it looked like just what it was, a renovated cotton plantation. Cletus knew it was Donovan's doing, a protection against intrusion. It would fool most of the world, but Cletus had seen it shift. He'd seen the years fall way, had drunk whiskey bottled before the Civil War had ended. He'd walked through the doorway underneath the stairs and found himself in a Brownstone in San Valencez, California. He knew the old place was more than it seemed, but he also trusted it, and his friend, to make it a haven when one was needed.

"You live here now, Cletus?" Lenny asked, glancing around the large foyer, and up the stairs toward the second story. "I thought this place was ready to fall down."

"A rich friend from California bought it," Cletus said. "He has more money than sense, so he had it restored. I'm sort of like, the caretaker. I still live in my trailer for now. Place makes me feel a little weird, after all these years."

Jasper and Bubba went straight into the main sitting room. Bubba put the drone case down on the floor, and Jasper headed for the bar.

Cletus nodded after them, and Lenny followed.

"You look like you could use something," Jasper said. "Bourbon?"

"That's fine," Lenny said. "Whatever."

He took a seat and Jasper brought him an old crystal tumbler with a couple of fingers of dark liquid. He watched as Lenny took a sip, waiting. At first, there was nothing. Then, staring at the glass in his hand, Lenny took another sip and glanced up. "What is this? My god that's smooth."

Jasper grinned. "No idea, but I think it's safe to say it's older than your pa."

Lenny glanced over at Cletus.

"It's fine. One of the perks of being the 'caretaker' is that the bar is always full, always different, and not on my tab. I believe what you are drinking is some of the original Old Crow, back before the guy who invented it died. At least that's the story."

Lenny stared at the drink. He took another sip, closed his eyes, and grinned. "Don't really care, I guess. This is one of the weirdest days of my life already, and this seems like about the best thing that's happened. I mean, what was I doing in that field? What if you hadn't been there?"

"That's what we aim to find out," Cletus said.

Among the antique paintings, tapestries, and odd, old-world lamps hanging on the walls of the old plantation house, there was also a large screen TV mounted on the wall. Cletus picked up a remote and turned it on, fiddling with the inputs.

"Can you connect to that?" he asked Bubba. "From the tablet?"

"Sure," Bubba said. "Turn it on and hand me the remote."

A few moments later the screen came alive with the video feed from the drone. The only sound, at first, was the whirring of the rotor blades. The four men sipped their drinks and watched as the camera drew near to the small grove of trees. There was an odd flicker, almost like someone had applied a filter to the video, but it cleared as the drone passed the outer line of trees and tracked across the treetops.

"What the hell was that?" Jasper asked, pointing to the lower right corner of the screen.

Cletus had seen it too. A glimpse of motion, like a large, pale light, moving through the shadows. Almost immediately there was another on the left, and a third near the center. Whatever they were, they were moving in the same direction as the drone, toward the Hemphill farm.

"I didn't see those before," Bubba said. "In the field, I mean. Just the trees."

As the far side of the grove came into view, a sound rose that managed to overpower the buzzing of the drone. It was rhythmic, like a pulse, or a strange drum, and the closer the drone came to passing over the last of the trees, the more it began to sound like a chant, or a strange song.

Lenny rose from where he'd been sitting, and Jasper only just caught the tumbler he held as his hands released it, preventing a spill.

"What the...?" Jasper fell silent, shooting a glance at Bubba.

"Maybe you outta shut that thing off..."

"Not yet," Cletus said.

One of the light-forms shifting through the grove had solidified. As it passed the tree line a woman came clearly into view. She had long silver hair that trailed into the sparkling light. She wore a white dress and appeared to be barefoot.

Ahead of her, they saw a small cottage, and standing in front of it, moving slowly toward the grove, was Randy Hemphill. He had one arm held out, as if reaching for the woman.

Then there was another sound. There was no explanation for it. The sound of rotors simply died. Very low, very plaintive, and somehow soothing, the sound of sheep lowing floated out from the big screen's speakers. No one in the room breathed. The woman cocked her head to the side, like she was listening, and turned her head toward the pens and the small barn.

Then the rotors roared back to life, and Randy Hemphill glanced up—directly into the camera—as if he saw them. His face was so clear it was impossible to miss the anger, the sense of betrayal, in the man's gaze. The drone spun back toward the grove—and the woman was gone.

The rest of the video was the quick flight back across the trees. The flicker occurred once more at the same point as it shot out over the trees, and Bubba stopped the replay. Jasper took Lenny by the arm and led him gently back to his seat. As the screen went blank, and the room fell silent, Lenny shook his head, took a deep breath, and looked around as if he had no idea where he was.

"I think," Cletus said, "It's about time I went out and had a talk with Randy Hemphill. Probably should've done that from the start instead of sending in that double-D Goddam drone. I don't think he means to be hurting anyone, but whatever he's doing, it's reaching out beyond that grove."

"You think that's a good idea?" Jasper asked. "He didn't look happy when we interrupted…whatever the heck that was. Maybe he won't be happy to see you."

"I don't expect he will, but unless you think we can chase him away from the land his family has owned since what, a hundred years before

Old Mill existed, I don't see an alternate plan. Also, he may be angry, but he may be angry for a good reason. The only harm we've seen, so far, is that whatever is going on out there is affecting his neighbors. It's not like he's going to shoot me."

"If he did," Jasper said, "he has enough money and connections to make you disappear."

"Well fine, Jaz, that makes me feel a hell of a lot better. I'll take Dog. He'll know if something is wrong better than I will."

"Maybe he'll talk to the sheep," Jasper snorted.

Dog, who had followed them in and was curled up by the door, raised his head and looked at Jasper. After a moment, Jasper averted his gaze. Cletus laughed.

"It's okay Jaz, I think he just might, you know? Lenny, you're staying here tonight, and Bubba? I wouldn't play that video for anyone else until we figure out what the double-D goddam hell is going on with it. It didn't affect you, or me, but it sure as heck called out to Lenny, and if it's some sort of thing that can spread, we don't want to be the ones spreading it."

"You going to call Donovan?" Jasper asked.

Cletus shook his head. "I think we're good, for now. He's a busy man, and there's no telling what kind of mess he's already mixed up in."

Jasper glanced at the door under the stairs and shook his head. "I'm going to grab some beer and head back home. Pap will be worried, and it looks like we may be busy again tomorrow. You want me to go with you to Hemphill's?"

"I'll call you after," Cletus said. "At least by then I should know if we have a real problem, and, hopefully what to do about it."

Five

Cletus started out early, dog on the seat beside him, heading for the road into the Hempshill place. It was a long one, and it was posted, but he decided that bridge had already been crossed when the drone entered that space. Worst that was likely to happen was he'd be escorted back out at the wrong end of a shotgun. He'd met Randy a few times, and the man hadn't impressed him as violent, or angry.

The fields on either side of the road grew greener, somehow lusher with each passing minute. The closer they came to that grove out in the center, the less it looked as if they were in North Carolina. Then it happened. The air shimmered. Dog sat up, ears perked, and let out a yip. It lasted only a second, hardly enough time to be certain there had been anything at all, but Cletus knew. It was the same thing that had happened to the drone. What it meant, he had no idea, but on the other side of whatever it was they'd passed through, there was something—a soft buzzing in the back of his head—a tingle running through the hairs on his arms.

Dog glanced up at him. He didn't appear to be upset, but his head canted to one side, as if he was thinking *WTF?* Cletus laughed and concentrated on the road.

"I have no idea," he said, "but I guess we're about to find out."

The way ahead widened. Off to one side of the cottage there was a small, well-kept pen, and beyond that a barn. There were sheep in the pen, and for some reason the sight made Cletus grin.

"How did I not know all of this was here?" he asked Dog. "I mean, I knew he lived here. I knew there were sheep. I could see that grove. I've even made jokes about it, but… this."

Dog woofed softly. Cletus felt the odd tingle of connection between the two of them. There was no fear in Dog's gaze, but Cletus felt a familiar wariness. Something was off. It didn't feel threatening, but it felt so alien that such a judgment could easily be premature without context.

"Guess we stepped in it again," Cletus said. He was almost certain dog grinned at that. "Yeah, yeah, well don't leave it by the door."

When he parked near the cottage, Cletus saw that Randy was seated in a chair out in front, staring off at the grove. He didn't even look up when Cletus cut the engine, stepped out of the truck, and made his way across the lawn. Dog trotted slowly at his heels, scanning the property with his nose in the air. Cletus stopped a few feet away and cleared his throat.

"Morning, Randy," he said. "Hope you don't mind the intrusion. All things considered, I thought it might be best if the two of us had a talk. And I'm sorry about that drone."

Randy didn't look up. His dog, Bro, turned his head. Cletus felt something pass between the animal and Dog and shivered. He sensed no threat.

"She was here," Randy said. His voice was so soft, so quiet it was difficult to make out what he was saying. "I never really believed. Not until I started living out here, you know?"

"Can't say I do," Cletus said, "but if you want to talk about it, I'm game."

"Guess I'd better. I imagine this place brings up some questions."

Cletus glanced around, looked at Randy, and nodded. "Reckon it does. Things just don't grow like this around here. That grove... I don't even know what kind of trees those are, but they look like they might have been here when the snake got us booted out of Eden."

Hemphill laughed. "Older than that story," he said. "Different god, different place. Bigger problem. At least currently."

"Problem?"

"There was a shepherd," Randy said. "So long ago that the place where he lived, and the names of the cities and towns were erased by the centuries. My grandfather told this story once. You ever hear of a writer named Ambrose Bierce?"

"Isn't he the guy with *The Devil's Dictionary*," Cletus asked.

"That's the one. This was a long time before that though. He wrote a story about my ancestor, Haita. He was a shepherd. He lived alone, cared for his flock, and he was very faithful to his god."

"I'm guessin' you don't mean the Old Testament guy."

"I do not. That god's name is Hastur. He was the god of shepherds, among other things. Here's the part I never believed. He was so faithful that, on his request, Hastur turned away a great storm that would have washed over the land. No one knew he'd saved them, but Haita wasn't looking for fame, or fortune. He was human, though."

"Over time, he started to lose focus. He wanted more than just the hill, and the flock. His worship started to fade. That's when he saw her."

"Her?"

Randy nodded toward the grove. "You saw her too, I expect? Assuming you had video?"

"We did, but nothing was clear. Like a bright light, a bunch of lights, really, were moving through the trees. Then one got brighter than the others and left the trees. I saw what looked like a woman then, and that's when you caught us. The minute you quit watching, everything in that grove was just... Hell, it was just trees again. There was nothing."

"She was there," Randy said. "Just like she appeared to Haita so long ago. When he saw her, his world changed. She is the most beautiful woman I've ever seen, and she was coming out. To meet *me*. Just like my father, and my grandfather, and their grandfathers dreamed of. She was there, and then..."

"We ruined it." Cletus said.

"Maybe. Maybe not. There's more to the story. When she appeared to Haita he tried to speak with her. He asked her questions. He wanted to be with her every moment of every day, and every night, and then... she was just gone.

"He returned to his worship, hoping it would help, that he could regain his god's favor and that the woman would return. Eventually, she came back. There are a lot of versions of this story. Some say he tried to own her. Some say he simply smothered her, clung to her as if worshipping her would make her stay. In the end, of course, she left. Or was gone. Or who knows. Maybe he dreamed her into existence. That's what I would have thought, I think, except..."

"Except she was here."

"And you saw her. It couldn't have just been in my mind."

"Maybe she'll come back?" Cletus said.

"Not sure that's a good idea," Randy said. "How about you tell me why you were out there trying to spy on me?"

"You know Lenny McMullan?" Cletus asked. "Owns the farm on the far side of the field, just beyond your grove?"

"I know *of* him."

"How long have those lights been showing up in the grove?" Cletus asked. "I mean, if something changed, when did that happen?"

"There's been something strange about the grove since I was a kid. Probably, there has always been something strange about it. It's only been the last month or so that I started noticing that things were changing. I'm here every night, me, and Bro." He nodded at his dog. "I guess I saw the first light, or shadow, or... something... about two weeks ago."

"Two days ago, Lenny was in his field. He was staring at your grove from the far side. He stood there a long, long time. Said he saw light and heard whispers. This is probably the weirdest part. He said he couldn't reach the sheep, and that the trees were calling to him. When he woke up, or, whatever, he went to the Cotton Gin. That's where Jasper found him."

Randy didn't look up, but he nodded. "I should have thought of that. Should have bought the land farther out, kept people safe. I've been too caught up in this place, in the family 'business,' I guess, to think about anything else. My family has been waiting for what is happening right now for longer than there has been a United States. We've been here a long, long time, Cletus. I reckon your grandpa saw this grove in his time, and I can tell you without any doubt, it looked exactly like this. We brought it from the old country. The soil, cuttings from the trees that were carefully cultivated, even some of the rocks. If Ambrose Bierce had visited this place, he might have recognized it. That altar over there?" He gestured toward the small pile of stones. "That's the same one that Haita worshipped at. It's exactly like the altar that he used to speak directly to Hastur. It's how he found and lost the woman of his dreams."

"All for a woman?" Cletus said, shaking his head. "That doesn't track."

"Not for the family, no. They had bigger goals. They believe the old stories. They believe that Haita's faith prevented a storm from destroying their ancestral home. Unfortunately, that faith trickled down about as well as Reagan's economy. The grove is here, and our family has tended it for all these generations, in the hope of tapping into that connection, communing with a god, and using that power. I believe that is why it's happening now."

"To… give you power?" Cletus said.

"I don't want power. I never did. I want the experience. I want to know that woman. I want to try to be what my ancestor wasn't."

"What?"

"Worthy. I'm afraid, though, I might have missed that boat. I'm glad you came out here, Cletus, because honestly? I'm a little scared."

"Of the woman, or the grove? The lights?"

"Again, nope." Randy reached over to the table beside him and picked up a tablet of some sort. He brought the screen to life, flicked his fingers across it a couple of times, and held it out to Cletus, who took it and glanced at the web page that was open.

The headline was bold, and ominous.

HURRICANE CLARA GAINING STRENGTH

There were a lot of lines and predictions and paths on the page, but the very center of all of them took that storm straight across the Outer Banks and dead on toward Old Mill. Cletus handed the tablet back.

"I have *got* to start paying attention. How long has this been coming?"

"That's the thing," Randy said. "It was just a tropical depression. No one thought it would be much of anything. Then the lights in the grove started growing closer to the altar, and things started getting… stranger. I expect it began growing in strength about the same time your friend Lenny heard that call. Only a couple of days. Government is in a panic, and I'm guessing they'll be starting an evacuation any minute, if they haven't already. You remember back when Isabel hit? That was category one. This one is four and growing, and it's headed straight for us."

"Well…hell. I expect you'll be heading out then?"

Randy shook his head. "It's a test. Haita's faith saved a village from a similar storm many years ago. I have to try to do the same. For all I know, I'm the reason the storm is coming."

"That's crazy talk," Cletus said. "Storms hit here all the time. I mean, they start to hit here, and then they bounce back to sea, but that's geography, not religion. Next thing you'll be trying to pray the chem trails out of the sky or something. You've got no protection out here. Wind from a cat four, or even a cat two could blow you and your grove right out of the state."

"This grove has been here through a lot worse than Isabel, Cletus. I told you. Generations. You get a chance, look up the San Ciríaco Hurricane of 1899. By modern standards that would have registered as a category four, most powerful to hit here. Ever. The grove was here then, and, I know I've said this—it looked exactly as it looks now. Exactly. My great grandfather, Ezekiel, was the member of the family assigned to it that year. When the storm cleared and they made their way back out here, he was… gone. The altar was here, right there where you see it. The grove was here. The cottage he'd lived in had simply disappeared. We rebuilt, and the next generation moved in."

"What did he do?"

"He drank. And he was having an affair with a woman over near where Hertford is now. He kept up the journals, but we found others, a separate set. He never really believed. I'm not blaming him; it's far-fetched, right? Hastur gave him the chance, and he let it slip away. Along with many, many homes and towns and lives. Sometimes I think our family is blessed with… this," Randy waved his arm to encompass the trees, the sheep pen, "and other times I'm convinced it's a curse."

Cletus stared at the trees. Nothing moved. There were no strange lights. "Not sure you can take all that on your shoulders," he said. "It makes a compelling story, but there have always been storms. Your great grandpa may not have been an ideal family member, but I have a hard time blaming him for a hurricane."

"I don't blame him either," Randy said. "I don't believe Hastur sent the storm. I do believe, though, that Haita's faith turned one away. I don't know if Ezekiel could have prevented it, or weakened it, but I *do* know that he could have tried. I know that he chose himself over all the generations of our family, and, whatever else you might think, I can tell you for a fact that things are—*different*—around this place. You can see it in the fields. Where else have you seen plants and flowers like we have out here, and then, just stopping at our border? I don't know how far it reaches, but apparently, it's grown a bit, if it reached McMullan.

"There is power here. In that altar. I'm a rich man, Cletus. I don't think anyone in Old Mill realizes how rich. We've tended the grove, and it has watched over us. The altar, all of it. I could have done anything in the world I wanted to with my life, but I'm happy here. Just me, Bro," he nodded at the dog, "the sheep. It's all so simple, and yet, the most complex pattern I can imagine."

"If you stay here, you're likely to find out that the double-D goddam hurricane doesn't much care," Cletus said. "I'll tell you, believe me or not, I've seen things. I've walked roads people wouldn't believe on a quart of shine. I've managed to walk away, but barely. When gods, or someone wearin' a god disguise, gets involved, it never works out well for us."

Randy smiled. "I sensed something." He glanced over at Dog, who met his gaze. "You and he are connected. I can feel it. So does Bro. Probably why he just let you wander in like you belonged. It's the same with us, and with the sheep, too, I suppose. They listen to me. They react to my emotions. They know that storm is coming, and they aren't afraid. Or, if they are, they are resigned to whatever comes. I feel the same. I believe I'll be fine, no matter what happens, though I can't offer that same to you."

"Reckon Dog and I have our own … protection," Cletus said. "Don't know how my trailer will fare, but that Plantation House? It's not just there, if that makes sense."

"Get your friends in there, then," Randy said.

At that moment, several helicopters flew overhead, passing on toward the Coast Guard base. Both men watched until they were out of sight.

"Reckon they'll be evacuating everything near the coast," Cletus said. "You sure you don't want to come with me? I got plenty of room, and I have a friend I'm pretty sure you'd have a long, very interesting conversation with once this blows over."

"You go," Randy said. "I'm going to spend my time at that altar, taking care of the sheep, walking the grove. There still may be time. Funny thing is, I know I should be scared stiff, but I'm not. I told you; my family has been waiting for what's happening for a very long time. I'm going to see it through. I think maybe I owe it to Haita, and maybe to those folks who died back in 1899, even if it wasn't our fault."

Cletus stood and offered his hand. Randy rose and took it. From the far side of the cottage, the sheep lowed, and it felt like the purring of a giant cat rippling through the ground. There was a spark where their hands touched. Very soft, and painless, but bright and undeniable. Dog let out a soft woof," and Cletus laughed, turning away.

"You know, I think you might be okay here after all."

With dog at his heels, he headed for his truck, already dialing Jasper to have him gather his pap, and Bubba. Then he called Willow White and told her he would pick her up at the Cotton Gin. It was closing and everyone was heading inland.

"Here we go again," Cletus said to Dog. Then he hit the gas, spun the truck in a circle and headed back toward Highway 17.

Six

Randy watched Cletus' truck wind out of sight through the fields and caught the strange flicker as it passed beyond his land. He turned back to the grove. The clouds overhead were already dark, and he knew no tropical storm or hurricane should form that quickly, so near to North Carolina. It wasn't natural, and just for a moment, he felt a chill dance down his spine.

He walked to his cottage and entered, crossing to the mantel above his fireplace. There was a small wooden case there, and he opened it. Inside was a short reed pipe. It was old, preserved by loving care and restored many times over. Randy had been playing it since he was a small child, and as he lifted it free of the case, it felt like an extension of his hands.

Turning back to the door, he returned to his old Adirondack chair, overlooking the altar, and began to play. The song was old, so old it had probably been copied and re-purposed and warped a thousand times. Randy knew it by heart and knew it was pure—the original. He knew where the music had been written down, and where the parchment that held it rested. As always, after a time, the notes shifted away from the original and became his own. He closed his eyes and leaned back, sensing motion in the trees and a strange breeze playing at the hair over his ears. He knew that, beyond the borders of his land, the winds were rising. The sky had grown darker still, but he felt no fear.

When he had played for a while, he slipped the pipe into his pocket and moved toward the pens where the sheep waited. Entering, he walked among them, running his fingers through their fleece, singing softly. He walked to the bins where he kept their feed and dipped out a handful of grain. An offering. He turned and made his way through the flock, exiting through the gate and turning toward the altar once more. Then, he stopped.

In the distance he heard engines. More than one and moving swiftly. Randy frowned. No one ever interrupted him. Could it be police? Had Cletus decided to come back for him?

He turned toward the cottage, glancing at the sky. The clouds blocked out all light, and though he heard nothing near the grove, he saw that the wind had picked up beyond the odd barrier locking him in. He walked to the corner of the cottage and glanced around. A string of solid black SUVs rolled slowly up the road, fighting the wind. Randy watched for only a moment, then turned and went to the altar.

He knelt, sprinkling the grain onto the stone surface. He offered a short, soft prayer in the ancient tongue, and closed his eyes. He had feared this moment—the moment when he would be required to reach out to Hastur, to beg his help. The moment his family would appear to wrest that moment from him. He didn't intend to allow it, but he was not the oldest, or the wisest. Bro lay beside him on soft ground and stared at the altar, as if listening.

Then there was a sudden, grinding noise, a scream, and a crash. It didn't sound as if one of the vehicles had hit something, and the engines didn't grow quiet. Randy cleared his mind and ignored it. Whatever had happened, maybe it would slow them down and give him time. He didn't know how the family planned to control a god, but his prayer this night would be a warning, as well. He heard the sheep lowing, their voices rising to drown some of the intruder's noise, and he closed his eyes.

"Aw hell," Bubba said. "I thought I had it."

Cletus ground the truck to a halt. It shivered in the grip of the wind and rain splattered against the windows. Ahead, like an eerie fishbowl in a field of fog, the Hemphill cottage, and the grove, were clearly visible. Heading in at a slow pace was a small fleet of dark vehicles.

"I'm surprised you got that double-D goddam thing in the air," Cletus said. "I don't think it's rated for hurricanes."

"I know, but if we could've gotten it through that—whatever it is," Bubba pointed at the dome of light ahead, "we might have been able to see what the hell is going on."

"You got their attention," Cletus said, laughing. On the seat beside him, Dog woofed urgently.

Bubba rewound the video on the tablet and hit play. It was hard to tell exactly what was going on at first. The rain was thick, and the drone jerked erratically through the air. The lens was covered with water, and it was dark. It rose a little higher. They got a quick glimpse of the weird energy dome that had cut the cottage off from the world, and the drone dove toward it, losing control, then dipping back on target, only to be caught in another powerful gust. Before Bubba could react, it dived headlong for the road ahead, crashing into the lead vehicle of the small caravan they'd followed off Highway 17.

It was difficult to make out the damage. Blinking red brake lights flashed sideways, then skewed back straight.

"Hell with this," Cletus said. He slammed his foot onto the gas, veered off road into the muddy field, and reached with a practiced hand to shift into four-wheel drive. The truck skewed sideways, slipped in the wind, then the tires gained traction. As Cletus roared around and past the floundering fleet of SUVs, Bubba let out a whoop and raised his fist. It smacked into the truck's ceiling, and he drew it back with a howl.

"You might want to save that enthusiasm," Cletus said, fighting the wheel to get the truck over the curb and back onto the road. The lead vehicle, its windshield shattered, was backing very slowly back on track. Cletus cut them off and roared ahead, passing suddenly through the edge of the strange veil of energy draped over Randy's home. Once inside he hit the brakes, hard. Bubba barely stopped himself from hitting the dashboard.

"What the hell, Cletus?" he said. "You trying to kill me?"

"Get out, Bubba." Cletus said. "Get out and get clear. I'm going to try and keep them out."

Bubba glanced at him, saw his serious expression, and opened the door, leaping out. Before he was even clear, Cletus had thrown the truck into reverse. Dog, who was still on the seat beside him, glanced up curiously.

"I don't know why," Cletus said, "but I think it would be very bad if they get in there and disturb Randy. You better brace yourself, I don't have a dog seatbelt."

Dog stared at him balefully, and Cletus nodded. "I know, I know. You can take care of yourself. Just get ready to jump. My side."

Cletus released the brake and drove backward at full speed.

Seven

Randy cleared his mind. The sounds behind him grew louder, momentarily, and then faded. He felt a sense of calm flowing around him, emanating from the altar, and from the trees. He couldn't hear the sheep, but he felt them, felt the vibration of their combined voices washing over and around him. They seemed to be drawing closer. He risked a glance and saw they had escaped the pen and were marching toward him in a line, eyes bright. Bro gave a soft woof but didn't rise. The sheep showed no sign of needing his guidance.

Randy sensed someone approaching from his other side, as well. He heard nothing, but the air shifted. He caught the scent of flowers, and leaves. He knew she was there but focused on the altar. He was pleased, but he was not at the altar for her, or even for the sheep, though they were all part of it. He reached out to Hastur, offering himself, his breath, his life. Softly, he spoke his version of the words Haita had spoken so long ago, and hoped they had meaning, that they were not part of some fairy tale that never happened... that he was worthy.

"I thank you," he said, "for sheltering me, and my flock, for providing protection against the storms, as you did so long ago for my ancestor. But I am not worthy of protection above the needs of others. The towns and cities, the people will die. I am your servant, but I cannot continue as such if you will not protect them as well."

A hand dropped softly onto his shoulder, and it was all he could do not to turn, not to see her, to speak to her, but he knew. He did not know what the translation of her name would be in the ancient tongue, but she was happiness, fleeting and uncertain. He could not control her, but he might be able to do something more. He was already happy. He was content with his life, with Bro and the sheep and the cottage, and with the grove. If she stayed, that would be a good thing, but he could not allow himself to concentrate on that, or to wish for it.

He felt a wave of something—approval?—wash over and around him. He heard voices calling out behind him. He heard what sounded like gunfire. He trusted Hastur to protect him, to protect the flock. He did not react, and though the sounds grew closer, and he could make out words, and familiar voices, he held his peace. He'd known the family would come. They believed him naïve. They'd groomed him for this position, for this moment, but they'd never been honest about their intent. He'd known for a long time, perhaps insight granted by his proximity to the grove, or his communing with Hastur, what they intended. He knew other things, as well.

Bierce was not the only one to write tales of Hastur, and those other tales weren't pleasant. Most, in fact, balanced out the protection of shepherds, and the rewards of faith, with acts so dark that when he'd tried to read them, he'd been unable to finish. Somehow, he knew there was truth in all of it, that words have power and the inspiration for stories often came from deep places better left untouched. His family, though, believed only in their history, their obsessive recreation of a moment in time, and their greed.

In that moment, all that mattered was proving his faith, and so, though he heard screams and more gunfire, the barking of a dog, and more, he knelt, and he prayed.

Cletus and Dog had cleared the truck, and road, just as their back bumper crashed into the already limping lead vehicle behind them. There were shouts and cries. A few engines revved, but there wasn't time to try and sort it out.

"Let's get in there," Cletus said. He rose, fighting to remain upright in the blasting wind. Dog huddled close, and the two fought their way down the side of the road toward the dome, where they could see Bubba on the other side, trying to see them through the slashing rain.

With a final lunge, Cletus dove into the clear, quiet space beyond the strange veil. As he went, he grabbed Dog by the collar and dragged him along. The two tumbled through, rolling once and rising quickly, stunned by the sudden lack of wind, rain, and sound. Cletus heard the sheep, lowing softly, but he didn't have time to worry about Randy.

"Bubba!" he called out. "Get over here and get away from that wall. I don't know who is out there, but I know they're coming, and I know they're pissed."

Bubba glanced up, just noticing he wasn't alone. He was holding the tablet still, somehow, and he was staring at it intently.

He crossed where the road met the misty veil, and the sudden crash of gunfire broke the silence. Bubba jerked, glanced to his side, and then took off at a run, heading straight for Cletus. As he drew near, Cletus turned and started off toward the cottage and the grove. There was more gunfire, but either those on the other side were not good shots, or something in the veil was throwing off their aim. Nothing even came close.

As they approached the cottage, Bubba slowed, and then stopped. He was staring at the tablet again, his face awash in fear.

"What?" Cletus said. "What are you looking at on that double-D goddam thing? The drone crashed."

Bubba looked up, then he held out the tablet.

"The camera is still live; it's stuck on that first SUV and pointed right at us. Sort of." Bubba glanced toward the grove, where they could see Randy, kneeling at his altar, and the trees beyond. The woman they'd seen stood just behind and to one side of Randy, her hand on his shoulder. She paid no attention to anything but Randy. Cletus followed Bubba's gaze, then glanced down at the tablet.

It was aimed at a cocked angle directly at the grove, and Cletus nearly dropped the tablet when he saw what it displayed. Randy and the woman were there, as they had been when he'd last looked, but the sheep! In their place, lined up and striding slowly toward the road, were tall, robed figures. He couldn't make out their faces, and even when he zoomed in, all he saw were masks. There was a dim, yellow glow surrounding them, like the dust of pollen that coated his truck every spring. Their eyes were hidden, but their attention was unwavering.

And that wasn't all. There was no grove. Instead, the video showed a city, tall and stark, dark streets without life, temples, and strange obelisks, impossibly tall and out of place.

Cletus tore his eyes away and looked hurriedly toward the grove. Nothing had changed, except, the sheep were moving in a slow line toward the road. Randy was very still, kneeling before his altar. Bro lay by his side, silent. The woman rested her hand on Randy's shoulder.

Cletus took a last look at the yellow-backlit city, and his heart filled with a dread he could barely stand.

"We have to get out of the line of fire!" he said. "The sheep… if they're double-D goddam sheep, aren't using their pen. Let's get in there."

Bubba nodded, taking the tablet back, turning, and heading for the cottage and the pen beyond at a run. Cletus and Dog were hot on his heels, and moments later, they closed the gate behind them and slipped into the small barn. There were several stalls inside, and Cletus chose the first. Once they were inside, he closed that gate too, fully aware that it was only about four feet tall and protected them from nothing. Then they sat against one wall, on a bed of straw, and waited.

Eight

Outside, in the storm, the invading troops gave up on their vehicles, hunching over and running for the veil. Not knowing what to expect on the far side, they sprayed random shots through to clear any further resistance. Elspeth Hemphill, heart pounding, shouted orders that had to be repeated down the line to be heard.

"Get inside and form up. We haven't much time."

And they did. Slowly, they bulled their way past the wind and driving rain, dove and rolled and lunged through, and then, finding themselves unnervingly in dry silence, dripping water from soaked uniforms and clothes, they gathered in a ragged line. Some had managed to retain their weapons. Many looked bewildered.

Elspeth, old as she was, took it in stride. She knew her grandson had somehow done what generation upon generation of her family had failed to. She knew he'd reached through to another world, to a power that could change everything. She also knew he would not take advantage of it, and that she had to.

"Gerry!" she called out. "Gerry, get up here."

Most of those she had brought were mercenaries. They'd been paid, briefed, and probably believed they were collecting very fat checks from a madwoman. The only other member of the family who had been available was Gerry, her nephew, and Gerry barely believed in any of it. At least, before tonight. She'd sent emails and texts out to branches of the family, but no one was going to make it through the storm to help, so it all fell to her.

Hastur. While Randy believed, Elspeth yearned. She was old and very aware that she had this one chance, this one in a million-year opportunity to confront a power that might change things. Might make her young, and beautiful. Might give her power. If it could truly be reached… and if it could be controlled. If the research was correct.

Gerry stepped forward, disheveled and wild-eyed. She saw him coming and handed him the gun she'd been carrying. Without a word she swung the pack off her shoulder and gently lowered it to the ground. Then she unzipped it and, almost reverently, pulled out a silk-wrapped object from within. She held it, calming herself, but glanced up sharply when Gerry let out a scream. He was already raising the gun.

"Hold your fire!" she said, rising quickly. "Hold your damned *fire*, Gerry. What are you…?"

She turned and followed his gaze. Elspeth had been to this cottage thousands of times. Short visits, bringing in supplies, visiting with Randy. She knew it as well as she knew her own chambers, back at the larger family mansion that had been her home all the years of her life. What she saw was impossible, and her courage nearly faltered.

The grove was gone. In its place, where the gate that had held the ancient sign with the single word Haita, a road wound off into a city. Not a city that would have fit in the grove, or even the field. It was vast. Towers stretched up into a sky of swirling clouds against a backdrop of ambient, yellow light that seemed to rise from the soaring buildings and the streets below. Groups of hooded figures wandered the streets, and it seemed they might have noticed her as she noticed them.

She was barely able to look away from that place, but she had to know. She turned toward the altar, toward Randy. She could just make him out behind a line of robed figures much like those she saw in the distance, but closer, and darker. One turned its head slightly and she gasped. It seemed for an instant that the thing's face was made of bone, but she saw that it was a mask. The group started slowly forward and Elspeth moved to greet them. As she did so, she let the silk around the object she carried slide softly and silently to the ground, revealing what she carried.

When there were only a few feet remaining between her, and the approaching creatures, she raised her hands and, her voice and hands shaky, said, "Stop."

There was a moment's hesitation. The things shivered, almost flickered out of sight, and strained forward, and then they stopped still. Watching her. Waiting. In her mind, sibilant voices whispered, working their way through leaks and cracks in her thoughts. They all said the same thing. "Take off your mask."

She shook her head and held the stone circle in her hand higher. It had cost millions, endless failures and blackmail, murder, and blind luck to locate the thing she held. They had followed a thousand false leads, paid exorbitant fees to charlatans and, in the end, found what they were after in a remote cave in New England. It was a circular stone amulet, large as a dinner plate, and heavy. There were symbols carved around its outer edge, and inscriptions etched deeply in its center. She felt it hot in her hands, and a deep red luminescence had begun to seep out into the darkness, and down her arms.

The creatures moved backward, very slowly... a single step. They did not remove their gaze from hers, even to glance at the stone she held. Her arms wavered. The weight of the thing seemed to have doubled as the red glow flowed from within. She steeled herself and took a small step forward.

"Bring me your king," she said. Her voice was soft, as if she had no air to push the words forth, but speaking gave her new strength, and she repeated her demand, more loudly... "Bring me your king!"

The line split, forming two columns, and the far end of the path they created between led directly into the city. Far off, a larger group, almost an army, of the things moved slowly outward toward where she stood. Behind them, or maybe in their center, something rose. A litter? What were they called... a *palanquin*? Someone rode in that, alone. Taller than the others, and though it was too far away to be certain, that figure appeared to be robed in a sickly yellow that burned the eyes. Elspeth felt eyes searching, felt that other trying to meet her gaze, and turned back.

"To hell with this," Gerry said from behind her. She glanced at him, saw him raising the barrel of the rifle, and she half turned, trying to call out to him, to break the hold the stone had on her arms and body, weighing her down. Then another voice broke the silence, loud and angry. It was the howl of a dog, but so much more, with a ferocity that chilled Elspeth's heart. As she turned, again, to follow that sound, the weight of the stone over-balanced her, and she tumbled toward the silent line of creatures. As she fell, she screamed. One of the creatures had reached up to grip the upper edge of its mask.

Nine

Cletus nearly jumped out of his skin when the howl rose. It was unearthly, like a wolf or coyote on steroids, loud, and long. Dog's ears pricked, and before Cletus could react, Dog had cleared the gate to the stall and was rushing for the door.

"What the double-D goddam hell?" Cletus said. He sprang to his feet and followed. As he ran, he reached out to Dog, tried to find the connection they shared, to understand. It was there, just out of reach. He caught glimpses. He vaulted over the fence surrounding the pen and glanced toward the road. He heard Bubba chugging up behind him, and he knew the man was calling out for him to wait, but he couldn't stop. Whatever was out there, if Dog was going in, Cletus was going to be there, too.

What he saw made no sense. He saw a group of strangers, the men and women from the SUVs, he supposed. In front of them a woman was toppling to the side. She had a stone in her hand and was encased in a deep red glow. Behind her, a man stood, soaking wet, in a black trench coat. He had a rifle in his hands, aiming it straight ahead... at the sheep. They stood in a group, faced off with the intruders as if they could protect the cottage, and Randy, and the altar.

The grove flickered again, lights moving in and out among the trees. There was something off about it, except, when he looked back at the man with the gun, and saw the trees in his periphery, everything was fine, and he felt a sense of calm. That man's face was a weird etching of terror, like a Halloween mask.

Just as Dog reached the back of the line of sheep, Cletus saw Bro, several yards ahead, launch over the falling woman at the man with the gun. The man saw Bro at the last second, staggered back, firing pointlessly up into the sky, and Bro hit him, hard. Dog was right behind him, and suddenly, the sheep were moving. They followed Bro, and broke into an odd, springing run at the men gathered behind.

For a minute, Cletus was afraid the two dogs would be shot, but those men were glancing at something off in the trees, and at the advancing sheep, and suddenly they dropped their weapons, turned, and fled back down the road. Only the two remained, the man with the gun, and the woman on the ground, struggling to rise.

She made it to her feet, dazed. There was something on the ground, something red, and glowing, but there was no time to think about that. Cletus ran forward, raising his arms and shouting. "Don't shoot. Do *not* shoot!" but there was no one left *to* shoot. Bro had let go of the gunman and circled behind, and two of the sheep followed. The man looked terrified. Cletus couldn't figure out why the guy would be terrified of sheep, but figured maybe he was from the city and just didn't understand.

Bro and Dog moved with the gathered flock, and began, very slowly, herding the woman, and the man, toward the trees. They stumbled, and looked back, but the sheep had formed a solid wall of fleece, marching toward them relentlessly, and they began moving slowly. Cletus passed them by, turned back to look toward the altar and check on Randy, and in that second, the world shifted. He saw the city, and the robed figures. One of them was pulling a mask free of his face, and the woman seemed captured by his gaze. Dog, sensing what he was seeing, shifted, and drove the group to the right, and everything shifted again. He saw the woman and the man he didn't know shuffling off into the trees, the line of sheep closing in behind them, but stopping at the tree line. Bro and Dog stopped directly behind them. Moments later, there was nothing left but the trees, the sheep, and the two dogs.

Bubba caught up then, following Cletus' gaze.

"Where are they going?" he asked.

"I'd like to say into the grove, and they'll be back, but..."

"Yeah," Bubba said.

They turned and walked slowly toward the altar. Randy raised his head then, as if just becoming aware of his surroundings. He rose and turned. Bro trotted over and leaned on his leg, and Randy reached down to scratch his ears.

"What about that?" Bubba asked. He pointed at the circle of stone on the ground.

Cletus glanced at it. Not far away was a backpack, and a large piece of cloth. "I'll get that," he said. "I think we'd better take it home and get it to Donovan. He'll know what to do with it."

Bubba nodded. "Got some killer video."

"You might want to think about it, though. Maybe—at least—some editing. Remember what happened to Lenny in that field? I have the sense that whatever just happened here is over. I don't think you want to be inviting it back."

"Probably right," Bubba said. "And whatever those things were, they weren't aliens…"

"You got that right."

Randy was walking toward them, and Bro had returned to his side. Dog trotted over and leaned on Cletus' leg, much like Bro had done with Randy. There was a jolt of connection, and he leaned down to scratch Dog's head.

"Sorry about my family," Randy said. "I was afraid this might happen."

"Not sure I want to ask you what *did* happen," Cletus said."

"One day," Randy said. "Maybe I'll come visit that magic house of yours."

Cletus looked startled, and Randy laughed. "Sorry. I know about the house because Bro knows about it. Another long story, I think."

"We probably both have a couple," Cletus said. "You going to be okay?"

"Yeah… I think everyone is," Randy said. He pointed toward the road. Cletus and Bubba turned and stared.

Beyond the veils surrounding the small cottage and clearing, the clouds were clearing. The rain had turned into a soft drizzle, and the wind was all but gone. The sky showed patches of black with stars. The storm was all but gone.

"I wouldn't ask too many questions," Randy said. "I'm glad I am here. I'm glad I could help. I don't know what will happen with the rest of my family, but I suspect they will try to shut me down…"

"I don't think so," Cletus said. He turned to Bubba.

"We have some pretty interesting video," he said, "and you have the two of us as witnesses as well. If you have no objection, I'm going to take that thing your—grandmother?—was carrying to a safe place and get it locked away. I think maybe if you play your cards right, and they know what might happen if they disrupt things…"

"You may be right," Randy said. "Elspeth was the worst of them, and I'm pretty certain she's gone. The rest could be convinced to listen to me. I need to be here, though. Maybe you could help me with negotiations and communication?

"I'll do that," Cletus said, "but I'll also bring in a friend of mine. If I can't convince them, I know that he can. And we have Bubba's video."

Randy stepped forward and drew Cletus into a hug. Then he stepped back. "I have the feeling the two of us will be friends." He glanced at Bubba and grinned. "Sorry, *three* of us. There will be time, but for now, I need to tend to the sheep, and get some rest."

"You wouldn't have something we could borrow to drive, would you?" Cletus asked. "I think I planted my truck in the grill of the lead SUV earlier."

"Take any of the others that runs," Randy said. "I own them all, and I'll be getting someone out here to clear away the rest. I guarantee you will not be reading about this in the news."

Cletus grinned. "I won't guarantee the same about the tabloids, but… thank you." He turned to Bubba. "Let's get back and make sure everyone is okay."

Bubba nodded. The two of them turned and, with Dog trotting at their heels, walked down the road and out of the strange, beautiful, terrifying clearing near the grove. As they went, they heard the lowing of the sheep. It was, at the same time, calming and horrifying. They hurried their steps.

Ten

Everyone left the room while Donovan watched the video from Bubba's drone feed. Cletus had seen it once, and decided that was once too many, and Bubba seemed to feel the same way. Jasper had taken one look at Cletus's expression and bowed out. Willow hadn't even pretended she was curious. She was on the porch, staring into the night sky. It didn't take long. It was less than a minute before Donovan turned off the feed and left the room.

"I'm going to need to put that somewhere safe," he said. "There are some visions you can't shake, and there is a very real danger of being... controlled. Your friend Randy appears to have appealed to a benevolent aspect, but I'm familiar with Hastur, at least from research. It's a very rare thing when his attention is something to be sought."

"What was that place?" Cletus asked. "I mean, from one angle it was a grove of trees, and there was a woman. There were sheep. From another angle that city, those... things. And something about a mask..."

"The city has a name," Donovan said, "but I'm not going to speak it. The best thing any of you can do is to forget what you saw. Maybe not the sheep. Probably not the woman. Everything else..."

"Never happened, far as I'm concerned," Bubba cut in. "I'm gonna have to replace that drone, but I won't be going anywhere near that grove with it."

"Lenny is going to go and talk to Randy," Cletus said. "I got the two of them in contact. Better if Randy looks after him, since he's so close, and his family. Wouldn't be surprised to see that grove expand a bit. I don't think there's any other way he gets through it."

"You're probably right," Donovan said. "You and I will have to visit your new friend and talk, but I believe he's a good man, and even if I didn't, the fact he appears to have prevented a major hurricane from touching ground would be points in his favor."

"There is that," Cletus said.

"I'll get that stone put away safely," Donovan said. "It's powerful and might have allowed that woman to speak with Hastur without losing herself... but it's as dark as that city, and it would have eaten her from within. It isn't something I can allow free in the world."

"Was kind of counting on that," Cletus said. "Happy to see it go."

"Well," Donovan said. "It seems you've cleaned this one up on your own, Cletus. You and Dog, and Jasper—and Bubba. Glad to see it, because there's another problem I was going to bring to you... something I could use backup on."

"What in the double-D goddam hell could you need help with that I could provide?" Cletus asked.

"Well," Donovan said with a grin. "It involves a lady and some goats..."

Cletus shook his head. "Swell. Just what we needed after the llamas and the alpacas and the sheep."

Donovan laughed. "I'll be in touch. Try not to let something end the world until then?"

"I'll do my best," Cletus said. Then he headed for the bar, ready to pour several fingers of very old bourbon and erase the yellow stain from his mind. "You can count on it."

The Pits of Hastur

A *Cthulhu Armageddon* adventure

By C. T. Phipps

Chapter One

The Gug lifted one of the pitiful human slaves in the air before biting their arm off at the shoulder. The bloody action caused the coliseum crowd to roar with delight. The stadium was built Roman style and filled with tens of thousands of Celephaïs residents dressed in robes, tunics, and the occasional blue jeans with t-shirt. They were a cosmopolitan band of citizens drawn from all over the Dreamlands and here for the Great Games of Hastur as hosted by their God King Kuranes.

The man who was my host.

I felt ill watching the violence below. I was familiar with gladiator contests, fighting for spectacle was as old as humankind, but found this display sickening. Most battles I'd witnessed had been designed to display the skill of the contestants, often fixed to inflate their heroism, but this was just gore for the sake of gore.

"You do not appear to be enjoying the Great Games, Lord Booth," the voice of my host spoke with a decidedly anachronistic upper crust English accent. He was unlike anyone else in his kingdom as well, resembling a 1920s actor I'd once seen a black and white photo of. He was also wearing a tuxedo, of all things, with an umbrella being held over him by a twelve-year-old slave girl.

Kuranes, though that was almost certainly not his birth name, was the most powerful Dreamer in a thousand worlds and perhaps the most powerful Earth had ever produced except for the missing Randolph Carter. Dreaming was akin to magic in the Dreamlands and one who mastered their nighttime visions had the power of a god. Kuranes had long since abandoned his mortal body and ruled this place, supposedly made from his childhood dreams, for centuries.

"Just Booth, or John Henry, not Lord. As for whether I'm enjoying this display, no, I'm not," I said, deciding that honesty was a better policy for keeping his attention. Kuranes was surrounded by flatterers and sycophants. I'd met several who'd dismissed me as a Wasteland barbarian and unwittingly served as the best introduction I could have gotten to a man bored of court life.

"Oh?" Kuranes asked, curious.

I nodded. "I see no value in slaughter for its own sake. The Wastelands provided me enough indiscriminate violence to last a thousand lifetimes."

"Which you may find also applies to life in the Dreamlands," Kuranes said, leaning back in his throne that existed in an alcove that dominated this portion of the area. My own chair was far smaller and to the side, letting the position of his guests remain clear. I was technically here acting as a representative of humanity's survivors in the far-off Republic of Carter. A position I had as much title to as the King of Oz or President of Made-Up-Ville. I did not know if he believed my bold-faced lie or not but, so far, he seemed intrigued enough to treat me with all the honors an ambassador deserved.

"Immortality is an exotic dish," I said, speaking as if I had any real experience in it. "But I've yet to see it among most people living here. The people down below getting slaughtered, for instance."

Kuranes ignored my not so gentle reproach to the bloodshed. "Dreamers are capable of living for eons here if their spirits survive the transition of physical death. It is the dreams, those poor fools being eaten by my Gug for example, who are doomed to short meaningless existences. Look at it closely and see the difference between it and its prey."

I reluctantly did so, wishing I was anywhere else. "Sure."

The Gug was a particularly hideous example of its species, standing eighteen feet tall and possessing a mouth that was large enough to swallow a man in two bites with teeth that were like swords. Its proportions were apelike with scales covering part of its body and ratty molted fur on other portions. Its hunger was unnatural, feeding a biology not even the strange alien biology of the Dreamlands produced but modified with the alchemy of Celephaïs as well as twisted human sciences to produce a creature that served an all-too-human evil: sport.

For the past ten minutes, the Gug had been "fighting" a group of eight men, dragging a tree-sized wooden club behind it while chasing the remaining helpless humans down as they tried to navigate the crude obstacle course set up in the center of the arena. There were things I recognized: a junked car, a streetlight, and a stone fireplace absent a house around it.

There were more alien things as well like statues of beings that had no human features, what could have been chairs made for beings that had had no legs, and an organic rock formation that seemed to shift with movement around it. They did little to separate the Gug from its prey and the humans below, slaves, had thrown down their weapons to hope to avoid the creature.

There were two left.

A blond-haired man in his mid-thirties and a woman of about fifty who was directing the former to try to keep the creature at bay with movement even if such a thing was probably futile in the long run.

"I doubt they view their lives as meaningless," I said, not sure how to respond. As much as I didn't want to be invested, I couldn't help myself. I wanted these poor fools to live even if it was impossible. There was a natural urge for humans to root for the underdog, particularly when they were from the Wastelands like myself. We were all underdogs there, even if I couldn't really count myself among them these days.

"Dreams exist for the dreamer," Kuranes said, his voice carrying only a hint of the mammoth disdain I felt from him regarding his subjects. "They are my immortality. But I will never forget they are just my imaginings."

"They are still people," I said, struggling with the concept that reality was so mutable even if I'd spent some time in the Dreamlands. "The dreamfolk love, live, and die like real people. So, they are real."

"Are they? The people below, the ephemera of my consciousness, live as long as I will them too. True Humans are not made for immortality," Kuranes said, his voice soft and sad, surprising me. "I sometimes wonder if it was not a mistake to cast aside my physical form and live here as a god king among my creations."

The middle-aged woman of the two survivors met her end at the hand of the Gug, grabbed in one hand and hurled against a burnt-out Toyota Corolla that I was surprised to recognize the make and model of. The Gug proceeded to smash down its club onto her corpse multiple times, getting greater cheers with each blow.

"How does one become a god king?" I asked, half-joking. I was trying to distract myself from the disgusting display around me. I was far from squeamish, having memories of both a man and an alien, but the sheer delight around me was making me nauseous.

Kuranes smiled at the prospect of speaking his story. All dictators, magical or otherwise, loved talking about themselves. "When I was still human, I dreamed of Celephaïs as an image of a bygone age. A landed gentry, I thought kings and knights were the highest thing to aspire to. It was a child's dream of bygone innocence and sanitized stories of Grimm mixed with Sir Thomas Malory. By the time of the Great War, I was homeless and wandering the streets of London with the war having consumed my wealth as well as sanity. But I still dreamed of this place where I was absolute ruler of its people and a hero beyond reproach. Eventually, I stopped doing anything but dreaming and what little pocket money I earned by begging went to drugs to keep me dreaming of it. I became a master dreamer, able to work wonders like flying by thought or talking to sentient glowing gases but I never could find my way back to the product of a mind without the weight of a world. I found my home, this place, once more, only when I ran out of money for drugs and threw myself into the sea. Only then did the knights of Celephaïs take me to this place, in the Valley of Ooth-Nargai beyond the Tanarian Hills, where I was to rule forever. My body undoubtedly eaten by fish or washed up against the shores of Innsmouth beneath some fat nouveau riche fool's mansion."

I disliked Kuranes' sing-song way of speaking, like he was a poet rather than a tyrant. "So, to become immortal, you have to die."

"Yes," Kuranes said, bluntly.

"Ah," I said, clearly not understanding nor sure I wanted to. I had known things that had come back from death, but the experience always left them changed in ways that were never improvements. What lay beyond death was apparently worse than Hell or oblivion.

"Earth is dead, at least our Earth," Kuranes said, sneering. "I thought this was Elysium, Heaven, or the final reward religions promised for countless years but the years, nay, the millennia wore on. The heroic battles I fought mattered little when I always won, the beautiful queens I had all became shallow caricatures as they were all the product of my fantasies, and the sweetest nectars I drank at fabulous banquets all became like ash in my mouth. By the time Randolph Carter came to my land, I was already sick of being God-King. I missed my beloved Cornwall and the sweet simple pleasures of being a mortal man. All that is left here is the memory of those things and the primal fears and lusts. You ask me why I revel in the violence here with my people? Because death is one of the few things that can still conjure even the memory of true emotion in me."

"Ah," I replied. "I understand."

And I did.

Kuranes frowned. "You think I am a brute."

"I think you are a madman," I replied, simply.

Kuranes burst out laughing. A thing that seemed to surprise him as much as it did me. It seemed likely he had not laughed in a very long time. "What are your motivations, then, Booth? You are far younger than me and I suspect have foolish sentimentality about the nature of man and life. A man who clings to the delusion that the gods are anything but dreams of bigger, better, and louder humans who judge or care about our every move."

I silently cursed myself for being so blunt with Kuranes and it was just the vagaries of fortune that he had taken it as a genuinely funny joke versus the serious indictment of his character that I'd meant it as. I was here, flattering the despot, because I needed access to his palace's heart. The Eye of Hastur, a gemstone of black ruby that contained magical power beyond imagination, was supposedly in Kuranes' possession. If I was to find a way to free the Dreaming City from its curse, I would need an object like it.

Unfortunately, to get close to the Eye of Hastur, I needed to share pleasantries with someone who was *fucking insane*. Oh, and had the power of a god. If he wasn't anywhere near the power of a Great Old One, he was certainly capable of doing wonders akin to the Small Gods of Earth like Zeus, Hypnos, or Nodens. They existed in the Dreamlands as well, the faith of their worshipers sustaining them long after the civilizations that revered them had died.

It didn't help I was distracted by the sole survivor of the blood sport below. Against my better judgement, I cared about whether he lived or died. He had screamed out at the death of the woman, the only person of his group he seemed to care about, and taken a spear up from the ground. It was a foolish move but that act of defiance was perhaps the only courage one could display in the face of such ritualized horror.

It did, indeed, inspire me with how to respond.

To quote a man who had lived his life free. *"I have known many gods. He who denies them is as blind as he who trusts them too deeply. I do not seek beyond death."* It may be a realm like yours Kuranes or the wonder and glory of the Deep Ones with their dragon-squid. Maybe even fluffy clouds and harps. Maybe nothingness. While I live in the Dreamlands, I am flesh and blood and blood and flesh are what I indulge in. Maybe as a god you have time to contemplate the ephemera of your millions of citizens but as a gunslinger, I only have a woman at my arm, a pistol in my hand, and a curse on my tongue to provide me my meaning."

Kuranes stared as if trying to remember some distant long forgotten wisdom. "You paraphrase the Cimmerian. He was nothing but a long-forgotten myth written about by Pulp writers in my time, like Gilgamesh or Hercules. The star of bawdy epics and boys' rags."

I shrugged. "I read those same rags as a boy. Though they were paperbacks and already decades old from when the Rising destroyed human civilization. Just because they were stories for children does not make them childish. *Let teachers and philosophers brood over questions of reality and illusion. I know this: if life is illusion, then I am no less an illusion, and being thus, the illusion is real to me. I live, I burn with life, I love, I slay, and am content.*"

There was something about my answer that annoyed Kuranes, more so than the direct insult to his face. "A simplistic answer for a simplistic mind, John Henry Booth. For me, there is only one god, and it is a god that we will all come to worship in the end: Hastur. The God of Madness."

"A strange deity to worship," I replied, trying to disguise my excitement at finally getting to a relevant topic. I doubted Kuranes would tell me where he was storing the Eye in casual conversation, but stranger things had happened. "I have heard a thousand tales of his worshipers but all of them speak of him as a malevolent deity. The Lord of Hali. The Master of Leng. The King in Yellow. The half-brother of Cthulhu. I was surprised to see him venerated here. Usually, his worship is outlawed and the masked traders of Leng killed on site."

I'd seen them everywhere in Kuranes' court.

Kuranes looked particularly disdainful of the last description. "That is what fools who think they are sane think. Hastur is the entropy inherent to the universe. The urge to self-destruction and horrific excess inherent to all thinking beings. Time wears down even the noblest of men but leaves only immediate gratification. When you have lived epochs, John Henry Booth, you will find that only staring into the spiraling abyss of everything's end provides any comfort."

Yeah, Kuranes was a madman who confused rapine for rapture. "Violent delights lead to violent ends. Spare the sole survivor in the arena."

It was an action that endangered my cover, and it was the height of hypocrisy to do so for this one fellow versus the dozens of individuals who I'd already seen killed. However, my emotions were piqued and if I had the attention of the self-styled God King then I might be able to do some small bit of good, at least as how humans defined it.

"So, you *are* invested in the games," Kuranes said, turning to me with a smile that seemed almost like he'd forgotten how to do it.

"As you say," I said, uninterested in arguing with him.

"So be it," Kuranes said, standing up and lifting a single hand with its palm outstretched.

The skies darkened over the coliseum with storm clouds rushing in across the horizon until it was as night, but no rain fell. From Kuranes' hands, though, not the sky shot forth a bolt of lightning like he was the King of the Olympians himself.

The bolt struck the man dead onto the ground before the Gug and left him twitching on the ground before death mercifully took him. It was an impressive but casual source of the supernatural powers at Kuranes' command.

The crowd was silent, shocked by the sudden action by their deity. It was a reminder of his terrible presence and power that could strike them down at any moment. A moment more of silence passed before the crowd erupted into wild ecstatic cheers, sincere or born from terror.

"That is *not* what I meant," I replied.

"I gave him the greatest gift possible," Kuranes said. "A chance to be martyred for his god. It was also a swift death, better than he deserved. Did you know he was a child-killer? A rapist? A serial murderer of women?"

"No," I replied.

Kuranes shrugged. "Neither do I. His crimes do not matter, if he has performed any at all. He lived and died at my will, just as you must—*shoggoth*."

My blood ran cold.

Chapter Two

Shoggoth.

That name. One that was reviled throughout the Dreamlands and among the survivors of Earth. If there was a more hated species where man's foot treaded, I did not know it. They were humanity's cousins, the Elder Things extracting the seed of consciousness from their modified slaves to create the sentient ape-men who would go on to father homo sapiens as well as all their offshoots like the ghouls, Serpent Men, or Deep Ones. The shoggoths themselves had been created from a marooned member of the Kastro'vaal species, creating a kind of sickening Great Chain of Being that extended from the Old Ones to the dreamfolk below.

It was difficult to say why the shoggoths were so reviled but there was no place in the Dreamlands I explored that they were not loathed more than the cannibalistic Skor or the plague-bringers of Tarkati. Somehow both dreamer and dreamfolk recognized enough of a kinship with the shapeshifting protoplasmic horrors that they desired nothing less but their enslavement or extermination on sight. Other creatures, let us call them monsters, might invoke awe as well as fear or a desire to propagate but the shoggoth was the preferred subject of sorcerers seeking slaves to dominate their foes or the proverbial dragon to slay for heroes hoping to make their legend.

I, myself, had slain a shoggoth before discovering our twisted kinship. In the Black Temple, I had managed to use a pair of mystical objects in the shape of revolvers to cut one down as it tried to slay me. It was the formative event of my career as a Wasteland "hero" and yet I could only wonder now if the creature had been trying to communicate with me as a brother versus striking me dead. Or maybe I saw sympathy where none existed, for it was not as if blood kinship prevented humans from slaughtering each other like ants over territory or starving dogs over a bone.

Kuranes' words were as such that the entire city would rise against me at his word, not that they wouldn't for any other words from him, and burn me alive. If I was known as one in the Dreaming City, I would also be killed along with all my associates. The Deep Ones might keep shoggoths as slaves but even they feared their power.

"I do not know what you—" I started to speak, stupidly.

Instead, I felt the air ionize around me and my words catch in my throat. I had no doubt that Kuranes could unleash ten kinds of magic upon me that would be as real as any flame, lightning, or explosive. I had survived things that would kill any normal man, which I was not, but shoggoths for all their reputation were still creatures of material matter. Immortal to the years but not to being killed and among the lesser creatures of the Dreamlands, only terrifying to humanity and their descendants. Kuranes may be playing God here, but the world was playing along with him. If he could dream me dead, I was dead.

"Yes," Kuranes spoke, clearly speaking to my thoughts rather than my words. "I could dream you dead."

"What do you want?" I asked, feeling a light rain pour down. Underneath Kuranes' umbrella, none of it touched him and I suspected it might not even do so should it have not existed. We were trapped in his mad twisted dream—which I probably should not have thought of given the revelation of his mind-reading power.

"Oh, I am mad," Kuranes said, clasping his fingers together and staring forward. "I'm mad. You're mad. We're all mad here. Charles Dodgson had it right. As for what I want, it is simple: amusement. You are a man who craves something from me and wishes to kill me for it. I do not know what it is, it is hidden from my mind, but I will have it."

I did not yet breathe out a sigh of relief for the fact he did not know that I craved the Eye of Hastur meant the spells my lover Mercury had woven, ones infinitely more complex than the meager sorceries I'd managed to master of pre-human civilization, were holding still. Still, it would not take much to guess it was my quest's object and the greatest defense I had now was that no one was supposed to know I had it.

I had learned it from the Crawling Chaos himself.

In, of all things, a dream.

"I do not wish your death, Kuranes," I said, speaking truthfully. "I feel you are a mad king, wasted by time and corrupted by power. However, if I was to kill every man destroyed by such things then I would have to spend every day of my life murdering every ruler in the

Western Dreamlands. I would have to kill myself. I have lived too long as well and intend to continue to do so."

"So, your defense is you just intend to rob me?" Kuranes asked, eyes twinkling as if the ridiculousness of it all was enough to spare my life for the next few seconds. I had no doubt he could turn me into snow, music, or ash with a wave of his hand. This was his realm, and I was just a guest if even that.

I decided to do the most human thing possible in this situation and lie. "I seek the missing Dreamer, Randolph Carter, Kuranes. The one you knew from your early days as god king. With his power, we can dream up a new Earth and create a home for the people of our planet if not an entirely new habitat for humanity with no Old Ones to threaten it. You are the last one to have seen him in living memory other than Nyarlathotep and he cannot—"

"Do…not…mention…that….being," Kuranes spoke, snapping his finger like a man summoning a waiter.

No sooner had Kuranes made his gesture, than I found myself falling on my knees against the dusty blood and viscera-splattered cobblestones of the arena. The smell that assaulted me was revolting, mixing the intestines and gore with the discharge of men in their death throws. The rain was doing little to deplete the smell even as the winds from it carried out the noxious scent of the Gug that was perhaps three or four yards away. The smell a foul bacteria-ridden musk mixed with chemicals from other worlds toxic and hostile to human life. It was a creature that smelled of sulfur, sweat, and the dead men it was splattered in the gore of.

The Gug was considerably more impressive in person than viewed from the stands, towering over me like a storybook giant. Its bizarre alien biology, though I was no one to talk, had made it vaguely resemble a man with connotations akin to a giant ape, but its extra arms flexed in anticipation of a kill that it had clearly not gotten enough of. The monster's mouth was the wrong direction, horizontal like a Venus Fly trap and its eyes, if such sensory organs functioned like the ones on Earth, were on its malformed face's side.

"We have a new challenger!" Kuranes' voice echoed throughout the coliseum. "The Wastelander John Henry Booth, Son of Two Worlds, versus Gug the Never Dying! May those who are about to die salute the God of Madness!"

I gave the God King my own salute with one finger before rolling on the ground to grab at the spear of one of the dead men. I'd almost certainly ruined any chances of getting out alive, let alone with the gemstone I sought. But I had no regrets. The opportunity to tell that slaving asshole what I thought of him was worth the remainder of my supposedly immortal life. One either died as the man one wanted to be or lived as an unrecognizable collection of lies.

"Arghooooooo!" The Gug made a noise that deafened me, spreading out its arms and charging toward me.

I dodged out of the way of the creature, cutting at it with the steel tip of the weapon, but if it was able to pierce the thick hide of the monster then it was not revealed in that moment, bouncing off as if striking rock. I considered in that moment assuming my true form, or at least what passed for such among a race of shapeshifters, to go after the beast. The crowd would consider me just another monster and Kuranes would keep me as a creature for his menagerie, no doubt, but at least I might have had a fighting chance. Besides, Kuranes had all but confirmed he knew who and what I was.

Unfortunately, that avenue had denied me as well as I found myself unable to make myself stronger, faster, or covered in alien armor. I was a poor shapeshifter, too much identification with my human form, but that was still better than being a helpless mortal against a creature that was as much alien matter as dream or flesh.

No, I cannot think that way, I muttered, standing tall. *The moment I think of my humanity as a weakness, the moment I am doomed to succumb to the same madness as Kuranes.*

I embraced that delusion as the Gug turned around like a charging bull, facing me with its open salivating mouth.

"Come on, you bastard!" I snarled, raising my spear. "Let's see how you do against someone who actually knows how to fight back!"

The Gug responded by lifting the Dodge Charger off the ground with two hands and proceeded to hurl it my way. I only barely managed to somersault forward, sadly bringing myself only closer to the creature as it smashed behind me. That was when the Gug moved forward, anticipating my movements.

Shit.

It could *think*.

A more philosophical man might have pondered the fact we were both being forced to combat one another for the amusement of a jaded crowd and a bloodthirsty wizard-king. Instead, I focused on the pure atavistic urge for survival while trying to tune out the crowds' screams beside. They were sincere in their cheering now, glad to see something more properly resembling sports instead of just simple murder.

I stabbed at the Gug again even as it swung its arms to the ground, sending up a cloud of dust that choked my lungs while its other arms reached for my body. I managed to move out in time, only for the steel to once more strike against a thick rock-like texture beneath its fur. The Gug had an exoskeleton underneath its flesh or musculature that was like coral.

"Arghhhhoooo!" The Gug blew hot breath that almost choked me with its nightmarish smell, tasting of the acids and chemicals in its stomach even as I saw the soft dark flesh leaking from two canals down its throat.

"Fuck it," I muttered, doing something very stupid and charging forward. The Gug grabbed me with two of its arms and lifted me up, the other two of them went to rip my arms off, only for me to jab the spear straight down its mouth into what I hoped was its brain. As I'd hoped, the creature's defenses were strong from the outside but not the inside as the spear pierced some sort of organ and it let loose a roar that was of a distinctly different kind than the ones it had thrown my way earlier.

I pressed the spear down with all my strength, forcing both hands to hold tightly while using the Gug's own arms as a base. The creature fell over, collapsing on the ground as it twitched violently with disgusting black ichor pooling in its mouth before it ceased its death throes. Modified or not by Celephaïs alchemy, the Gug had been mortal enough to be killed. So, its name as the Undying was ironic.

Then it started to move again.

Goddammit.

"Ratto! Ratto! Ratto!" The crowds chanted, genuinely excited now and leaving me with the impression I was even more screwed than before.

My knowledge of Celephaïs language was not great. It was the kind of language a child would invent for his fictional fantasy world, close enough to English to be understood but with a hidden code to those 'in the know.' Ratto was not a word I was familiar with.

It means resurrection, Kuranes spoke in my ear. It was as if his presence was right behind me even though I could see him from his royal box. *Tell me, John, have you ever killed the immortal?*

A couple of times, I thought back, cursing myself for thinking it would be this easy. *I guess I'm going to have to repeat the feat.*

I watched the corpses of the dead gladiators start to get up off the ground or crawl their way toward the body of the Gug in unnatural stop-motion like style. They started attaching themselves together to form a sickening form of armor around the Gug while the crowd went wild. There was a home team champion here and it was obviously not me.

There is another option, Kuranes whispered. *Submit to me, be my slave, and I will spare your life.*

Never, I thought, preparing to die. *Not all of us are afraid of death.*

I had been a slave once before. The Dunwych tribe had held me prisoner away from my family for a year and used me as breeding stock among other indignities. I would not submit again even if it would be to escape again.

Not everyone has the chance to escape it forever, Kuranes said, seemingly genuinely surprised by my response, but undeterred. *But perhaps not slave. Thrall. Servant.*

I prepared to do battle with the giant undead monstrosity that now had a dozen arms. The faces of the dead men merged into its flesh, opening their eyes and mouths in looks of abject screaming horror.

Alien tongues slithered out of their mouths as something wholly new animated the corpse of the Gug along with its fleshy new additions, some nameless nightmare thing from beyond even the Dreamlands. Perhaps it had always been and would simply move to a new host after today. Golden yellow puss leaked from its body and bones stuck out of its head in a surreal parody of a crown.

"Hastur! Hastur! Hastur!" The crowd chanted, clearly treating the thing as a manifestation of Kuranes' mad god.

Perhaps it was.

"The answer is no," I said, looking for another spear and finding none that weren't broken or in the hands of the monster's own many hands. I was unarmed and had no chance, perhaps not even if I'd been fully armed and capable of calling upon my alien heritage. I cursed the fact I would die here, though, for no cause. In my youth, it would have been easy because my children were looked after, and I had faith I'd lived my life well spent. Now, in my monster years, I had only each moment to live for and a handful of loved ones I could not say would live in heaven or hell depending on the Dreamlands' mood.

How about if you simply say please? Kuranes whispered, knowing my heart.

I closed my eyes for a moment and hated myself for my response. *Please.*

I hated myself in that moment for acquiescing but that was in part because I didn't trust Kuranes to honor any promise he made. Honor may exist among thieves, but no one had ever gone broke betting against the integrity of kings or priests. I doubted god kings were any different.

My suspicion seemed to be justified as the Gug was now more like a centipede of living death with a long tail of dead bodies in place of its legs, incorporating the bodies of not just the victims of the initial fight but the bodies from previous battles fought in Hastur's name. The creature was far faster than it was before, and it slithered at me. I had no choice but to run now, jumping around and navigating the obstacles throughout the area, watching the abomination smash through them as if they were a child's toy blocks.

Accompanying the carnage and my less-than-heroic flight, I tried and failed to find any way that I might harm this horrifying thing. Resigned to the idea that this was my end, and I would have it witnessed by thousands,

I heard the war horns of Celephaïs. Kuranes' voice echoed through the coliseum, "Welcome, Nybbas, Hunter of the Immortal!"

My attention briefly turned to an unusually tall woman, over six feet in height, muscled and dressed in furs that seemed less like the product of a barbarian race and more designed to evoke that by those marketing a product. She was beautiful in an unconventional way with long red hair cascading down her shoulders and eyes that were green without pupils. In her hands, she was wielding a sword made of orichalcum or Deep One gold. The gold weapons were almost impossible for a mortal man to wield due to their weight but struck down things that did not exist entirely in this world.

Supposedly.

If this was Kuranes' idea of help, then he was amusing himself at my expense to no end. That was when the woman charged forward, leapt into the air higher than any human could and struck the Gug's head off with a single blow that might as well have been cutting air. The undying creature's head rolled away as the yellow puss poured out in a river of golden fluid, spraying every direction. The head tried to reunite with its body, only for the woman to spear it to the ground with her golden blade.

Dismembered, the creature that could not die continued to roll around its body like a dying fish before falling into a pitiful set of twitching that was barely noticeable. It was not dead but no threat to anyone.

The crowd's cries turned from cheering to rapturous joy. "Nybbas! Nybbas! Nybbas!"

I stared, stunned. "Huh."

Chapter Three

It was hours after the slaughter of Gug the Undying that I finally found out the price for Kuranes' help, well more than the "please" he had claimed but far different from the eternal servitude that was his opening offer.

Kuranes, Nybbas, and I were standing on the balcony overlooking the gladiator barracks, there was no other word for it, that contained the God King's collection of hand-picked warriors. They were a motley collection of creatures ranging from Deep Ones, ghouls, Serpent Men, and humans from other parts of the Dreamlands with qualities showing alien or otherworldly heritage. There were perhaps as many as a hundred of them but room for many more in the extravagant building. The scent of death was here and by the sense of the beings beneath me, I could tell that these were not particularly cared for or valued warriors despite belonging to Celephaïs' dictator.

"You want me to coach your gladiator team," I said, not sure I'd heard him correctly.

"Yes," Kuranes said, bluntly.

"I was expecting something a bit more esoteric," I replied, surveying the warriors below. Some of them were clear veterans and covered in scars as well as walked with a killer's swagger, others looked significantly rawer.

"Your soul, if such a thing exists?" Kuranes asked. "Don't be gauche. You are a warrior and killer, so I want you to do something related to war and killing."

I didn't feel inclined to point out that my first gladiator battle had been just a few moments ago and doing battle in the arena was inherently different than doing it in the Wasteland. "My first piece of advice is to arm your gladiators with weapons that can actually kill the things they're fighting and then face them against monsters that are killable."

"Cute," Kuranes said.

"Yeah, I'm not joking," I said, not sure what would set off the mad tyrant. "Besides, you already seem to have a master gladiator."

Nybbas had barely spoken two words to me since her display in the arena, even to acknowledge my thanks for saving my life. Instead, she stared over the balcony at the gladiators with a look of contempt on her face.

"Nybbas is a supreme killer, the blood of Kadath runs through her veins, but her capacity to work with others is limited," Kuranes said, sounding almost apologetic.

Kadath was the Mount Olympus or Asgard of the Dreamlands, if not where those places were located. The Small Gods of Earth dwelled there, feeding on the worship of the humans they stole away in ancient times and bred like cattle to continue their relevance long after the Great Old Ones had devoured Earth's last civilization. In simple terms, it meant she was a demigoddess and possessed of her own power.

"How would you prepare this group?" I asked, still hoping to engage her in conversation. I'd like to say for reasons other than she was simply a statuesque figure akin to Atlantea or old pulp illustrations of Dark Agnes but that certainly didn't hurt.

"Let the blood flow between them and cull the weak among them," Nybbas said, her voice filled with a kind of cat-like purr of anticipation. "The strongest will emerge from them and die or triumph on their own merits."

"I see," I replied, nonplussed.

"Wars are won with strategy, tactics, and teamwork," Kuranes said, as if this was some great triumph of insight on his part. "I wish you to pick twenty men from this group and teach them to work as a proper collection of warriors against whatever threats can be thrown at them in the next Great Games. The rest can die or be resold as you wish. You have my complete authority for this and access to my treasury to make it so."

I blinked. "The next Great Games."

"Yes," Kuranes said. "A year from now, the Great Pasha of the Leng Empire will visit Celephaïs and bring with him one thousand of his Sorcerer Lords. We have a wager between us that must be won. Whoever's team emerges triumphant will receive their heart's desire. For the Pasha, it will be the Eye of Hastur that was stolen from his father by Randolph Carter and given to me for safe keeping. For me, it will be sublime apotheosis."

I blinked, trying to process a rather large number of revelations in but a few seconds. "I thought you were already a god."

Nybbas snorted at that, drawing Kuranes' distasteful gaze.

Kuranes did not correct her, though, and turned to me. "I am worshiped as one, but true divinity eludes me. The Great Pasha knows the true name of Hastur the Unspeakable One and if I repeat it three times, the King in Yellow will appear to grant me a wish. I will cast aside this feeble shell the way I did my mortal form and live among wonders and glory forever in the court of my god."

I'd chosen the path of war over the path of wizardry, but I had an unusually high education in the occult, hell an unusually high education period, for a man who'd grown up in the Wastelands. I'd read the Alan Ward translation of the *Necronomicon*, the 17th century Joseph Curwen penned edition of *The Book of Eibon*, and even a yellowed mass market paperback of the *Re'Kithnid* from Dunwich House. I needed none of these to know that mortals who summoned up gods, demanding to be made into one of their number, was a story that never ended well. The Ancient Greeks had even coined the term hubris for this very reason.

Explaining that, especially when he could read my mind, seemed like it would end poorly, though. "I am not sure I want to spend a year here in your fair city, no matter how intriguing I might find the job. You saved my life, but I point out you were the one to imperil it in the first place."

Also, being restricted here would make any attempt to acquire the Eye of Hastur more difficult rather than less. The gladiator stable was far from the palace and being part of its staff would restrict my movements greatly.

Of course, Kuranes knew this even if he didn't know precisely what I was after. He might suspect, though, and that was as good as being exposed. "Oh, Mr. Booth, I believe you will want to agree to my terms."

Ah, yes, here came the threats. Sucking in my breath, I looked into his eyes. "And why, may I ask, is that?"

"Because I found your spy," Kuranes said. "The lovely redheaded girl of Eurasian descent who fancies herself a witch. Sadly, her sorcery may be fine for the world she came from but is nothing to a place that absorbs and exhales magic with every breath. The woman called Mercury."

I blinked. "I see. I take it something untoward would happen to her if I don't cooperate?"

Kuranes patted me on the shoulder. "Not at all, because you are going to. She will be kept in the finest lodgings and given books of magic that will allow her to increase her power tenfold. Just as you will be kept in the finest quarters and availed every luxury while you train my slaves."

"I'm not a slaver," I said.

"Promise them their freedom then," Kuranes said. "Yours as well. If you defeat the Pasha's own team of slaves and monsters then I will give you what you seek, whatever it is. If you want Celephaïs itself, then the kingdom shall be yours to wear the crown of on a troubled brow. I will have no need of it. If you want Nybbas—"

"I choose my own partners, wizard," Nybbas interrupted, her voice sharp and condemnatory. "I also kill shoggoths, I don't fuck them."

Kuranes, much to my surprise, lowered his head. "Of course."

"I am not a shoggoth," I replied. "I am me."

Kuranes turned to me. "And if you do not win, I will strip your mind of everything human within you. I will toss slaves to you to impregnate and breed a host of monsters that I will spend the next thousand years killing then feeding to you."

"That is a very vivid image," I replied, cooly.

"I've done worse for less," Kuranes said, smiling. "Do we have an arrangement?"

"I feel very much like a gladiator coach now," I replied. "Go team."

"Splendid," Kuranes said, his voice lowering an octave. "I am glad we have an accord."

And like that, Kuranes was gone. There was no puff of smoke, crack of thunder, or flash of light. No, he was simply there one moment and then gone like a frame of a movie reel badly cut together.

"You realize he's going to kill you after the contest, right?" Nybbas asked, looking at me without the disgust I expected because of her earlier words but, instead, good natured pity.

"Are you familiar with the old Muslim proverb about the singing horse?" I asked.

"Indulge me," Nybbas replied, turning to me and crossing her arms.

"A thief is brought to the sultan and sentenced to be executed," I replied. "The thief then says, 'wait, no, I can teach a horse to sing!' The sultan, surprised by this, says that he'd like to see this and agrees to spare the thief's life for a year. One of his associates asks why the thief would make such a stupid promise. The thief says, 'A lot can happen in a year. Maybe the sultan will die, maybe he'll be overthrown, or maybe he'll forget all about me. And who knows, maybe in a year the horse will sing.'"

Nybbas nodded. "Ah, so it's a stupid proverb. None of that will happen to Kuranes."

"Probably not," I admitted. "But it is a year and that gives me some time to figure out an alternative."

Nybbas shook her head. "Your best bet is to abandon your comrade and flee. If you seek the Eye of Hastur, it is a fool's prize. Kuranes' land did not start decaying and his people starve until he began gazing into its depths. The sights of alien vistas and glorious magnificence exposed his paradise for the pathetic little fantasy world it was. If you think it will give you great power, you are a fool."

"I don't seek great power," I said, staring at her. "I seek the freedom for my people. The sole survivors of my Earth. Specifically, my family."

I had no idea why I was opening up to this stranger.

"Other shoggoths?" Nybbas asked.

"Man, monster, and otherwise," I said, staring at her.

"Find another Earth," Nybbas suggested. "There are an infinite number out there in the World Tree of Azathoth's branches. You don't even have to dream them up. Maybe that is what Randolph Carter did like in that outrageous lie you told or maybe he died long ago. Hastur touched him too and set him on the path to Unknown Kadath, ruining his brief mortal life the way that he ruined Kuranes'."

"Hastur ruins a lot of lives," I replied.

During my journeys across the Dreamland, I'd discovered my son was a Dreamer. Far more powerful than me or Mercury and he'd turned to the King in Yellow to try to find ways to save his fellow humans on Earth. He'd taken over Randolph Carter's own dreamlands, made in the image of New England, and turned them into the Republic of Carter. There was always a price for magic, though, and if I could kill any of the Great Old Ones then it would be him.

"Hastur does not exist," Nybbas said.

I blinked. "Excuse me? I'm pretty—"

"He exists only in the minds of his followers," Nybbas said. "He is not like K'Tullu, who is an alien older than worlds, or Yog-Sothoth, who is the incarnation of the universe's physical laws respectively. Nor even the Crawling Chaos, created by Azathoth in a blind moment of insanity, to give purpose to a chaotic primordial universe. Hastur is the first of the true gods, those beings that living things create in their dreams to justify the helplessness they feel. He is the Eldest of the Elder Gods and exists only in the heads of his faithful. He is yellow because the first gods are dreamed of coming from the Sun, and The Lord of the Dreamlands, and with less substance or will than thought. By being all things, he is nothing."

"It sounds like Nyarlathotep," I said, half expecting Kuranes to show up and punish me for saying his name.

"Hastur is the shadow of him on the wall in a dimly lit room," Nybbas said. "Which is why your master has sent you to recover his property as well as punish its thieves."

"He is not my master," I replied, dryly. "I am neither his slave nor his friend. The True Gods don't have either. They have toys and pets. I'm just the turtle he occasionally puts on its back to see if it can right itself."

"And yet you sometimes can," Nybbas said, surprising me. "You are unlike other shoggoths, John Henry Booth."

"Like I said, I am not a shoggoth," I said, denying it to myself as much as anyone. "I am a human being."

It was a lie, but a lie I'd repeated so often I hoped it would be the truth someday. After all, the Dreamlands were made of wishes and lies. Long after Earth had been consumed by Yog-Sothoth, it would remain a world of fiction and broken promises. In my travels, I'd even seen the remnants of the dreams of races destroyed by their own Great Old Ones—peoples billions of years dead and the shattered remnants of other universes that had existed like bubbles. There one day and then suddenly not.

"They are the same race," Nybbas said, surprising me. "The human mind and capacity for Dreaming, consciousness, came from the Elder Things inserting their slime into the apes evolved on your world. They are just trapped in one form and death when they could be awakened to so much more."

It was a strange statement to make, especially when she looked so very much like a human woman. But the Dreamlands were full of things that could appear to be something very different from what they truly were. "So, what is your story?"

"Do you know the phrase talk is cheap?" Nybbas asked, looking at me with her deep impenetrable eyes of solid green.

"Yes," I said.

"Whoever said such was a moron," Nybbas said, putting her hand on her sword pommel.

"Fair enough," I said, looking away. "I was merely asking because we're going to be working together."

"Together, perhaps. As brother and sister in arms, no," Nybbas said.

"My feelings are decidedly less than brotherly while you're in that outfit," I replied. "It gives remarkable support for animal skins."

Yeah, I was pathologically incapable of not being a jackass. On the other hand, some females found it endearing. Others turned into giant snake women with detachable jaws.

I'll share that story sometime.

Nybbas snorted. "You do a fair impersonation of a human, John Henry Booth. So, I will give you a hint. I was born on Kadath to the Lord of the Great Abyss. I am a goddess of the hunt, and my brothers and sisters are the nobility of the night sky, not frail humans. Our fathers are enemies, John Henry Booth, and I am here to slay a kingdom."

I was getting real sick of everyone and their delusions of godhood here. However, unfortunately, that was about as common as roadside shrines and bad food in the Dreamlands. "So, you're a goddess of the hunt like Artemis? Does that mean you're a virgin goddess?"

Nybbas shook her head. "Just focus on training the warriors below. I must win the next Great Games. The others winnowing the competition will make it easier."

"What do I have to work with?" I asked, switching topics.

"Rapists, murderers, and scum," Nybbas replied. "The only reason they're not in the pit to feed to monsters generated from the Hastur worshipers' nightmares is because they're marginally better at surviving than the ones used to quench the masses' blood thirst."

"Good," I replied. "Then I won't feel bad about reducing their ranks to twenty. Kuranes was clear about the number of the team he wants. I was afraid I'd have to do something decent and give the others their freedom."

"Free men have something to live for," Nybbas said. "Think of that when motivating them."

She then walked away, leaving me alone with my thoughts.

Chapter Four

The year passed quickly.

Such a thing should not be easy for any mortal man to say but the nature of the Dreamlands was such that a year, ten years, or millennia could pass with barely the blink of an eye. Time was always fluid within dreams and had a quality of otherworldliness that prevented it from being wholly similar to life in the "real" world.

But yes, I could say I almost enjoyed being Kuranes' gladiator coach. The warriors he'd assembled were all hardened killers from the four corners of the Dreamlands' Known Kingdoms. However, they were an eclectic bunch of murderers and each of them had stories to tell that reminded me of the time I'd been among fellow soldiers. I'd forgotten how much I'd missed the camaraderie of fellow warriors and Nybbas' description of them as scum did not include the fact most had done nothing worse than what I had.

Which was less of an endorsement than a reminder I had little room to judge the evils of men. Either way, there were only a few days left until the Great Games, and I had still a few choices to make for the final team to face the Great Pasha's Janissaries. Unfortunately, that choice would be decided by blood rather than deed. For example, I was about ready to strangle one of my best gladiators if he didn't shut the hell up.

"The universe is perfect, absolutely functional," Socrates the eight-foot-tall four-armed praying mantis spoke in a surprisingly human voice. His people were called the Callisto and had written the *Al-Azif*. "The rules sustain it, let it grow, develop. It is sublime. Unfortunately, it has reflections, imperfect copies echoing through spacetime, filled with holes, imperfections, flaws in the system that the true universe has long discarded. We live in one of those. Like all the flawed reflections, it's temporary, dying, soon to succumb to entropy, which is just the name of its most obvious hole. Beings in these dying universes can escape the end of their realities by leaving through those holes, entering other universes, where they don't belong. The more stable the universe, the longer they can survive there. They can survive here in Celephaïs for hundreds, if not thousands of cycles. But their very existence degrades the worlds they find themselves in. They are living embodiments of our own limitations. But these dying worlds also need us. Our order, our dreams, is all that stands between them and nothingness. And these dreams will trap us if we let them."

"Shut up and fight!" I snapped at Socrates, holding a two-handed great sword with a cat headed pommel. "You're here to kill, not philosophize!"

"I can do both!" Socrates said, dodging past an ax coming for his throat with the speed only an inhuman creature could achieve.

Socrates and I were in the practice arena, little more than an octagon twenty yards long surrounded by fence. The Callisto and I were fighting on the same team against two other gladiators: Reaver the Ghoul and Bodhi the Vanir.

Reaver the Ghoul was like most of his kind in that he was a furry werewolf looking figure with a canine head combined with just enough human features to be terrifyingly wrong. At least to human eyes. In his two hands, he held double-bladed axes that were made from the bones of unnamable creatures. He was naked and only the length of his fur kept it from being distracting. Armor slowed the creature down and he moved like lightning.

Bodhi the Vanir, by contrast, was a heavily tattooed redheaded man with yellow skin. He preferred a pair of short, curved swords with jagged teeth edges that moved like dancing fireflies, burning with magic that he conjured with spells from his long-dead homeland. The short swords were engraved with runes that caused them to burn without ever being reduced to slag and were capable of searing the flesh off unearthly monsters as well as dreamfolk.

"Speak well, abomination," Bodhi said in a sing-song voice. "It will be your last conversation on this realm's soil. I shall offer your ichor to the Great God Hastur that I have abandoned Ymir and Muspell for. He lives inside my brain and compels me to kill."

Bodhi was one of the few slaves I fought with and promised freedom to that I knew the actual crimes of. He was a serial killer, and his crimes were both gross as well as against innocents. However, in the Dreamlands where bandits and armies were allowed to plunder freely by their masters, it had only gotten him thrown in here when his rapine had gone poorly against a village under Kuranes' protection.

I wanted to kill Bodhi when I'd first heard his descriptions of his crimes and would have if not for the fact that I'd gotten to witness some of the Janissary team at work during the final days of last year's Great Games. They were guests of Kuranes and yet killed a dhole, a shoggoth, and an Elder Thing in rapid succession. They were nine-foot-tall giants each and wore smoky black metal armor that disguised their true natures. I'd released eighty of our crew from slavery over the past year, but of the twenty-three remaining, Bodhi was the strongest other than Socrates, me, and Nybbas.

Too bad he was a traitor.

"Die, half-man!" Reaver hissed, going for me with his two bone axes. The ghoul had revealed little of his past or interests in the year we had together, but had apparently chosen his side when his attacks were not meant to disable, but to kill.

I dodged out of the way, ducking underneath his blows before kneeing him in the stomach then punching him in the face. It was like striking a brick wall even as I struck hard enough for the ghoul to feel it by the noises he made.

Our audience was the remainder of the team with them watching the battle with mixtures of boredom as well as curiosity. I had not won much loyalty from the twenty despite my freeing them and offering coin as well as other rewards to those who agreed to stay. They were aware that this was a bloody game and who got them through it alive was their friend, rather than who made the most lucrative promises. If I fell at Bodhi or Reaver's hands, they would be the leader and Kuranes would barely notice.

Watching us in the battle was the person who held the loyalty of the gladiators despite, or perhaps because of the fact, that she made no pretensions of caring whether they lived or died. Nybbas wore a large horned helmet with an ornate dragon (or perhaps night-gaunt) themed carved into its face. We'd grown *closer* during the past year despite her avowed hatred of shoggoths but I wasn't sure I'd made any sort of dent in her emotional armor. It was kind of sleazy to use sex to try to make an ally in this hell pit but, well, you used whatever methods you could, and it wasn't the first time I'd been a slave who'd tried to manipulate their master that way.

"You are leading us to our doom, Booth!" Bodhi hissed, going after Socrates rather than myself with his flaming blades. "We all know it! You think you're one of us, but we know you're one of them! Our only salvation is in Hastur and the Lords of Leng!"

The speech wasn't for me, and I had the strong suspicion that I now knew the source of the discontent among the gladiators I'd recruited. Bodhi had been spreading rumors about me this entire time and undermining my leadership. The worst part was I couldn't really refute them either. I was working for Kuranes after all, and he had no intention of living up to any promises I made in his name. I wasn't here for them either, but to acquire the Eye and get Mercury back. If that meant leaving them behind, well, that was something I'd do.

But it's not like Bodhi was better. "Yes, selling us out to the people who are going to fight and kill us in the arena is so much smarter. Why not just throw down your swords and die. It'll save you some time in the long run."

I was hoping Reaver wasn't completely lost to Bodhi's side but that went out the window when he lost control over his animal rage and went for my throat with his powerful jaws. The rotting meat smell of spoiled flesh and worse on its breath made me nauseous but didn't stop me from going under him to toss him over my shoulder. The ghoul was momentarily taken aback by basic wrestling instead of savage combat and that was when I slammed down my Ulthar steel sword through the back of his mouth before pinning him down with it. Blackish blood and a look of horrified terror passed through his all-too-human eyes as death took him. Until this moment, he hadn't thought I'd kill him. That was another problem the others had: they believed my desire not to kill them made me weak.

Examples had to be made.

I hated making examples.

"You cannot stop the coming of the King in Yellow!" Bodhi shouted, slashing away one of Socrates' arms with his flaming sword then forcing the Callisto over. "He has spoken in my dreams! I have seen the coming destruction of Celephaïs! You are all meat for the God of Madness! He will—"

Bodhi turned around to charge at me only for me to stand perfectly still, taking advantage of the fact my two-handed sword had significant reach advantage. I pulled up the sword from the ghoul's mouth a moment before he was in swinging distance and spun it around in a perfect arc that was matched with the speed of a half-giant's strength.

Bodhi's head rolled off his body.

Almost immediately, the Vanir warrior's body began to rot, splitting open and pouring out one-inch-long yellow human-faced maggots with mandibles attached to their faces. I stabbed my sword down again into Reaver's twitching body, picked up one of Bodhi's swords, and tossed it on his body. The flaming sword's magic spread across whatever foul sorcery had kept him alive since the Hyborian Age, and caused the maggots to scream as they died.

I gestured to the body. "Is this the kind of thing you want to follow? A corpse animated by the magic of Leng wizards and eaten for all eternity from the inside? He would sell you out to horned devils of that land and call it God's will. He is a traitor who sold you out for black rubies."

I reached down, and ignoring the pain from the hellfish flames that were eating at the body and licking my hand, I pulled off a small leather pouch from Bodhi's side. Or so it appeared. I opened it up and poured out the contents, revealing a bunch of black garnets and a few very flawed rubies from Bodhi's payout. It was a cheap payment, but I believed it would make the bribe more believable.

The Great Pasha had no need to pay great riches for destroying our team.

It was also a lie.

I'd had the payment hidden on my person the entire time. Bodhi had never needed payment to undermine our team, its morale, or me. I'd speculated on his motives, ranging from jealousy over Nybbas, jealousy over not leading the team, hatred of my race (shoggoth or what I appeared to be), or simply the fact he was an enormous asshole.

Either way, the Iago to my Othello was dead, and I hoped to turn that into an advantage.

"Better a traitor than a shoggoth!" a voice called from the back that was trying to disguise itself, but I recognized as Pinch. Pinch was a human pickpocket who had somehow survived a dozen gladiator fights, deluding himself into believing that great riches, as well as fame, awaited him if we won.

Perhaps because I'd told him so.

"If I was a shoggoth," I said, knowing now what Bodhi had done to destroy their faith in me, "then our chances of actually winning would go up greatly. Wouldn't they? You would have a monster on your side rather than be in its path."

That caused a ripple of confusion among the group and was perhaps the one thing I could say to sow doubt Bodhi's dissension. I'd never shown them my true form, but I was stronger than any normal human as well as healed far faster. That was hardly an unknown set of abilities among this collection of oddities, though. One of them was a man made of clockwork, wood, and tin that could only exist in the Dreamlands.

"Are you a shoggoth?" Pinch asked, no longer disguising his voice.

"You will find that out when we are about to lose, which we shall not, or if I decide to kill you all," I replied. "Now go back to your training. Tomorrow, we fight, die, or triumph."

It was not exactly the Saint Crispin's Day speech, but actions spoke louder than words. Bodhi and his chief hatchet man were dead as well as exposed as traitors. Whether they believed it or not, the doubt in him had been sown. That doubt caused them to question the words Bodhi had spoken and hopefully would have them follow me to the end. The group broke up at that point and returned to their exercises while I turned to Socrates.

"Are you alive?" I asked, staring down.

"Losing an arm is not much to my people," Socrates said, lifting its charred remnant. "Socrates will still be able to fight at most of my capacity."

"Most but not all," I replied. "If I had sorcery to—"

"Socrates would turn it down," Socrates said, shaking its head. "Sorcery is evil no matter what world it comes from and destroyed my people. You are tainted by it more so than any alien heritage you have, Booth, and it will bring nothing but misery to you. I suggest you abandon whatever quest you are on here in Celephaïs."

"I don't know what you mean," I said, helping him up. He weighed a little over four hundred and fifty pounds of exoskeleton and chitinous plates.

"You have a look of a man chasing magic," Socrates said. "Like all wizards, it will be your ruin."

I had no rebuttal for it. Magic had destroyed my teacher, Alan Ward, and it had ruined my wife, Martha. My son had taken to sorcery and become a worshiper of Hastur the same way that Kuranes had. What would it do to Mercury, and would the allure of it eventually consume me the same way it had them? At what point would the dark allure of true names and occult rituals overcome my love of the sword or gun? Had it already? I was, after all, here for a year of precious time seeking the Eye.

Socrates skittered away, still as fast as ever.

Nybbas jumped over the wooden fencing and headed to me. "A nice show, Wastelander."

"We're going to miss Reaver's and Bodhi's blades during the Great Games," I muttered, wondering if I'd made the correct choice.

"Having two less blades is a good thing when they're pointed at your back," Nybbas said. "But I remind you that you don't care what happens to these fools any more than they care what happens to you."

The bluntness of her statements was usually endearing. Not so today. "I was a soldier once, I had brothers in arms."

"And these are not them," Nybbas replied. "They are a distraction you are using every bit as much as they are using you in hopes of a vast payday. Or have you forgotten your true goal?"

"No," I muttered. "I have not."

"Good, because Kuranes hasn't," Nybbas said. "He has lost his mind."

Things had gotten worse in Celephaïs over the past year. A drought had caused devastating famine and the king's hydromancers had been able to do little about it. Riots had spread throughout the God King's city, and he had dispatched his zealots to put them down. Roving press gangs wandered through the streets, grabbing people at random for the work crews that were expanding the coliseum for the Great Games, and human sacrifices to both Hastur as well as Kuranes were performed weekly. It was said that every slave galley to Leng was full and that payments were no longer black rubies but exotic monsters for gladiator pits.

"I'd ask if he ever had it but I know what you mean," I replied. "I do not know what it says about a man's psychology that the people he dreamed into existence now curse his name."

It was treasonous talk but the spies in the arena were dead at my feet and very little could suppress it anymore. I knew Kuranes wanted me in that arena for his own reasons and would not strike at me now. I just had to figure out how to turn it around on him and that required the aid of forces beyond this stable. They were, as Nybbas said, a distraction.

"Dreams take lives of their own," Nybbas said, shrugging. "How else could you explain my attraction to a Spawn of Nyarlathotep?"

That was her latest way of referring to me instead of shoggoth and I wasn't sure it was an improvement. "I have drills to do and weaponry to inspect, Nybbas, unless you have something else—"

Nybbas lifted a bullet up in the air. It was sized for a revolver and engraved with tiny writing that was filled with orichalcum, Deep One gold.

"A gift," Nybbas interrupted. "From your woman in the palace."

She meant Mercury. My lover and closest companion with an infinitely more ruthless spirit than I had ever possessed even at my most alien. I had only seen her a handful of times in the past year at Kuranes' gatherings (more often orgies of debauchery and waste) but she seemed in good health. Indeed, true to his word, he had deluged her in ancient mysticism from the Lost Cities of Yith to the black rites of Acheron. I tried not to love her for all the murders and dark arts she practiced but the heart wanted what it wanted. The fact I was with Nybbas out here and she'd cultivated a harem of adoring young men in Kuranes' service changed little of that.

"What is it?" I asked.

"A bullet," Nybbas replied.

I glared. I was in no mood for jokes.

"She claims to have found Kuranes' true name in her research, possibly weaseled out of him in bed," Nybbas said, showing the first signs of jealousy or cattiness in our association. "The bullet is inscribed with it to remind the God King of his mortality. The metal is supposedly made from Randolph Carter's sword when he quested for Kadath."

I took it and nodded. "With this, we can kill Kuranes."

Nybbas smiled.

Chapter Five

So it was time to teach the horse to sing.

The twenty gladiators I'd chosen for this battle were gathered in the darkness of the coliseum's depths, having waited for the Great Games to reach their main event with increasing apprehension and disgust. Kuranes had ordered the entirety of the city to be assembled in the arena and the populace that tried to flee had been slaughtered or used as fodder in the Great Games.

Even then, most people in the stands were not the residents of the city itself but bloodthirsty crowds assembled from across Leng, Ulthar, and even the distant Republic of Carter I'd falsely claimed to be representing. The whispers of fantastic beasts, monsters, legendary warriors, and spectacle for these games were those that had stirred places not even known to humans.

I had seen obese Deep One potentates, ghouls covered in glamours I only recognized by the telltale signs I'd learned from my friend Richard, and even one of the foul Elder Things that was a special guest of Kuranes. The obese multi-stalked thing was supposedly being served meals of fresh human flesh that even ghouls did not kill for but only scavenged.

In the darkness of the dungeons below where we armed and outfitted ourselves, we could not see what was going on but I could tell from the sounds above that no matter whether the fact the people were starving or insane, it was the show of a lifetime.

"I was a potter's son," Pinch said, lacing up his boots. He was a brown-haired man of Celephaïs descent and it still surprised me he'd made it this far over godlings and hardened veterans. "My father lost my sister and mother to his creditors. I ended up enslaved myself when I tried to steal enough to get them back."

"So why did you stay?" Socrates asked, his missing arm replaced with a prosthetic attached to a shield.

"Booth got my sister back at least," Pinch said. "No telling what happened to my mother. I barely recognized her and there was nothing left of her behind her eyes, but she had two children. I had them shipped across the Silver Sea with a bag of silver as well as a letter of credit. But you'll always be someone's slave if you don't have money. So, I'm here. Even if I die, they'll be taken care of."

Yes, I had said that. I'd already taken the money out for his family, but the Other Gods knew whether it would ever reach them given how many crooked hands it would have to pass through before it reached them.

"Socrates has no people or hive," Socrates said. "They fight for knowledge instead."

"Knowledge," Pinch said, surprised.

Socrates pointed a clawed appendage with prehensile tendrils sticking out of the side at his chest. "This one has studied at universities as far off as the Yithian Learnarium of Pnakotus to the Shadow Archives of Miskatonic at Carter. None have given the secrets necessary to journey across the multiverse and find either his people or a reasonable facsimile. Across Yog-Sothoth I must go to be among people like myself. The God King may be the last option I have to send me to such a place or teach me how."

"A man who beseeches the gods for salvation is bound to be disappointed," Nybbas said, staring into the reflection of her polished sword blade. "Besides, what makes you think Kuranes will be impressed enough to do you any favors?"

"Both you and Booth are doing this battle for him," Socrates said. "Both of you have walked the rivers of time. Magic has a price I cannot pay but there are other secret knowledges I pursue. Thus, I follow you in hopes of finding a path home."

"How long have you been looking for a way home?" Pinch asked.

"Millions of your years," Socrates said. "Socrates would spend millions more for the comfort of the familiar."

I didn't have the heart to tell him that, yes, there was a way to find a portal to another universe where the Callisto still existed. The cults of the Key and the Gate or the Yithians both could have given him the secret. However, the Callisto had been destroyed so humanity could exist and the Yithians could eventually replace them. I had been the one to destroy the original Al-Azif, the book Abdul Alhazred had claimed contained the secrets of chittering insects, that had been their portal to this world. Not telling Socrates was the least of my betrayals. Perhaps he knew, though, as sorcery had been the downfall of his people as it had been Kuranes'. Unless he succeeded in becoming a god tonight, the God King would be overthrown or invaded by his neighbors. Already there had been failed plots against his life and mine would just be the latest.

"Survive and I'll lead you to a portal where your people still live," I lied, wishing it was the truth. "You have my word. For whatever its worth."

"Do you think we'll live?" Pinch asked. "That we really have a chance."

"Yes," I said, pausing. "Just not all of us."

From the expressions on the faces before me, they believed me. It had taken up to the very end of our time together, but I'd finally earned their trust. Unfortunately, the chances of us winning were nonexistent according to even the most generous betting pool.

Despite the fact we all had blades capable of piercing steel like paper, armor that was enchanted to turn even alien claws, and had trained extensively in squad tactics, well, the Janissaries of the Leng Empire were the most feared soldiers in the Dreamlands for a reason.

They were made from children stolen from the many victim states of its armies and subjected to experimentation that hideously mutated them to a level even Gug the Undying might loathe. It was said that a headless man with strange fluids in a bag had killed them at the height of their power and resurrected them as revenants without fear of death as well as an unholy bloodlust that could never be quenched. It could be bullshit but who knew in the Dreamlands?

"It's time," I said, feeling the cold steel in the back of my pants as I'd hidden the carefully crafted holster underneath my long coat. The other gladiators wore very different armor, choosing to forgo their usual displays of flesh, but I'd gone for a 'cowboy' theme that coincidentally hid my weapon. I still sported a greatsword since they weren't about to allow a gun in the arena, however useless such a weapon was against most creatures of the Dreamlands. It was presently tied to my back, which was normally a ridiculous place to put a holster but apparently Velcro wasn't a thing in Kuranes' quasi-medieval kingdom.

There was an itching in the back of my mind that I couldn't put into words, but it was a sense I was playing into the hands of parties infinitely stronger than myself. Perhaps it was Nyarlathotep or Hastur, though it was arrogant and stupid to believe either of them cared about the goings of humans more than a spider they removed from a web or flicked away at night. Hastur might not even exist outside of the avatars conjured by his worshipers, a god made by men and brought to life by our desire for a vengeful judgmental king.

Did Kuranes suspect I was plotting against him? Almost certainly. However, I was probably one of thousands doing so. There was also the fact that he was mad, driven to megalomania by too much power and staring into the abyss of his own insignificance too long. Which sounded like a contradiction until one realized that those who felt the need to prove their power constantly were those most insecure in it.

Then there was Nybbas. It seemed ridiculous to believe the gladiator was pulling the puppet strings around me, but she felt far more in control of her destiny than anyone else here. She was no more human than I was and dropped cryptic hints as to her true nature constantly. Then there was her claim she was here to destroy a country, which I wasn't sure meant she was plotting a revolution or something more literal. Certainly, she was excited and supportive of the plot to kill Kuranes. Indeed, it was what had gotten her to become intimate.

Ahem.

But there was no time to ponder the machinations about me, and the twenty of us walked down the underground passages of the coliseum before gathering in four rows of five before the Southern Warrior's Entrance. The enormous steel door lifted through the power of Gugs turning enormous wheels. Light filtered from underneath as it slowly rose, the light reaching our feet first then slowly rising.

"Now for the main event!" Kuranes voice filled the ears of everyone in the arena, myself included. "A battle between the legendary Janissaries of Leng and the greatest heroes of our fair city-state!

Whoever wins will be made immortal through the glory of their deaths and showered in wealth beyond imagination!"

Pinch muttered something about imagining quite a bit.

Socrates, by contrast, said, "Immortality in death seems a poor substitute for the real thing."

It seemed my sense of humor had rubbed off on them.

"Remember the strategy," I replied. "Kill them one at a time, three on one and stay out of individual engagements whenever possible. Turn their size against them and go with killing blows against their throats or back legs. It's where their armor is weakest."

"And if any of them is a sorcerer?" Nybbas asked, looking positively eager with her nightmarish yet ornamental armor that seemed made of black monster bone but shaped with themes venerating the Great Lord of the Hunt.

"Kill him first," I replied, knowing she was referring to Kuranes.

We departed into the light of the arena, and I thought myself familiar with carnage then I found myself swiftly disillusioned with my experience. Kuranes had organized whole battles and mass melees with the results left to rot as well as fester in the light of the dying sun that seemed to burn brighter than usual. The corpses were piled up to the first row of bleachers as the stink wafted upward.

Kuranes stood in a row at the very front this time, almost level with the warriors he had enslaved. He was still giving announcements before his throne that had a miniature version of it beside him for a single guest: Mercury. Beautiful Mercury, short and redheaded, wore a crown and translucent sheer evening dress as she sat at his side.

I had no doubt of her loyalties because she was ever someone who was primarily loyal to herself. Still, if Kuranes hoped to convince me she had defected to his side, he was bound for failure as long as I had the bullet chambered for his assassination. That was when I was distracted by the sight of the glowing orb hovering above their heads.

It was a glowing, pulsating, sickening piece of matter that reminded me more of a beating heart than a gemstone. It glowed in dirty colors of neon purple, vomit orange, and shades that didn't really exist in the human spectrum, but I could see due to my alien heritage.

It changed shape the more you looked at it, but it was really just catching a glimpse of it from other angles. It was alive and hungry, eating time and dreams. Something was *inside* it, I could tell, and it was begging to get out.

The Eye of Hastur.

Any plan to steal the object immediately fled my consciousness and I cursed myself for ever following the advice of the Black Pharaoh in the first place. It was no solution to my problems and a year of my life, possibly my life itself, was wasted on a fool's errand. Whatever was contained within that was uncontrollable and it would take a madman to believe they could. Which, in retrospect, explained quite a bit.

Turning my attention to the opposite side of the arena, I caught sight of the Great Pasha of the Leng Empire and almost immediately retched. One thing I'd learned in the Wasteland was the price of immortality was always everything human about a person and the Great Pasha had ruled the Leng Empire for 10,000 generations. The creature was a hundred-foot-long dragon-insect thing that was surrounded by a hundred chained slaves whose neck collars all linked to a central one around its bulbous cyst-covered waist.

The Great Pasha's side of the arena was filled with his court of fawning sycophants, wizards, and petty nobility that was a glimpse into what Kuranes was slowly becoming. It was easy to imagine that once the Great Pasha had just been another human dreamer from either the Middle East, Middle Kingdom, or perhaps a far older civilization like Khitai. Time and the Eye of Hastur had turned him into the thing he was now. It would be my destiny if I'd attempted to harvest the Eye's power to save the Republic and my family there.

Looking at Mercury I debated taking the shot immediately, my life and everyone else's be damned, but she gave a very brief shake of her head that told me it was not the right time. Confirmation came a second later as I saw a bubble of barely visible shimmer around his box in the alien sunlight. Kuranes, for all his claims of immortality and godhood, had taken precautions against assassination.

Kuranes stood up and spoke. "You have seen our mighty heroes, the Champions of Celephaïs, but now it is time to see their challengers!

They are the most terrifying warriors of the plateau they hail from, raised to kill from birth and infused with powers even the gods may envy! I give you the Janissaries!"

The metal door across the arena opened and our opponents marched out in perfect synchronization. They were indeed giants and wore armor made of chitinous insect plating taken from giant creatures that inhabited Leng's dense jungles. Their faces were covered in disturbing exaggerated wax masks that I realized, only belatedly, were not masks at all. Their eyes burned coal red and their heads were covered in small metal helmets dipped in gold. Each of them wielded a halberd and had a scimitar at their side. I'd heard they also trained in the basics of sorcery but felt that was overkill even for the Pasha of Leng to get his toy back.

Especially given their numbers.

"Is it just me or are there a lot more of them than there should be?" Pinch asked what was on the mind of every gladiator I'd assembled here.

There were a hundred of them. Kuranes' treachery knew no limits and he'd made all the arrangements he had just to set us up in an impossible battle against people who outnumbered us five to one. This was not meant to be a battle but a slaughter and all of the tactics that I had prepared were worthless.

"What do we do?" Pinch asked, knowing it was as hopeless as I did.

Socrates muttered something in a reverent chittering tone that I wondered about being a prayer, perhaps to Yog-Sothoth or cleaner gods. I had no gods to pray to who could help me now but lowered my head in acknowledgment.

Fury replaced my resignation. "We fight and we die, showing them that we are not beasts for slaughter!"

Nybbas placed her hand on my shoulder, staring at me then looking at the others. "John and I will carve a way through them. We must merely wait for the distraction."

"Distraction?" I asked, not having made any such plans.

Nybbas smiled enigmatically. "You will know it when you see it. Until then, embrace your inhumanity."

Nybbas transformed before my eyes, casting off her human form like a snake shedding its skin or an insect emerging from its cocoon in a way that was both horrifying as well as beautiful. The creature that emerged was bat-like and majestic but also terrifying. It was no Earthly creature so any allusions I made could not adequately describe what it was but there were many things it reminded me of. It was like some great majestic beast man with mighty horns, covered in an oily black skin that lacked sexual characteristics. Its leathery wings spread out from its back, absorbing all the light around it like a vampire consuming the sun. A long thin prehensile barbed tail dangled from its back. No face existed on its pointed, goat-like head, instead being so smooth as to be reflective.

I knew the creature as one of the most fearsome and dreadful beasts of the Dreamlands. One that terrified individuals as much as the shoggoths but without the revulsion that came from humanity's secret shared heritage with them. It was a night-gaunt, a creature that served the god King of Kadath, Nodens, and stalked the monsters of the Far and Near Nightmare. Nodens was said to be enemy of Nyarlathotep and because people believed it, it was true. They were predators of predators, the kind that fed on shoggoth like an owl might a mouse.

But Nybbas, instead, flew into the ranks of the Janissaries.

I loathed myself for what I did next, but I did not even look to my fellow gladiators before abandoning myself to the inner beast. The monster inside that did not think like John Henry Booth but wore his face as well as personality like camouflage. I feared every time I indulged its immense power because I carried a bit more of the alien immortal monster with me each time that I returned to who I was. Something that I would simply forget one day and cease to be able to do, becoming the thing I most despised.

Death.

Destroyer of worlds.

I can't say who or what happened next as everything I did as a shoggoth was so wholly removed from human senses. It would be like attempting to describe a battle to someone blind, deaf, and without a sense of smell. The senses of a shoggoth were dozens more and they overwhelmed the meager organs of humanity with their incomprehensible feedback. Whoever I was when I became a Kastro'vaal, a Primordial One, was also not me. They acted on instincts and memories that I could barely comprehend and was terrified of when I did.

If you assumed this was an easy slaughter, though, then I am unhappy to inform you it was anything but. Of the alien series of images and nightmarish urges I experienced, I remembered enough flashes to know the Janissaries fought back fiercely and inhumanly with weapons that bit through dimensions of flesh as well as spirit.

The wounds created were enough to have killed a normal man a hundred times over and eventually I was forced to withdraw back into myself and the human side of me. The pain was agonizing and it was a struggle to pull my mind back from the fury. Even so, I felt like my blood was burning as the alien matter struggled to keep itself together. I was naked and covered in slime in my human form, barely able to stand. I would need Mercury's magic were I to recover, though it would be hours or days until I died should I not gain access to it.

The carnage around me had gotten worse and fifty of the Janissaries lay dead but that left half of their numbers still capable of fighting. That did not mean this was a heroic victory in the making, though, for I could barely move due to the pain of the invisible injuries my alien biology struggled to heal. Nybbas, herself, was on the ground with several holes in her right wing and a bleeding slice across her side with greenish ichor pouring out.

As for our brothers and sisters in arms?

Dead.

All of them.

I saw Pinch had been torn in half, his body still twitching as his eyes stared up into the sky. Socrates was surrounded by the bodies of four dead Janissaries, having gone down battling them but succumbing to their sheer numbers. The others? Growl, Lysharra, Venom, and Stoneheart? All of them had died at the hands of their enemies in bloody as well as awful ways. Would we have won if Kuranes hadn't betrayed us? Did it matter? The game was rigged the entire time. I didn't get a chance to think more as Nybbas' voice spoke in my mind. *It is time.*

Time for what? I asked, confused.

A group of five Janissaries with nets and drawn swords, abandoning their halberds for more close and personal means, approached me when I heard the sound of screeching in the air. Turning my gaze upward to the dying sun, I saw it was blanketed by the black and horrifying forms of night-gaunts. Hundreds of them. Thousands.

I did not know which side they were on, if any, until they began picking up the Janissaries around me and descending into the crowd to their screaming terror. The Great Pasha of Leng was as vulnerable as any with five of the bat-like creatures tearing apart Kuranes' rival god king while his court were feasted upon by beings who had no fear of their power or wealth. Whatever magics the sorcerers wielded was also ill-suited to combat against the abyssal predators.

"You are ruining my ascension!" Kuranes shouted, his voice echoing throughout the coliseum. The God King levitated upward and over his box before he started to approach me. A night-gaunt descended upon him, only for him to make a dismissive wave that disintegrated it as if an errant dream.

I searched the ground for the pistol I'd prepared that had been lost with my clothes and saw it halfway underneath the corpse of a fallen warrior. I threw myself in a roll, almost vomiting from the stresses of the movement, only to feel the cold steel of the weapon in my hands. I had one shot at this and aimed the weapon at the God King. His eyes were firmly affixed on me, and I had only a second before he obliterated me like he had that night-gaunt. It would be an epic story, truly, a warrior assassinating the tyrant in the middle of the arena surrounded by monsters.

An epic story.

Perfect for a god's origins.

A terrible god but a god nonetheless.

You clever bastard, I thought, adjusting my aim ever so slightly and fired.

The bullet sailed not into Kuranes but the Eye of Hastur above him, shattering the jewel or at least the prism for whatever was inside it. I only got a momentary glimpse of what was inside, but it was enough that I was tempted to rip my own eyes out. An equally memorable image was Kuranes' look of absolute shock and horror at what I'd done. It was followed by a glowing yellow light spilling out, over him first, then everything beyond, consuming everything it touched at a glacial pace that was so much more terrifying than instantaneous death. Mercury had run to my side and wrapped her arms around me as Nybbas moved the folds of her wings around my body. I closed my eyes and readied myself for death.

But death did not come.

Nybbas, instead, carried us off into the alien skies of the Dreamlands, as Celephaïs disappeared into the maw of the King in Yellow.

The King in His Court

By Eric Malikyte

"Well, now I know what a colonoscopy drone feels like."

Slab Panther sighed, inadvertently inhaling the putrid stench of the dungeon's deepest layer. After spending an embarrassing amount of in-game time gagging, he heard his group's armored boots clanking up to the precipice.

"You gonna piss and bitch about it all night or fight the boss?" Mirrorz said, their voice echoing through the dungeon's stone corridors—the dank and dark halls, freshly emptied of their demon denizens.

Mirrorz was decked out in some Legendary golden armor. Their elf ears poking through the sides of their +2 *Great Helm of Burning Wounds*.

"You're the fucken tank, Slab," Fl@ky-Band@ge666 said, striking a pose for her followers in front of the flesh pit's opening. Anything to show off that Ultra Rare enchanted loot she'd picked up in the last raid. "Gotta have a stronger stomach, yizz."

Fl@ky-Band@ge666, or Flaky as they always called her, was a super cute anime fairy princess with eyes the color of a dying sun.

"Naw, I'm with Slab here," Mirrorz said. "They keep making these smells more and more real and people gonna wake up from a dive covered in vom."

"There's a market for that, Mirrorz," Flaky said, winking.

"A'ight," Slab coughed, straightening his back and peering over the edge. "I'm good. Ready to clear this dungeon?"

"Was waiting on you in the first place," Mirrorz said.

With a dramatic nod few would find cool, Slab dove off the precipice into the flesh pit. His superhero landing generated a miniature tidal wave of blood that rang out against the walls of the boss room.

Flaky and Mirrorz landed behind him.

They didn't have long before the boss hatched.

"Mirrorz, keep those spells coming," Slab said. "Flaky, be sure to keep us good and healed."

"No shit, Slab," Flaky said, readying her *Wand of Glorious Restoration*, which only vaguely resembled a dick. "By the by, if we lose, I'm invoicing your ass. Spent way too much cred on this as is, so keep your dukes up no matter what."

"Dukes?"

"Somethin' my grampa used to say, yizz. Means fists."

"Your gramps is dumb AF."

"Shut up," Mirrorz shouted. "It's hatching!"

Light erupted from the other end of the boss room, revealing pink fleshy walls that bordered a lake filled to the brim with blood and the floating bodies of all the players who'd died that day.

The blood lake surged; the corpses rode the waves.

Any moment now, the boss would emerge.

Any moment.

Any...

"Do you think it's a glitch?" Flaky asked.

"How the fuck should I know?" Slab asked, shrugging.

The beacon of light froze; the blood lake's surging waves stopped like a paused video file. Old world Internet jank.

"That's not supposed to happen, right?" Slab asked.

"No, Slab, that's not supposed to happen at all," Mirrorz said, making their way out of the frozen pool of blood. Curiously, while everything seemed to be frozen in time, blood still dripped from their armor when they emerged onto the fleshy walkway. "Fucken devs! Always cuttin' corners and makin' us pay for the fixes!"

Slab watched Mirrorz walk up to the frozen beacon of light, taking out their *Mage Staff of Flame* and prodding one of the glowing beams.

"Think they'll give us a refund?" Flaky asked.

"You signed the waver, Flaky," Mirrorz said, "you honestly think that's in the cards?"

"Fuck," Flaky sighed. "I spent this month's rent on my portion!"

"Sucks to suck," Mirrorz said.

"Least you can't blame this one on me," Slab said, chuckling.

"Why are you always so fucken mean, Mirrorz?" Flaky shouted.

"I'm pissed off, that's why!"

Mirrorz kept poking their staff at the beam of light, raging emojis exploding over their avatar's head.

"You dun have to take it out on us!"

"Mu'fuckah, ProdInt is lookin' to pull eminent domain on my block. Gonna wreck the whole neighborhood to put in a mega-skyscraper, so I'ma have to move next month to a place that hopefully has a spot for a full deep dive rig."

"We all got problems, Mirrorz, doesn't mean you have to—"

Their bickering voices faded like background noise as he looked into the light.

Slab held his head.

A wave of nausea.

As the frozen light loomed and his vision waffled, he couldn't help but think the light was turning yellow.

Next thing he knew, he was nose-to-nose with the frozen glowing beam.

For some reason, he felt compelled to reach through.

And when he did, the entire chamber turned that same sickly shade of yellow.

Mirrorz and Flaky both stopped their bickering and turned to him.

"What in the fuck did you—"

A guttural voice, like none he'd ever heard, processed or organic, boomed through the boss room.

"SACRIFICE QUOTA REACHED!"

The light faded.

The blood lake unfroze, emptying into the dark.

"YOU HAVE FOUND THE YELLOW SIGN."

When his Heads-Up-Display cleared, he could see that the boss room had transformed into a long stone corridor. In the stonework of the corridor, tiny lines of yellow light pulsed with a familiar rhythm. Like the beat for some kind of music.

"Sacrifice quota?" Flaky said.

"Yeah, weird," Slab said. "You mean all the bodies that were here?"

"Where'd all the blood go?"

Slab gestured down the hall. "This way?"

Mirrorz was first down the new corridor.

"I'ma find the boss if it's the last thing I do," Mirrorz said.

Flaky sighed and followed after them.

Slab brought up the rear. He couldn't help but wonder if he'd come out of this dive to find his fat ass covered in chunks of half-digested pizza tacos.

Mom was gonna kick his ass to the curb if she had to spend another mint on a premature laundry session. Plus, he'd used her credit line to pay for his portion of this little adventure. She still didn't know.

He could practically hear her voice now:

"You're pushing sixty and still don't have a steady job, Clarence!"

The yellow stone corridor seemed to go on and on and on.

Each step brought a surreal sense of knowing to Slab. Like he was in two places at once.

While he made his way through the corridor, he could also see his bedroom.

He watched as mother's custom, hourglass body stomped into his bedroom, freshened up and ready for a night at the MilkyWay Unlimited Holiday Gala.

As the proportions of the corridor twisted and transformed into a tunnel, its stone blocks betraying new geometries unfamiliar to his eyes—simultaneously—he could see mother gesturing with all the demonic rage of King Hastur at his limp body.

"You're worthless, Clarence, I wish your father had pulled out!"

His expression was blank, drool hanging from his mouth as lights flashed behind his eyes. The cables and wires snaking from the ports in his skull blinked with an urgency that alarmed him.

His rig was under a massive amount of strain, loading bars with strange yellow characters up on the monitors.

Another vantage point in mother's apartment. Mother storming around, gathering her purse before one last bump of designer super-coke.

"Next kid I push out better be CEO material, I swear!"

If this was real, it was a cause for concern.

"Whoa!" Flaky grabbed his shoulder.

Slab covered his eyes.

The tunnel ended abruptly. And when his avatar's digital eyes finally adjusted to the light, he could see rolling green hills beyond the tunnel's mouth and the hazy outline of towering structures.

"Where the hell are we?" Slab asked.

"Maybe we unlocked a new area?" Flaky said.

"I didn't hear shit about a new area being added to the game," Mirrorz said, flames practically shooting out from their helmet.

"Are you sure?" Slab asked.

"Mirrorz got an inside source for leaks within InnerCircle Productions. Why their socials always get the big views."

Mirrorz took their helmet off. The Book of Hastur™ featured full facial expression mapping for players in deep dive. And right now, Mirrorz's eyes were wide. Even with Slab's shit grasp on social skills, he could tell they were afraid.

"What is it?" Slab asked.

Mirrorz shook their head. "Let's take a closer look. Maybe we'll get some answers in town."

"All right," Slab said, gesturing toward the structures in the distance. "Lead the way, boss."

Flaky gave him an uneasy look, her avatar's ruby red eyes glimmering in the pink sun's light.

It had to be a new area, right?

It was a scene right out of a big budget fantasy movie. One of the classics, too, not the AI generated crap that gets hashed and rehashed every couple months.

The three of them wandered into a town square, their armored boots clanking atop a worn cobblestone path. They were surrounded by multi-storied buildings made of cobblestone and wood, with proportions that made Slab certain they would collapse in the real world. A strange thing for a game that was known for its grim and gritty realism.

Thatch rooftops crumbled atop each structure, broken windows and windowpanes accompanied them.

Slab poked his head into one of the houses. It was fully furnished with decaying tables and chairs, a rusting ancient stove in the corner. Food rotted away on the kitchen table.

"You seen anyone?" Flaky asked.

Slab withdrew his head. "Nope."

"Cast Detect Life Form," Mirrorz said.

With a wave of her wand, Flaky cast the spell.

Or, at least, that's what *should* have happened.

Flaky gave the wand a good smack and shrugged. "It's not working."

Mirrorz shoved a hand into their satchel and retrieved some spell components. After a chant and some hand signs, a brilliant...

Well, a brilliant nothing..."happened."

Mirrorz cursed, stomping on the ground like a child throwing a tantrum in the middle of a tech kiosk.

That's when Slab noticed the gathering storm on the horizon. "Maybe they ran away from that?"

"I'll bet that's where the boss is!" Mirrorz shouted, sprinting ahead.

"Wait for us!" Flaky screamed.

They trailed after Mirrorz, running past abandoned taverns and shops and cottages.

They were practically halfway through the dreamlike town when Slab's lungs were about ready to explode.

He protested, dropping to his knees. He managed to yell for Flaky and Mirrorz to wait for him.

"What is it now?" Mirrorz asked, looking a tad winded themself.

"Stamina buffs," Slab managed, wheezing, "not working! Armor feels...too heavy!"

"Yeah, now that you mention it, my gear is really feelin' heavy," Flaky said, ripping at her helmet and tossing it to the ground.

Slab couldn't help but point. "Flaky, your hair..."

Her avatar's brilliant green hair was gone now. In fact, as she tossed her armor pieces to the cobblestone path, Flaky's shapely breasts and hourglass figure were gone too, replaced with what looked like a teenage boy's body.

"What?" Flaky stood there blinking.

"Slab..."

Mirrorz was practically face-palming. "Your fat is showing."

Slab tried bringing up his character's inventory screen, even the third person cam, but none of the mental commands were working.

In fact, his HUD had entirely disappeared.

Even Mirrorz no longer looked like a tall, sexless alien elf with spiky hair. Now, they were a sexless human with a shaved head.

"What in the hell is going on here?" Slab asked.

"*Simple,*" came a dreamlike voice, "*you are all in Dreamland.*"

Their gaze fell upon a man that looked like he'd stepped right out of the 1930s, complete with a blazer, black and gold cane, and a top hat.

"Finally, a goddamn NPC!" Mirrorz shouted, approaching the strange man. "Who the hell are you and where the fuckballs are we?"

"*I have many names,*" the man said, a devilish smirk wrinkling his face. "*But you may call me...Carter.*"

"Okay, Carter, answer the second question before I tell all of my followers to review bomb this piece of shit!"

"*I already told you. You are in Dreamland.*"

"So it is a new area!" Flaky shouted, her voice cracking.

"Why are we here, Carter?" Slab asked.

"*Oh, my dear boy Clarence, I'm so glad you've asked.*"

"Clarence?" Mirrorz chuckled. "What kind of stupid fucken name is that?"

"*There's an old Earth saying, Fanny: 'One should not throw stones when one lives in a glass house'.*"

"How the fuck do you know my legal name?" Mirrorz asked.

Flaky snickered, "Fanny, heh."

"*Rather immaterial, isn't it? You're wondering why you're all here. And that's quite simple. You're here to see the King in his Court.*"

"What?" Slab shook his head. "Is the boss a king?"

"Has to be," Mirrorz said.

"*That is certainly a way to put it.*" The man gestured behind him. "*You all posses the Yellow Sign, yes?*"

"Hey, didn't the voice say that?" Slab asked.

"*Check your inventory.*"

"We've been trying this whole time, but the mental commands won't work!"

Carter's eyebrow rose. "*Have you tried your pockets?*"

"Oh, hey!" Slab shouted, taking out a black and yellow piece of loot. "I got something!"

"Me too," Flaky said, holding it real close to their right eye. "I wonder if it's enchanted."

"They're all the same?" Mirrorz asked. "Won't that drop their value on the secondary market?"

Carter sighed.

"*Come, the King does not like to be kept waiting.*"

Slab gave the man a nod. Something about him made him not want to try his patience.

The man led them through the remainder of the town, out the back gates, and up a large green hill.

"Is that some kind of gate?" Flaky asked.

The grassy slope ended in a sharp cliff, and something else.

What Slab could only describe as a window, or a mirror that ended in storm clouds.

"Is this the big bad storm that the NPCs all abandoned their town for?" Mirrorz asked. "Doesn't look that bad up close."

"Oh, no one has lived in this corner of Dreamland in a few hundred years at least. In another century, I imagine the abyss shall claim it altogether."

"This NPC talks really fucken weird," Flaky said. "Can we trust him?"

"Oh, it's not me you have to worry about, truly. Think of me as nothing more than a messenger. A guide even."

"So, what do we do?" Slab asked, gazing up at the mirror from the edge of the cliff.

Now it, whatever it was, appeared to tower into the heavens, as if it had grown several thousand stories in the short time it took to walk down the hill.

"You take a step through. Really, you're all quite lucky. These days, dreamers such as yourselves have to journey through The Plateau of Leng, the city of Celephais, and make their way far past the furthest reaches of the Underworld before they ever have a chance of finding the way to Carcosa."

Slab gripped at his chest. Something didn't feel right. Made him want to turn his fat ass around and run as fast as he possibly could in any direction that wasn't through that glass portal.

"This leads to Carcosa?" Mirrorz didn't seem too sure.

"Isn't that the planet King Hastur is from or something?" Flaky asked.

"Yeah, but it hasn't been built yet," Mirrorz said. "My guy said InnerCircle Productions were still working on that part of the game, it was supposed to be a huge update toward the end of the year or something."

"Maybe your guy was wrong?" Slab said.

"Shouldn't you be happy?" Flaky asked. "We were all worried about not getting our money's worth out of this pack, but it looks like we're gonna get something no other player has gotten!"

"Yeah, but why the weird glitch with our avatars and..."

"You're worrying too much, Slab!" Flaky said, walking right up to the mirror's edge before disappearing entirely.

"*What a brave dreamer she is,*" the man said, grinning ear to ear. "*In the rest of you go.*"

Mirrorz shrugged before walking through the reflective surface...like it was no big deal.

"Umm..." Slab was sweating. Felt like he was gonna have an asthma attack. "How are we supposed to fight King Hastur if we don't got any levels or spells?"

The man's hand was on Slab's shoulder. "*Who said anything about fighting?*"

Slab's breath caught in his chest.

Something heavy, like a god's fist, slammed into his back.

Gravity took hold of his stomach.

The man had pushed him off the cliff, into the waiting embrace of the mirror portal.

Liquid.

Black. Viscous.

It surrounds his plump body.

An ocean of ink.

He realizes he doesn't know how to swim.

Panic seizes.

Grips his chest.

Air.

He needs air.

Something wraps around his legs.

At first, he believes it's one of his friends.

Surely, Mirrorz will save him again.

Instead, the sensation continues. It slithers up his legs, around his gut, and wraps around his neck.

And it yanks.

Pulling with the force of an ion engine set to full burn.

His mouth opens in the black. Screaming into the void.

The rush of the current.
His head feels fuzzy. Alien colors dance behind his eyes.
If he doesn't get air...
If he doesn't cough up this foul tasting water...
His life flashes before his eyes.

Kindergarten through eighth grade.

Virtual classrooms. He's the only one who made his avatar look like himself.

The other kids tease him. Call him meat-sack, hamlet, and meat-space-fucker.

No friends.

No one to talk to.

While mommy whores herself out to anyone with a salary and a view.

He gets a hold of mommy's credit deets, orders SkyBox™ six times a day.

She doesn't care. Someone else is footing the bill.

And he eats. And he eats.

Synthetic grease clogs his arteries. Makes it hard to breathe.

Makes it hard to think.

Can't stand reality, so he uses a headset to escape to another world. His own personal Dreamland.

Slashing up demons and dragons makes it better.

Gotta get that EXP.

Gotta get that level.

Gotta spend mommy's rent money on the next expansion.

He's been gaming so long, MilkyWay Unlimited.EDU sends him a notification that he's been expelled.

Social score's trash now.

All that's left is the game.

His life is the game.

Is that so bad?

He even makes some friends.

Mirrorz says they're from ProdIntelligence.

Fl@kyBand@ge666 is just a small town girl in the big city. Or, at least, that's what she says. Claims she's got a husband with a big black—

He's seeing something else now.

Mommy in a small metal room. Neon LEDs flashing vertically off her lipstick as she checks her cleavage.

An elevator.

The doors open. Neon digits above tell him she's on the 700th floor, where the CEOs and big wigs are celebrating subjugating the masses, robbing unsuspecting fools like him blind.

In a sea of plastic, metallic eyes lock on mommy.

He's grabbing her ass and slipping his artificial tongue down her throat.

She's into it. Or, at least, he thinks she is.

He's high as fuck. Telling her all sorts of things.

Like how he's the CEO of InnerCircle Productions, a MilkyWay Unlimited subsidiary. How this little game is gonna crush Rackham Media's stranglehold on the content biz. How the devs discovered something incredible in the rotting, radioactive Frontier. The ruins of old America.

How it inspired them to create the greatest financial venture of the century.

No, of all time.

And then, Clarence is seeing it for himself.

Jungles infested with wild, radioactive boars. Vines and trees and weeds adorning the ruins of an ancient city.

A temple on the outskirts. Hidden from the unworthy.

Teams of three exploring its tunneling, dank depths.

Skeletons in the dark.

A bridge crossing the abyss.

A set of stone doors with a familiar symbol in their center.

One of their number presents the Yellow Sign. It gleams in the dark.

The doors open.

The others look nervous.

Inside is an altar. A single book lying open upon it.

He smiles. Hands sweaty in anticipation.

Laboratories and data processing chains.

The book's at the center. The man's skin is looking strange, gray and splotchy. It's okay. He's got the money for synthetic flesh.

The book doesn't need connections. It reaches deep into the network, takes on a life of its own.

With a single prompt, he's able to generate a world from its strange pages.

The world waits with bated breath for The Book of Hastur.

Eager minds, empty and ready to receive his message.

Gasping for air.

Fingers clawing through black sand.

White, burning sky speckled with black stars.

Vision's blurry.

He can't breathe right. Like the battery for his BreathAssist finally crapped out.

The first asthma attack he's had since it was installed.

Screams.

Echoing off glass towers with strange shapes. It's like information overload. Head feels like it's being dissected.

He struggles to get to his feet.

Ankle feels weak. Like it doesn't want to support his girth.

Somehow, he manages.

Manages to make his way through that city of immortal glass.

He wonders if he's gonna wake up.

He doesn't like this game anymore.

Rivers of ink lead him to an incredible domed structure.

It's miles and days and light years away.

He crosses the distance somehow. Somewhen.

And it swells in his vision. Growing larger and larger and larger still.

He wonders if he's still trapped in that blackened lake.

Still sucking its water deep.

The next time he emerges, he's yelling. Calling their names.

Their screams draw his eyes to the platform.

Mirrorz, clawing their eyes out. Black ink oozing from decomposing wounds.

Flaky crawling. Crawling. Crawling away from Him.

Now she's just a torso. Intestines splayed out like loose wires.

Vile, golden light. Pallid mask. Shifting, shambling silhouettes beneath His form.

Tentacles reaching, twisting, wrapping around her flat, boyish chest, climbing inside her rotting mouth.

And then she's still.

They're both still.

He tells himself they've lost. That they've woken up in their deep dive chairs, ready to send him nasty messages.

But in his mind he can see them, heads hanging back, mouths open, warmth leaving their corpses.

The figure turns His gaze on him.

Its pallid mask. No matter how much he wants to cover his eyes. He can't look away. Yellow Sign burning in his pocket.

"Please!" he cries. "Please let me live!"

No answer.

"I'll do anything!"

The figure stops. Tentacles slithering, making their way to his swollen feet.

"Please..."

As it makes its way inside his mouth and spreads its filth, he sees another life.

One where he finally gets out of that chair and makes his way out into the world.

Orders a SkyTaxi™ to see Mommy at the gala.

Rides the elevator.

He's got a present to give, it rests cool and shiny in his swollen hand.

The doors open.

She turns to see him.

Lust turns to rage. Accusing finger thrusted in his direction.

He doesn't care.

A sea of plastic flesh parts for him.

Mommy won't stop screaming.

And he places His gift in her hands.
"You have seen the Yellow Sign, mommy."

About the Authors

David Hambling

David Hambling is a journalist and author based in Norwood, South London. His fiction, starting with a collection, *The Dulwich Horror & Others*, explores the Cthulhu mythos in his own locale. His novels include the popular Harry Stubbs adventures, also set in the 1920s, and he has previously contributed to ST Joshi's *Black Wings of Cthulhu* collections. He can be found at:

https://www.facebook.com/ShadowsFromNorwood/

Matthew Davenport

Matthew Davenport hails from Des Moines, Iowa, where he lives with his wife, Ren, and daughter, Willow. When his scattered author brain isn't earning weird looks from the ladies of his life, he enjoys reading sci-fi and horror, tinkering with electronics, and doing escape rooms.

Matt is the author of the Andrew Doran series, the Broken Nights series (along with his brother, Michael), *The Trials of Obed Marsh* and *Satan's Salesman*, among other titles. He's also a self-styled student of the Cthulhu Mythos and exercises that influence in his stories and as an editor at the blog Shoggoth.net. You can keep track of Matthew through his X/Twitter account @spazenport. Matt occasionally updates his blog at davenportwrites.com.

Eric Malikyte

Eric Malikyte is a neurodivergent author, illustrator, science communicator, and video editor. He has published works in various genres, including Lovecraftian horror, dark fantasy, and cyberpunk. He has written for YouTube channels such as TopTenz, Geographics, and Biographics. He lives in Richmond, Virginia, with his wife and two cats, where he spends his spare time exploring used bookstores, Irish Pubs, and terrorizing the neighborhood children on Halloween.

Get a free copy of Eric's debut novel *Echoes of Olympus Mons* here: https://dl.bookfunnel.com/1cw07o2uyb

Tim Mendees

Tim is a rather odd chap. He's a horror writer from Macclesfield in the North-West of England that specialises in cosmic horror and weird fiction. A lifelong fan of classic weird tales, Tim set out to bring the pulp horror of yesteryear into the twenty-first century and give it a distinctly British flavour. His work has been described as the lovechild of H.P. Lovecraft and P.G. Wodehouse and is often peppered with a wry sense of humour that acts as a counterpoint to the unnerving, and often disturbing, narratives.

Tim is the author of over one hundred published short stories and novelettes, seven novellas, and two short story collections. He has also curated and edited several cosmic horror-themed anthologies.

When he is not arguing with the spellchecker, Tim is a goth DJ with a weekly radio show on The Feelgood Station, and the co-presenter of the Innsmouth Book Club Podcast & Strange Shadows: The Clark Ashton Smith Podcast. He currently lives in Brighton & Hove with his pet crab, Gerald, and an ever-increasing army of stuffed octopods. timmendeeswriter.wordpress.com/

Andrea Pearson

Andrea Pearson, *USA Today* bestselling author of several series including the Kilenya, Mosaic, and Koven Chronicles, lives with her husband and children in a small valley framed with hills. She graduated from Brigham Young University with a Bachelor of Science degree in Communications Disorders. Her Mosaic Chronicles has been lauded as "a little bit Harry Potter, a little bit HP Lovecraft," and most of her books exemplify an appreciation of the works of Lovecraft and his peers.

Andrea spends as much time with her husband and kids as possible. Favorite activities include painting, watching movies, collecting and listening to music, and discussing books and authors.

C. T. Phipps

C. T. Phipps is a lifelong student of horror, science fiction, and fantasy. An avid tabletop gamer, he discovered this passion led him to write and turned him into a lifelong geek. He is a regular blogger on "The United Federation of Charles":

(http://unitedfederationofcharles.blogspot.com/)

He's the author of *Agent G, Cthulhu Armageddon, Lucifer's Star, Straight Outta Fangton, Space Academy Dropouts,* and *The Supervillainy Saga.*

David Niall Wilson

David Niall Wilson has been writing and publishing horror, dark fantasy, and science fiction since the mid-eighties. An ordained minister, once President of the Horror Writer's Association and multiple recipient of the Bram Stoker Award. He lives outside Hertford, NC, with the love of his life, Patricia Lee Macomber, his children Zane and Katie, occasionally their older siblings, Stephanie, who is in college, and Bill and Zach who are in the Navy, and an ever-changing assortment of pets.

David can be found at: http://www.davidniallwilson.com

Or Connect on Facebook at

http://www.facebook.com/David.Niall.Wilson

Curious about other Crossroad Press books? Stop by our website:
http://crossroadpress.com
We offer quality writing
in digital, audio, and print formats.

Subscribe to our newsletter on the website homepage and receive a
free eBook.